"I WANT TO BE MORE THAN JUST A MEMORY TO YOU,"

he said, staring into her eyes.

"But you are wearing the wrong trappings." Ariane spoke in a broken whisper as she looked down at the blue sleeve of his Union Army uniform.

"It mustn't matter, my lovely Rebel," he said, sweeping her into his arms. Before she could protest, he pressed her tightly against him, his mouth hungrily covering hers.

The firm, sinewy feeling of his body against her triggered long-repressed yearnings. A wild surge of pleasure ran through her as she parted her lips, allowing him the deep, achingly sweet exploration of her mouth. All other thoughts fled before the force of their need as she returned his caress, stroking his back, then tangling her fingers in the ebony silk of his hair.

For a brief time there was no war, no fear of what tomorrow would bring—only the fire of his kiss and the rapture of his touch . . .

READERS ARE IN LOVE WITH ZEBRA LOVEGRAMS

TEMPTING TEXAS TREASURE   (3312, $4.50)
by Wanda Owen

With her dazzling beauty, Karita Montera aroused passion in every redblooded man who glanced her way. But the independent senorita had eyes only for Vincent Navarro, the wealthy cattle rancher she'd adored since childhood—who was also her family's sworn enemy. The Navarro and Montera clans had clashed for generations, but no past passions could compare with the fierce desire that swept through Vincent as he came across the near-naked Karita cooling herself beside the crystal waterfall on the riverbank. With just one scorching glance, he knew this raven-haired vixen must be his for eternity. After the first forbidden embrace, she had captured his heart—and enslaved his very soul!

MISSOURI FLAME   (3314, $4.50)
by Gwen Cleary

Missouri-bound Bevin O'Dea never even met the farmer she was journeying to wed, but she believed a marriage based on practicality rather than passion would suit her just fine . . . until she encountered the smoldering charisma of the brash Will Shoemaker, who just happened to be her fiance's step-brother.

Will Shoemaker couldn't believe a woman like Bevin, so full of hidden passion, could agree to marry his step-brother—a cold fish of a man who wanted a housekeeper more than he wanted a wife. He knew he should stay away from Bevin, but the passions were building in both of them, and once those passions were released, they would explode into a red-hot *Missouri Flame*.

BAYOU BRIDE   (3311, $4.50)
by Bobbi Smith

Wealthy Louisiana planter Dominic Kane was in a bind: according to his father's will, he must marry within six months or forfeit his inheritance. When he saw the beautiful bonded servant on the docks, he figured she'd do just fine. He would buy her papers and she would be his wife for six months—on paper, that is.

Spirited Jordan St. James hired on as an indenture servant in America because it was the best way to flee England. Her heart raced when she saw her handsome new master, and she swore she would do anything to become Dominic's bride. When his strong arms circled around her in a passionate embrace, she knew she would surrender to his thrilling kisses and lie in his arms for one long night of loving . . . no matter what the future might bring!

DIANE GATES ROBINSON
THE FALCON AND THE SWAN

ZEBRA BOOKS
KENSINGTON PUBLISHING CORP.

For all my good caring friends, supportive family, and kind acquaintances, who have made my life in Memphis truly one of good abode.

And

In memory of Belle Edmondson, a courageous Southern lady who lived the life of a Memphis spy for the Confederacy, as did my heroine Ariane; but sadly her story did not have Ariane's happy ending.

ZEBRA BOOKS

are published by

Kensington Publishing Corp.
475 Park Avenue South
New York, NY 10016

First printing: March, 1992

Printed in the United States of America

"Make war on men—the ladies have too long memories."

Stephen Vincent Benét,
John Brown's Body

Prologue

June 1862

Memphis. The name seemed to hang in the soft early dawn air like a plaintive melody that could conjure up feelings and memories best left in the past. Named for a city of antiquity in Egypt by the early settlers of Tennessee, it had meant to the ancient Egyptians "place of good abode," but for the tall lean man, dressed in the uniform of a Union medical officer, leaning against the rail of the Federal gunboat, the name was synonymous with heartbreak and old hatreds.

As the sun rose over the rushing chocolate waters of the Mississippi, the Union officer stared, his dark eyes full of pain and bitterness, at the ghostly outline of the city rising out of the river fog like an apparition. His lips, shaded by a thick ebony beard, twisted into a cynical self-mocking smile as he watched the fourth Chickasaw bluff rise out of the pearly-gray morning mist. It had taken one of the ironies of war to bring him home to the city of his birth. A home he no longer claimed, to people that no longer claimed him as kin. How they would all hate him, he thought with another twist of that thin-lipped smile, a Yankee captain returned to defeat Memphis, known as the clasp on the necklace of the Confederacy. Well, this morning, he thought with bitter satisfaction, the clasp was about to break wide open.

Thin wisps of early morning fog drifted off the vast expanse of the Mississippi River and clung to the lush verdant vegetation of the high bluff. The gray mist veiled the rambling tangled honeysuckle vine, the fragrant jasmine bushes swirling around the trunks of the tall oaks, the leathery emerald boughs of the magnolia, and the shaggy bark of the stately cedar trees. As the first golden rays of the sun broke through the mist of the summer morn a mockingbird gave its salute to the splendor of the day.

"You can see them! You can see the Yankee gunboats!" The excited voice of a young boy standing on the riverbank joined the shrill of the awakening birds. It was as if he had broken some spell of silence, for a hum of conversation followed his cry.

As the dawn broke over the bluffs of Memphis, the ever-widening rays of the sun fell on ten thousand anxious citizens gathered on the high banks of the Mississippi. They had come before sunup, some having spent the night, waiting to see the small Confederate squadron steam out into the flood waters to meet the Union fleet and its destiny.

Cheers rang out from the throng on the bluff. Men raised hats in the air, and women waved delicate lace handkerchiefs. A young boy played "Dixie" on a silver flute glistening in the sunlight. The tune the South had adopted as its own sailed out across the river on the soft, humid air that was blowing away the last of the fog.

In the shadow of a giant magnolia apart from the others stood a bay mare, her rider staring out at the coming battle with somber gray eyes. The young woman made no gesture of elation, no cry of excitement. The expression on the lovely oval visage was one of great sadness. If she noticed the sidelong stares of the other women, she gave no sign.

"That's her, that's Ariane Valcour," the good ladies of Memphis whispered behind lace-gloved hands to their companions. "She is the one who dressed up like a man to fetch her wounded father back from Shiloh. Buried her brother Charles there, I heard tell. Rode all that way with only one of the young grooms from the stables. Imagine a lady doing such a thing," they muttered in disapproval.

The fact that the object of their gossip was young, beau-

6

tiful, and wealthy only added spice to their conversation. Two of the Confederate steamers, hastily fitted out as gunboats, belonged to her father's company, Valcour Steamboat Line.

"Their loyalty to the South is unquestionable, I give them that," one stout, tightly corseted matron stated to another. "But the family has always been a bit odd, even if they do come from old Louisiana money people. Why the mother, Marie Louise, killed herself, course she was never quite right after Ariane's birth. It happens to some women, childbirth melancholy, but then I heard that a streak of madness ran in her family, the Dubois. They might own half of Baton Rouge, but some of them are crazy as bedbugs."

Ariane Valcour kept her delicate chin raised staring straight ahead at the Confederate gunboats drawn up now in a double line of battle before the city, as the Union gunboats came downriver in a single line of battle heading downstream for Memphis. She knew the old cats were gossiping about her, but she refused to let them know she heard. She had always been a loner, not caring how others thought she should conduct her life. Let them talk, there were more momentous events to think about on this heart-breakingly lovely summer morn.

As the massed citizenry looked on, the Confederates opened fire with their light cannon and the Union gunboats responded. Cheers again broke out on the bluff as the battle for the Mississippi at Memphis began.

"Miss Valcour, 'tis good to see you looking so well. May I inquire about your father." The rich, deep masculine voice at her side caused Ariane to turn away from the battle scene.

"General Thompson, I am surprised to see you here," Ariane replied, for most of what was left of the Confederate troop garrison had withdrawn from the city the night before. "My father is not well—the loss of his leg has left him despondent—but then the events of the last few days would certainly not lift anyone's spirits." With the capture of Fort Pillow upriver by the Federal troops a

7

sense of impending doom had come over Memphis.

"I am sorry to hear of his ill health. Please give him my regards, for I fear I will be unable to visit him. I shall be leaving shortly for Hernando, but I wanted to see some of the engagement for myself." The handsome brigadier general lifted his cockade hat with the red plume to several ladies and gentlemen he knew in the crowd.

Suddenly, as they all watched intently, the Confederates ceased firing. From beside the Union gunboats steamed two ram boats heading for the wooden Southern ships. These steel-nosed rams plunged into Confederate vessel after vessel cutting off their paddle wheels and sinking them. After a little over an hour, all the Southern boats were captured, sunk, or adrift.

"Well, that's it then," the general said with a sigh. "I shall be off. You'd best return home, Miss Valcour. The surrender of the city is upon us." Lifting his hat once more in farewell, he was gone.

Ariane listened to the stunned silence of the crowd as they realized it was over. They had lost. There was nothing left to do but surrender to the Union troops. She lifted the black veil of her tall ebony riding hat to wipe a tear from her cheek. She thought she had come beyond tears since Shiloh, that bloody battle where she had lost a brother and friends. She could never forget the horror of it. It haunted her days as well as her nights. For many in Memphis the horror of war was just beginning, she realized, and she shuddered for them.

The crowd, stunned and unbelieving, milling about the bluff, some moving toward the levee where a Union gunboat was preparing to draw up. The scent of gunpowder mingled in the hot air with the sickening sweet smell of the molasses that had been spilled from hundreds of kegs on to the cobblestones of the levee. Flies covered the sticky mess rendered useless the night before so that the Federal troops would be unable to capture it. The stench of burned cotton also hung in the humid air like an undertone. Hundreds of bales of cotton that usually stood waiting for transportation to New Orleans and the cotton markets of Liverpool,

England, were destroyed to keep them from Yankee hands.

Ariane found she was urging her mare forward with the crowd, drawn for some horrible reason to the spectacle of the city's surrender. She watched as three Federal officers disembarked from a Union gunboat and walked up the slippery cobblestones of the levee. They stopped once to pluck a copy of the last issue of the *Memphis Daily Appeal* to be printed in Memphis from a stand. The management of the paper had loaded its newspaper press and staff on a train the night before for Grenada, Mississippi, vowing that they would continue printing as long as there was a Confederacy. The Union officers were greeted by a few jeers from the crowd as they lined the street called Front Row to view in mostly stunned silence the surrender of their city.

Drawn by some strange force, Ariane followed the three tall officers as they made their way with rigid posture through the hostile streets of Memphis. Quickly she realized they were heading to the city's post office. Over the building flew the stars and bars, the Confederate flag. They could see it from the river.

Impervious to the hostile atmosphere, the three men made their way to the post office building at Third and Jefferson streets. As the sun beat down on the dark blue of their broad hats, the indigo plumes ruffling in the breeze like the feathers of some predatory bird, the men began to lower the Confederate flag.

Ariane sat watching from the back of her mare, a blinding anger growing as she saw once more before her the dying body of her brother Charles, gentle bookish Charles who had seldom even raised his voice in anger. He now lay dead on the haunted, blood-soaked ground beside the Tennessee River near Shiloh Church. She had found him after the battle in the mud as the rain fell across his handsome features. He had died not knowing that his young wife had preceded him a week before in the stillborn birth of their first child.

They could not do this without at least one shot fired in protest, she thought through a haze of bitter tears, one shot. With trembling fingers she slid out her father's pistol from the pocket in her skirt. Raising her arm above her head, she fired straight up in the air as the Stars and Bars reached the outstretched hands of the Yankee officer.

The captain lifted his head at the sound, his fierce black eyes searching the crowd. Then he saw her. An elegant figure in a black riding habit mounted on a sleek bay mare. Haughty gray eyes stared unrepentant into his. The sun caught a lock of red-gold hair that had escaped the chignon at the base of her neck, and it shone like spun gold. The face was beautiful, yet cold, full of disdain. Who was she and why did he feel as if he knew her?

Trembling, she slowly lowered her arm, but her gaze was caught by the penetrating black eyes of the Yankee captain. Even across the yards that separated them she felt as if he had reached out and touched her. She could see little of his features for he wore a black beard and mustache, but his penetrating eyes like those of a hawk bore into hers, rendering her for a moment immobile. It was insane, he was the enemy, but she could not turn her eyes from his. There was an air of isolation about his tall figure as if he was used to being alone, in fact preferred it. Surrounded by a crowd who despised him he showed absolutely no fear. In fact, he seemed oblivious to them. It was as if there were only two people in Memphis on this hot summer morn, the Yankee captain and Ariane.

"You best leave quickly, miss," an old man hissed. " 'Tis a brave thing you done."

The man's voice broke the spell in a way she could not do herself. Lowering her gaze, she thrust her pistol inside her skirt and turned Dancer away from the crowd. As the crowd parted so she could make her escape, she felt the burning eyes of the captain follow her although she had turned her back to him. A chill ran through her even though the day was growing sultry. She must escape from here and from him. Every vibrating nerve in her trembling form told her that such an instinctive powerful response to a man meant he was trouble.

Captain Justin Pierce clenched his fist as he watched her leave. He was amazed at his reaction—he wanted to go

10

after her. He wanted to touch that golden hair, pull it out of that prim bun and spread it across his fingers. His pulse quickened as he thought of that cold haughty visage softening into passionate surrender as he tasted those trembling lips that betrayed her courageous resolve. Would her skin feel as silken to his touch as it appeared?

He must be mad, he thought in disgust. It's this town; the sooner he left Memphis again, the better. It had been eight years since he had departed his hometown, and it had taken a war to bring him back. He was glad he was not staying with the occupation troops—there were too many memories here, memories that tore at his heart. A Memphis belle had almost destroyed him; only a fool let that happen twice. All the time he had spent in the North at medical school, and then in Europe, he had forgotten that sensual allure Southern woman could put on like perfume. On the morrow he was continuing on down the river. It was for the best. Memphis would remain in the past, the past he had tried so hard to forget all these years. It had taken an order from his commander to force him ashore to accept the city's surrender and to raise the stars and stripes. In a few hours he would leave again, and he would try to leave the memories as well.

"Let's get it over with," the young lieutenant beside him muttered, "before any more Rebs take a shot at us."

With a swift pull, they raised the Stars and Stripes and Memphis became a conquered city. The clasp on the necklace of the Confederacy was torn open. There was a mumble of displeasure by the crowd, a few jeers, but no more shots were fired.

Staring up at the fluttering flag, Justin Pierce knew that they may have conquered the city, but the people would fight them every step of the way. A pair of stormy gray eyes and red-gold hair flashed across his mind. With that spirit, she would never surrender. He wondered, with a ghost of a smile relaxing the pain that was in his dark eyes, what else she would do to bedevil her so-called conquerors. For a brief moment he forgot old hatreds, old pain, and wished he could stay and see it.

11

Part One

This Southern Confederacy must be supported now by calm determination and cool brains. We have risked all and we must play our best, for the stake is life or death.

Mary Chesnut,
Diary from Dixie

I hate and Love. You ask, perhaps, how that can be? I know not, but I feel the agony.

Catullus, *Poems*

Chapter One

June 1864

"Ariane, take this! Hurry!" The frantic young woman handed her friend several balls of opium as well as a box of morphine from the medicine cupboard. "Hide it in your pockets. Mine are full. Quick before Miss Schneider returns."

"There is to be a courier coming from Forrest's men tonight. I will have more for him than just information," Ariane Valcour whispered in triumph.

"Be careful. The Yankees are livid that so much is smuggled out of Memphis to the Confederacy. I heard tell that they have increased the guards on the road leading into the city."

"The grounds of Fleur de Lys are relatively safe even if we do have those Yankee officers they forced upon us staying there. They would never believe the gracious Miss Valcour would be capable of such an unladylike activity as smuggling and spying." There was a bitter contempt in Ariane's voice as she quickly stuffed the stolen medicine in the voluminous pockets of her plain gray dress under her nursing apron.

For over two years she and Felicity Sanders had been volunteer nurses in the Federal Hospital located in the old Exchange Building, taking care of Confederate prisoners and Union wounded. The Yankees allowed them to see to the wounded prisoners as long as they also nursed the Northern sick as well. Little did they know that there was another motive to the seemingly humane actions of the Memphis women. As nurses in the hospital, they had access to the Federal supply of medicine, drugs badly needed by the Confederacy. Ariane and Felicity had been smuggling medicine out of the hospital since the first day they began work. It never got any easier or less frightening, Ariane thought, feeling the perspiration trickle down her spine as she straightened her apron.

"Ladies, I believe there are prisoners who could use your help." The cool Northern tones of Hazel Schneider startled both young women as she entered the ward room, causing Felicity to spill the cup of coffee she had grabbed to cover her more furtive actions.

"Is it true a new doctor has been assigned?" Ariane questioned, trying to divert attention away from her friend so she might recover her composure.

"Yes. He just arrived from Vicksburg with the wounded aboard the steamer. We can use the help. The Rebs are losing, but fools that they are, they continue to fight their losing battles." The tall, raw-boned woman pursed her thin lips as she checked the roster of patients in the first ward. She seemed unaware of the effect of her words on the two young Memphis women.

Ariane made a slight motion with her elegant head signaling Felicity not to speak. Her hot-headed friend had often gotten into an argument with the tactless, plainspoken Hazel Schneider. But the woman was head of the Federal Sanitary Commission in Memphis and as such was in charge of the nurses at the hospital. She had discharged one Memphis woman that week for pinning a small Confederate flag to the blanket of a Southern prisoner who had just died. The woman had spent two days in the infamous Irving Block Prison just a couple of blocks away before a Union doctor had spoken to the provost marshal and had her released.

"Come, ladies, we have patients waiting. In this heat we will have our work cut out for us." Hazel Schneider touched a handkerchief to her flushed, pinched features.

She had arrived in Memphis the previous autumn from Ohio in the last cool days of November. This was her first hot humid Memphis summer, and it was taking its toll. She never seemed to be able to breathe, and her hair kept escaping the tightly wound braids about her head in stringy gray-blond wisps.

As they left the ward room, several Union officers strode past in a blur of blue coats and broad hats. Ariane turned to stare after them, taking note that they were new, meaning new troops had arrived as well. General Forrest would be most interested in that knowledge. She smuggled more than medicine to the Confederates, for she sent them information about troop movements as well.

"You will have plenty of time to meet the new doctor, Miss Valcour. I believe he is to be billeted with the rest of his fellow officers at your home." The sarcastic words of Hazel Schneider stung Ariane, but she gave no sign. The humiliation of having Union officers forced upon her and her father without any say on their part had long been turned to their advantage. She learned much about Union strategy from her "guests," information that made its way to the Confederate lines in Mississippi and the ears of General Nathan Bedford Forrest.

As the women entered the first ward, the stench of the wounded soon drove all other thoughts from Ariane's mind. If she had looked behind her, she would have seen that their appearance had not gone unnoticed.

"That woman, who is she?" the tall, lean captain with the intense black eyes asked, pausing at the door of the chief surgeon's office.

"One of the Southern women that come to nurse the Reb prisoners, I expect, sir," the young lieutenant replied, holding the door open.

"My God, it's she," Captain Justin Pierce muttered, rubbing his hand over his freshly shaved chin. It was still hard for him to get used to being without his beard, but in the heat it had become unbearable. On the ship back from Vicksburg he had shaved it off, leaving only the thick ebony mustache that didn't quite hide the deep merciless lines about his mouth.

He had thought about her at odd times during the last two years ever since that June morning. It had been usually at night, especially on warm spring nights when the Southern moon shone ripe and full and the air was filled with the scent of honeysuckle. Those nights caused the blood to pound with yearnings as he tried in vain to sleep. Again on the steamer as they made their way up the twisting, surging yellow-brown waters of the Mississippi to Memphis he had thought of her. No longer did the word "Memphis" mean only painful memories; now it also meant stormy gray eyes, red-gold hair, and skin like the petal of a magnolia blossom.

"Welcome to Memphis, Captain," the voice of the chief surgeon broke through the fog of his musings.

"Thank you, sir," he replied, returning the old man's salute. He had heard he was a stickler for protocol and it appeared the gossip had been right.

The rest of the afternoon was taken up with a tour of the mammoth Federal hospital, which took up the entire three-story building. The top floors had been the city hall and the bottom a medical college before the surrender. Although they saw many Memphis women helping the Northern women sent down with the Sanitary Commission, Justin Pierce did not again see the mysterious rebel belle of the red-gold hair.

"I am sure you are tired, Captain. The corporal here will see you to your quarters. The medical officers are billeted with local families. I am afraid the Hotel Gayoso is filled to capacity. You will be staying out at an estate called Fleur de Lys."

"Did you say Fleur de Lys? Is it still the home of Leander Valcour?" the captain asked, his voice a sharp rasp.

"Yes, do you know him?"

"I am originally from Memphis. He was a friend of my father," he replied, staring beyond the chief surgeon as if he were seeing pictures from another time, a time only he could see.

"I see. Well, it can't be helped. Be prepared, these Rebs

18

are still Sesch to the bone. Valcour is running his steamer line with an officer from the Provost Marshal's Office at his elbow. He doesn't take kindly to it, but is smart enough to realize it's the only way he can stay in business. I will see you in the morning, Captain." With a gruff dismissal and another salute, he returned to his office.

"Come on, sir. Your horse has been brought from the docks." The young corporal, not much older than a boy, gestured for Justin to follow him.

The lavender Memphis twilight was deepening into the gloom of night when the two men reached the gates of Fleur de Lys, located near the sentry post on the edge of the city. It had not changed, Justin thought as he spied the gray stone tower that soared above the giant magnolia trees. Leander Valcour's French chateau on the Mississippi. A famous New York architect had been engaged to create a Gothic castle in the latest fashion that had swept the country and England, the Gothic Revival. Located on twenty forested acres, it had been the talk of Memphis and cities up and down the river with its gray stone facade that resembled the châteaux along the Loire in France.

"These Rebs sure know how to live, don't they, Captain." The young corporal shook his head in wonder. "They don't have anything like this back in Indiana."

As they rode through the open gates guarded by four giant iron flambeaux, now darkened by the war, Justin remembered when they were lit every night by a slave. In those long ago days before the war, they looked like four flaming steamboat stacks. It was the steamboat trade that had given Leander Valcour the vast fortune that had built Fleur de Lys. He had come from old Louisiana planter money, but he had increased it tenfold with his steamer line. Everywhere on the estate were remainders of the Valcour Line, from the wrought-iron fleur de lys entwined in the iron fence, to the flag that flew over the tower of the mansion, a flag that was identical to the one that flew over every steamer. A gold fleur de lys rising from a bouquet of cotton blossoms on a deep blue field.

"Kind of spooky at night, though," the young corporal

19

muttered as they rode up the gravel path that led between the cedars and the giant magnolias, their blossoms glowing alabaster in the moonlight. "They say that his wife was crazy and drowned herself in that pond over there." He gestured to his right toward a small lake also shimmering in the light from the newly risen moon. "There's swans on it, even a black one. Now that's something I never saw before I came here, a black swan." He scratched his head in wonder at such a thing.

Justin's deep-set eyes darkened at his words as a memory from the past flashed across his mind. Little Bit, the funny sad little sister of his friend Charles Valcour. He hadn't thought of her in years. It had been a hot July night over nine years ago when Marie Louise Valcour had taken her life, seeking some relief from her tortured mind, unaware that her twelve-year-old daughter was watching from her bedroom window. What went through the poor child's mind was anybody's guess, but she had vanished in the turmoil. He and Charles had spent all night looking for her. They finally found her wandering around the dangerous riverfront district of Pinch Gut dressed in cast-off clothes of her other brother Beau. She had cut her hair short like a man's so it stuck out in orange wisps, and she told everyone her name was Andy. How the ugly little kitten had fought them, saying she was going to hire out on one of her father's ships as a cabin boy. She refused to ever go back to Fleur de Lys, saying she would rather live on the waterfront.

A slight melancholy smile softened Justin's taut mouth as he remembered telling Charles to leave them be, that he would see to her. How self-important he had been, just home from Harvard Medical School and thinking he knew all the answers. He had lifted her up in front of him and, holding that squirming little boy, had named her "Little Bit." They rode for hours along the bluffs of the Mississippi while he held her trembling, raging, and finally crying like some small, wild frightened animal. He gentled her as he had a wild young critter he found once caught in a trap till she trusted him and would allow him to comfort her.

20

What nonsense had he told her about how wonderful it was to grow into a woman, for through the tears and anger he had discovered that her woman's monthlies had come for the first time the night she saw her mother die. The frightened child had rebelled at the thought of her own femininity. Whatever platitudes he had uttered must have helped, for she let him take her home. What had happened to her, he mused, for he had not seen her again. It was a few weeks later on another sultry Memphis summer night that his world had been torn apart by Olivia, that Southern temptress who had cut out his heart and made him a stranger in his own home. He had left Memphis and never looked back until tonight.

"Looks like the others got here before us, Captain." The corporal nodded toward where several horses stood tied to the ornate hitching post. "Half the slaves run off, it takes them a while to see to all the horses."

Justin tied his mount with the others and thanked the corporal for seeing that his bags had been delivered earlier in the day. Striding up the broad stone steps toward the mansion's massive double doors, he held himself rigid as if to ward off what might come. In a few seconds he would come face to face with someone who would remember him as Justin Pierce of Cedar Rest Plantation. As he lifted his hand to raise the giant brass fleur de lys door knocker, the massive portal swung open.

"Welcome, sir, to Fleur de Lys." The aged black servant in the blue and gold Valcour livery stood back so he might enter.

"Caesar, is that you?" Justin asked as he crossed the threshold.

The old black man peered up at him in the dim light. Where once a massive chandelier had blazed in the huge foyer, now the light from one small lamp made the place dark and full of shadows.

As Justin swept off his wide-brimmed hat and turned to stare down at the old man, he heard a sound in the direction of the enormous curving staircase. "Don't you recognize me, Caesar?"

"No, sir, I . . . Lord Almighty it's Mister Justin!" he gasped.

"It has been a long time, hasn't it," Justin said softly as the old man stared at him like someone come back from the dead. Well, perhaps, in a way he had.

"Is this the new officer, Caesar?" the soft caressing sound of a feminine Southern voice floated across the foyer from the darkened staircase.

Turning, Justin was startled to see the figure of a woman come lightly down the stairs. The lamp she held aloft cast a halo of light around the shimmering tresses caught at the back of her head in a cascade of silken curls. He felt a hot rush cut through him. It was she—the woman who had come to symbolize Memphis to him. The lovely high-spirited Rebel belle. He had read somewhere that to fully appreciate a woman's beauty, one should observe her descend a staircase. That unknown author had spoken the truth.

"Yes ma'am," Caesar muttered uneasily.

"Welcome to Fleur de Lys, Captain," Ariane Valcour said in her soft husky voice as she glided across the stone floor. Her gauzy lavender gown, like some overturned flower blossom, billowed gracefully from her tiny waist. But as she reached him, and the light of her lamp fell across his face she gasped, "Who are you?"

"Captain Justin Pierce, ma'am, and whom might I have the pleasure of addressing?" he drawled, the accent of his home coming back deeper to his speech. It had been a long time since he had played the flirtation game that Southern women seemed to be born knowing.

Her delicate oval visage paled with shock at his words. It was he. She stared, unable to speak as a montage of memories seemed to move before her. Doctor Justin Pierce, her rescuer, her knight, how often she had thought of him, dreamed of him in those long-ago days when she had stood on the threshold of young womanhood. She had loved him with all her childish, newly awakened heart. When he had dueled with his own brother over Olivia Whitlow, and been disowned by his father, she had defended him to the girls at her school, who had called him a rogue and a scoundrel.

When he left Memphis, she had thought her heart would break. How many hours had she spent up in the tower staring out across the city to the Mississippi River, willing him to return on the next steamer that turned the bend. Gradually with the years he had faded in her memory as she grew to be a woman, but always she'd had a soft spot in her heart for the young doctor who had treated her with such kindness and delicacy in explaining what no one else had taken the trouble to explain. He had changed—before her stood a man who had seen a great deal of life by the look of him.

The inherent strength in his handsome visage had hardened with the years. There was, however, the same swarthy skin, bronzed even deeper by the elements, stretched over high cheekbones. The fine aquiline nose with slightly flaring nostrils, firm strong chin, but there was a hard, remote quality about him that changed him from the young doctor she had known long ago. She wondered with a stab of sadness if his tender kindness had gone as well. This man had a detached, brooding air about him. It was only in those deep-set, brilliant black eyes that she could find a hint of the man she had once known. His eyes told her he was not entirely cold and detached. Oh no, she thought with an unaccustomed ripple of sensual excitement. This was not a cold man, only a very controlled one.

"This be Miss Ariane Valcour," Caesar finally announced as the silence lengthened between them.

"But that cannot be. Ariane Valcour is a child," Justin replied in terse tones, not taking his eyes from the seductive figure that stood in front of him.

"That was nine years ago, Doctor Justin," she breathed softly, using the name she had called him those far-off years ago.

"My God, Little Bit," he muttered in disbelief.

"I have grown up." She gave a low husky chuckle at his bemused expression. She sensed that this self-possessed man with the wary eyes was rarely caught off guard.

"You certainly have." His dark eyes for a moment allowed a glint of wonder to lighten their ebony depths.

"I prayed for years that you would come back to me. You

23

see, I thought of you as my knight," she whispered, tears of remembered pain and loneliness misting her gray eyes. "I fear I've read too many romantic books as a child."

"Perhaps, Little Bit, I have come back to you," he answered huskily, stunned that he was saying such a thing. But then this had been a night for surprises. Gently, he reached out a tapered finger and brushed the tear that trailed down her cheek.

"But you are wearing the wrong trappings, my errant knight." She spoke in a broken whisper, staring down at the blue sleeve of his uniform.

"Does it matter, Little Bit, my lovely Rebel?"

Chapter Two

Smoke gray eyes stared up at him awash in a mist of tears that did not hide the flash of pain that flickered in those expressive orbs. "I wish I could say that it does not, but . . ." Her husky voice trailed off as she took a step back from him. A battle was raging inside her heart, and she struggled to put some distance between herself and his disturbing presence. He had returned to her, the hero of her lonely childhood, but in the uniform of the enemy, the enemy she had sworn to defeat any way she could.

"I see," he answered in taut cold tones as an inexplicable look of withdrawal came over his face. His gaze, however, continued to burn with a curious intensity that belied the ice in his voice. He wanted her with a hunger he thought he had become incapable of feeling after Olivia had torn out his soul. This beautiful seductive woman was his poor lost waif, his Little Bit. It was amazing.

"Daughter, we are awaiting dinner." The cultured, weary voice of a man broke the spell that hung in the air between them like a presence. "Caesar will see to the officer's bags. I am sure he is as eager for his dinner as we are." The bent figure of a man leaning heavily on a sturdy cane appeared in the doorway of a room on the right.

"Yes, Father, we are coming," Ariane replied, flashing a silent warning to Justin that was also a plea.

Puzzled, Justin soon understood as he followed her to

25

where her father stood. In the light from the many-branched candelabra on the long dining room table, he saw the man he had known as Leander Valcour. He was a ghost of his former prewar self. Deep age lines were cut across his brow and beside his mouth. His once golden hair had turned silver, and his blue eyes were blood-shot and rheumy like a very old man. There was a haunted look to his gaze that chilled Justin to the marrow. This man had seen hell and lived to tell the tale. It was a look he had seen on men whose physical wounds had healed but who had deeper wounds that still festered in the soul. He thought of them as the walking wounded. They were irrevocably changed, never in spirit the men they had once been. The loss of his leg at the knee was tragic, but the loss of all hope in his eyes was heartbreaking.

"This is Captain Pierce, Father," Ariane said softly as they reached the older man. " 'Tis Justin Pierce, Papa, Charles and Beau's friend. He has returned to Memphis."

Leander Valcour raised his leonine head, and for a moment there was the fiery pride and strength of character shining out from that aristocratic visage. It was the man Justin remembered. "I am glad your father is no longer alive to see this day. You, sir, have forfeited your honor. How can you have joined his enemy? He and Charles died fighting men who wore that uniform," he thundered. Then as if the memories were too much for him, he stopped, staring off into space past them all. "They're all gone, all gone," he whispered, shaking his head in disbelief.

"Come, Papa, perhaps a tray in your room. It has been a long day and you are tired." Ariane put her arms around his shoulders. He was shaking with silent sobs as his wounded mind relived the horror of the past battle of Shiloh, where he had lost his oldest son, and Justin's father, his best friend.

"I take him upstairs, Mam'zelle Ariane." A still attractive woman of color dressed in the blue muslin dress, white apron, and tignon of a house servant appeared at her side.

"Thank you, Sable." Ariane stepped aside so the graceful woman could take her father's arm and lead him from the room. Dear Sable, who had come from Baton Rouge all those years ago with her mother. The still lovely quadroon woman ran the huge house now as housekeeper. And sometimes only Sable could quiet her father when the past became too much for him to bear.

"You must forgive him. He would never have said those things if he were . . . were more himself," Ariane apologized, quietly, only the trembling of her soft, delicate mouth revealing the depth of her despair at her father's condition.

Justin had to clench his fist to keep from reaching out and pulling this beautiful, poised young woman into his embrace. He remembered that scruffy little girl fighting against fate with her childish courage. She had grown into a beautiful woman but had lost none of her pluck or mettle. How he admired her control and grace in a situation that must be breaking her heart.

"How long has he been like this?" he questioned in a professional tone, instead of pressing her to him and caressing that red-gold hair, kissing the pain from the pale oval of her face as he wanted to with every fiber of his being.

"Since Shiloh. He was too old to go, as was your father, but they insisted. He saw Charles . . . Charles killed, before taking a bullet in his own leg. They had to amputate part of his leg in the makeshift hospital in Corinth. He almost died, but I managed to bring him home. He has never really regained his health, but insists on going to the offices every day. I fear it is too much for him."

"You were there . . . at Shiloh?" There was disapproval and a kind of wonder in his voice as a sharp stab of pain cut through him at the thought of his old friend's death. He had heard of his father's mortal wounds—his brother had sent word through their attorney—but he had not

27

known about Charles.

"She rode through the lines dressed as a boy to look for her father and brother. Miss Valcour is quite a legend in the city," one of the officers billeted at Fleur de Lys remarked from where he stood with the other two officers beside their places at the table. They had risen when she'd walked into the room and were still standing, having witnessed the confrontation with her father.

"Not really a legend, gentlemen." Ariane smiled in their direction, but it was a smile Justin noticed didn't reach her stormy eyes. "Please be seated so Roman can begin serving. Captain Pierce, since you are an old family friend, perhaps you would take my father's place." She gestured to the place set at the end of the long table. The other three men hurried to pull out her chair, but the black serving man reached it first, to their chagrin. They observed Justin with interest. The gossip about him would be all over the hospital on the morrow.

From where he sat at the foot of the table, Justin could observe his beautiful hostess as she made sure her "guests" were served and made idle polite conversation with them. She was the perfect Southern hostess and lady. It was this observation that disquieted him, for there was something wrong about it all. She was too kind, too gracious, to these officers whom she saw as the enemy, and the seeds of doubt about Ariane Valcour began to grow.

"Captain Pierce, you must have some of our chess pie," his hostess called out to him from where she sat at the other end of the elegant mahogany table with its gleaming silver and Staffordshire china. Magnolia blossoms swam in the shallow tiered centerpiece, their clean lemony fragrance wafting in the humid, sultry air and eliciting in Justin's turbulent thoughts a myriad memories of other Southern nights.

"I should enjoy that, Miss Valcour, 'tis a dessert you can only get in this part of Tennessee," he replied, staring out across the wavering light of the tall ivory tapers to capture her gray eyes for a moment before she turned away. He could look at her all night, those alabaster shoulders, the soft tantalizing mounds of her half-revealed breasts, the way she tossed her red-gold curls when she talked or laughed at something one of the other men said in jest. He hated their mere presence, that they, too, could enjoy the sight of Ariane Valcour.

She was conscious of his gaze, that too intense gaze that seemed to devour her from out of the shadows at the opposite end of the table. What trick was fate playing on her to return him to her now, at this time. The other officers were easy to fool with a few light flirtatious glances, but Justin was a Southerner born and bred. He would notice and understand all the subtleties the others did not, and worst of all for her, he knew the grounds of Fleur de Lys like the back of his hand. She must somehow play the game without alerting him to what she was really up to with her gracious hospitality. Tonight she was to meet her brother Beau, who was a scout with General Forrest's raiders, at the tomb of her mother in a remote part of the estate. If he could slip through the sentry's post at the edge of the city, they would rendezvous at midnight. She would signal him from the tower if all was clear. It had to be tonight. She had to tell him of a shipment of arms coming in on the Memphis and Charleston Railroad. If General Nathan Bedford Forrest's raiders could stop that train outside Memphis, they could capture guns and ammunition badly needed by the Confederacy.

"Gentlemen, if I might be so bold as to suggest we adjourn to the parlor, Caesar will delight you with his special mint juleps. They are just the thing on such a hot night. And I shall endeavor to entertain you with several songs on the melodeon." Rising to her feet, she nodded to the aged butler. She had already told him to double the bourbon in the drinks and to keep them coming till the men were worse the wear for drink. She needed sound sleepers in the house tonight.

29

What was she up to, Justin mused. Mint juleps and a music recital—certainly that went beyond the bounds of the General Order in Memphis of not interfering with the enemy. Why would the spirited woman who fired the only shot in protest at the city's surrender suddenly be so friendly with the very Yankees who had killed Charles? Something was wrong here, very wrong. Forcing his attention back to the words of his beautiful hostess, Justin rose and followed her graceful figure from the dining room. Her hoop skirt swung provocatively from her tiny waist as they crossed the darkened foyer. The parlor was just as Justin remembered it, elegant with its rosewood and mahogany rococo Belter furniture. Decorated in shades of blue and buff with twenty-foot ceilings and long French doors that opened onto the veranda, it was a cool retreat from the hot, humid Memphis summer. Crystal vases of deep red roses and shallow silver bowls where alabaster magnolias floated perfumed the chamber with an almost overpowering perfume.

" 'Tis always such a relaxing way to spend the evening, Miss Valcour. The hospital seems so far away," one of the young doctors commented as they followed her into the shadowy room lit by several globe oil lamps. The young man's face was damp from the heat and he passed a handkerchief over his brow frequently.

"I always find Fleur de Lys several degrees cooler than in town." Ariane gave him a gracious smile as she seated herself at the gleaming walnut melodeon, the ivory keys creamy in the glow from the hurricane lamp.

"Gentlemen, yo' drinks." Caesar appeared with silver mint julep cups, beads of moisture clinging to them in the heat. The doctors all helped themselves with relish to the old black servant's specialty.

"Captain Pierce," Ariane said, interrupting him as he reached for a julep. "Would you do me the honor of singing to my accompaniment. I remember what a splendid voice you had when you and Charles performed duets."

"How can I refuse such a charming request," Justin replied, letting Caesar pass him by.

"Is 'Lorena' all right?" she asked, smiling up at him as he joined her at the delicate, pianolike instrument.

He nodded, standing close behind her so he might read all the melancholy lyrics that both the North and the South had taken to their hearts. Standing so, as his rich baritone filled the sultry chamber, he couldn't help staring down at her soft alabaster shoulders with just a hint of gold in their creamy texture. He felt a tightening in his loins as her perfume floated up to him, a fragrance he had not smelled anywhere else but in the South. It was the sweet, seductive scent of heliotrope. From now on, it would always remind him of her, of Ariane.

It was as if they were alone in the room, just the two of them in the soft, hot night, held together in the small golden circle of the lamp light. He had to force himself to keep from reaching out and brushing the red-gold tendril that fell across her temple. Strength deserted him when it came to averting his gaze from the voluptuous mounds of her breasts that teased him from the low line of her bodice. He drank in the sight of them and envied the locket that nestled between their ripe softness.

She was so aware of his nearness she thought she could feel the heat from his body. She felt his gaze soft as a caress move over her neck and shoulders and down to the depths of her bosom. There was a tingling that ran through her, causing every nerve to vibrate in a way she had never known before. It was as if she had never really been alive, not in this way. The music seemed to pour out of her soul into her fingers and they flew over the ivory keys like darting swallows.

"*A hundred months have passed since, Lorena. Since last I held thy hand in mine. And felt the pulse beat fast, Lorena. Though mine beat faster far than thine,*" Justin sang, starting the second verse as he stood close behind her. Suddenly the poignant words of the song seemed to have been written especially for them.

The sound of his voice touched Ariane deeply, causing

31

an ache to rise in her throat. She was glad she knew the music almost by heart for the mist of tears in her eyes clouded her vision. She could barely read the notes. His presence, his voice, even the scent of his bay rum shaving lotion struck a vibrant chord deep within her. Every word of the sad refrain cut into her heart.

"A hundred months, 'twas flowery May, when up the hilly slope we climbed, to watch the dying of the day, and hear the distant church bells chime. To watch the dying of the day, and hear the distant church bells chime," his deep voice ended the song as her hands rested over the keys.

There was a silence in the chamber for a few seconds as if the others did not want to break the spell of the tableau they had just seen. Memories of home and sweethearts filled the sultry stillness till it became too much, and first one man then the other two began to clap in appreciation.

As Ariane rose to accept their applause, Justin took her hands and raised them to his lips in salute. The touch of his mouth to her skin sent the shock of him through her body till she thought she couldn't breathe. Reluctantly, he lifted his lips from her fingers and captured her gaze with his intense black eyes. There was both an invitation in those burning depths as well as regret. It was as if he could probe her mind and soul and knew that what they both wanted could never be, not as long as they stood on opposite sides of an enormous chasm known as war.

The chiming of the tall clock in the foyer reminded Ariane that there were three hours left before she was to signal Beau from the tower. Turning from Justin's probing gaze, she signaled Caesar for more drinks and then with a flirtatious smile asked for requests from her guests.

" 'The Girl I Left Behind Me,' please, Miss Valcour," one of the officers called out as he helped himself to another mint julep.

"Captain Pierce, an encore?" she asked with another

flash of her practiced smile as she seated herself once more in front of the melodeon.

"Perhaps we could all join in," he replied, noticing the flushed faces of his fellow officers. Ariane was deliberately trying to make them drunk, and it looked like she was succeeding. Gesturing to Caesar for one of the silver cups he was passing around with such lavishness, he lifted the drink to his lips. The fumes of the bourbon were strong, too strong for one of Caesar masterpieces. As he swallowed the liquid, the strength of it almost choked him. In the days before the war he had often sampled Caesar's famous juleps. They had been delicious— the right mix of sugar, mint, and bourbon. It seemed since the war he had gotten heavy with the bourbon, way too heavy. Staring at the red-gold curls of his hostess as they danced to the spirited tempo of the song, he wondered if it had been her orders to make the drinks so strong. There was a certain feeling in his gut that told him he was right, but why did she want her guests in a state of inebriation?

As the night wore on, Ariane played every song she knew as her guests became more and more the worse for drink. After the first few sips, Justin had put his cup aside. He would need all his wits about him this night. His lovely Rebel had some plan behind her actions. He was going to find out what it was that required such a devious plot.

As Ariane played, her drunken guests crowded around the melodeon, singing with abandon. She caught herself glancing uneasily over her shoulder in Justin's direction He had taken a seat at a distance, not drinking the mint julep Caesar had given him. She could feel his eyes upon her, questioning her motives. There was a growing sick feeling in the pit of her stomach. Her mouth felt dry and hurt from her forced smile. The chiming of the half-hour, telling her it was ten-thirty, made her decide she had to end the evening before she gave herself away.

"I declare, gentlemen, but you have worn me out. This

heat does make any activity all the more exhausting. Perhaps it is time for us to retire for the night." Ariane rose to her feet, firmly closing the lid over the keys.

The officers, with elaborate protestations, gave in to her request. After bidding her good night, they staggered off to their various chambers on the second floor. Only Justin remained, staring out the open French doors. A full moon was casting ivory streams of light on the long grass and turning the magnolia blossoms to glowing alabaster globes.

"I have had Caesar put your valises in Charles's old room. I did not think you would mind," Ariane said softly from where she stood beside the silent instrument. She had extinguished the hurricane lamp to hurry the men on their way, and now the only light came from two night candlesticks Caesar had placed on the foyer table, to be taken upstairs. The moon shone into the room, making ghostly patterns on the Aubusson carpet.

"Thank you, I am honored to have Charles's room, but do you mind, my dear Ariane, having Yankees thrust upon you?" He turned to face her, and she felt the strength of his speculative gaze even though she could see only his outline silhouetted by the moon.

" 'Twould make no difference if I did," she answered, unable to keep the resentment out of her voice.

"You sound remarkably resigned. I wonder what happened to that spirited Rebel belle who fired the only shot in defiance when Memphis surrendered." He came closer to where she was standing.

"How do you know that?" She was barely able to control her gasp of surprise.

"I was there."

"There!" Her body stiffened in shock. "You were one of those three men," she repeated slowly as she realized what he was saying and its implications. The one with the piercing eyes . . . of course, she thought. "How did I not recognize you? The beard—you wore a beard then. How could you participate in humiliating the city of your

34

birth? How could you do such a thing?" Her mood had veered sharply to anger and she spat out the words contemptuously.

"I believe Tennessee was wrong in leaving the union. It has caused only bloodshed, death, and destruction. There were other ways that could have been used to solve this country's problems. Seceding from it solves nothing. The South will be defeated in this bloody war and it will take years to recover, if ever, from what has been irretrievably lost." A thin chill hung on the edge of his words.

"Do you hate us that much? I know you were treated badly by many after the duel with your brother, but is that any reason to turn against the South, to turn against your own people?" Ariane reached out her hand as if in supplication, begging to understand what was, to her, beyond comprehension.

"I could never hate you, my sweet Ariane." He clasped her outstretched hand and lifted it to his heated lips, the soft fur of his mustache brushing the back of her trembling hand. Turning over the tiny hand, he pressed his mouth to her soft palm in a tender intimate gesture that bespoke his ardor.

A shudder of longing ran through her at the touch of his mouth, the light pressure of his tongue. She had to clench the fingers of her other hand to suppress the almost overwhelming desire to reach out and caress the ebony satin of his hair that fell in a slight wave across his brow and curled over his collar. This man was the enemy, she repeated over and over silently as if to burn it into her mind and soul.

"Please . . ." The whispered cry came from the depths of her tortured, confused heart.

"Please what?" he asked quietly, raising his head from her hand but keeping it tightly clasped in his long tapered fingers. There was a probing query in the depths of those all-knowing, depthless eyes.

"I . . . I do not know," she answered in confusion, struggling to conquer her involuntary reaction to the hunger she saw reflected in his gaze. From deep within her it was kindling, a fire that threatened to be inextinguishable. She had to get away from those eyes, that touch, this man who struck some hidden chord she had thought was long forgotten.

"I think you know, Little Bit. We have both known since I entered this house." His voice broke with a sensual huskiness as his hands reached out for her, pressing her to him as he had desired since that long ago hot June morning when Memphis had surrendered.

She buried her face against the welcoming sanctuary of his chest, tears of joy and regret falling on the hated blue uniform. Her arms wrapped tightly around him as if they had a will of their own. Stay away, her mind cried, but her heart wanted the feel, the touch, the taste of him. With a sob, her heart won, and she melted into him, her soft curves molding to the contours of his lean form.

"Do not cry, my sweet, I have come back to you. You are not alone any longer. Dear, sweet Little Bit, hush, hush now," he whispered into her hair as he gently rocked her back and forth in the circle of his embrace, lightly kissing the wispy tendrils at her temples.

Not alone any longer, she thought. Oh, if it were only true. But at this moment, held close to this strong caring man, she realized how alone she really was. She had chosen a solitary road. Because of who she was and her deep abiding love for her native land, her Tennessee, she could take no other course, but oh how hard it was, how lonely it must be. Honor, family, friends, her beloved Fleur de Lys, because of all these she must do what she had promised, but the cost would be great. For a brief moment she did not know if she could put all this before what her whole being cried out for—the total surrender of her heart and soul to this man who had been from her first awakening as a woman her perfect cavalier, her knight-errant, her imagined lover.

The chime of the clock penetrated through the torment of her conflicting emotions. There was no time for the luxury of indecision. Somewhere in the dense woods surrounding Fleur de Lys waited Beau, her brother. Family loyalty gave her the strength to pull away from the beguiling sanctuary of Justin's embrace.

" 'Tis late, I must see that my father is all right," she whispered, pulling back from his chest, turning her head from those all-knowing dark eyes.

"Do you want me to look in on him," Justin asked quietly, feeling the tension in her slender form, still holding her in the circle of his arms.

"No!" she exclaimed, then realized she had overreacted, for her father had only been an excuse to leave him. "I . . . I mean that it would probably just excite him to see you."

"Of course, you are right. If, however, you should need me for any reason, don't hesitate to wake me. Promise?" He lifted her chin till she stared up at him in the dim moonlight.

"I promise," she whispered as his finger moved up to trace the soft outline of her mouth.

"Then, good night, my sweet Rebel," he murmured as his mouth brushed hers in a light tantalizing kiss.

Her mouth burning from the touch of his lips, she turned away and fumbled for the night candle Caesar had left. She had to leave now while she still could. Without looking back, she started up the staircase.

"Little Bit, is Charles's room still at the head of the stairs next to yours?" he called after her.

Pausing halfway up the staircase, she turned to stare down at him. The wavering light of the tall taper he held caught the smoldering fire in his ebony gaze. "Yes," she stammered at the implication in his voice.

"Good," he answered, his deep voice filled with a barely checked passion. Never had she haid so much implied in a single innocent word.

Her hand shook as she lifted the candlestick high above her head to light the way, her skirt clasped in the other hand. How long was she going to be able to keep her much-needed control with Justin staying beside her in the next chamber. It had been the only room left, but she realized she should have moved one of the other officers to Charles's chamber. She had not wanted a Yankee staying in his room—somehow it seemed a stain on his memory—but Justin was different. Was he? He wore that hated blue tunic, but somehow it was different, and she realized that was what made him so dangerous. She had to be on her guard, not so much because of Justin, but because of the feelings he caused to burn within her heart. Oh, dear God, did she have the strength? Even now she could hear his boots on the stair coming up behind her in the dark hot night.

Chapter Three

Ariane stood with her back pressed against the locked mahogany door of her bedchamber. Was she locking Justin out or herself in away from temptation? She felt her heart skipping a beat as his footsteps paused outside her door. It was as if she could feel his tall lean presence through the thick portal. Her hand caressed the satin of the wood as if she could reach out and touch him. Torn between desire and duty, she had to bite her lower lip to keep from calling out to him. A hot ache grew in her throat as she fought the overwhelming desire to tear open the door.

The sound of his footsteps walking away brought both disappointment and relief. It was for the best, she told herself, trying to still the longing that throbbed like a wound. There was much to be done and not much time left before midnight. Crossing the darkened room, she lit the oil lamp on her dressing table with the tall taper she carried. From her basket beside the huge four-poster draped in a cloud of mosquito netting, a black-and-white springer spaniel rose to greet her mistress.

"Bess, we have work to do tonight." Ariane bent down to stroke the silken fur of her pet. Walking her dog was a perfect excuse to be outdoors at night if ever she was unfortunate to be caught in her midnight strolls. Bess was getting on in years and known to be greatly indulged by her mistress.

Sitting at the white and gold Louis IV writing desk, she unclasped the locket she wore around her neck. When she pressed a tiny button beside the delicate cameo top, the locket sprang open to reveal a brass disk. Ariane took the small disk from the locket and placed it on the polished surface of the table. From an embroidery case she took out a pair of wire-rimmed magnifying glasses. The work she was about to do required excellent eyesight and she was a little far-sighted. Placing the glasses on her nose, she picked up the brass disk and began to move the tiny inner wheel to line up with the letter *A* on the outer wheel. The disk was a cipher used to encode messages so that even if the courier was caught, the enemy would not understand the message. Taking pen in hand, she dipped it in the inkwell and began to encode the message she was sending to General Forrest.

By the time the full ivory globe of the moon shone down on the grounds of Fleur de Lys at midnight, Ariane was ready with her message hidden in an empty pocket-watch. The smuggled morphine tablets and quinine were in a long, hollowed-out loaf of French bread. Placing the bread in a basket she carried over her arm, she attached Bess's leash to her collar. Picking up a tin lantern that had pierced sides to let out small streams of light when the sides were closed, Ariane left her bedchamber, closing the door quietly behind her. She stood in the hall for a moment listening, but all she heard was the sound of men snoring behind their closed doors. Good, she thought; the mint juleps had done their work well.

Quietly, as the huge clock in the foyer downstairs struck midnight, she walked Bess down the hall to where a small staircase led up to her refuge as a child, the tower overlooking Memphis and the surrounding countryside.

Once up in the glass-enclosed room, with the door

closed behind her, she stared out across the tops of the trees toward the Mississippi, where the moon turned the water to a glowing silver ribbon. It all looked so peaceful out there from this great height. She sighed. If only the land were as it appeared, but the Federal Army held Memphis in its grip. The city was quiet only because there was a curfew, and if anyone was caught out on the streets, the infamous Irving Block Prison would be his resting place for the night. Shuddering at the thought of Beau hiding out there, somewhere waiting for her signal, she quickly unsheathed the lantern. Moving to the far window, she began to swing it back and forth in the signal she had been taught by her brother. This signal meant all was clear; meet her at the tomb.

Leaving the tower, she made her way down the stairs and out the back door. The light from the moon was so clear and bright she closed the sides of the lantern so only a few streaks of light came from the pierced design on the sides. Feeling a sense of exhilaration, she realized once more she had pulled it off, leaving the house without being seen. Hurrying across the kitchen herb garden, she made for the path around the lake.

What the hell was she doing, Justin mused as he stood at his window staring down at the slight figure, her dog at her side, moving determinedly away from the house. Unable to sleep, the memory of red-gold curls, full alabaster breasts, a tiny waist that hinted at the curving hips beneath threatened to drive him mad. The elusive scent of heliotrope seemed to linger in the soft, sultry air, taunting him till he wanted to go to her—even if it meant breaking down her chamber door. He wanted to strip the night rail from that ivory-gold body, pull those red-gold tresses free till they were her only covering. He wanted to span that tiny waist with his two hands to see if it was as small as it appeared. He had to taste those crushed rose lips under his so he might drink his fill.

.My God, he thought as he lit his pipe, hoping the smell of tobacco would drown out the flower-drenched scent of the air. Southern nights—how long it had been since he'd experienced their seductive allure. They got inside a man like a fever, making his blood pound with desires best left hidden in the deeper recesses of his being.

As he stared down at the moving figure, her dress white in the moonglow till she looked like some enchanted, celestial creature that appeared only on starry midsummer nights, he mused once more on what would cause her to leave the house at this late hour. A swift shadow of anger crossed his usually cool, aloof features. Was she going to meet a lover? The thought gnawed at his gut, causing a muscle to flick angrily in his tensed, firm jaw. Those who had felt his wrath would recognize the signs of his disturbance. He was a self-contained man who had learned to show little emotion, but there was a certain tenseness about him like that in a large predatory jungle cat who stalked his prey with careful deliberation. This curious waiting quality would alert those discerning enough to notice that he was filled with a cold rage.

Watching her disappear into the dark shadows of the trees, Justin could stand it no longer. He had to follow her, he had to know what she was doing, whom she was meeting.

It became darker the farther Ariane walked from the house and gardens. The giant cedars cast long, ghostly shadows across the path around the lake, their thickly furred boughs blotting out some of the moonlight. But Ariane knew her way—she had walked these paths from childhood. Every beloved inch of Fleur de

Lys was familiar to her sure step.

The spectral outline of her mother's tomb with the weeping angel atop it appeared on a slight rise overlooking the lake. A stream of silver moonglow caused the white marble angel to glow with an unearthly light. The scent of the night-blooming jasmine was stronger here, for the tomb was surrounded by the tenacious plants. The scent had been Marie Louise's favorite, and after her death, Leander Valcour had planted them in her memory. The African slaves claimed the place was haunted, and avoided the site. The story worked to Ariane's advantage, for it was here she could meet her brother without fear of detection.

The hoot of an owl sounded above the undertone of crickets and katydids, adding to the symphony of peeper frogs. This, however, was an owl with a decided human intonation. Ariane gave an answering hoot as Beau had taught her years ago as a child. It was their final signal.

"Sis, over here," the familiar beloved sound of Beau's voice hissed from behind the spreading branches of an ancient magnolia.

" 'Tis all clear, Buba," she called to him, using that Southern term for "brother" that had been her affectionate name for him since she was a little girl and couldn't pronounce Beau, let alone Beauregard.

He came toward her, and in the bright moonlight her heart broke at his appearance. Rail thin, his tattered gray tunic hung over the dyed butternut breeches. His knee-high boots were worn, and scarred. His broad-brimmed gray felt hat was battered, but one side was still turned up jauntily and bright cock feathers replaced the long-gone scarlet ostrich plume. Beau, the handsome cavalier whose attention the belles had fought to catch at long-ago balls, was a lean, hardened warrior. A thick golden beard covered his chin

43

and a wary look had come into his blue-gray eyes.

"You are so thin," Ariane exclaimed as he gave her a hug, tears filling her eyes. "I have been searching for gray cloth for a new uniform, but the Yankees put Felicity's cousin Camelia in Irving Block for trying to smuggle a uniform out of the city to her brother. When she wouldn't tell what company in Memphis had sold her the gray cloth, they refused to let her out. She's been there for weeks, the beasts!"

"Miss Camelia is in Irving Block?" Beau's voice was filled with horror. The blue-gray eyes she knew so well now gleamed with a cold hate. They were not the eyes of her fun-loving cavalier brother; they were the eyes of a man who had seen too much, a man who had killed many times.

"Forgive me, darlin'. I forgot about you and Camelia." Ariane's voice was full of regret. How could she have mentioned such a thing. In those heady days right after war had been declared, when the young men had rushed to join the Confederacy, they had formed drilling companies. As the companies marched off to war, each soldier tied the handkerchief of a chosen lady to his rifle, like a knight of old wearing his lady's colors in a tournament. As Beau had marched off to Shiloh, he'd adorned his rifle with a scrap of lace belonging to the delicate Camelia. How could Ariane have forgotten?

"Damn them all to hell!" Beau stared off across the tranquil lake and the look in his eyes was murderous.

"There is not much time. I am frightened for you to spend so long inside the Yankee lines," Ariane whispered, alarmed by the look on her brother's hardened visage. He seemed like a stranger to her. She tried to distract him from his thoughts about the unfortunate Camelia. "Here is my message to General Forrest. 'Tis important he read it immediately. And inside the bread is medicine we were able to smuggle out of the hospi-

44

tal. Morphine and quinine. I will try to get more next time. There is food in the basket for you too, darlin', and Father insisted on a bottle of his best brandy for General Forrest as well as a pack of those cards you said he would like."

"The Wizard of the Saddle does like his poker," Beau said with a thin smile, taking the packs of food to put in his saddlebags. To his men, and the South, the brilliant General Forrest had come to be called affectionately by the nickname Beau had just used.

"So I have heard," Ariane replied with a sad smile. Beau and his brave comrades had nothing but worn-out clothes, guns and ammunition they had to steal from the Yankees at great risk. Their only food was what they could forage for or steal. But this small regiment of men outnumbered by the Federal Troops under General Hurlbut and General Washburn were bedeviling the Yankees. They had them held up in Memphis reluctant to venture out into the surrounding countryside held by the Confederates led by the Wizard in the Saddle. Mempis was an island of Yankee strength in a sea of partisan Rebel troops. She would do anything to help these valiant, gallant men she had known all her life. Their exploits were the only bright spot in the bleak lives of Memphians held under the strong oppressive hand of Yankee occupation.

"Be careful, sis. The word out from our intelligence is that Grant has sent someone to Memphis to help those idiots in the Union Command discover who is in charge of the smuggling and spying activities in the city. Forrest says that he doesn't want anything to happen to his beautiful Memphis Swan."

Ariane gave a husky chuckle at the code name the general had given her. "I do believe the general has a romantic streak."

"Try and tell that to the Yankees," Beau joked as he bent down to kiss her cheek in farewell.

45

Suddenly Bess gave a low growl, startling them both. "Quick, leave. This time next week," Ariane whispered, giving her brother a brief fierce hug. Then he vanished into the dark wood surrounding the small lake.

"Who goes there?" Ariane called out, tightening her hold on Bess's leash. Turning to face the direction of the house, she saw the tall silhouette of a man approaching her through the shadows.

"I might ask the same question."

"Justin, 'tis you," Ariane said with a sigh of relief.

"Whom were you expecting?"

"Why . . . no one," she stammered.

"Really. Why else then would you be out at this hour?"

"I couldn't sleep. 'Tis so hot and I had forgotten to walk Bess. She is getting on in years and needs to go out more."

"Ah, the dog of course," he replied in dry tones of disbelief. Leaning down, he let the animal familiarize herself with his scent before trying any further contact. Soon she was rolling over in the grass, allowing him to stroke her belly.

"Do you recognize her?" Ariane asked quietly.

"You mean this is the puppy I sent over from Cedar Rest all those years ago?"

"Yes, I named her Bess. She has had several fine litters of hunting dogs, but now she is too old to breed. She was just what I needed then. I . . . I wanted to thank you but you left Memphis soon after, after all that, and I never was able to tell you what she meant to me." Her face was a pale flower in the moonglow, the large gray eyes sad with remembered pain.

"Little Bit, I am sorry. I should have thought to inquire . . ." His words trailed off. How could he reconcile the image of that scruffy, lonely little waif he had sent one of the puppies from his father's prize hunter

46

in a long forgotten gesture with this exquisite woman.

"It was a long time ago. I am just glad I can finally say thank you. Time has changed many things, but my memory of your kindness will always stay with me."

"I hope I will be more than just memory to you," he said softly, staring intently into Ariane's eyes. How lovely she looked in the moonglow, her hair turned to spun gold, her gown a misty cloud about her slender form. There was an ethereal quality about her beauty that made him breathless when he remembered the strength of her spirit.

She looked away from that too penetrating gaze and stared out across the lake. The swans were roosting for the night on the tiny island in the middle. Now that he wore that hated blue uniform, what else could he be to her but a sad memory of what might have been. Tears choked her throat as she thought of how so much had been changed by this heartbreaking war, so much lost, never to be again.

"No, Little Bit, don't," Justin muttered in a husky whisper, sweeping her into his arms. His hard-fought battle with control was lost. He had wanted her since their eyes had met across the angry crowd that June morning, and now to find her again was too much. Before she could protest, he had her pressed tightly against him, his mouth covering hers with a hunger that knew no bounds.

The pressure of his hands, the firm sinewy feel of his body against hers, triggered long repressed yearnings. It was as if the vague desires of her girlhood dreams were somehow coming to life. A wild surge of pleasure ran through her as his mouth opened over hers, his tongue tracing her full lips as it sought entrance to that more intimate part of her. Fire racing through her veins, she parted her lips, allowing him the deep, achingly sweet exploration of her mouth. All other thoughts fled before the force of their need, and as if it had always been so, the scarlet ribbons of their tongues entwined in a slow circling dance of love.

His long tapered fingers learned the planes and hollows of her back as he caressed her slowly, wishing he could strip the huge bell of her hoop skirt from her delicate, petite form so he could touch her everywhere. He gloried in her tentative, yet ardor-filled touch as she returned his caress, stroking his back then moving up to entangle her fingers in the ebony silk of his hair where it curled over his tunic collar.

It was a deep drugging kiss that her tired, battered soul could melt into. For a brief time there was no war, no fear of what tomorrow would bring, only this splendid sense of reunion with Justin, her long-lost girlish vision of the perfect cavalier.

It was the sound of thundering hoofbeats then the burst of rifle fire from somewhere on the other side of the lake that destroyed their moment suspended outside of time. Ariane's every nerve tensed at the sound. Beau! Had he been seen?

Justin felt her slender form go rigid with fright. Reacting instinctively to protect her, he raised his head from her trembling lips and pressed her head into the corner of his shoulder. Bending his tall muscular body around her as if a shield, he led her into the dark shadows of the cedar trees. Bess followed with a low growl.

"We will be safer here. The moonlight doesn't penetrate these overhanging boughs. Out there we were too easily seen. 'Twas most likely some trigger-happy sentry shooting at the shadow of some animal," Justin tried to reassure her, but there was such an emotional bond between them he sensed her continued distress.

"Hush, Bess," Ariane whispered, pulling away from Justin to reach down and gentle the animal with a few pats.

"What is it? Why are you so frightened at what

48

must occur quite regularly with the city occupied by Federal troops?" He questioned her in sharper tones than he'd intended, raising her back up to face him.

"It does not mean I have to like it," she replied in terse tones, not looking up at him but over his shoulder into the night.

"Who is out there, Ariane?" His words were cold and clear as ice.

"I have no idea." This time she looked at him through slightly narrowed eyes that were veiled and remote, meeting his accusing gaze without flinching. " 'Tis best we return to the house if the sentries are trigger-happy as you say, for they will be shooting again at shadows. I don't wish to be one of their mistakes."

It was as if she had put up an invisible wall between them, he thought as he stared down at that cool, upturned visage as beautiful and remote as the moon above them. She had retired behind the facade of hauteur and good manners she had been taught as a Southern aristocrat. It was a perfect mask to hide behind, but what was she hiding? All of his suspicion came flooding back.

"Was that your lover the sentries were shooting at?" He couldn't stop himself from asking the question, for a coil of jealousy was growing inside him at the thought of another man touching her.

"My lover! How dare you!" She spat out the words with contempt. Her gray eyes darkened like thunderclouds as she glared up at him with an angry, reproachful gaze.

"Why else would you leave the security of your bedchamber to walk these darkened path in the dead of night. Oh, yes, Bess. Surely she does not require such a lengthy exercise. Would not the kitchen garden serve her purpose." His thin lips, which had given Ariane such pleasure, now twisted into a cynical smile of triumph. He held her forearms in his strong hands so she might not escape him, forcing her to listen to his questions. His jealousy was driving him to act so cruelly, but he was unable to stop. Even when she made him angry, he still wanted her. She had somehow, with only a glance, broken down all his carefully erected defenses and found a vulnerable place inside his hardened heart.

Frightened for Beau, and stunned that Justin could think her capable of meeting first one man, then dallying with another, she stared, unable to speak. Where was the kind, gentle knight of her girlish dreams? Gone, she thought with deep bitterness, gone when he put on that blue uniform.

"Let me go!" she ground out through clenched teeth, throwing him a look of utter disdain. "If you call yourself a gentleman, let me go."

"Ah, yes, the perfect retort for unbecoming behavior in the South. But perhaps, my dear, I am no longer a Southern gentleman. Perhaps I no longer play by those rules," he said with a bitter edge of cynicism in his deep voice.

"That, sir, I can believe," she countered icily. Puzzled by his abrupt change in mood, and the glimpse of pain she had briefly glimpsed in his now sardonic ebony eyes, she took refuge in a cool remote facade that depicted an emotion she didn't really feel. She was caught in a turn of events she couldn't explain to him, for he was the enemy. Her brother's life, and perhaps her own, depended on no Yankee finding out she was the "Swan," General Forrest's spy in Memphis.

"I am tired and this conversation has become distasteful to me." Ariane tried once more to pull away from him. Surprisingly this time he lifted her arms and gently kissed each wrist. She shuddered at the touch of his lips, for in spite of everything, she was drawn to him. There was some tangible bond between them that was stronger than anger, stronger than war, and she was afraid stronger than honor.

"Go, my sweet, but remember how close I shall be to you, just next door. And this Yankee has a code all his own." He released her with a low husky chuckle at her look of confusion.

Picking up Bess's leash, she turned on her heel and walked away from him with as much dignity as she could muster. He was a rogue and a scoundrel as the gossips had said all those years ago, but oh what an effect he had on her susceptible heart. She would have to fight her feeling for him every second, and as he said, he would be so near, so close. And, she thought with a sinking heart, he would be watching her. The one thing she didn't need at this time was a Yankee captain shadowing her every step. Suddenly the sultry Memphis night seemed to have a chill as an undercurrent to all that perfumed humid heat.

As he watched her graceful figure with its swaying bell-shaped skirt walk back toward the house, Justin saw from the corner of his eye a basket lying in the long grass not far away. Picking it up, he saw a small piece of fresh bread clinging to the bottom. The basket had not been there long or the bread would have gone stale. Looking up at the figure of Ariane disappearing into the shadows of the night, he realized it belonged to her. Why had she brought a basket, a basket of bread out with her on her walk. The famous Valcour swans were roosting on their island—it could not have been for them. If she had been meeting a lover, it was damn odd to bring a basket of bread to a midnight rendezvous. It all didn't make sense, none of it. The too strong mint juleps, the lavish entertaining of Yankee officers, a midnight stroll with a basket of bread. There was something wrong about it all. What was Little Bit up to, or rather, what was the beautiful Ariane Valcour up to? "By God, I am going to find out," he muttered into the soft, secretive Southern night filled with the sweet scent of flowers, some of which he remembered were deadly poison.

Chapter Four

"Mam'zelle Ariane, those Yankee doctors have left for the day," the soft French-accented voice of Sable spoke quietly in her mistress's ear in an attempt to awaken her as she pulled back the mosquito barre.

"Thank you. I didn't want to have to put on my polite, charming mask so early in the morning," Ariane sighed, struggling to sit up so Sable could put her breakfast tray in front of her. "How is Father? Has he left for the office yet?"

"Your papa is determined to do just that, but, *ma petite,* he is not up to it. He has one of his headaches and you know how sick they make him feel," Sable replied, her lovely arched brows drawn in a concerned frown. "He wouldn't allow me to ask one of those doctors to see him, not even Doctor Justin. I thought they might be able to give him some medicine for the pain."

Ariane felt her pulse quicken at the mere mention of Justin's name. Her sleep the night before, when it finally came, was disturbed by dream images of being pursued through the woods of Fleur de Lys by a shadowy masculine figure dressed in a blue uniform.

"Hand me my peignoir, Sable. I will try to talk Father out of leaving the house today." Thrusting the bed tray aside, Ariane took the gossamer white garment from her maid and, tying it about her waist, slipped her white kid mules on her small feet. "There is fever in the city.

Papa doesn't need to take such a risk in his condition."

"I hope you have more success with him than I did. He is on the terrace having his breakfast, Mam'zelle Ariane."

The house was still cool and shadowy this early in the morning, but as she walked out through the French doors on to the stone flags of the terrace, she felt the heat of the July sun.

"Coffee, Miz Ariane?" Caesar asked from where he stood by the tray table containing the breakfast chafing dishes.

"Yes, please," Ariane replied, seating herself across from her father at the white wrought iron table with its lace cloth. A war might be raging all around them, but the formalities of polite living were still adhered to at Fleur de Lys.

"You are rather *en déshabillé* this morning, *ma chère,*" Leander said with mild disapproval as he lifted a spoonful of grits to his mouth.

"I didn't have time to dress, Father. I wanted to speak with you before you left. There is fever in the city. I wish you wouldn't go to the office today," Ariane pleaded with him, noticing his use of the French of his Louisiana boyhood, always a sign he was upset. "Sable tells me you are suffering from one of your headaches."

"A little food and some coffee and I will be as good as new," her father insisted, signaling Caesar for some more of the dark, strong New Orleans coffee always served at every meal.

"Please, Papa, you are not well. There is no need to go into the city. I could go to the office and check with Sam Riley and tell you what, if anything, he needs when I return from the hospital."

"You know I do not like you nursing in that Yankee hospital, daughter. 'Tis not fitting for a lady to do such a thing, see such sights."

"Ladies all over the South are doing just such things, Papa," Ariane answered. "The Confederate prisoners in

54

that hospital need our help." There was no way she could tell him exactly how she was helping the South, by stealing and smuggling medicines from under the Yankees' noses.

"That is why I must go to the city, daughter. I, too, in my own way am still helping the Cause," he told her in cryptic tones, sipping hot coffee from an egg-shell-thin cup.

Her gray eyes met those of her father's in a look of perfect understanding. The rumors she had heard, and Beau's veiled references, were true. Valcour Line Steamboats were leaving the city loaded with goods and food for other cities of Yankee occupation. Once they left Memphis, however, they traveled up bayous and small rivers feeding into the Mississippi, where Rebel boats were waiting to transfer some of the supplies on to their ships for the needs of the Confederacy. Manifest lists were then changed to agree with what was left.

The sounds of the mockingbirds in the tall cedars, the lemony scent of the huge ivory magnolia blooms, the deep richer scent of the climbing crimson roses, the humid soft air that was like a caress, all made their intentions for the day seem all the more unreal. On this lazy Memphis summer morn danger seemed impossible and far away. A dangerous thought, Ariane mused, for it could make one careless.

The sound of horses thundering up the front drive startled Ariane out of her reverie. Her father rose from his chair, wavering for a moment before he got his balance by leaning heavily on his cane.

"Go to your bedchamber, daughter, while I see what trial the Yankees have decided to thrust upon us this time."

"Papa, let me stay with you," Ariane pleaded, for she knew her father's emotional state. One disrespectful word from one of the soldiers and there was no telling what he would do.

"You are not properly dressed. Do not give these blue bellies reason to insult us any more than they do," her father said firmly. "Hurry through the house while I head them off," he called over his shoulder as he walked slowly toward the front door.

Throwing her napkin on the table, Ariane obeyed, running across the terrace and through the French doors. She needed to dress quickly and join her father before his anger made him say words they would both come to regret.

Sable was making up the huge four-poster bed when Ariane returned to her chamber. She turned in dismay as she saw the expression on her young mistress's worried visage. "What is it, mam'zelle?"

"Soldiers, Sable. Father is talking with them now. I must dress. Heaven only knows what the Union Command has up its sleeves now to bedevil Memphians."

Since Union Generals S. A. Hurlbut and Washburn had taken over command from General Sherman, conditions in the city had gone from bad to worse. All manner of Northern speculators and traders had flocked to the occupied city to pick it clean. It was said by the natives of the city that Yankees seemed determined to turn the city into a paradise for thieves. Under Generals Hurlbut and Washburn, the Federals discovered all manner of what they called "abandoned" property. If they wanted a place, they said it was empty no matter how many Rebels lived there. They simply threw them out, and took over the house or business. The citizen had no recourse, for the head of the Abandoned Property Department, Captain Eddy, worked hand and hand with the chief of the Detective Office. Both men were allowed any outrage by the Union Command.

"You wash, *ma petite*. I will fetch a day gown." The graceful maid strode to the huge armoire that dominated one wall of the elegant chamber. As she opened the carved double doors, the lemon scent of the herb southernwood along with pungent tansy and the mint fra-

56

grance of pennyroyal floated out from the sachet bags placed inside to repel insects.

"The gray dimity, Sable. This is my morning at the hospital," Ariane instructed over her shoulder as she stripped her night garments away and began to wash from the flowered porcelain basin. She didn't have time for a bath so she would have to make do with a quick wash with the heliotrope soap Sable made from the herb grown in their garden.

She had just been helped into her chemise and pantalets when her chamber door was flung open.

"Mon Dieu!" Sable cried out. *"Vite!* Go! Go!" My mistress is dressing," she told the grinning soldiers who stared from the portal. Leaving Ariane's side, she strode toward them and made pushing gestures with her apron as if they were a flock of chickens she could intimidate out into the hall.

"Hold on there, darky," one leering sergeant snarled. "We're here by order of the Provost Marshal's Office. Supposed to confiscate all Secesh items. Now I don't see a Reb flag hanging here, but I do see a pretty little Sesch item." Thrusting Sable aside, he sauntered into the room and headed toward Ariane.

From the corner of her eye, she saw her locket with the Confederate cipher inside lying on her writing table. Biting her lower lip in frustration, she cursed her own carelessness. Why hadn't she placed it inside the hollow-out romance novel she usually hid it in or even fastened it about her neck.

"How's about it, girly, are you a tried-and-true Reb?" He grabbed her chin and the whiskey fumes hit her full in the face. "Is that waist as tiny without those corsets you Sesch belles like to wear?" He placed his other hand at her waist where her pantalets began and squeezed her hard.

"Let go of me, you oaf!" she hissed, raising her hand to slap him hard across his face. Bess, watching from her basket where she had been awakened by the noise, began to bark.

"Why you little Reb bitch," he muttered, grabbing both her wrists and pulling her up against his chest. The metal buttons on his uniform cut her soft breasts through the thin chemise.

"Let her go, sergeant." The deep masculine voice was low and controlled, but edged with menace. "Now."

"She hit me. I'm takin' her in," he snarled, dragging her around as he faced the tall captain.

"Justin," Ariane murmured, relief washing over her in waves. Bess ambled to her side, sensing her mistress's relief.

"She was, I believe, defending herself against a drunken attack. The Provost Marshal's Office would be interested in knowing that you drink on duty, Sergeant." There was more than a threat in Justin's words as he fixed the soldier with a cold stare.

"Well . . . now I thought she might be harboring a gun or a Secesh flag. Guess I was wrong, Captain. This room has been searched thoroughly, men," the chastened sergeant muttered to the others watching from the hall. "Come on, there's the rest of this place." As he angrily left the chamber, Sable ran after him, frantic the men would destroy the house.

"Are you all right?" Justin asked, turning toward Ariane. He stared down at where the buttons from the sergeant's tunic had left an impression on her ivory and peach skin.

"We thought you had gone to the hospital," she replied, trying to stop the trembling in her hands by clasping them together in front of her.

"No, thank God. I have been walking by the lake where we were last night. There was something I wanted to check. I heard the horses and came to see what was going on."

"My father . . ." Her voice trailed off as she realized

58

her legs weren't going to hold her up any longer. Slumping forward, she felt strong masculine arms support her and lift her up.

In a few lithe strides, Justin carried her to the bed. Bess, deciding in her canine head that her mistress was in good hands, lumbered back to her basket. The lavender silk counterpane felt cool like water to Ariane as he laid her down upon it. A feather pillow in its lace and ribboned sham was put tenderly under her head.

"Take a deep breath and now let it out slowly, and another, one more. Good. Your color is better. Lifting her wrist, he took out an ornate pocket watch and flipped open the embossed case.

" 'Tis lovely. Is that bird a falcon?" she asked, staring at the intricate design on the lid.

"Yes, my mother gave it to me before my departure from Memphis. It had belonged to her father. It was the last time I saw her," he said tersely, putting the watch away after he had checked her pulse. "My only regret is that I was not here to tend her when the cholera struck, but I was at the University of Edinburgh in the course of my travels. The family lawyer wrote me of her death. Not a word, of course, from my father."

"Your father was a hard man, even Papa said that and he was his best friend. Do not blame yourself for your mother's death. Many people died in Memphis during the cholera epidemic. There was little the doctors could do," Ariane said softly, wishing there was some way to ease the pain she saw for a moment in his expressive black eyes.

"This doctor says you have had a shock, but that you will recover," he said lightly, moving his fingers down her wrist till he enclosed her hand in his.

"Again, you have come to my rescue, valiant knight." She managed a small, tentative smile.

Her beauty and spirit smote his heart. Seeing that scum with his hands on her had driven him mad. Something had snapped in him, and if the sergeant hadn't stopped, he thought he would have killed him there in cold blood.

"Although I wish I could, I can't always be with you. Be careful. I don't know what is going on here, but there is something. Are you sure your cause is worth sacrificing everything for, Little Bit?" His expression had stilled and grown serious, his ebony eyes flashing her a gentle, but firm warning.

"Charles thought it was worth his life." There was a light bitterness to her voice. Her gray eyes clouded with a misty sadness, but never left his gaze. You can't frighten me, those large soft eyes were saying in a mute appeal for understanding. There is no other way for me.

"Then you admit you are doing something to aid the Confederacy?" he said sharply, his fingers involuntarily tightening on her hand.

"No, I said only that there are some things worth defending, some things one has to do in the name of honor even if it means sacrificing one's life."

"Charles was my friend, the only one who came to say good-bye after my disgrace. I hate the waste in this war, the deaths of good men like Charles," Justin said with sadness and a tinge of anger in his voice. "He wasn't even political, just enjoyed his Sir Walter Scott and tales of knights and fair ladies. Chaucer and Shakespeare, those were his passions."

"Yes, you are right, he did not want Tennessee to leave the Union, but when it happened, he felt he had to defend his home," Ariane explained. "He said his heart would always be with the South. There was no way he could lift his hand against another Southerner. So he did what he thought he must, as others have done and will continue to do."

"This war is madness. The sooner it is over, the better," Justin muttered. "Stay out of it, my lovely sweet Rebel, or it will destroy you as well."

60

"Why are you telling me this?" Ariane asked, sensing there was more beneath the warning. There was something he was not saying, something he was hiding from her. For the first time since his return to Memphis, she wondered about the strange circumstances that would send him back to his old hometown, a town that held only painful memories. Why had he joined a regiment sent to the western border of the Confederacy, one sure to come to Tennessee. Had it been merely coincidence or something much deeper, more significant?

"Because, damn it, I care." His voice cracked with a self-mocking weariness. "I wish I didn't, Little Bit. It would be easier."

"For whom?"

"For both of us." His words were a husky whisper as he leaned down to caress his mouth across her lips.

A small sound of wonder came from her throat as she lifted her arms up to pull him down, down. The whisper-light contact of their lips sent a tremor of pure desire through her. Her mouth opened to him in mute invitation as the rest of the world vanished for them. Her senses were singing with the glory of his touch, the strength of his embrace, the masculine scent of him that was bay rum, pipe tobacco, and that more elusive male musk scent that was his alone.

Justin's blood was afire with the sweet agony of wanting her. When she had reached up for him, her reaction had delighted him in its innocent seductiveness. Was she as chaste as she seemed? Did it matter, he thought as he fought to control the hunger she had aroused. He wanted to stroke the satin of her skin. It was unlike any other woman's skin he had ever seen or felt. Cream ivory with a touch of gold, the skin of a true blond. She was like some rare flower that he wanted to touch and admire, but keep from the common eyes of others. How could he want to ravish her, make her sigh and cry out with her passion, and yet at the same time want to protect her,

61

cherish her. Fool, he thought as his tongue swirled the hidden corners of her moist heated mouth—when had he ever wanted to cherish a woman? Take them, use them even, for every woman taken and discarded easily was a reminder that no woman could ever hurt him, destroy him the way Olivia had done that sultry Southern night. But this fragile porcelain doll he held in his arms, this wistful child-woman who spoke of honor and duty, had him completely bewitched.

In his arms she forgot everything; nothing mattered but the here and now. How starved she had been for touch and affection, she realized with amazement. She had known little of either, for her brothers and father had been busy with their own lives. Shy, growing up alone, trying to hide from her friends at school the fact of her mother's mental state, she had remained aloof from others. They took it for conceit and called her a snob. In her bewilderment and hurt she withdrew all the more. Only with her brothers, when they allowed it, did she find some sense of belonging. Now in Justin's embrace she felt a warmth, an acceptance that made her feel she had come home.

His tender kiss grew more fervent as he felt his control slipping away. Raising his hand, he stroked the curve of her shoulder and gently pulled down the lacy strap of her chemise till the rose bud of one taut nipple was exposed. Cupping her soft ivory breast, he learned its contours as his thumb caressed in sensual swirls the throbbing peak. He took his time, allowing her to become used to the idea of his touch, to learn to enjoy the pleasure he could give her.

How wonderful it was to have a man touch her in such an intimate way. Glorious! She could never have imagined there was this much pleasure between a man and a woman. The only kisses she had experienced were a few rough fumbles from young men during barbecues and dances before the war. Her manner had put most of the gallants off. She was too serious, too shy, only her beauty had attracted them, but it had intimidated them also. Consequently most had been rather drunk before they got up the nerve to ask her out on the terrace, where most of the kisses and embraces took place. But this wasn't some awkward boy rather the worse for drink; this was a mature man who now was kissing her in such a wonderful way she thought she would die of the pleasure.

"Yes, yes," Ariane moaned as his mouth left hers to sear a path down her slender neck to her breast. His tongue circled the hard coral bud, arousing her even more as he teased and suckled the swollen tip while his hand exposed the other breast to his knowing touch. His lips moved from one throbbing peak to the other as she arched up like a silky kitten, reveling in what he was teaching her about her own body. Her fingers entwined in his midnight black hair, enjoying the sheer tactile feel of it, pressing him closer to her, so aflame with desire she never wanted him to stop. If this was madness, it was sweet, but then the world as she had known it had gone mad.

How far they would have gone in their joy of one another, they weren't to know, for outside forces drew them apart where their own control had failed. It was as Justin caressed down to her tiny waist, marveling at how petite she was, how perfect she was, that a shot was fired out in the hall. It echoed down the long corridor and then was joined by the horrible piercing scream of a woman. The spine-tingling sound hung in the hot morning air, intruding on their private paradise.

Chapter Five

"Stay here," Justin ordered, lifting his head from her delicious breast.

"Father?" Ariane called out, sitting up, her mouth still swollen from Justin's kisses.

"I will see to him. You must stay away from them, especially if there is trouble," Justin cautioned, rising swiftly to his feet. "Here, cover yourself." He handed her the peignoir Sable had laid at the foot of the bed.

Pulling up the straps of her chemise, Ariane rose from the bed and slipped the garment on, tying it securely at her waist. She watched with her heart in her throat as Justin opened the door and quickly exited the chamber.

Finding her satin mules, she thrust her tiny feet into them. If he thought she was going to cower in her bedchamber while her father was in danger, then he didn't know her very well.

The morning seemed to have gotten hotter, she decided as moisture beaded her upper lip and her palms grew clammy. Whether it was the humid heat or fear, she wasn't sure. Nervously, she brushed damp tendrils of hair from her cheek. Taking a deep breath for courage, she gently opened the heavy mahogany door.

The scene in front of her chilled the blood. Her father stood with an outstretched arm, pointing a pistol at the sergeant coming from his dressing room. Looking down the hall, she saw what had angered her father.

The Yankee soldier held Charles's sword in its leather scabbard. A small hole in the wall beside the sergeant's head showed where her father had barely missed him.

"Put it down, Sergeant," Justin ordered in a voice that was full of the authority of command.

"He damn near killed me, Capt'n," the man whined, his shifty eyes rolling with fear in his sweating face.

"That was my son's sword, sir," Leander Valcour thundered, holding the pistol still out at arm's length, ready to fire again.

"Put it back where you found it," Justin told him tersely, his eyes narrowed, his chiseled features cold with disdain.

"It's a Secesh sword, Capt'n. We confiscate Secesh swords. This 'en belongs to me."

"You are stealing, Sergeant, not confiscating. I weary of this farce," Justin drawled, pulling a navy six-pistol from the holster at his belt, cocking the trigger as he pointed it at the trembling soldier. "Put it back."

With a flash of hatred in his porcine eyes, the sergeant laid the sword on a table beside him. "Reckon which side you're on, eh, Capt'n?"

"Not on the side of thieves, Sergeant. Now take your men and leave here immediately." Justin kept the gun trained on him as he shuffled down the hall toward the stairs, his men behind him. One of the men carried a gold pocket watch dangling from his hand.

"That belongs to M'sieur Charles too," Sable snapped, grabbing it from the startled man's hand.

"The Provost Marshal's Office will hear about this, you can depend on it," the Sergeant called out as he started clumsily down the stairs.

"They certainly will hear about it, Sergeant, and more, I can assure you," Justin replied with a steel edge to his words.

"Papa, put it away," Ariane called out, running to

where her father stood weaving on his cane, the extended hand dipping up and down as he began to lose control. Quickly, she took the gun from his shaking hand.

"Lean on me, M'sieur," Sable told him, as she hurried to his side, placing her arm around his chest. " 'Tis the *mal de tête,* the headache." He nodded in the affirmative.

"Yes. We must get him to his bed," Justin agreed, returning his pistol to the holster. Coming to their aid, he half carried the old man to his bedchamber.

Ariane hid the gun in a drawer in her room then followed them to her father's bed. She helped Justin loosen the collar about her father's neck and slipped the boot from his remaining leg.

"Fetch my bag from my room, Sable," Justin ordered as he began examining his patient. "He is not well enough for such strenuous emotions."

"I did not want him to go to the shipping office today. I told him so," Ariane explained, pouring cool water from the pitcher on the washstand into the porcelain bowl. Taking a clean linen, she wrung it out in the water then placed it across her father's forehead and eyes. "The light bothers his eyes so when he has an attack of the migraine."

"They have trained you well at the hospital," Justin commented, lifting her father's wrist to take his pulse.

"Miss Schneider is a martinet, but she works as hard as anyone," Ariane admitted reluctantly.

"She is head of the Sanitary Commission, I believe," he replied with a faint smile softening his stern mouth. "I have heard that she runs a very tight ship."

"Indeed, she does. I think she feels all Southern women are lazy empty-headed belles used to being waited on hand and foot. We are trying to dissuade her from that opinion," Ariane told him in wry tones.

"And have you?" He looked up at her with a glint of admiration in the depths of his onyx-black eyes.

"Miss Schneider has very fixed, unshakable opinions, but we continue to try. But that reminds me, I must send word to the hospital that I will not be in today. I must go to the shipping office in Father's stead."

"I am leaving shortly. I will convey your message to the formidable Miss Schneider," Justin told her as he stood up. "Mr. Valcour, sir, you need a great deal of rest, at least a week before you return to the shipping line. Then I must request it be mornings only."

Leander Valcour nodded his head that he understood. The pain was so intense he could not speak.

"Sable has brought me my bag, sir. I am going to give her a powder to mix with water that should help your pain. It will make you sleepy, so give in and let nature take its course."

Ariane watched the strong self-contained Justin minister to her father with kindness and great sensitivity. Never had she felt so attracted to him as she did now, watching those long tapered hands that had touched her with such sensual pleasure tend to her father with such tender expertise. As a nurse at the Federal hospital, she had watched many of the staff doctors attend the wounded and sick. Some were perfunctory, treating their patients with what almost amounted to rudeness, but Justin was not one of these. There was a sure caring in his touch and it communicated itself to her father. She saw him relax as he responded to Justin's unspoken respect and concern for his patient. It was another measure of the man who had captured her heart all those years before. But oh it would be so much easier if he wore a coat of gray instead of blue.

"Come, we will leave your father in Sable's capable hands. I wish to speak with you," Justin said, closing his leather bag. Taking her arm, he escorted her from the room, pulling the door shut behind them.

"Thank you," she said simply as they paused in front of the long ceiling-to-floor window that overlooked the back garden at the end of the hall.

"You must be very careful from now on, Ariane, my lovely Rebel," he began with quiet emphasis. His gaze that traveled over her upturned visage was as soft as a caress. "The sergeant is not a forgiving man. He will be out for vengeance."

"You think he will be back, then?"

"He knows I am billeted here. That may keep him away for a while. But even if he does not come back, he will look for some other way to gain his retribution. Be aware every minute, and weigh everything you do, knowing there is someone watching you, waiting to find something he could use to put you in Irving Block Prison." A melancholy frown flitted across his cool, darkly handsome features.

Once again Ariane experienced a strange sense that there was a hidden message behind his words. In the humid heat of the morning, she felt a shiver go up her spine. Sable had told her that was the feeling of someone walking over her grave, and meant that fate was sending her a warning of her own mortality.

"I must go." Justin's voice was husky with unspoken desires. "Remember to take care, Little Bit." He touched her trembling mouth with one slender bronzed finger in a brief tender gesture of farewell.

She watched with an ache of longing in her throat as he moved with long lithe strides to the staircase. There was such a sense of firm strength about him that she basked in the warmth of it when he was with her. For a brief bittersweet time when she was in his magnetic presence, she felt unafraid and no longer alone.

Staring at the empty hall, where there were only the golden shafts of sunlight coming from the tall window to break the gloom, Ariane felt a stab of despair. For a moment she wanted to cast aside her pledge to General Forrest and be only a young woman in love. Turning, her glance fell on the glimmer of Charles's sword where it lay on the table. Her brother had done what he thought honor required of him, could she do any less? Her eyes filling with tears, she pulled the blade out a fraction from its scabbard to touch the engraved name "Charles Valcour" and then up to where the letters "C.S." for Confederate States were engraved, surrounded by finely etched tobacco leaves and floral decorations. She could not abandon her brother's memory, her beloved South, the very concept of honor that had been ingrained since childhood. Her word had been given, she had taken a stand that could not be forsaken no matter how hard it might be, no matter the personal cost. So many had already given so much, including their lives; she could not ask any less of herself.

Wiping the tears from her eyes with the back of her hand like a forlorn child, she was assailed with a terrible sense of bitterness. How fate was toying with her to send Justin back to Memphis at this time. Straightening her shoulders in an unconscious gesture of determination, her fingers tightened about the handle of the sword. With one swift motion she returned it to its scabbard, then turned and walked with sure steps to her bedchamber.

As she donned her gray dimity walking dress, she had the carriage brought around from the stables. With her red-gold tresses caught low on her neck in a chignon, simple pearl studs in her ears, and sensible short boots called balmorals in gray kid, she appeared cool and competent.

"Not the Dolly Varden hat, Sable. I am not going to a party or a barbecue. Something more somber, I think," she mused, slipping on black lace fingerless mitts.

"You best take a parasol, mam'zelle, if you are going to wear that tiny chip bonnet. The sun will ruin your complexion," Sable warned, placing the black straw hat on her golden hair, tilting it low over her forehead in the latest fashion. A black grosgrain ribbon was caught under her chignon to hold the bonnet in place. Rose and white silk flowers rested on a filmy cloud of gray chiffon across the low brim, while a black half-veil was pulled to the end of her retroussé nose.

"The only good thing one can say about the Yankee occupation is at least some of the stores have stock in them once more," Ariane commented in wry tones, fastening the all-important locket with the cipher key inside around her neck. Justin's warning came back to her. She wanted nothing hidden in the house for the sergeant to find if he came back.

"Your parasol," Sable replied, holding out the light rose-pink silk sun shade with the gray fringe and her gold mesh reticule.

"Thank you, Sable. Please watch over Father. Do not let him leave that bed," Ariane called over her shoulder as she bent down to stroke Bess good-bye. The sleepy canine regarded her for a brief moment from half-open brown-velvet spaniel eyes, before returning to her interrupted sleep with a deep sigh.

"The dog is the wise one, sleeping in this heat instead of running all over and tempting the fever," Sable commented with a worried frown.

" 'Tis necessary I go. You know why." Ariane paused with her hand on the porcelain doorknob with the tiny gold fleur de lys painted on it.

"Go with care, mam'zelle," the maid cautioned, fear in her dark eyes.

"What is it? Have you seen something?" The fine

hairs on the back of Ariane's neck seemed to quiver in the hot still air. Sable had a certain reputation in Memphis as a seer. Many said she was a priestess in the local Voodoo cult, which met on dark nights in a secluded glen known as Voodoo Village. Ariane could not be sure if the rumors were true, but often as a child she would see the maid slip out of the kitchen house late at night. Where she was going, Ariane had never asked, for she was supposed to have been asleep, instead of stealing up to the tower room she had considered her magic sanctuary.

" 'Tis only a feeling, mam'zelle. But I caution you, I fear your destiny is a troubled one with many twists and turns before you find what you seek."

"And what do I seek, Sable?"

"Only you can say, mam'zelle," she answered in the cryptic tones that Ariane had heard before.

She wished she could dismiss what Beau had always called Sable's mumbo jumbo, thought Ariane as she jostled in the Valcour carriage on her way into Memphis. Poplar Street, which could be a sea of mud when it rained, had dried out in the heat, but was now full of deep hard ruts that shook the barouche with each turn of the wheel.

The road was thick with traffic as they crossed over Bayou Gayoso and into the city. Union drays and mounted troops were everywhere, a constant reminder of Memphis's occupation. Wagon loads of cotton rolled past. Cotton was worth 300 dollars a bale in gold. Ariane narrowed her eyes in anger as she watched the Yankee profiteers rape her Southern land of its white gold. Plantations where the owners had been driven out, or burned out by Union troops, were taken over by the Yankee rabble that had come following in the wake of the advancing army. In many cases, she thought in satisfaction, Southerners outside the Federal lines were

71

able to send cotton into Memphis by loyal house slaves where speculators would turn a blind eye to where it came from and eagerly buy it. The money in turn brought badly needed supplies for the families and the Confederacy. The Southerners then smuggled the gunpowder, guns, and other munitions they received for their cotton bales often with the full knowledge of Union soldiers or speculators who looked the other way as long as they were getting rich on cotton. Every Billy Yank soldier dreamed of adding to his meager Army pay with a bale or two of cotton. Thus Memphis had become, during the Federal occupation, a rough city where every kind of corruption flourished.

Ariane gave a light shudder of distaste as the carriage pulled on to Front Row, the street that ran across the top of the bluff overlooking the Mississippi. Garishly dressed women called out to passing soldiers as the wooden sidewalks teemed with the riffraff that had followed the Union Army to Memphis. There had always been a wild side to the city—it was, after all, a river town—but before the war, the prostitutes had stayed in the gambling hells and brothels of Beale Street or in the riverfront dives of the area called Pinch Gut. Now it wasn't safe for a lady to leave her carriage to shop for the barest essentials. Every Southern woman was open to insults and propositions.

Ariane leaned back against the seat, away from the open window and leering masculine eyes. She breathed a sigh of relief when they pulled up in front of the huge double doors of the Valcour Steamboat Line. The blue, white, and gold Valcour flag flew from a brass pole in front, as did the Union flag at the order of the Provost Marshal's Office.

Stepping out on the carriage block with Roman's assistance, she heard the whistles and rude calls, but lifted her head with cold disdain. She would not allow them to deter her or frighten her from her task. It was, however, with a sigh of relief that she closed the double doors behind her, shutting out the sounds of the street.

"Miss Ariane, what are you doing here?" the rough voice with the lilt of Ireland called out to her from the winding stairs that led to her father's office.

"Sam Riley, just the man I am looking for," Ariane replied, moving toward the stairs, nodding at those surprised men she passed on the way. Sam Riley was her father's best captain and good friend as well. The Irishman had been with her father since the beginning of Valcour Steamboats, when Leander Valcour had first come up from Louisiana.

"Come up here, lass," the large-framed man gestured, moving toward the head of the stairs. "Where's your father?" he asked as she reached him.

"I will explain inside, Sam."

Opening the heavy door to her father's office, Sam stood back so she could enter. The floor-length windows behind the long mahogany desk framed the mighty river below, revealing the vast panorama of the docks. It was a sight Ariane loved, but today she had no time to enjoy the view.

"Sam, Father is quite ill. He never really recovered from Shiloh, and I fear he has been working too hard here at the office," she explained, turning to face him as he closed the door behind them. "One . . . one of the doctors who is staying with us has examined him and advised him to rest for at least a week." Ariane watched the concern come over Sam Riley's weathered features and the worry in his Irish blue eyes at her words.

"Miss Ariane, I need to speak with your pa. It's real serious," he told her, nervously running a large hand through his fading red hair, now grizzled with gray.

"I would rather you didn't go out to the house today.

73

He needs his rest, and if he thinks anything is wrong, he will get up out of bed. If it is that important, Sam, I think you better tell me."

"Well, lass, I don't think this is really in your line." He paused, staring at her with indecision in his worried blue eyes.

"Sam, there is something I think you should be aware of, and I know I can count on this going no further than this room. I know that you and my father are helping the cause, as am I. There are certain contacts I have with General Forrest that might prove helpful in an emergency. You must realize my father may not be able to make the vital decisions that are needed for some time. I am prepared to take his place and his responsibility for the Valcour line. I need and want your trust or our use to the Confederacy will be greatly damaged."

"You always did have plenty of spunk, lass," Sam said. "I reckon there is naught else to do but what we must in these bad times. Anything you need from me, well, just say the word, and you got it. I'm proud to know you, lass, and that's a fact."

"Thank you, Sam," she said softly, touching his arm for a moment in affection. "Now, I think you best tell me what the problem is, and between the two of us, perhaps we can find the answer." She walked over to her father's high-back chair and, with a graceful movement of her skirt, sat down, placing her parasol and reticule on the polished surface of the desk.

"It's them Yankees. They want us to use Valcour steamers to take prisoners to that hellhole prison upriver called Rock Island. Now your pa and I had other plans for those paddlewheelers. It was working out real nice taking their supplies for them, making stops along the way, if you understand my meaning." Sam gave her a knowing wink as he sat

74

down in a chair across the desk from her.

"Do you think they have caught on to what was happening?" Ariane inquired.

"No not yet. Money has greased the way up till now," he answered thoughtfully. "Many a blue coat doesn't mind looking the other way if it means a little extra money in his pocket. We have been warned, though, that General Washburn is out to make a name for himself in Memphis, and he thinks to start by stopping all this smuggling out of the city. Seems some of those Northern newspapers are raising quite a fuss about Memphis being the supply depot for the Confederacy since the surrender," he chuckled, his blue eyes twinkling. "Bet he'd like to find who writes that column 'A Secesh Captive in Memphis' in the *Memphis Appeal*. Hell's bells, excuse me, lass, but he can't even find who the writer is, let alone keep the columns from being sent through the Yankee lines to wherever the newspaper is that week."

"Yes, the column is . . . interesting," Ariane replied with a slight smile. She wondered what Sam would say if he knew she was the journalist who managed to smuggle the articles out to Beau. He passed them on to the two valiant editors of the Memphis paper who had taken the presses from the city the night before surrender. They now continued to publish the newspaper in exile, keeping the presses on railroad cars, often just one step ahead of the Union Army. The *Memphis Appeal* was circulated throughout the Confederacy and widely read and enjoyed. It continued to be a symbol of Southern resistance and as such had become the bane of existence to the Federal authorities.

"It's a warning we should take serious, though. That's my dilemma, Miss Ariane. I can't raise much of a fuss about those prisoners—why, that would put the Yankees' backs up. They would be watching us somethin'

75

fierce. But it pains me to see our boys, sick boys from that hospital, taken up to that hellhole."

"Those are the prisoners they are sending upriver, the patients from the hospital?"

"Yes, and it's a shame, that's what it is."

"I agree that they are in no condition to travel, most of them, but perhaps they will send only the ones that have recovered," Ariane said thoughtfully.

"No, they are sending sick ones too. In fact, there is supposed to be someone from the hospital to check the ship. The Provost Marshal's Office is sending someone today," Sam told her. "I have tried to warn everyone that this is different from the supply runs, and to keep their mouth shut. You know some of the roustabouts aren't too bright, but all we can do is hope for the best that no one talks about our other arrangement."

"I don't see as we have any other choice, Sam, but to go along with the Yankees on this. If we put up any objection, they will simply take the steamers anyway and take over control of Valcour Shipping."

Sam nodded sadly in agreement. They were caught and that was all there was to it. The road they were walking was a dangerous one—one misstep and their destination would be Irving Block Prison.

A sharp authoritative rap on the door roused them from their musing. Before Ariane could answer, the door was rudely thrown open by the lieutenant assigned to the Valcour offices.

"Yes," Ariane said in terse tones, rising to her feet, her face a cold mask.

"The liaison officer from the hospital is here. Where is Mr. Valcour? We must speak with him," the young lieutenant demanded.

"My father is ill. I represent Valcour Shipping in his stead," Ariane retorted, staring at him with haughty rebuke.

"You're a woman," he answered, floundering before the fury in her gray eyes.

"She certainly is, Lieutenant," the rich timbre of a familiar masculine voice drawled with quiet emphasis.

"You!" A soft gasp escaped Ariane as she stared at the tall lean figure that seemed to fill the threshold of the office.

Chapter Six

Justin stared back at her, one finger lightly stroking his luxuriant mustache, dark eyes glittering with some unreadable emotion. Those who knew him well would recognize this gesture as one he unconsciously used when in a situation not of his choosing. Sweeping his broad hat with the dark midnight-blue plume from his ebony hair, he entered the chamber with a sure step and commanding air that rankled Ariane.

"It seems the Provost Marshal's office changed my plans for the day," he told her with a wry smile.

"When I heard they were sending someone from the hospital, I thought it would be Miss Schneider of the Sanitary Commission," Ariane replied, hating the slight trembling in her voice.

"Although Miss Schneider is certainly quite able, I believe they wanted an officer to handle the loading of prisoners. The *Southern Lady* is in port, I understand."

"Yes, this is her captain, Sam Riley," Ariane said coolly, trying to mask her inner turmoil with a deceptive calmness in her manner. It was very difficult to control her swirling emotions at seeing Justin as a symbol of Union Authority. The blue uniform had been hard enough, but now to have to deal with him as the representative of an army she hated, commanding her to do something she abhorred. It shook her to her very core, for while hating everything he symbolized, she was tormented by the involuntary reaction of her body

78

to his presence, to the penetrating look in his knowing onyx eyes that recognized the conflict within her. How could they feel such a bond when everything in their lives was against it?

"Good. Captain Riley, I would like for Miss Valcour and myself to tour the steamer with you this afternoon to make sure everything is as it should be before we start loading at three. Shall we say at two."

"You are going to load this afternoon?" Ariane questioned sharply in surprise.

"Yes, we expect another trainload of wounded this afternoon. Some are prisoners. There is a shortage of room in Memphis hospitals, as I am sure you know, Miss Valcour," Justin said tersely, hating the look of revulsion and bitterness he saw come over her delicate features.

"Sam, can the *Lady* be ready by three o'clock?" Ariane turned toward the Irishman, who was watching the exchange between the two of them with interest. He wasn't so old that he couldn't feel the sparks igniting as they spoke. The atmosphere in the chamber was like that before a violent summer storm.

"It will be tight, ma'am," he answered, aware that her real attention was centered on the tall, darkly handsome Yankee captain, even if she was turned toward him. He knew there were Union doctors billeted at Fleur de Lys, and wondered if this captain was one of them.

"It has to be ready, Captain Riley," Justin ordered in a voice that allowed for no dissent.

"You heard Captain Pierce, Sam. The Union Army gives an order and it must be obeyed or . . . or what, Captain? Irving Block Prison?" Her gray eyes were like glacial ice and each word was etched with bitterness as she turned back to stare at Justin.

Looking as if she had struck him, his hand tightening on the brim of his hat, he managed an impersonal polite tone as he said, "I will see you at the *Southern Lady* at two. Please be there on time." Turning, he shut the door hard behind him as he left.

"I best be gettin' down to the docks and hurry the men along," Sam said, rising to his feet. "Appears to me that Yankee captain means what he says about expectin' to start loading at three."

"If there were only somebody else to send upriver, Sam, I would be happier. I hate to see you gone for that long a time, right now with Father so ill. Will you pass the word with the other captains that I am now in charge and nothing has changed."

"That I will. You can trust them all, Miss Ariane. To the last man, they are true to the Cause. Capt'n Patrick Bradley is your man if things don't seem to be goin' right, or if the Yankees start givin' trouble. He and the *Natchez Belle* will be in port in two days' time."

"Thank you, Sam. I will meet you at the *Southern Lady* this afternoon for our tour." Her voice emphasized the last word with heavy sarcasm.

"I'll have one of the office boys run down to the Gayoso House and bring back a basket for your luncheon. Often's the time your pa did that when he was busy," Sam informed her as he bid her good-bye.

A summer storm had come up suddenly while they had been talking, and Ariane walked to the long windows to watch its fury. Lightning flashed across the angry purple-gray sky as huge drops of rain slanted across the glass panes. Somehow she hoped to quiet her own inner turmoil by focusing on the furor of nature. Staring out at the downpour, she could see only Justin's handsome, unyielding visage, the intensity of his gaze that saw all too much.

The gusting winds stirred the rushing ochre flood of the Mississippi as the heart of the storm reached the river. All manner of boats were tossed and turned like toys as they lay tied to the floating wharf hulks. The elaborately carved white confection, like a many-layered wedding cake, that was the *Southern Lady* stood out in bold relief against the leaden sky. The Valcour Line flag flew proudly, whipping in the gusty air. Ariane hoped that the storm was only a brief summer shower for the sake of the men to be loaded that afternoon onto the *Lady*'s decks.

No matter how long she stared out the window, all she really saw was Justin, a Justin who was the enemy. Never had that been clearer to her than when he appeared at the Valcour offices as a representative of the Provost Marshal. A deep rumble of thunder that rattled the windows seemed to run through her like a premonition of despair. Lifting her fingertips to her trembling lips, she thought of the feel of his mouth on hers that morning. How wonderful it had felt, how right, but no, she shook her head—it could never be right. Her own traitorous body was betraying her resolve as she felt even her breasts ache for the touch of his hands, his gentle sensuous mouth. He had awakened senses, feelings, hungers in her that would have been best left dormant. Her brain warred with her heart, her body, till she felt sick with the struggle within her being.

The object of her musings was having conflicts of his own within his heart and mind. Striding out of the Valcour Offices, he had walked without direction, clenching his fists that wanted to both strangle and caress the proud, beautiful woman he had just left behind. The first drops of rain roused him from his melancholy. Ducking inside the doorway of a cotton factor's office, he pulled out his pocket watch to see how much time he had till he must be at the docks. Two hours to kill, he realized, snapping the cover shut. There wasn't time to return to the hospital, and the rumblings in his stomach reminded him he hadn't eaten breakfast. The

Gayoso House was just down the street. Maybe after a meal and a smoke, he would be able to put this morning in some perspective.

The tall, white elegant columns of the Gayoso House were a welcome sight to Justin as he made his way down the crowded wooden sidewalks. Mule-drawn drays, carriages, Union supply wagons, and mounted soldiers all dashed down Front Row, kicking up the mud in the street now that the rain was turning the hard ruts to sink holes. Trying to avoid the flying muck, he made his way through the jostling crowd into the civilization of the fashionable hotel.

Shaking the water from his hat, Justin marveled at the two-story vaulted ceiling in the lobby. The luxurious hotel was one of the wonders of Memphis and the South. Built by Robertson Topp to give the city a more sophisticated air, it was considered one of the best hotels in the country. The latest word in all modern conveniences, it had its own waterworks, gasworks for gas lighting, bakeries, wine cellar, sewer and drain system, something the rest of the city needed badly, and of course, indoor plumbing. In an era when nearly all Memphians had privies in their backyards and washtubs for bathing, the Gayoso bragged of its hot showers, marble tubs with silver faucets, and the latest marvel — flush toilets. If the rest of the city had been as well planned, maybe it wouldn't smell so bad in the summer heat, Justin thought in disgust, noticing the mud on his high boots, which had been well polished that morning.

"Why, I don't believe it." A husky feminine voice in Justin's ear caused him to whirl around with a sinking feeling in the pit of his stomach.

"Olivia," he managed through clenched teeth, fighting the flood of memories that familiar seductive voice invoked.

"A Union officer — well, I can't say I am surprised.

You always had a sense of survival and more brains than most of the men in Memphis put together," she drawled, tilting back her exotic delicate face, which was strangely like a cat's. The movement caused her ebony tresses to ripple down her back in thick ringlets. She was trying to entice him. My God, she thought with a sensual shiver, what a handsome man he had become with the leashed sense of danger about him.

"If I remember correctly, Olivia, you were the one who honed her survivor instincts on my young susceptible heart," he replied with a light cynicism. She has grown older, he thought with satisfaction, noticing the fine lines at the corners of her knowing eyes. There was a certain hardness about her that reminded him of expensive whores he had known in Europe. She was still lushly beautiful, but like a rose that had reached its full bloom and was now starting to droop about the edges.

"La, but you still know how to flirt with a woman. It's what I hate about some of these Yankees, they are such boars, such pigs. They do not understand the joys of the chase, prolonging the satisfaction," she murmured with deliberate sensuality. Her small pointed tongue resting for the moment on her full lips in a gesture of sexual invitation as she gave a low husky laugh.

"I should not think my brother would allow you such intimate knowledge of the Union Army," he responded coldly, dislike flickering in his black eyes.

Stiffening with surprise, Olivia said quietly, "Clay is dead. I thought you knew, that our lawyer had written you."

"I have not been easy to find these last two years. When did he die?" Justin was shocked at the pain her words caused him. Had there been some part of him that hoped someday to reconcile with his brother, who had had the misfortune to also come under Olivia's spell?

"He died of the measles in Corinth after the battle of Shiloh. Not a hero's death as he would have wished," she said, brutally honest.

"Cedar Rest?"

"Burned by the glorious army of the Union." She gave a bitter smile as she spoke.

"But you seem to be doing well," Justin pointed out with some sarcasm, looking at her fashionable if rather garish costume.

"I have, shall we say, a protector." She spoke with a light bitterness. "And here he comes now." Pasting a brilliant smile on her face that didn't reach her calculating eyes, she greeted a rather portly major with the flushed visage of a drinker.

"My dear, may I introduce my brother-in-law, Captain Justin Pierce. Justin, this is Major Horace Osgood." Olivia purred the introductions while her eyes flashed Justin a glance that said, Yes, he is as bad as he looks. For a brief surprising moment, Justin felt a stab of pity for her.

"Major, Olivia, if you will excuse me, I must dine quickly, for I fear I have a busy afternoon." Having made his apology, Justin thankfully escaped to a corner table in the lavish high-ceilinged dining room filled with potted palms and huge lacy ferns under cut-glass chandeliers. After perusing the huge red-leather-bound menu with its numerous items listed in gold script, he gave his order to a waiter dressed in scarlet livery.

The room was filled with Union officers and their ladies, although it would be stretching it to call some of those women ladies, Justin mused. It seemed Olivia was not the only female in Memphis with a protector dressed in Union blue. Most were not the belles of the city, however; no, those Southern ladies were home trying to cope with the trials of occupation. The surrender of Memphis had attracted prostitutes of all shapes and sizes, and the better-looking with some pretensions sat in the Gayoso House. As he sipped his coffee, Justin thought of Ariane, his brave beautiful Rebel. She had clung to the edges of his mind all day. His hands could still feel the perfect shape of her breasts, the sweet nectar of her mouth. If her father had not made his pitiful attempt to stop the rabble from looting his house, where would it have ended? He wanted her with a passion he had never felt for any other woman. Seeing Olivia had only proved how strong his obsession was for his proud Little Bit. But it was the wrong time, the wrong place for them. Could she ever see past the uniform he wore, and if she knew his real purpose in Memphis, could she ever forgive him?

Throwing his napkin on the table, he signaled for his check. A long walk down to the docks would clear his head, strengthen his resolve to put a wall around his emotions where Ariane Valcour was concerned. There could be nothing between them, for ultimately it would bring only pain to both of them. As long as they were on opposite sides of this ghastly war, they had no future. Somehow he must remember that fact.

The rain had stopped and the street streamed in the humid heat. Any coolness that the rain had brought had evaporated, leaving the air sultry as a brief storm would often do in Memphis in the summer. He had forgotten how tropical the climate and how soft and steamy the air. It seemed to seep into a man's blood, teasing him, caressing him like the soft touch of a woman's hand on his heated skin, making him dream sensual dreams.

Plunging into the throng of the sidewalks, he made his way to the docks and the *Southern Lady*. He noticed the crowds were less brisk now that the sun had come out. Red-faced Union soldiers wiped the sweat from their faces as they rode past, the mud in the streets now drying but still as thick as molasses in places.

The seductive scent of magnolia and honeysuckle drifted above the more mundane scents of the street as he neared the promenade that overlooked the wharves. Taking a narrow cobblestone street down the bluff, he was soon in the bustle of the docks.

Ariane saw Justin's tall figure as he made his way through the throng of wagons, horses, soldiers, roustabouts, and passengers, who crowded the cobblestone landing. Her pulse had pounded at the sight of him, and she hated it. Even from a distance he radiated a vitality that drew her like a magnet, destroying all her resolve that this time his mere presence would not cause her to act like a lovesick child. She had taken the carriage the short way from the Valcour offices down the bluff to the docks, for it was no place for a woman alone. How glad she was that she had, for here she was hidden from view and could gather her wits about her before meeting him face to face. His commanding aura made him stand out from all the rest, for even in a crowd, his presence was compelling. Always she noticed the air of isolation about his virile form as if he was indeed a solitary man who kept his own counsel. Sable had called him a lone wolf.

Deliberately turning away from him, to give herself time to control her swirling emotions, Ariane stared out at the riverfront she loved. It, like the Mississippi, held an endless fascination for her. She loved the grand steam packets that rode side by side with keelboats, flatboats, and all manner of small river craft as well as the mighty army and navy boats of the Federal forces. The steam packets, like the *Southern Lady,* were the queens of the river. Ariane hated to see such a beautiful ship used for an odious purpose. However, it was simply another indignity of this awful war, that a Valcour steamer was to be used to transport Southern men to hellish confinement in one of the worst Northern prisons. It was an unbelievable irony. Push your anger to the back of your mind, or you might give yourself away to the Yankees, she reminded herself, clenching her hands tightly together till her fingernails cut into her skin.

She breathed deeply of the humid air perfumed with the scents of the ship's cargo to ease her nerves. The mingled scents drifted through the open window of hemp, smoked meats, rum, tar, tea and coffee. Everywhere there were huge bales of cotton. Cotton had been stored from the harvest the previous fall, and now that the Union encouraged exports, it was ready to be shipped to Northern and English markets. The bales, some half covered by rough burlap, towered even above the carriage. The market was high, and each steamer that left Memphis with its decks piled high with the fluffy white-gold was worth a fortune.

As the carriage pulled up alongside the *Southern Lady,* Ariane straightened her veil. Taking a deep breath, she ordered herself to act coolly competent in the discharge of the distasteful task ahead. Remember, show no emotion, she cautioned herself one last time as Roman opened the door and helped her out.

"It would appear your Sam Riley is true to his word," Justin said as he moved to her side from where he stood next to the gangplank. "The *Lady* appears to be ready."

"He is most trustworthy," she answered coolly, opening her parasol against the rays of the afternoon sun. Looking up at the elegant steamer with its intricate white gingerbread filigree trim sparkling in the late afternoon sun, she could avoid meeting those midnight eyes that penetrated too deeply inside her soul.

Justin held out his arm. "Shall we go on board. I believe I see Captain Riley coming down from the Texas deck."

Placing her hand on his sleeve, she felt a tremor of excitement at his nearness as they walked up the gangplank. Lowering her parasol as they reached the ship, she stumbled on a piece of rope left lying on the deck. Firm masculine hands spanned her tiny waist, helping her regain her balance.

"Thank you," she stammered, all too aware of the strength and warmth of those hands. As they lingered a fraction longer than needed, she felt a quickening in her blood as she remembered the pleasure those long tapered fingers could elicit from her body.

"My pleasure." His voice was a husky whisper that sent a ripple of awareness through her that he, too, had thought of their intimate moments together.

"You can take your hands away. I am quite all right," Ariane managed to say in a choked voice.

"If you insist," he replied, the huskiness lingering in his tone. He stood so close to her she could feel his warm breath on her neck like a kiss.

"Miss Valcour, Captain Pierce, the *Southern Lady* awaits your inspection." Sam Riley joined them from the top deck. He couldn't help feeling that he was intruding on a private moment; and he couldn't help the grin on his weathered visage. These two were as skittish around each other as a mare in heat with her first stallion, he thought in his earthy way. Being a captain on the river, he had seen all kinds of people come and go, but there was something that never changed and that was when a man and woman took a fancy to each other. They gave out sparks, and these two were giving out enough sparks to set the whole ship ablaze. It was a real shame, he thought, for there wasn't much of a future for them, not with this war.

The tour didn't take long, for Sam Riley had been

true to his word—the *Southern Lady* was ready to sail. Ariane had tried to keep her mind on the reason for this visit, tried to remember that this mercurial man beside her was her enemy, but it was so very hard. She was so aware of him beside her, his nearness made her senses spin. She felt ashamed that she had so little control over that part of her that ached for his touch, the fulfillment she somehow instinctively knew would come from his lovemaking.

"It seems we were just in time," Justin commented tersely as they returned to the lower deck. Mule-drawn federal Wagons loaded with prisoners accompanied by mounted soldiers were rattling down the steep cobblestone road of the bluff.

"Can't they go slower?" Ariane cried out in exasperation. "None of those wagons have springs, and the jarring of the cobblestones will make some of the men start to bleed again." Picking up her top hoop, she hurried down the gangplank to meet the first wagonload of prisoners. Justin followed close behind her.

Prisoners who had recuperated enough to walk were used as stretcher bearers. The rail-thin men dressed in their tattered uniforms climbed down and immediately began, under a Union officer's direction, to carry the more seriously ill and wounded up the gangplank. The air was filled with the sounds of harsh coughs, and the moans of those who were in pain.

"Miss Valcour, is this one of your boats?" a Southern voice called out.

"Jeff, are they taking you?" Ariane called out as she hurried to the side of a young man, not more than eighteen, who was being borne on a stretcher. He had been one of her patients, a Tennessee boy from the town of Jackson. She had become quite fond of him. He played a harmonica to while away the long hours in the ward and his playing seemed to cheer up the others.

89

He never complained although he had lost part of one leg. It had been a miracle he'd survived the battlefield amputation, for only 10 percent recovered from the operation, done many times without any other anesthesia besides a good swig of bourbon.

"Appears they are doing just that, ma'am," he replied giving her a weak but valiant smile.

As she leaned down toward him, she saw blood seeping from the bandaged stump of his amputated left leg. The ride had broken open the wound. If it wasn't treated, the boy would bleed to death.

"Captain Pierce!" Ariane called out to Justin, who was directing the stretcher bearers. "Over here!"

Justin heard the panic in her voice and came swiftly to her side. Glancing down at the young soldier, he saw immediately what was wrong. "Over there on the grass," he directed the white-faced bearers. The two older men also knew what was happening to young Jeff, a favorite with all of them. "Gently, gently," he cautioned, pressing down on the main artery of the leg to try and stop the bleeding.

Kneeling down beside the stretcher, Justin tried his best to stop the hemorrhage, but even his skilled hands could not work swiftly enough. Ariane watched from the other side of the stretcher as Jeff's life blood seeped out into the grass and wild black-eyed Susans that covered the bluff.

"Miss Valcour, will you write my ma and tell her I was thinking of her and pa, and . . . I love . . ." His voice trailed off as he lost consciousness.

"Yes I will," she whispered, holding his hand as he died. Gently she closed his eyes then leaned over and kissed his forehead. "For his mother," she whispered to the men who stood watching, their eyes filled with a haunted grief.

"Come, you must leave here," Justin said, motioning

for the men to carry the young boy's body away for the burial detail. Rising to his feet, he lifted the stunned, trembling Ariane up from the grass. She slumped against him for a moment, then as anger surged through her, she found the strength to stand alone.

"It would never have happened if they had not tried to move him so soon. He would not have died if they had only waited," she cried, glaring at him with burning, reproachful eyes. "He was only a boy, a boy!" She threw the words at him like stones, her gray eyes dark with her fury. "You should have stopped it, you're a doctor for God's sake."

"Quiet!" He grabbed her arm and pulled her toward her carriage. Her hat had fallen off; her parasol lay on the deck with her reticule. Her dress was spattered with blood, and her cheeks were stained with tears. Never had she looked more beautiful to Justin, but if he didn't get her away from there, she was going to incite a riot. The men were watching from the wagons, and as she passed by them, there were low cheers of encouragement.

Reaching the carriage, Justin yanked open the door and thrust Ariane inside. "Go home and write that letter you promised the lad. Cry it out, but leave here. I have work to do," he told her tersely. As a physician, he had learned to conceal his feelings, to erect a wall around his heart in order to be effective in his work.

"How can you do this to your own people?" she cried out, her eyes dark with despair and pain. "You are not the man I knew. He was kind—you are a stranger, a Yankee stranger." Her accusing voice stabbed into his heart. "The Justin I knew could never go along with this kind of treatment."

"This, my dear, is war. It is not kind, nor is it glorious. It is blood and waste, terrible waste, and young boys are dying, both Northern and Southern boys. Now go home where you belong." Stepping back, he ordered Roman to leave.

As the carriage pulled away, Ariane saw through tear-filled eyes his tall broad-shouldered figure silhouetted in the rays of the setting sun. "I hate you," she whispered, then wiping away her tears with a trembling hand, she murmured, "And I love you. God forgive me, but I love you." Leaning back against the seat she closed her eyes, feeling torn in two. She was overwhelmed with the torment of knowing where her loyalties must lie, but wanting a man with all her heart who was wrong. Would she ever be able to conquer her involuntary reactions to his dark eyes that spoke to her without words, or the bond between them that knew nothing of conflicting loyalties.

Chapter Seven

The shaft of moonglow fell across Ariane's writing desk from the long window of her bedchamber, but she had no time to enjoy the starry night. Her gold wire-rimmed glasses on the thin bridge of her delicate up-turned nose, she bent in concentration over the column she was writing for the *Memphis Appeal*. Tonight was the night she was to meet Beau for their weekly rendezvous, and she would give him the copy to smuggle out to the exiled Southern paper along with more stolen medicine from the ward. Pleading a headache after returning to the house from the hospital, she had had her evening meal sent up on a tray so she would not have to entertain her doctor guests.

Reading over what she had written, she sat back in her chair to rest her eyes. The seductive scent of the night-blooming jasmine perfumed the soft, sultry night air, making her strangely restless and interfering with her concentration. It was a night for a stroll in the garden in the moonlight with an attentive man by her side. She gave a sigh at her own foolishness. The masculine visage that obsessed her disturbed slumber had been seen in rare moments these last two weeks since the afternoon of the loading of the *Southern Lady*.

Justin returned to Fleur de Lys late each night and was gone at first light. Even after her father had returned to the Valcour offices in the mornings and Ariane had been able to return to nursing, she had rarely seen him at the hospital. It was as if he was avoiding her. Perhaps it was for the best if they did not see each other, she thought with a rush of mixed emotions.

Turning up the oil lamp, she resumed her labors, trying to banish the memory of his burning mouth that had kindled a like fire in her own blood. It was as if her thoughts had conjured up the object of her desire, for she heard the sound of a lone rider approaching the house. The drumming of the steed's hooves on the ground was like the rapid beating of her heart when she thought of Justin coming home. Some instinct told her it was Justin and no other. How she knew with such certainty, she had no idea, but then how could she explain the bond that drew them together when it was so impossible.

Drawn to the window, she took off her glasses and moved like a sleepwalker to the open casement. Staring down, she saw the lean sinewy length of him as he tied his horse to the iron hitching post. Then as if he could feel her eyes upon him, he turned and looked up at where she stood. Silently, he took off his broad-brimmed hat and, holding it at his side, stared up her. For a moment he studied her intently, the bright moonlight showing the brooding, almost angry expression on his classically handsome visage. Held by his dark eyes that glowed up at her with an insolent, savage inner fire, she couldn't move away from the window. A shudder passed through her and she could feel her breasts tingle against the sheer muslin of her bodice.

With a sudden gesture, he inclined his elegant head, sweeping his hat in front of him in a mocking bow. Then with one last burning look up at her, he turned on his heel and walked inside the house.

With trembling limbs, she ran to her chamber door and turned the lock with shaking hands. Pressing her fingers to her lips, she stood transfixed, listening for his footsteps in the hall. Hating the hunger she felt surging in waves through her. Where was her strength, the steely will that made her one of General Forrest's best spies in Memphis.

The sound of boots on the wooden floor echoed down the hall, but he did not stop at her chamber door. Ariane hated the odd twinge of disappointment that ran through her as she heard the sound of his door closing. She experienced a let-down feeling, an inexplicable feeling of emptiness. What had she expected, she thought in self-disgust, that he would break down the door and sweep her into his arms. Why did he always make her think such wanton thoughts?

Shaking her head at her own foolishness, she settled back down at her desk to finish her article on the latest insults and terror the Yankees had visited on the citizens of Memphis. Another family had been forced to leave Memphis in retaliation for Confederate guerrillas shooting at the coaches of the Memphis and Charleston Railroad when Union officers were aboard. Ariane felt especially bad about this for it was she who had told Forrest and his men that arms were being shipped on this particular train. While she was happy they had been successful, her heart was heavy that innocent women and children were going to pay for it. There was no sense of chivalry among the Federal command in Memphis. The family, consisting of a woman, her mother, and her three small children, were given only a few hours to pack up what they could carry in their carriage pulled by a mule. They were then escorted to the boundaries of the city and the Federal Lines and sent out into "Dixie," as the Yankees called it. Ariane could only hope the unfortunate family would find shelter with some Southern family as had her good friend Elizabeth Meriwether, who, when eight months pregnant, had been forced to leave Memphis with her two small boys in the cold of November. Her column about the gallant Southern lady had been widely read. The pitiful story of a pregnant woman setting forth through a stark countryside ravaged by war in a cold driving rainstorm in retaliation for a guerrilla attack on a Federal boat tore at the heartstrings of Southern readers. Her story had been a continuing one in Ariane's column as she told of Elizabeth's brave journey with only her carriage and faithful mule Adrienne to take her and her boys through cold rains and muddy roads. Traveling a month in these conditions, she finally reached Columbus, Mississippi, and refuge in the home of a Mrs. Rebecca Winston in time to give birth on Christmas Eve to her third son. She named him Lee after Robert E. Lee. Later her friend had had to move one step ahead of the Union army. Ariane had received another letter from Elizabeth smuggled to her by Beau that told of her hitching the mule to her Rockaway carriage once again this spring and moving once more with her three children. Ariane added Elizabeth's continuing story to the end of her column.

Satisfied with her copy, she rolled it tight, wrapping it in oilskin so rain wouldn't make the ink run. She wanted this column to make it intact to the *Memphis Appeal,* wherever it was now on its travels. General Forrest would know and make sure the article got there.

She had lost all track of time, so engrossed had she been in writing. Suddenly it was almost midnight. Surely her "guests" had settled down for the night. Placing the pilfered medicine in oilskin packets, she slipped them inside the lining of an old dove gray jacket that had belonged to Charles. The merchants in Memphis were not allowed to sell gray material that could be used to make Confederate uniforms, but she had gone up to the attic and found this packed away. After seeing Beau in rags, she was determined to find him something to wear. She was also taking him two white shirts and a pair of tan breeches. The Confederacy couldn't be fussy about regulation clothing anymore. All that was important was that they have something to cover themselves.

Placing everything in a small covered basket, she slipped her coded message into the hollow handle of a hunting knife. The message told of a country funeral, only the coffin, instead of carrying a body out of Memphis, would be filled with new Enfield rifles and ammunition.

Tonight she had decided to wear a peignoir over her night rail inside of a day gown. She had told everyone she had a headache so she must look as if Bess had awakened her for a call of nature. The basket could be explained as containing her dinner things, which she had decided to return to the kitchen to help the house staff, who were so short-handed since half the servants had run off.

Before she left the house, she had to check and make sure all was quiet, everyone asleep. Lighting a tall taper from her oil lamp, she carried the silver candlestick to the door. Quietly she slipped open the bolt and opened the door. Standing in the hall, she listened for anything that would tell her someone was awake. She heard only night sounds coming through the open windows. Taking no chances, she walked down the dark corridor then stopped once more to listen. Satisfied, she turned to walk back to her chamber to fetch Bess. Then she heard the creak of the floorboards under someone's step. Hurrying inside her chamber, she shut the door behind her, turning the lock.

"Who is it you are afraid of?" a familiar deep masculine voice queried from out of the shadows of her chamber.

"Justin," she gasped, her hand lifting the taper high so that she might see him.

"Is that an answer or a question?" he murmured, coming toward her out of the gloom. "You do have a penchant for wandering around late at night. Or is it old Bess again. Don't tell me you were sleepwalking." He came to stand in front of her, taking the taper from her hand and placing it on the table.

"What are you doing here?" she asked, hating the quiver she heard in her voice.

"I couldn't sleep. You really shouldn't look at a man that way when he returns home and expect him to go straight to sleep in his bed alone." There was a dark, sensual huskiness to his words as he caught her chin between his thumb and forefinger, lifting her delicate visage up so she would have to look at him.

His black eyes were staring at her with scorching intent. She flinched at the raw wild hunger she saw on his lean handsome features, in the depthless onyx gaze. "Tell me what you are doing on these midnight strolls of yours. Is it a lover you go to in your nightdress?"

"Let me go," she whispered, even now feeling herself flowing toward him as she sensed the barely leashed fury and hunger inside the sinewy length of him.

"To go to him, I think not," he answered raggedly, trying to control the urge to strip the thin wrapper and gown from her body. "Tonight, my lovely wanton Ariane, you will have only this man in your bed." With a groan acknowledging his lost control, he swept her into his arms, his hot mouth kissing first the hollow in her ivory throat then up the tingling cord of her neck to capture her moist waiting lips.

Her mouth opened under the assault of his kiss that was both punishing and tender as his arms pinned her to his broad chest. She should try and resist, she thought dimly, then the knowledge that this was Justin, her Justin, the knight of all her girlish dreams, swept over her and she molded against him. As his tongue began a deep achingly sweet exploration of her mouth, she gave in to the wild surge of pleasure that sang through her veins. Shyly at first, then with the strength of her passion urging her on, she met his tongue with her own and they danced together to a silent melody of rapture.

He had not meant to do this, he thought even as he was overtaken by the intense hunger that ruled him. How many nights had he lain awake listening for any sound from her room, since his late return the week before when he had seen her drifting into the house in the early hours. He hadn't seen anything but the bell of her skirt as she vanished up the back stair, but the lingering scent of her perfume, the seductive scent of heliotrope, had hung in the air, telling him that she had just passed.

It had driven him to a white hot fury to think of her meeting a lover in the garden or the summer house by the lake. Who was he, he had mused, staring at the other three doctors that stayed at Fleur de Lys when he met them at the hospital.

He had tried to stay away from the house as much as he could to keep her from his mind, but tonight when he returned and saw her at the window, he had experienced such a pang of longing he thought he would go mad. There had been no question of sleep for him; he had waited to hear her step in the hall. When he saw her through the crack in his door dressed only in her wrapper, he had been driven over the brink. She had become so brazen as to meet her lover in the house, perhaps go to his chamber. It was one of the other officers, he thought through a red haze of jealousy. He had meant to follow her when he had stepped on a squeaky floorboard and she had heard him. Then his only thought was that she would not lie in another man's arms tonight, for he would have her again and again till he drove her out of his soul.

Unlike Justin, Ariane was under no illusions—she was in the arms of the man she had worshiped and adored since childhood. A man who must not discover what she was really doing on her midnight strolls. Although she knew she loved him now with a woman's heart, she also had commitments to a cause that claimed her entire loyalty. She could not jeopardize the lives of the gallant men that fought beside her for the South. If spending the night in Justin's arms was what it took to distract him from his pursuit of the truth, she would do it. And throwing caution to the winds, she would revel in it. For in the splendor of his warm embrace there was no right or wrong—only the circle of his arms and the taste of his heated mouth. Pressing against him, she returned his kiss, eager to become a complete woman in his arms.

Her response only inflamed Justin, his blood leaping in his veins, his manhood erect and throbbing, pressing against the softness of her thigh. Feeling the heat of her skin through the thin material that separated them, he ripped it from her body. His hands could not get enough of the satin feel of her as he traced down the long graceful curve of her spine to cup the soft roundness of her delightful bottom in his hands. His mouth moved down her throat, blazing a fiery trail of kisses. Then she was swept up into the cradle of his arms as he carried her the few feet to the bed. Pushing the mosquito netting back with his elbow, he laid her down on the soft linen sheets that smelled also of heliotrope from the sachets Sable had placed inside the pillowcases.

She stretched back against the feather pillows like a contented kitten as he stripped the clothes from his back. His midnight-black eyes never leaving her face, they burned into her with the promise of rapture yet to come. In the golden glow of the candlelight, he was as beautiful as a Greek statue of Apollo—lean and lithe along the entire well-muscled length of him. His swarthy bronzed skin glowed under the soft black fur of his chest. Trembling, she lifted her arms up to him in a gesture of welcome.

With a low moan that was somewhere between rapture and pain, he was beside her on the bed. As he enfolded her in his arms, his mouth sought the succor of her breasts as a man dying of thirst finds a crystal clear spring and drinks his fill.

Her body felt as if it were being consumed with fire as his tongue circled the taut throbbing nipples, sensitive now to the lightest tough. Aflame, driven by instinctive hungers and needs she had no control over, her fingers tangled in the black silk of his hair, pulling him closer to her as she arched up, lifting the ivory mounds of her breasts to him as a gift. A languorous heat spread throughout her body and centered in her loins as she rubbed the smooth of her legs against his long sinewy masculine thighs. The rigid shaft of him was pressing in gentle erotic thrusts into the inner softness of her thigh, hinting at what was to come.

"So sweet, so perfect," he murmured as his mouth trailed down to the soft roundness of her belly. His long tapered fingers gently traced the curve of her ribs, the indentation of her tiny waist, and down to the swell of her slender hips as if he were memorizing everything about her. As his fingers found the silky auburn-gold triangle at the top of her Venus mound, his mouth kissed her sensitive inner thigh in tender adoration.

When he touched her, caressing the silky intimate curls till Ariane's breath caught in her throat, she arched up instinctively, seeking the complete fulfillment. Her moans filled the dark, hot room as he parted her inner petals and gently stroked and caressed her to the peak of sensation. She was all quivering fire, writhing under the knowing fingers that played her, eliciting the joyful music of her ecstasy as if she were a fine instrument made for the rapture of loving.

As she neared the pinnacle of her passion, he gently moved her legs apart and rose over her. Staring down at her, the fiery sunset of her tangled tresses fanned out about her ivory shoulders, the erect coral peaks of her ivory breasts, he was made breathless by her beauty. The sultry wanting in her gray eyes was his undoing.

"Look at me, sweet Ariane, look at me," he commanded as he opened her to receive him.

"My love!" she cried out, reaching for him as he entered her. "I have waited so long, so long for you." Her body trembled as he cupped her silken buttocks, lifting

101

her up to receive the long erect length of him.

As he thrust forward, he met what he did not think would still be there, the proof of her maidenhood. His fierce black eyes widened in shock as she smiled up at him.

"Do not stop, my love," she whispered, arching up in a movement as old as time.

He could not stop, not when she looked up at him with her whole heart and soul in her soft gray eyes. In her lovely smile that struck deep within him. "Ariane! My Ariane!" he moaned as he took her in one swift thrust.

After a brief pain that was quickly gone, she gloried in the knowledge that he was inside her and they were one. She pressed up closer to him, nearer to his lean, hard body.

Slowly, he began to make sensuous movements that took her breath away at the pleasure they gave her. At first, her hips tentatively met each thrust, but quickly she became all emotion and sensation. Then she was a wild wanton creature that could not get enough of him, of his long full length, the taste of his mouth on hers, the masculine scent of him. The movement of her hips became wild as she met each of his thrusts with one of her own. All the lonely years when he had been only a dream were gone and now she was filled with him. She thought she would never get enough, that she would go mad with the joy of it, when suddenly the exquisite wild pleasure of their joining seemed to explode within her, and Ariane knew for the first time the wonder of fulfillment.

Hearing her sweet cry of complete gratification sent a shudder of pure satisfaction and joy through Justin. Letting go of all restraint, he drove into her and found his own total release.

Holding him to her, she caressed the soft curling length of his hair at the nape of his neck till his ragged breath quieted. Then slowly he eased himself from her to lie beside her and take her in the curve of his arm.

"Oh, Little Bit, I should not have done such a thing," he murmured huskily against her temple. "There has been a wildness in me since I returned to Memphis, in truth since that first day I saw you. Still, if I had known that you were . . . were still a maiden . . ." He stopped, for indeed he didn't know what else to say. She was not what he had thought, or had that been only an excuse to himself to quiet his conscience so he might take what he had wanted since the first time their eyes had met across the square. "Of course I shall speak to your father."

"You will what?" she sputtered, sitting up and staring at him as if he had lost his mind.

"To ask for your hand in marriage," he said softly, a grin lurking at the corner of his usually stern mouth. "What did you think I meant?"

"I don't know," she replied slowly, lifting her fingertips to her lips, which trembled in a bittersweet smile. Turning to face him, her gray eyes misted with unshed tears, she said sadly, "Please say nothing, for you must understand . . . I cannot marry you."

"And why not, Little Bit?" he asked, gently wiping a tear from her cheek. "You just showed me your love."

"Because there is too much against it, against us," she answered in a heartbroken whisper.

"Because of the uniform I wear," he stated with sudden bemused clarity.

"Yes," she sighed. There was more bitter sadness in that one word than he had ever heard in a human voice.

"The South is going to lose this war. Perhaps then you will see that it matters not what side we are on. I can't believe that tonight meant so little to you," he told her harshly, angered now by her allegiance to some cause that was already lost. He was in no great hurry to marry; in fact, before tonight he had vowed he would never marry. He had only made the offer because, despite everything, he found to his surprise that he loved this headstrong, beautiful woman with her old-fashioned sense of honor

103

and loyalty. To have her reject him because he wore Union blue instead of Confederate gray cut him deeply and made him strangely all the more determined he would wear her down and make her his wife. A thought crossed his mind, causing him to give a thin-lipped smile. She might even now carry his child—he would see how she felt about marriage to a Yankee then.

"It meant more to me than you will ever know, but it doesn't change my mind. There are other things that are important to me as well," she explained, looking up at him, trying to make him understand.

"The glorious Cause," he said with biting sarcasm, his black eyes glittering dangerously.

"I think we should not talk of this," she said quietly, looking away from him. "Perhaps you should leave. Sable would be shocked if she came with my breakfast tray and found you beside me." She made an attempt at humor to defuse what was rapidly becoming an argument.

"I will go this time, Little Bit, but I will be back. And I will be watching you, I don't know what is going on here at Fleur de Lys, but if it has anything to do with your glorious cause, let me warn you, you are playing with fire. Stop it, don't waste your life on something that is already lost," he told her harshly as he dressed. "Women who help the Rebs are considered traitors, and they are put in Irving Block Prison. It is not a pretty place. They haven't hung a woman yet, but General Washburn is determined to stop what he sees as Secesh feeling among the women of Memphis. You have a beautiful neck, my dear Ariane. I don't want to see a rope around it."

She watched as he strode from the room without a backward glance. Even in the sultry humid heat she felt a chill. It was as if she felt a trap closing in on her. There was no way she could meet Beau tonight. On the morrow she would have to send word to him by their other emergency courier. With Justin watching her, she would have to be more careful. She had to talk with her brother to make some other arrangements. How to do it, she mused, biting her fingernail. Then she remembered her cipher message to General Forrest — she would have to send it with the courier, but add a post script that somehow they must make other arrangements because she was being watched.

Leaning back against the pillow, she caught the faint fragrance of Justin and she felt a stab of pain in her heart. If only everything were different, she would be proud to be his wife. How much would this war take from her? Her hand went to her throat and his words came back to her, making the fine hairs on the back of her neck stand up. Was there any hope for them at all, or would the war destroy their love as it had so many lives.

Chapter Eight

"Caesar, I have put the note in the watch, and my column has been rolled up inside the hollow handle of the carriage whip. My brother's clothes are hidden under your seat. The Yankees wouldn't think of looking there. What is it you are going to say when you are stopped by the sentries on the Raleigh Road?" Ariane asked the old black servant, handing him the hollowed-out watch case.

"Ifen they ask wheres I'm goin' and why, I says that I'm takin' my master's wagon out to the Raleigh Springs Hotel on the Raleigh Bluffs to fetch some of that fine medicinal water from their famous curative springs. My master he swears that water will cure stomach problems. He always went every summer before the war during the fever season, but now 'cause of the curfew, he sends me to fetch the water," Caesar said solemnly from his seat atop the wagon.

"Good, you have your tin containers." Ariane checked the back of the wagon where they had put several empty containers. "Remember, after meeting with my brother at the spring house at noon, you be sure and fill up those water jugs. The Yankees might check on your way back. Perhaps there is something to the legend that the water is a miracle curative. The summers we spent out there at the hotel we never did suffer from the usual summer stomach complaints."

"Yes, Miz Ariane, Sable done swear by it. Efen your ailing with the bellyache, she only lets a body drink that bottled Raleigh spring water she buys at the apothecary tills you're well. Good for the baby colic too, I hear," he told her, picking up the reins of the two old harnessed mules, Napoleon and Josephine.

"Thank you, Caesar, for doing this. Be careful." She touched his sleeve for a moment, her gray eyes misted with emotion, her delicate features strained with worry. She and Beau had made provisions that if she did not send him the all-clear signal, the next day Caesar would meet him out at the Raleigh Springs at midday.

"We can't let Mister Beau go around in rags worrying why you didn't meet him last night. I raised that boy up to manhood, taught him to ride his first pony. No matter hows I feel 'bout this war, I don't turn my back on you or Mister Beau. We's all family, I reckon. Don't you worry none, missy, I tell him what he needs to know," Caesar told her with quiet dignity as he snapped the reins. "Get up there, ole mules."

Ariane stood watching the wagon pull away into the rising sun, the straw hats bobbing up on the mules' heads. They were Caesar's special pets and always in summer wore raggedy straw hats, sometimes decorated as they were this morning with black-eyed Susans stuck jauntily in the red bandanna hat bands. Caesar was right, she thought with a lump in her throat. They were all family in some strange way.

But even in families, certainly among friends, this war was tearing apart bonds and straining individual loyalties. Even between lovers, she thought, staring out across the lake where the graceful swans glided on the green-blue glass of the still water, their feathers glistening ebony and alabaster in the streaming rays of the morning sun. It all appeared so normal and tranquil, but it was only a facade. As if her thoughts conjured up the object of her unease, she saw the flash of a blue tunic come around the corner of the house.

"You are up early, and dressed for the day too I see.

May I ask where Caesar is going with that wagon?" Justin's coolly impersonal tone broke the stillness of the morning as he approached where she stood beside the kitchen herb garden. It was as if they had never made love, as if they were only polite strangers.

"I sent him to the springs in Raleigh for fresh water. Sable claims it is a curative for summer stomach ailments," she replied matter-of-factly, but felt a trickle of fear run down her spine. This morning he was a Yankee officer and she hated him for it, for his cool, remote demeanor that put a wall between them.

" 'Tis a long way for him to go for fresh water, although I agree the Memphis water from Bayou Gayoso is foul this time of year. Raleigh is outside Federal lines— are you sure that is the only reason for Caesar's trip?" He frowned down at her, his dark eyes holding hers, analyzing her reaction to his question.

"What other reason could there be?" she replied, never flinching from his gaze.

"Do not tempt fate, my dear, or should I say, do not tempt the patience of the Provost Marshal." His voice, though quiet, had an ominous quality.

"Is that a threat, Captain?" Her delicate features flashed him a look of disdain.

"Never a threat, Little Bit, only a warning." His voice had a husky catch in it as he gently touched her chin, one tapered finger tracing for a moment the curve of her lip.

She couldn't control the shudder of longing that ran through her at his touch, the shock that ran through her body. Clenching her fists at her sides, she fought the urge to reach out to him. For a moment she closed her eyes against the raw desire she saw in his tender gaze.

"Do you think I could dismiss last night from my mind, when even now my mouth hungers for you, my hands ache to feel the touch of your skin," he murmured in a harsh raw voice, letting his hand drop to his side.

"Please . . ." Her voice was a low moan as she turned

her head away, knowing if she looked at him, she would be lost. This was madness—they were in full view of the house with the servants going about their daily tasks, but as usual when they were together, it was if nothing else mattered in the world.

"God help me," he muttered, turning on his heel and striding quickly toward where his horse had been brought around by Roman.

A brushing on her skirt caused Ariane to look down where the kitchen cat, a disreputable black-and-white tom with a distinctive black patch around one eye, chased a butterfly flitting across the lemon balm. "Oh Pirate, what am I going to do," she sighed, stroking his silky fur.

"Miz Ariane, you be wantin' the carriage?" Roman asked politely as he came toward her.

"Yes, I will be leaving for the hospital directly. Let me fetch my parasol. I will meet you around front," she directed him, heading for the house.

Poplar Street was crowded with the usual early-morning traffic, drays delivering milk and vegetables to the wealthier homes in the city as Roman drove Ariane to the hospital. Clouds of dust rolled through the open windows of the Valcour carriage as did the numerous mosquitoes that bedeviled the citizens of Memphis in spring and summer. The summer mosquitoes were so thick and swarmed with such a vengeance around one's face that inhaling them was a common occurrence. Thus most ladies such as Ariane wore a veil on their bonnet that came down to their chin and tied high in the back when outside.

The entrance to the hospital was thronged with people even this early in the day. A train of wounded must have arrived at the Memphis and Charleston depot this morning over on Lauderdale, Ariane mused as she climbed with Roman's help out on the carriage block. The three-storied Exchange Building was huge, extending from Poplar Road to Exchange Street. The lower floor that had been a medical school before the war had now been turned into wards, but even so, she wondered where they were going to put all the sick and wounded. Army wagons used as ambulances were backed up to the front door, where soldiers were pulling stretcher after stretcher off the crude vehicles. The moans of the wounded greeted Ariane as did the stench of blood, pus, and human excrement. For a moment she felt faint and leaned against the wall till she could catch her breath. Dear Lord, would she ever get used to the stink of war and its residue from battle. The humid heat of July only intensified the fetid odors of festering wounds and sick men. Struggling to gird herself for the day, she looked up and saw a tall familiar figure making sense out of the confusion with a few terse commands.

Justin had come out of the hospital and was carefully checking each stretcher as it passed him, then directing the bearers to the proper ward. His mere presence seemed to give her strength, the fluid muscular grace of his movements, the impression of energy barely contained that seemed to emanate from his dark lithe form. He was sanity in an insane world.

"Miss Valcour, you could certainly do more than remain a spectator." The tart, sarcastic tones of Hazel Schneider shook her from her musings.

"Yes, I am sorry. I felt faint for a moment," Ariane apologized.

"This wretched heat is affecting everyone, but I would have thought you were more acclimated to it. Come, I need your help. That young Reb's leg has festered badly; there is naught they can do but take it off today. I thought perhaps you could sit with him till they're ready," Hazel Schneider explained brusquely, but Ariane could see the sadness in her pale blue eyes. "He is one of your own, comes from some small town in Tennessee, and is barely nineteen."

Sometimes Hazel Schneider surprised her and showed a

110

compassion Ariane didn't think her capable of, but then she had reason to hate the Confederacy. One brother had been killed at Bull Run and the other at Antietam.

Having placed her bonnet, parasol, and reticule in the wardroom cupboard, Ariane donned a long white apron that covered most of her blue muslin gown. Taking a novel by Sir Walter Scott from her reticule, she stuck it in the pocket of her voluminous apron. She was thankful she had thought to bring it. Maybe the words of the South's favorite author would help the young man pass the terrible wait for his amputation.

As she followed Hazel down the long corridor to the surgeon's wing, the persistent, sickening fumes of chloroform seemed to surround her. Entering the ward nearest the surgery room, Ariane could feel the apprehension and fear of the men like a looming presence. Walking down between the rows of cots, she heard some men moan and writhe with pain while others quietly wept. It mattered not to her in this room if the men wore blue or gray — she felt only an overwhelming sadness and had to fight to keep from giving in to a sense of despair. Was anything worth this carnage, she thought.

The young Southern prisoner lay still and white on his cot, staring up at the ceiling as the two women approached. The smell of his gangrenous wound hovered about the bed like a cloud. "Lieutenant Pendleton, I have brought Miss Valcour to sit with you. She is from Memphis, I thought you would like the company of another Southerner at this time," Hazel said quietly before leaving.

Ariane touched his hand reassuringly where it lay still on the sheet of the cot. So young, she thought, to be a lieutenant. The South was losing men and had only boys to replace them.

"Is there anything I can do for you, Lieutenant?" she asked softly, sitting down beside him on a rickety chair Hazel had put there for her.

111

"Just talk to me, ma'am. I would like to hear a Southern woman's voice once again before I die," he whispered in cultured, educated tones, turning huge brown eyes her way, eyes from which all hope had gone.

"What is your first name, Lieutenant?"

"Wade, ma'am."

"Well, Wade, the Yankees have very good surgeons in this hospital and they will do their best to see that you don't die," she told him, wiping the dampness from his brow with a dry cloth. "My name is Ariane. I have a book of Sir Walter Scott's with me. Would you care to have me read to you?"

"Yes, Miss Ariane. I would like that very much indeed."

She smiled down at him and began to read, her voice a counterpoint to the moans of the sick and dying. She could feel Wade Pentleton's eyes fastened on her as if she could give him some last reprieve from what was to come. When they came for him, she walked beside his stretcher, holding his hand until they reached the door of the surgery room. As they carried him in, Ariane turned white, for there on the floor in a large basket lay the bloody remains of previous operations, a hideous basket of legs and feet. She turned away, her hands pressed to her mouth. She had to get out of there. Hazel Schneider was slowly dripping chloroform over a linen cone mask on Wade Pentleton's face. He was past needing her support.

Hurrying down the hall, she sought the fresh air outside the wards. Pushing past a group of convalescing soldiers, she sought a small inner courtyard that the staff used as an island of calm in the sea of pain and misery that was the hospital.

Thank God it's empty, she thought as she sought the shade of an oak tree, sinking down with trembling legs on to a wrought iron bench. She needed a few minutes of solitude to regain her control. This morning had brought back those hideous days after the battle of Shiloh when she had searched for Charles and found him dead. The memory of those hellish hours she had spent nursing her father after he'd lost his leg seemed to run over and over in her brain. And the thought that it could have been Beau in there under the surgeon's knife turned her blood to ice water even in the sultry heat. Shuddering, she placed her hands over her face, as if she could somehow blot out the terrible sights she had seen.

"Are you all right?" the deep masculine voice asked, breaking the heated silence of the courtyard.

Slowly she took her hands from her face and looked up into Justin's concerned gaze. "I thought it could no longer reach me, that I had built the wall around my heart high enough," she whispered. "I was wrong."

"If it didn't touch you, it would mean you were no longer human, no longer able to feel anything," he said softly, coming to sit beside her on the bench. "And that would be a real tragedy."

"Then it does bother you," she said, raising huge gray eyes full of pain and wonder to meet his clear, direct gaze.

"Yes, but I have to continue on because it does bother me. If I didn't do something to make a difference, then it would all be for naught," he told her quietly, staring out at the pattern the sunlight made on the flat stones.

It was as they sat enjoying the simple stolen pleasure of a few moments in each other's company that they heard the shouts of men and the protests of a woman. They rose to their feet just as the door to the hall was thrown open and a white-faced Felicity Sanders ran out into the small courtyard, a soldier right behind her.

"Stop her, Captain!" the corporal yelled as he chased her around the tree till she stood trapped up against the brick wall of the building.

"What is the meaning of this?" Justin demanded as Felicity stood trembling like a frightened animal that could see no way out.

"I saw her take quinine tablets out of the medicine cupboard and slip them in her pocket," the Union soldier said, pulling his service revolver from his holster and pointing it at the terrified young woman.

A cold knot forming in her stomach, Ariane recognized the young soldier. He had taken an interest in Felicity from the first day he had been assigned to the hospital and had tried to strike up a friendship with her. Fiercely loyal to the South—and to her fiancée, who was serving with the Fourth Tennessee Infantry—Felicity had spurned his attentions. He had continued to watch her with longing, and now his avid attention had been her downfall, that and his need for revenge.

"Is this true, Miss Sanders?" Justin questioned, his voice cool and exact.

Felicity darted a frightened glance in Ariane's direction. Her fists clenched at her sides, she refused to speak.

"Can't you see she is too terrified to think, let alone answer your questions. I'm sure she was only taking the medicine for a patient, but the corporal has frightened her so that she can't think rationally," Ariane countered icily, amazed she could lie so smoothly.

"Then isn't she lucky she has her good friend to answer for her," Justin said sternly, with no vestige of sympathy in his voice. Staring at Felicity, he demanded, "Empty your pockets, Miss Sanders."

With trembling hands, Felicity pulled packet after packet of quinine tablets from her deep pockets. They fell from her shaking fingers to lie in a pile at her feet.

"Well, obviously these were not meant for just one patient. I think you had better accompany me to Major Hawthorne's office," Justin told her tersely, not looking at Ariane. "I think she can walk without your escort, Corporal, and with all the staff about, I don't think she can escape," he told the soldier as he grabbed Felicity's

114

arm.

"Courage, honey," Ariane called after her friend as Felicity gave her a despairing look over shoulder before disappearing into the hall, where curious patients and staff stood watching.

"Miss Valcour, I could use your help with some of the incoming patients," an angry-voiced Hazel Schneider commanded from the doorway.

"Yes, I am coming." Ariane hurried after the brusquely moving figure. "How did the lieutenant endure the amputation, if I might ask?"

"He died on the table," she said over her shoulder, never slowing her pace.

Ariane felt a stab of pain run through her at the woman's terse words, but kept on walking. She had to be strong for Felicity, for Beau, for all those of her friends who were daily risking their lives. She would cry tonight for the gallant young lieutenant, tonight when she was alone, away from all these hostile eyes.

All the long day Ariane kept looking for any sign of her friend, the worry and anxiety taking its toll along with the intense heat. As the late afternoon sun was setting in the west, sending its glaring heat through the long windows and turning the wards into ovens, Hazel Schneider dismissed her for the day.

"You are not looking well, Miss Valcour. I can't afford to lose another nurse. Perhaps you better leave for the day," she advised her. Ariane swayed as she rose to her feet after changing a patient's bandages.

Gathering up her reticule, parasol, and bonnet, Ariane gratefully escaped from her duties. Taking a small bottle of perfume from her reticule, she opened it and touched the stopper to her wrists and behind her ears. It made her feel fresher and took away some of the stench.

As she was leaving, she passed by the surgeons' offices and saw Justin was alone at the desk, filling out the day's reports. Sick with worry about Felicity, but afraid to draw

115

Miss Schneider's attention to the charge against her friend, she had not inquired what had happened. But she could trust Justin, she thought as she slipped inside the office, closing the door behind her. He was a Union officer, but he was Justin, born and bred in Memphis, a Southerner in his heart.

"Yes." He looked up at her without any welcome on his stern visage. His features seemed to have become molded steel, his black eyes wary as he stared at her for a moment before rising to his feet in a fluid movement of courtesy.

"I . . . I wanted to ask about Felicity," Ariane said in a choked, hesitant voice.

His eyes narrowed and his back became ramrod straight as he said, "She has been taken to Irving Block Prison." The words hung in the heat between them like an invisible barrier.

"On what charge?" Ariane managed to ask, her anguish almost overcoming her control.

"Stealing, smuggling, spying, giving aid and comfort to the enemy, take your pick." He flung the charges at her like stones, the chill of ice shards in his voice. His expression darkened with some unreadable emotion as he stared at her, waiting, watching, giving her no quarter. He had a strong suspicion, as did others at the hospital, that Felicity was not in this alone, although she had refused to speak under interrogation. Even the threat of prison had not shaken her resolve, and that fact had infuriated the major. In anger, he had called the guards to take her to Irving Block immediately.

"How could you be a party to sending one of your own to that hellhole?" she cried, flashing into sudden fury. "I thought I knew you, but I am realizing I don't know you at all."

"As I am coming to understand about you, my dear Ariane. What exactly is the game you are playing with me?" His accusing gaze was riveted on her, burning

116

through her.

She flinched at the tone of his voice and the derision she saw in his black eyes. "Think what you will, or what you must of me, there is nothing I can say that you would understand, for it seems we don't speak the same language. You are not the man I thought you were all these years. The Justin I loved as a child was just that — a childish fantasy. Good-bye." She turned and walked from the office, slamming the door hard behind her.

"And you, my beautiful tormenter, are exactly what I think you are. By God, how am I going to live with that," he muttered, staring after her. The faint scent of heliotrope still lingered in the stuffy heat of the room, reminding him that no matter what, deep, deep in the innermost depths of his soul he still burned with an overwhelming desire to caress her, to taste the honey of her mouth and feel her trembling beneath him. He could not ever forget her, he knew that, but how could he deal with the conflict she raised within him? It was a conflict between loyalty to an abstract concept and the fiery flesh-and-blood reality of Ariane. Even now when he was filled with anger at her, at the words she had thrown at him, he wanted her. She was a sickness in his blood, a sickness that had no cure.

Chapter Nine

The long purple-mauve shadows of twilight were falling over the grounds of Fleur de Lys as Ariane paced by the side of the tranquil lake. Trying to quiet her turbulent thoughts, she watched the swans circling in graceful motions across the glassy surface of the dark green water.

Having returned from the hospital hot and tired, she had taken a long cool bath in the brass sit tub in her bedchamber, but the visions of Felicity in the hellhole that was Irving Block Prison would not leave her. Feeling trapped in the hot stuffy room, she had dressed in a cool gown and left the house to await Caesar's return.

The music of the sad-voiced whippoorwill singing its last song to the dying day filled the early evening air, echoing the melancholy in Ariane's heart. Snapping open the ivory lace fan she carried on a silk cord at her wrist, she fanned her heated face, the familiar fragrance of heliotrope drifting on the still sultry air from where Sable had placed a few drops of perfume on the lace folds.

How could Justin have sent Felicity to Major Hawthorne's office? He had to have known he was sending her to prison. But he was a Yankee, she reminded herself, and his loyalty lay with the uniform he wore. She must go on the morrow to Irving Block and see if she could speak with her friend, and then she would have more to tell Mrs. Sanderson about her daughter. She had wanted to go straight there after leaving the hospital, but there was a sundown curfew for the residents of Memphis, the Southern residents of Memphis. She had barely made it home in time, for as she reached the estate's grounds, she had been stopped by the one of the many Union sentries that patrolled the streets of the city. She had shown her pass that stated she was a nurse and explained she had been kept late at the hospital. He had let her pass on into the gates of her own home, she thought bitterly, but she was worried about Caesar. Although the soldiers were more lenient with former slaves, they questioned any that still showed loyalty to their former masters. She had told Sable to send the old man to her as soon as he arrived.

Hearing steps on the gravel walk that circled the lake Ariane called out, "Caesar, is that you?"

"Has he not returned?" The deep masculine voice sent a delicious shiver up her spine. After everything that had happened today, the very sound of his voice could still send a tingling of wild yearning through her that was impossible to stop.

"No, I think not," she answered with caution as Justin came out of the shadows of the huge cedars to stand beside her. Remember, she told herself, regardless of his honeyed words, he is the enemy. If he knew the truth about her, would he even hesitate to send her to join Felicity?

" 'Tis dangerous for him to try and enter the city after dark. I came to tell you that General Washburn has declared martial law today. He is tired of Confederate sympathizers providing aid and information to Forrest and the Rebs. He means to hold Memphis in an iron grip," Justin said in terse tones, watching for her reaction.

119

"But why now after all this time?" Ariane gasped, turning away from his too probing gaze to stare out at the swans and their serene water ballet.

"Forrest has defeated General Sturgis on his sortie into Mississippi. He has lost not only a quarter of his army but all his artillery and most of his supply wagons. Forrest was waiting for him. Someone in Memphis had alerted him of the troop movement. Washburn and Hurlbut will have their retribution."

"Why are you telling me this?" she asked softly.

"It went harshly for your friend. She is sentenced to Irving Block for the duration of the war. But she is lucky she wasn't hung as a traitor." His voice was filled with exasperation.

Ariane's shoulders slumped at his words as her heart sank. How could Felicity survive in such a place? She had heard stories of the wretched conditions. The guards were inhuman, the food inedible, the living space filthy and crowded.

"I must see her. Can you arrange for me to see her, take her some personal items," she pleaded, turning to face him, anguish in her misty gray eyes.

"That is exactly what you must not do. They are looking for her contacts. She was not alone in her misguided attempt to help the glorious cause—of this they are very aware. If you go to her, they will assume you were in it together. They don't need proof, my dear. They are the law in Memphis and the concept of habeas corpus was abolished with the stroke of Washburn's pen." He reached out and caught her arm, forcing her to look up into his dark eyes.

"She is my friend. I cannot let her think that I don't care what happens to her," Ariane replied, rancor sharpening her voice.

"If she is your friend, she wouldn't want you to be put in danger because of visiting her. This is not a game, my dear Ariane, this is deadly serious. I wish you would understand that if nothing else, for I am sure your friend Felicity does by now. Your glorious cause has cost enough good men their lives I don't think the South requires the blood of their women as well."

"I don't know what you are talking about," she spat back at him, looking him boldly in the eye.

"Oh you know all right, and from now on I will be watching you, your every move, your every breath. There is nothing I can do for your friend, but by God, I can make sure you do not follow her."

"There is nothing you can do for Felicity now, since you were the one who put her in that hellish place."

"I am an officer of the Union Army and as such I had no other choice."

"Of course, it was your duty," she sneered. "Believe me, I am only too aware of the uniform you wear. Please take your hand off me. I have a dinner table of your fellow officers to preside over."

He stared down at her for a long moment, then lifted her arm to his lips and placed his warm mouth where his fingers had gripped her delicate skin.

The touch of his tender kiss sent a shimmer of heat through her body, burning away her every thought but the memory of what it was like to feel those lips on every part of her trembling body. She felt tears pick her eyelids at the knowledge that it was all wrong for them, no matter how deep their feeling was for one another. There was no future for their love—their strong sense of honor and duty kept coming between them.

Suddenly the black swan and the white swan rose in the air and flew to their roosting place on the small island in the middle of the lake. Ariane and Justin turned at the sound, and hands clasped, they watched the lovely spectacle.

"Is it true they mate for life?" he asked softly.

"I am not sure, but 'tis a lovely thought," she replied with a catch in her throat. As the graceful birds sought their night sanctuary, the man and the woman turned and walked slowly back to the house.

The mansion was ablaze with light as they entered the foyer. Men's voices rose and fell from the parlor as the other officers had a smoke before the evening meal was served.

"Mam'zelle, may I speak with you?" Sable greeted them as they entered.

Justin left them to join his fellow officers. As soon as he had left, Ariane turned to the maid, anxious to know if she had heard from Caesar.

"He is in the kitchen house, mam'zelle," Sable replied to her query, looking quickly over her shoulder to make sure they would not be overheard. "The trip was successful, but Mister Beau wanted you to know that they killed a Union courier outside of Memphis. He was carrying a coded message in his saddlebags for General Washburn from Brigadier General Dodge. They only broke the code this morning at General Forrest's headquarters. It seems that one of General Dodge's field agents is working here in Memphis. The agent is one of their best operatives and his assignment is to find and apprehend all those in the city who are giving information to Forrest and his men."

"Did the message give a name?" Ariane asked in a whisper. General Dodge's network of agents working in the South were notorious for their cleverness and stealth in operating in and out of Confederate lines. It was rumored some were Southerners, who, with their familiar accents, were able to masquerade as loyal Confederates while gathering information for the Union commander.

"No, only a code name—Falcon. Not even Washburn is to know the agent's real identity," Sable murmured.

"But your brother says this agent is dangerous. A Yankee operative in New Orleans was responsible for the capture of several Confederates working within the Yankee garrison and in Vicksburg too, after the city was taken. They think this may be the same person."

The sound of masculine voices coming from the parlor silenced the woman as the Union officers filed into the foyer at Roman's announcement that dinner was being served. Ariane turned with an automatic smile at her guests as her mind turned over feverishly the information Sable had confided. There was something about what she said that had struck a familiar chord, but Ariane couldn't quite grasp what it was that had triggered a memory. It hung there on the edge of her brain, teasing her, but she was unable to focus on it. Giving a shrug of her delicate shoulders, she smiled at Captain Norris as he held out his arm to escort her into the dining room. Turning her back on the scowl etched in Justin's stern visage, she allowed Captain Norris to accompany her to her chair.

Ariane gestured for the men to take their seats as she nodded to Roman to start serving. Leroy, the cook's young boy, sat in the corner pulling gently on the cord that caused the rosewood fan suspended over the table to waft slowly back and forth. This helped keep the numerous flying insects of a Memphis summer from the food.

"Father," she said in startled tones as Leander Valcour appeared in the doorway. He had had his evening meal in his room since the day the Union soldiers had searched the house. It was his own small attempt at showing his dislike of the men thrust upon them by the Provost Marshal's Office.

Leaning heavily on his cane, he glowered at the Union officers from where he stood, not moving into the room. "Is it true that martial law has been declared

123

in Memphis and that every man who desires to work at his business in the city must take the iron-clad oath in person."

There was a heavy silence in the chamber as the men avoided each other's gaze. Ariane felt a throbbing in her right temple. Rising to her feet, she told him, "Have a seat, Father, you look tired. A bit of food will do you some good."

"Are you all deaf or is there not one of you man enough to admit to one more barbarous act by that gang of cutthroats that call themselves the commanders of this army of rabble." He fairly shouted the words, ignoring Ariane's plea.

"Yes, sir, martial law has been declared," Justin replied in a quiet, yet controlled tone as he rose to his feet. "I understand every man will be expected to take the iron-clad oath or be considered a traitor."

"And, sir, what do you consider yourself if not a traitor to your own people, to the South," Leander Valcour thundered.

"I think, sir, that you are tired and should seek the rest of your bed," Justin answered quietly, his face a frozen mask.

"Father, please," Ariane murmured, coming to his side so quickly her skirt swayed like a bell. "This will do no good. The doctors are not responsible for a decision made by General Washburn. Come, let us help you upstairs. Gentlemen, please continue your dinner without me."

"I won't do it, daughter," he told her with a heavy sigh as she helped him up the curving staircase.

"Yes, Father, I know," Ariane replied with pain etched on her delicate features. Her father's refusal to take the oath that stated he would never give any help or comfort to any Confederate soldier no matter the circumstances, even if he was dying and asked for a

124

drink of water, could result in his imprisonment.

"They push us too far, daughter." Her father sagged against her as they reached his chamber, where Caesar suddenly appeared to help her take his master into his bed.

"I take care of him, Miz Ariane," the black valet told her, taking her place beside the old man. "Sable done told you what you need to know?" he asked over his shoulder.

"Yes, I got the message."

"You be careful. They getting right mean and serious, ma'am," he told her as she turned to leave.

"It appears to be so," she agreed, more shaken by the night's events than she cared to admit.

Justin was waiting at the foot of the stairs as she descended, her face clouded with uneasiness. He stared up at her, the golden light from the oil lamp falling over the hard angular planes of his handsome visage. They were the features of a hard controlled man, but in those dark expressive eyes dwelt a naked pain. He had let the cold remote mask slip for a moment and the depth of his anguish smote her heart. So close was this invisible bond connecting them that for a moment it was as if they were one person, and she felt his pain as if it were her own.

"Is he all right?" he asked as she reached the bottom stair.

"Caesar is seeing to him," she answered, but their words had no connection to the conversation they were having with their eyes. That was quite different. There was nothing mundane about the depth of wanting, the sheer need and understanding of that need, in spite of everything.

"I think we should join the others," Ariane said softly, turning away while she still could, for his nearness was overwhelming. She longed for his touch, yet

125

knew that nothing would change because of it.

The rest of dinner was strained and everyone was relieved when dessert was finished and they could leave the table. The men knew that tonight there would be no friendly singing in the parlor, so after excusing themselves, they drifted off to read or engage in a game of chess in the library. Justin, with a taut goodnight, went upstairs to his chamber.

Ariane, her nerves jangled, knew that she would not be able to find release from her anxiety in slumber. Instead, she strolled out onto the terrace. The night was sultry, not a leaf stirring in the still humid heat. The moon hung like a ripe melon in the velvet night sky, casting streams of an eerie alabaster light through the branches of the cedars and magnolia. Fever weather, she thought with a melancholy sigh. There were as many sick patients at the hospital as wounded ones in this heat, especially since most of the soldiers were not acclimated to a Memphis summer.

Strolling idly near the open French doors of the library, she heard Captain Norris speaking to his friend and fellow officer as they sat over a chessboard. "I heard we are to be expecting more wounded in another few weeks. Seems General Sherman was outraged by Sturgis's defeat at the hands of Forrest. He's tired of hearing Washburn do nothing but complain about Forrest and Rebs keeping a large part of the Union Army holed up in Memphis. He's sending General Andrew Smith and a force of 18,000 men out of the city and into Mississippi to catch Forrest. Says he doesn't want to hear anything but that they finally caught that devil."

Ariane stood outside the door, memorizing every word. She had to get word to Forrest, she thought, her hands balled into tightly clenched fists at her sides. He had to know what was coming toward him. It was not

126

the first time she had discovered important information about Union troop movements from her "guests." She marveled at how lax they were in keeping vital statistics to themselves. They discussed anything, and everything, in her house with little thought to whom might be listening. She must have stood outside the library door for an hour, but heard nothing else of any importance.

Slipping upstairs to her bedchamber, she felt like a tightly wound spring. She had to get the information to Forrest, but how? It would look too suspicious to send Caesar outside the city boundaries once again. There had to be a way—she just had to think of it.

Justin stood at the long open window, the blue smoke from his pipe curling out on to the perfumed night air. A night-blooming jasmine vine clung to the stone wall outside his window and the seductive scent was overpowering, stirring memories and desires better off kept buried deep inside him. He had heard her light step on the stair and the gentle closing of her chamber door. In spite of his resolve to stay away from her, the image of red-gold hair fanned out as she lay beneath him haunted and teased him. An involuntary smile softened his stern mouth as he was filled with the remembered pleasure he had found in her petite ivory form, the depth of her passion. The smile, however, turned to a frown as he heard again her refusal to marry him. She had given her maidenhood to him, but had declined to be his wife.

Turning away from the window, he cursed himself for a fool. Sitting at the desk that had once belonged to Charles, he tried to concentrate on a letter he was writing to a colleague in Edinburgh, Scotland. He had become well acquainted with an English surgeon named Lister while studying at the medical college there. The young physician was developing an interesting theory that cleaning wounds, as well as the doctor's hands, with soap and water and then with a solution of carbolic acid drastically cut down on the mortality rate of patients. Justin had tried his methods, to the amusement of the rest of the medical staff, and had found them to be sound. Fewer patients died when their wounds were treated with the Lister method. He was writing to his old friend of his findings.

Concentrating on his letter, Justin lost track of time, having put the image of Ariane in the back of his mind in a fierce act of control. But the soft sound of a door opening and then closing drew him from his writing. The door was Ariane's. Checking his pocket watch, he saw that it was five minutes after midnight. Putting down his pen, he knew he had to follow her. The midnight wanderings were beginning again.

The darkened hall gave no clue to her whereabouts, but as he looked down the long length of it, he saw her silhouetted against the long window as the moon shone a silver unearthly light through its many panes. She moved with an intent grace in some flowing garment without hoops, holding a tin lantern in one hand. This time the dog Bess was nowhere to be seen.

Keeping to the shadows, he followed her, determined to know her secret. Suddenly she vanished, but as he hurried to where she had been standing, he saw a door he had not noticed before. It had not caught completely when she had shut it. Prying it open gently so as to not alert her, he found a narrow staircase. With a careful step, he followed her up the twisting stairs.

After frantic deliberations, Ariane had decided that she must alert Forrest's scouts led by a Captain Thomas A. Henderson, who stayed near the city. They hid in the thick woods near Fleur de Lys at night. In the daylight they harassed the Union troops and reported their movements, shooting at Union riverboats that were leaving the wharves as well as troop trains. The con-

128

stant harassment angered the Union Command, but they were helpless to stop it. The Reb scouts knew the countryside around Memphis like the back of their hand. There were a hundred escape routes they could take. Ariane had a standing agreement with these desperate men that they were to check the tower of Fleur de Lys every night between midnight and the half hour. If they saw the signal light flash, they knew to have a scout meet her outside at a certain cottonwood tree on edge of the estate two hours after first light. She hated to use the signal device too often for she was always afraid the Yankee sentries would also see the flashing signal from Fleur de Lys. But Forrest must know as soon as possible what the Union troops were sending against him.

Going to the open windows of the tower room, she lifted up the lantern, pushing up the sides to allow the most light to shine forth when she signaled the hidden Reb partisans.

"What do you plan to do with that?"

Ariane whirled around to see Justin standing in the doorway with arms folded. There was a sardonic twist to his mouth and his eyes glowed with a dark fierce fire.

She stared wordlessly across at him, her heart pounding, her mouth dry as cotton. The silence grew between them like a cloud. She sensed that everything was going wrong and she was helpless to stop it.

"I come up here when I can't sleep," she explained, finally finding her voice. "This has always been my retreat since I was a little girl. It is safe, above everything like a nest, or so I used to pretend." She forced her lips to part in a curved, stiff smile. Somehow she must bluff her way through this, for he had seen nothing. He had only his suspicions.

"Why the lantern?" he asked in a mocking drawl that

129

told her he didn't believe a word of it.

"I can hardly find my way up here in the dark. I am not a cat," she responded sharply, meeting his accusing gaze without flinching.

"My dear Ariane, I think you could do almost anything if you put your mind to it." With a lithe stride, he was beside her, cupping her chin with firm fingers that forced her to stare up at him. "What kind of game are you playing with me?" he murmured. "Haven't you realized yet that we are two sides of the same coin. That, my sweet devious Little Bit, you have finally met your match?"

Chapter Ten

"I have no idea what game you might be playing, but I am only trying to find some peace in this overcrowded house. However, I am beginning to understand that General Washburn intends to spy on Memphians even in their homes," Ariane retorted.

"Have you anything to hide?" he whispered harshly, his fingers tightening on her chin.

"As my father stated earlier this evening, you Yanks push us too far. Please let me go, I wish to retire to my chamber since even here I am pursued and spied upon."

"You better get used to it, my beautiful Rebel, for I never intend on letting you go," he murmured, his voice low and raspy with desire. Gently he moved his fingers from her chin in a caressing motion down the column of her ivory throat, as his other hand pulled her to him, pressing her slender form against the long sinewy length of him. Holding her to him, he pulled the pins from her chignon at the base of her neck, allowing her silken red-golden hair to pour over his hand like water and down her back to her narrow waist.

She heard the moan torn from deep within her as his mouth followed his fingers down to the tender hollow of her long elegant neck where her pulse throbbed like a trapped bird. She made no attempt to resist. All control had fled at the first touch of his heated mouth. He would always be her Justin, and her heart overrode any attempt at logic when she was in his embrace. Yielding to him, she bent like a willow in the wind, pressing against him as his arms held her with the strength of his ardor, allowing no escape.

When his mouth found hers in an urgent bittersweet kiss of such yearning hunger and despair, she could do naught but open her lips to encourage him. Lightly, she touched his tongue with her own in recognition of the bond that held them in spite of everything. He responded by kissing her a long heart-stopping time, as if he could never get enough of the taste and feel of the hot sweetness that was her mouth.

The silver moonglow caressed the swaying couple that were so intertwined they appeared one entity. It was as if the sultry perfumed night was encouraging them as nature put on its most exquisite show of light and warmth. The air seemed to whisper that it was a night for love and the fulfillment of desire as only a Southern night can do in midsummer.

Ariane felt the caress of the soft humid air from the open tower windows as Justin slipped the peignoir from her shoulders and let it fall to her feet. Only the thin batiste of her nightrail veiled the perfection of her feminine form. Tenderly, he lowered the small cap sleeves with their delicate lace trim, then peeled the garment slowly, reverently downward, downward, till she was revealed in all her naked perfection. With her ethereal, delicate visage, and long golden tresses half veiling the alabaster satin of her hour-glass figure, she reminded him of a painting he had seen in Italy, and only now remembered. He had stood in front of Botticelli's *Birth of Venus,* at a deserted gallery in Florence one rainy afternoon when he had felt a moody depression at the wandering life of exile he had chosen from his native land. Somehow the painting had revived his despairing spirit at the tragic farce of the human condition. If only such a woman existed, he had thought, then jeered at his foolish romantic fantasy.

132

Hadn't life and Olivia showed him what women were really deep in their souls. He was a physician, for God's sake, and he had seen every wretched kind of female creature in his study of medicine. But here before him stood the embodiment of his goddess of love and beauty rising from the lace of her fallen garments as Botticelli's Venus had from the foam of the sea. And he knew that she was as beautiful in her heart and soul as the perfection of her body, and that was what made it all so much harder for him. It would have been so much easier if she had been only a lovely shell of a woman, without a heart like Olivia.

"Don't move. Let me look at you so I might remember always, always," he whispered, devouring, memorizing, worshiping her with his intense ebony eyes that touched her everywhere.

She stood almost embarrassed, but then as she saw the wonder in his burning gaze, her head lifted with pride, and she gloried in the homage she saw on his darkly handsome visage.

Slowly she reached out her arms to him, the moon making her a figure of silver and ivory. "Beloved," she whispered, and the word was both plea and acknowledgment.

He caught her to him with a cry of need and surrender to that need, his mouth covering hers with a hard, hungry passion. She returned his kiss with an urgent hunger of her own. Tongues swirling, tasting, as if they could never get enough.

"I must have you, I must," he muttered, like a man lost, as he lifted his mouth from hers for only a moment to pull the cushions from the windowseats that lined the tower room, till they made a soft bed on the floor.

She stood watching as if in a dream as he stripped the clothes from his lean, sinewy form. They faced each other in the moonlight unashamed, for this was an enchanted night when the heart ruled.

Slowly he knelt down in front of her to press his lips to the soft mound of her belly in a gesture that was both tender and reverent. He heard her gasp of pleasure and his name torn from her being. It was the sweetest sound he had ever heard. He wanted this lovely strong-willed woman so desperately that he could hardly endure the exquisite agony of her hands grasping his shoulders with a rapture she could not control as the tiny pearls of her nails dug into his skin.

She felt shudder after shudder of desire flow through her as his lips trailed fiery kisses down to her soft inner thigh. His hands were caressing, kneading the soft mounds of her bottom, pressing her to his moist hot mouth. Then he was pulling her down, cradling her in his arms as he laid her on the velvet cushions.

His breath was quickened to ragged gasps by her unearthly beauty as she lay below him, her hair muted to a soft gold by the dim light. Her erect nipples were like tiny rosebuds in the silvery moonglow. He bent down and traced each peak with his tongue, the air touching the moistness left by his mouth to tease her with a new erotic sensation.

She felt no shyness with him, for he made it seem so right, so natural, an expression of the overpowering feelings they had for each other. This was only another facet of the strange bond that held them ensnared, that made everything else in their life pale in comparison. It was as if this was what they were made for, that their past life had been only a prelude to this acknowledgment of the depth of their feeling.

She loved to look at the male beauty of him, the hard planes and the thick black fur of his chest and thighs, which felt so masculine against her own sleek feminine softness. How could a mortal man have the virile grace of an ancient Greek God?

Then there was no more time for thought as his hands stroked and caressed down her body, memorizing the curves and hollows till she writhed under the splendor of his touch. Her hands reached out for him, following his lead as she kneaded and caressed his shoulders and down the sinewy planes of his back. She loved the leashed strength of him as he withheld his own urgent need to rouse her to the peak of desire. Every nerve was tingling, aroused to an intense sensitivity, so each stroke and caress of his hand sent rivers of fire through her to center in the innermost depths of her throbbing womanhood.

Sensing that she was ready for him, he gently parted her thighs and caressed the soft inner petals of her woman's flower till she was moist and aching for him.

"Please, my love, I can bear it no longer," she cried out to him, her fingers digging into his back as she arched her slender hips up in circles of ecstasy.

"Nor can I, my sweet," he whispered, his voice husky with his passion.

Rising over her, he caught her hips in his hands and lifted her up to the erect velvet length of his thrust. After the first invasion, which filled them both with the joy of union, they lay for a moment savoring the total bliss of man and woman joined in a love knot that was as old as time. But they felt as if they'd discovered something that no one else had ever known.

Enfolded in his embrace, his heated mouth on hers in a deep drugging kiss, the long masculine length of him deep within her, Ariane knew that no matter what else ever happened to her, she would always remember this night, this perfect night when they loved as if there were no tomorrow.

Suddenly she could control herself no longer and she arched against him, wanting more of him, all of him. She was wild with her need, moving her hips wantonly, sucking his tongue, till he caught her mood and with a deep wild cry moved with her in frantic circles, thrusting again and again till they reached the pinnacle of their rapture and found their complete fulfillment. And when it was

135

done, they still clung to each other, panting, exhausted by the depth of their passion, but reluctant to part, to once more be two instead of one.

"Even now I cannot let you go," he whispered, against the silk of her hair as she lay with her head on his chest.

"Yes, I know," she replied with a sigh. She wanted to remember all of it, the scent of the night-blooming jasmine coming through the window on the soft night air, the way the moon shone a shaft of light across the small room, veiling everything in a silver glow of enchantment, but especially the wonderful sense of love and belonging she felt in the circle of Justin's embrace. She hadn't even realized the depth of her loneliness till it was vanquished, if only for a few brief moments, in the splendid joining with this man who was like no other.

As he stroked her upper arm with a tender little circle, she moved her head and smiled up at him. In doing so the cameo pendant that was still clasped around her neck slid from the valley between her breasts on to his chest. Giving her a light affectionate kiss on the tip of her tiny nose, he reached down and picked up the locket, whose metal back had felt strange on his skin.

"I have noticed you wear this always. In fact, I cannot remember ever seeing you without it," he mused, holding it in his hand so a shaft of light fell across the cameo.

"It belonged to my mother. 'Tis all I have left of her. It belonged to her mother and her mother before her. I believe it came from France as that is where my mother's family were from originally. It is of a lady and her two swans. 'Tis why father has always had swans at Fleur de Lys. They were a symbol of my mother's family back when they lived in France, and Swan's Rest is the name of their plantation outside of Baton Rouge. I . . . I never really knew my mother, for from the time of my birth, as you know, she was never well. I guess I feel it is my only link to her," Ariane explained calmly, but she felt a cold knot form in her stomach. What she said was true, but instead of pictures inside, she had hidden the circular cipher key.

"It is quite large for a locket. Does it open?" he asked, turning it over in his hand.

" 'Tis so old I don't, for fear the hinges would break," she answered, trying to keep her voice even, not showing in any way the turmoil that was raging inside her.

Justin, however, was acutely sensitive to any change in her mood, for their bond was that close. He knew immediately that something was wrong. Placing the locket back between her breasts with a tender gesture, he asked, "What is it, Little Bit?"

She swallowed with difficulty, her throat suddenly so dry she could not speak. Taking a deep breath, she found her voice and replied, "What do you mean?"

"Did you think our relationship such a shallow thing that I would not know when you are upset," he said with quiet emphasis.

"Must we talk of my mother and that night that I cannot ever forget," she asked in a voice that even to her sounded stifled and unnatural. Unable to lie in his arms and tell him falsehoods to distract him, she pulled away from him and sat up to stare out at the starry night.

"Yet you wear her locket—that must be a constant reminder," he continued softly, stroking the graceful plane of her back.

" 'Tis a memorial to her life, a link to my heritage, not a reminder of her horrendous death," she told him, choosing her words carefully.

"We shall not speak of it again as I see how it bothers you. I do not ever want to bring you pain, little one," he said ruefully with infinite compassion.

"Oh, beloved, I know you do not." She spoke in a broken whisper that held regret at the masquerade she must play even with him.

"Then might I have the pleasure of holding you to my heart for a bit longer?" His dark eyes glowed with a gentle fire as she came back eagerly into his arms.

They lay not speaking, content to enjoy the comfort of the other's presence. For a while they even slept, but as the night grew toward dawn, a storm rolled in over the far Arkansas bank across the river to drench the city. They woke to the sound of thunder and the jagged slash of lightning.

"Ah, I think Mother Nature is telling us we should retire to our chambers. I fear it would be hard to explain our sojourn in the tower to your father," Justin murmured against her temple, gently bringing her from the far realms of Morpheus.

"I think you are right, but I hate to leave our enchanted bower," she said with a yawn, sitting up and stretching her arms.

The rain was blowing in the windows in furious gusts as another roll of thunder shook the high tower. Dressing quickly, they shut the windows against the storm and placed the cushions back on the low windowseats. Ariane stood for a moment, mesmerized by the fury of the summer storm seen from their vantage point high in the air. Justin stood behind her, his hands on her shoulders, his lips against the silk density of her hair.

"I had forgotten how severe these summer storms could be," he murmured. "But then I had forgotten so much about the South and Memphis. The wild, lush, overblown quality of the land that seduces with its sensuous allure. I wanted to hate it, but I find it impossible to resist. I fear I was lost from the first moment I set foot on the cobblestones of the wharf that day in June. Lost from the moment my eyes saw a certain Memphis belle with a spirit as fiery as her hair," he added in a lower, huskier tone that contained a tinge of wonder

Ariane felt tears mist her eyes. She leaned back, pressing against his body till she could feel the lean sinewy length of him. With a sigh she asked, "Why then can you still continue to uphold the orders of a command who has done everything to make the lives of your fellow Southerners a hell on earth?"

"To love something or someone does not blind you to their faults. The South brought this on itself when they fired the first shot at Fort Sumter. Granted I feel that there has been a vindictive hatred, as well as greed, motivating many of the actions of the Union Command, especially here in Memphis. But the South has lost, my dearest Ariane; it is only a matter of time till it realizes it can't win. When that day comes, I hope to be one of the saner voices to speak for a healing of the bloody wound that has torn this country apart, precisely because I love the South and perhaps can ease her transition back into the Union as a part, an important part of this country." He felt her stiffen at his words, but she had not pulled away, only held herself at a rigid attention as she listened intently to his reply.

A sudden jagged bolt of lightning lit up the sky as the tower shook with the deep crash of thunder. They watched in horror as a huge cypress tree was split in half, the huge branches of one side falling to the earth only a few feet from the tower. The fire on the trunk was quickly extinguished by the heavy rain till only a few smoldering wisps of smoke evaporated into the lashing wind.

"Come, we best go downstairs. This is not the safest place to be in such a storm," Justin said firmly, picking up the lantern. The candle had burned down to a stub so the light was a dim wavering one at best.

"I will have Roman see to the tree in the morning when it is light. Perhaps part of it can be saved," she said with a sigh, turning to join Justin. "It was almost a hundred years old. I hate to think of it destroyed."

"We shall hope that the damage it incurred wasn't fatal, and with care it can be restored to its former strength," he said softly, standing so she might descend the stairs. He thought with a sudden clarity that the same could be said for the country once this bloody, heart-wrenching war was over.

The house was dark and quiet as they made their way with caution down the wide hall to their separate bed-chambers. Stopping at her door, Ariane turned to Justin and gave him a light kiss on the stern mouth she loved so much. Then taking the lantern from his fingers, she quietly opened the door. Before she stepped inside, she whispered in a voice thick with tears, "Whatever happens, my beloved, I shall never forget this night, when there was only our splendid love between us."

Stunned by the anguish he heard in her voice, he reached out to touch her, but she was gone. He heard the key turn in her lock. Staring at the secured portal, he puzzled over her last words. It had the ominous sound of a final farewell, but that was nonsense, he thought as he turned to enter his own chamber. She was his, regardless of her foolish romantic loyalty to a cause already lost. He wanted her as he had never wanted a woman—even, he realized in shock, more than he had wanted Olivia. And he always got what he wanted. In time she would realize that he was never letting her go. When the South was on its knees, she would forget this ridiculous idea that because they were on different sides there could be no future for them. She was young, he thought with a wry smile. Her youthful idealism would soon tire in the face of life's harsh reality.

But Justin underestimated Ariane's commitment to the Confederacy. While he slumbered, she paced the floor. Bess watched from her basket with sleepy eyes, unable to return to her canine dreams while sensing her mistress's agitation.

Ariane had to get the information to Forrest. The only way left to her, now that Justin's presence made it unwise to use the tower, was to leave word at a certain tavern in Pinch Gut. A shudder ran through her at the thought of the most disreputable, dangerous district in the city. It would have to be in daylight; even men didn't go to Pinch Gut after dark without being armed. But it had to be done and without attracting Justin's attention or that of any of the other officers. And Hazel Schneider was expecting her at the hospital in the morning. There were a hundred different loose ends that would have to be seen to if she was not to be discovered.

Slipping between the sheets of her bed, she stared up at the canopy, exhausted but unable to stop thinking, going over and over her plan. It had to be infallible. Forrest had to know what the Yankees were planning; there was no alternative. She could not let Beau and the other gallant men walk into a trap. But an icy fear twisted around her heart. She had to be careful that she didn't enter into a trap set for her, a trap that General Washburn was setting to capture every Southern spy in Memphis. As fatigue finally claimed her, and she drifted into an uneasy slumber, she remembered Sable's warning and wondered who was the Southern traitor turned Union spy who was now working with Washburn in the city. It could be anyone, someone she trusted. She must be so careful, so very careful if she didn't want to join Felicity in Irving Block Prison.

Chapter Eleven

"Yes, sir, Mam'zelle Ariane is indisposed this morning and asks that you convey her regrets to the lady at the hospital that she won't be coming in today," Sable told Justin as he had his breakfast with the other officers.

"Perhaps I should see her and make sure she is all right," he said, rising to his feet as the other men exchanged amused glances. The chemistry between Ariane and Justin had been obvious and a source of gossip when the two weren't around.

"No, sir. She is sleeping sound, just a touch of the heat and not enough rest," Sable assured him, pouring another cup of the coffee the Valcours were given by their "guests." The rest of Southern Memphis made do with an ersatz made from chicory or herbs. They couldn't buy in the Union-controlled stores without taking the iron-clad oath, which most refused to do no matter how hungry they were for the delicacies of life.

As soon as Ariane heard the sound of the officers' horses leaving for the city, she finished the breakfast Sable had secretly brought to her and sent for her bay mare Dancer. Her father had left in the carriage earlier for the Valcour Line offices. Picking up a box wrapped in brown paper in one glove-clad hand, she looped the gray linen skirt of her summer riding habit over her other hand. Her riding boots echoed in the empty hall as she walked downstairs, Bess trailing at her feet.

"Be careful, Miz Ariane. Pinch Gut is no place for a lady," Caesar cautioned her as he helped her mount Dancer.

"I will," she assured him with a smile. "Watch Bess that she doesn't try and follow me."

"That dog's spirit may be willin' but her legs gettin' too old," Caesar chuckled, leaning down and rubbing behind the ears of the gentle spaniel.

Ariane sadly agreed, then signaled Dancer and they were off down the long alley of cedars that led to the Poplar Road. The intense heat of summer even this early in the day had slowed everything and everyone to a crawl on the deeply rutted road that led into the city. Not a breeze stirred the leaves of the oaks and sycamores that lined the avenue. Even the mud was quickly drying in the strong penetrating rays of the subtropical sun. Army wagons driven by sweating drivers not used to the climate and made short-tempered by the heat passed Ariane with barely a glance. She received a few admiring looks from some mounted Union officers, but none stopped her as she passed the sentries stationed at the city's boundaries a few feet beyond the gates of Fleur de Lys.

Joining the throng that was making its way into Memphis, she was unaware that she was being followed. Pulse pounding with anxiety, she urged the mare on, not looking at her surroundings. Numerous farm carts going to the large open-air markets added to the confusion and the clouds of dust that rolled from under the hooves of horses and mules. Skittish in the turmoil, Dancer needed all of Ariane's attention. There was no time for her to see the tall figure of the man in Union blue who rode several yards behind her.

The veil that tied over her face then up to her tall black hat kept out some of the swarms of mosquitoes, but they interfered with her vision as she tried to keep Dancer on a tight rein. The insects worsened as they crossed over the plank bridge that spanned the Bayou Gayoso.

143

The stench from the sluggish yellow-brown stream was awful, Ariane thought, pulling a scented handkerchief from her pocket and holding it to her nostrils. The Yankees had tried to clean up Memphis—she had to admit that—but people still dumped all matter of refuse in the narrow bayou, and in the heat, the smell was appalling.

Keeping to the side streets, Ariane avoided going near the hospital. She did not want to be recognized—not that that seemed likely, she realized, for Memphis had become a different town since the Union occupation. It had always been a river town with its wild side. A city of rogues where fortunes were made in the cotton trade and lost again on the turn of a card in the many gambling hells. Cotton had been king in Memphis, and numerous cotton factors had had their offices on Front Row, where trade was based on a my-word-is-my-bond system, and every man carried a concealed pistol. Memphis had been the hub of cotton country around which revolved the plantations of the rich alluvial delta of the Mississippi River. And with the cotton boom there had come a layer of gentility spread over the city with the many fine city residences of the planters who brought their wives and daughters in for the season. Looking at the people that thronged the wooden sidewalks, Ariane saw that all pretense of gentility was gone.

Rough-looking men in garish suits hurried down the crowded streets—they were some of the speculators that had followed the Union Army, looking to pick the remnants of the South clean. Lost-looking ex-slaves, who had fled plantations to Memphis in search of food and shelter, stood or lay against storefronts and the many oak trees that dotted the streets. The only white women she saw were the great number of prostitutes that could be seen sauntering up and down the wooden planks in their brightly colored silks and satins. They flirted and sometimes called out to any prosperous-looking male who met their gaze as they passed by, each with a small black child holding an elaborate silk parasol over his mistress's intricately coiffeured head. The child also distributed fliers with a roughly drawn likeness of his mistress and the address of her particular house as well as the lady's specialty printed on it.

The crowd grew rougher and more frightening in appearance as Ariane passed along what was known as Smoky Row on the east side of Auction Square. The street was so called because those who used to wait to attend the slave auctions before the war camped there amid the slave pens, and their cooking fires and antimosquito smudges thickened the air.

Men called crude propositions to her from the mudspattered wooden sidewalks. Soldiers passing by in muledrawn drays stared at her in surprise, for she was entering an area of town that seldom saw a woman so well dressed, riding a Thoroughbred. Holding her head high and staring straight ahead with steely determination, she could only pray that it was not much farther to the Bell Tavern.

The area known as Pinch Gut had originated in the early days north of Memphis at the mouth of the Bayou Gayoso where it emptied into the Mississippi River. Tired, rough flatboat owners, worn out from fighting the strength of the river, had stopped at the quiet eddy over the years and built mean structures out of their wooden boats. These buildings were little more than shanties and often full of poverty and disease. Because the inhabitants had to hitch up their belts a notch during bad times to stifle their hunger pangs, the area became known as Pinch Gut. It had grown through the years and, with the Union occupation, had become filled with the many street walkers that had followed the troops. Their cribs lined the streets and it was rumored all kinds of the meanest sort of vice could be found in the district. One of the largest brothels in the South known as the "Iron

Clad" stood on the south side of Winchester. Grog shops were numerous and Ariane shuddered as she saw men in all states of inebriation on the streets, some passed out and lying facedown in the rapidly drying mud. Pinch Gut was a favorite with the roustabouts of the river as was the infamous Natchez-under-the-hill and the Swamp in New Orleans. They could all be seen here, the flotsam and jettison of the Mississippi and the war.

Ariane gave a sigh of relief, for ahead of her and to the right stood a weather-beaten wood building with the crude sign saying BELL TAVERN nailed over the entrance. Riding up to the hitching post, she motioned for a small black boy to come over. Handing him the reins, she dismounted onto the stone carriage block. Giving the boy some money after he tied the horse, she told him there would be more if he watched over Dancer. He agreed, staring in some surprise that such a lady would come to the Bell Tavern.

He was not the only startled resident of Pinch Gut that morning, for as she entered the darkened interior of the tavern, the few men that were left over from the night before lifted drunken heads from the scarred tables to stare in amazement at the elegant figure of Ariane in her spotless gray linen riding habit and tall black silk hat, a package in one hand and her skirt looped up around her other wrist. Her only weapon seemed to be her riding whip. They didn't know that in the pocket of her skirt was her father's loaded pearl-handled Colt.

With a haughty glance at the patrons, she strode quickly to the long bar, empty except for one man at the far end. The beefy man behind the bar stared at her from under massive black brows as he wiped the surface of the counter with a dirty rag.

"May I speak with Paddy McRooney?" she asked in a low voice, only the tapping of her riding whip against her boot showing her nervousness.

"Who wants to know?" he growled from under a massive mustache, his small black eyes like currants in the white dough of his fleshly face.

"One who seeks complete victory," she answered in a whisper, using the cipher key word phrase of the Confederacy for that month, the same phrase she had used to encode her messages to Forrest. It changed frequently so that by the time the Yankees had broken it, it was meaningless to them.

"Liberty or death. It's Paddy McRooney your talking to," the man replied, putting down the rag and giving her a slight grin that didn't reach his cold, watchful eyes.

"This then is for your daughter. I heard from Sam Riley that it was her birthday, and he thought she would so like it." She placed the package on the bar. It was then she saw the flicker of fear in his eyes, and looking up at the cracked fly-spattered mirror behind him, she saw the tall figure of a Union officer coming into the gloom of the tavern.

"Thank you, miss. It was real kind of you to bring it to her, her being sick and all," he said in a loud voice that carried across the room.

"Nonsense, I had some shopping to do, and I know Sam won't be back in Memphis till the end of the week," she lied, catching the lifeline he was throwing her.

"I will take that," a deep familiar voice commanded from behind her. A hand with slender tapered fingers, fingers that had caressed her body, reached out and pick up the package from the scarred surface of the bar.

"Justin!" she gasped, turning to stare up into the remote mask of his handsome visage, the black fury of his eyes.

"I see you have recovered." His voice was etched with contempt, and a bitter weariness.

"Why aren't you at the hospital?" Ariane asked, shocked at how much the look in his eyes tore her apart.

"Something told me that you might not be as ill as Sable wanted me to believe. You are becoming predictable,

Miss Valcour." He ground the words out with exasperation.

"As are you, sir, for it seems I now have a Yankee spy following my every move," she replied defiantly, meeting his accusing eyes without flinching.

"I would not banter the term 'spy' around if I were you," he replied with contempt, placing his hand on her arm with an iron grip. "Come out of here before you cause any more talk and even I can't get you out of Irving Block Prison. This isn't a romantic game, Ariane." His expression was grim and tight with strain.

"And my gift for Mister McRooney's daughter?" She could not believe she had asked, but it was so vitally important Forrest receive her coded message.

With his visage a glowering mask of rage, he yanked her to him. "One more word and so help me I will tear this package open right here. If you don't follow me out of here, I will carry you out."

The customers of the bar were now sitting up with some sense of alertness, fascinated by the scene that was being played in front of them. Only Paddy McRooney stood with beads of sweat trickling down his pasty cheeks, his hands clasping the edge of the bar to stop their shaking.

"I'll take the package, Captain." Another Union officer had entered the tavern unnoticed by Ariane and Justin. He held out his hand for the box wrapped in brown paper.

"Captain Whitney Frank, Chief of United States Detectives, Sixteenth Army Corps," he said in a commanding voice as Justin hesitated.

Ariane felt a sheer black fright sweep over her at his words. Captain Frank was notorious in Memphis for his corruption and hatred of Southerners. His office thought nothing of confiscating the property of someone considered a Southern sympathizer and throwing the owner out in the street. Why hadn't she listened to Justin, she thought with a sinking heart.

"I am quite capable of handling this myself, Captain Frank," Justin answered in cold clipped tones, his eyes narrowed in a frigid anger.

For a moment Captain Frank seemed to hesitate at the look of contempt that was etched on Justin's stern features, the feel of barely controlled fury that seemed to emanate from his being. Aware, however, of the interested stares of the bleary-eyed customers, he was determined not to lose face to this fierce man whose steely gaze seemed to go right through him.

"Don't want to share the little Secesh bitch, I guess. Well, can't say as I blame you," he sneered with a leer at Ariane. "That one I would enjoy interrogating."

"Leave us!" Justin snarled, but his attention was diverted for just a fraction of a second, enough time for the other man to grab the package from his hand.

"Not before I see what's so God-awful important about this box." With a triumphant smirk, he tore the paper from the box and lifted the lid. He stared in humiliated surprise as snickers from several customers filled the dingy room. "It's a doll," he muttered, holding the small doll with its painted china head and arms and legs in his beefy hand.

"And what else would you give a child, Captain?" Ariane queried, reaching out and taking the doll from his hand before it could drop to the floor and break the china head. Inside the small delicate head was the coded message to Forrest. For a brief moment Captain Frank had held her life and Paddy McRooney's in his hands and had never even realized it.

"By God, what's going on here?" he thundered, his small restless eyes darting around the tavern in suspicion.

" 'Tis only a lover's quarrel, Captain Frank. I am sure as a man of the world you understand these things." Justin spoke in a low, conciliatory voice. "She can be the

149

very devil, but as you can see, with beauty like that I can forgive these little tantrums of hers."

"Hot-headed fillies, these Rebs, but all the more fun to tame I should imagine." Captain Frank smirked, his hot avid eyes traveling over Ariane in a way that made Justin want to kill him.

"Yes, well, can I count on your discretion on this matter. As you can see, I have it well in hand, Captain. I know a busy man like yourself has more important things to do than referee a lover's spat." All the while he had been speaking, he had been leading Captain Frank to the door.

With one last hungry lustful look at Ariane, the chief of detectives vanished out on to the street. Turning back, Justin stood for a moment glaring at the patrons. They quickly looked away and began talking among themselves or slunk out of the tavern.

In a few lithe strides Justin was beside Ariane. He stared down at her, and his mouth took on an unpleasant thin-lipped smile that contained no humor. "I don't know what you are up to, Little Bit, but we best get out of here before our rather dense friend comes back."

"Yes, I think you are right," she replied, turning and placing the doll on the bar. It was going to work, she thought with a rush of elation. This afternoon a woman courier and her child carrying the doll would cross through the Union lines, going to their farm in Mississippi. Once outside the city at a safe house, one of Forrest's scouts would meet them and twist off the doll's head to find the coded message. With a slight smile at McRooney behind the bar, she turned and, picking up her dragging skirt, walked from the room with head held high. Justin was right beside her.

"I don't know what you are up to, but I admire your style, my dear Ariane," Justin murmured as he helped her up on Dancer. This time there was a flash of admiration in his black eyes and his mouth quirked for a moment in what was almost a smile as he mounted his own horse tied beside her mare.

"Where are we going?" she asked as he motioned for her to ride beside him.

"Eventually to Fleur de Lys, but now I wish to see the bluffs. If I remember there is path along the river."

"What about the hospital?"

"I have the morning off," he said quietly.

"You only pretended to leave with the others," she replied softly, her eyes narrowing.

"Yes. I waited in the woods near the gates. You did not disappoint me."

"I didn't think I was so transparent," she muttered as they rode out of the Pinch district into the long grass of the bluff overlooking the Mississippi.

"Only to me, Little Bit, but then I know you like no one else," he said with a husky sensual tone to his deep voice.

She didn't trust herself to look at him, for his words had been like a caress that set every nerve tingling. How right he was, she thought with a bittersweet pang. And if this had been any other time or place, how wonderful the bond between them would have been. Sadly, now it only complicated a situation that was becoming more and more dangerous.

They rode for a while, not speaking, through the tangled honeysuckle and jasmine vines that ran wild over the top of the bluff and down the side to the chocolate rushing water of the Mississippi below. The heady scent of the blossoms rose from underneath the crushing hooves of their steeds in the soft hot air. In the distance the plaintive whistle of a steamboat broke the primeval stillness, sounding its high trills as it neared the Memphis docks. The tawdry sight and sound of Pinch Gut were left far behind them.

They couldn't go too far, Ariane knew, for Union sentries were up ahead, but right now it seemed in this deserted place that they were alone in the world. It was wonderful, she thought with a sigh.

"What is it?" he asked. "You sighed," he explained at her questioning glance.

"Only that I am happy," she said shyly.

"As am I," he murmured, reaching over to touch her cheek for a brief heart-stopping moment.

"Do you remember the last time we rode together along these bluffs all those years ago?" she asked softly, staring across into his dark eyes that caressed her tenderly with the light of remembrance. He had been her knight in shining armor that hideous night when her mother had taken her life and she had run away to Pinch Gut. And once more he had come to her rescue.

"What a beautiful woman that scruffy little girl has become, but the fiery stubborn spirit hasn't changed," he commented, a husky catch to his voice. "You are still fighting against the inevitable."

"Charles always said I was the most contrary brat he ever knew," she joked lightly, but there was a sad catch to her words at the mention of her brother's name.

"Shall we stop here," he said, and it was a statement, not a question.

Dismounting, he tied his horse to the spreading branch of an oak tree, then turned to help her down. She slid from Dancer's back into his arms. And as naturally as the river willows swaying in the wind, she leaned into his embrace. Tearing the top hat and veil from her face till they fell forgotten to the ground, he held her against him as if he would never let her go. She could feel his uneven breathing on her cheek as he held her close.

"I have wanted to do this all day," he whispered, his lips slowly descending to claim her mouth with a deep drugging kiss.

The world for a few wonderful moments vanished and there was only the touch, the taste, the sense of completion that came when she was in Justin's arms, lost in his kiss. She clung to the solid strength of him as his hands caressed the length of her back and down to the tiny span of her waist.

"You drive me to distraction, Little Bit," he moaned softly as his burning mouth lifted from her to kiss the tendrils of red-gold that blew across her temples. "I could take you now, here on the grass, but it wouldn't begin to end my hunger for you. You are a fever in my blood that has no cure."

"Then I, too, have caught the fever, for I cannot resist you. When I am with you, nothing else matters, for everything pales in comparison to my feeling for you," she whispered into his neck, delighting in the sensuous touch and the faint scent of bay rum that was his skin.

"If only that were true, I would breathe easier," he said in wry tones.

"You do not believe me?"

"Would you give up your precious cause for me?" he asked softly, feeling her stiffen in his arms.

Whatever she would have answered, he never knew for before she could speak, the rapid sound of gunfire was heard from a thicket a hundred yards to the right of them.

"Hurry, mount Dancer," he ordered, helping her up on the mare that had stood patiently only a few feet away. Quickly untying his mount, he was up on his steed, and they were off racing down the bluff back toward Memphis.

Her hat forgotten, her hair came loose and fell about her shoulders in the wind as their horses galloped into Pinch Gut. Their idyll was over. The war had intruded once more, for she knew the gunfire came from Confederate Scouts firing on a steamer that was making its way to the harbor. She should know, for she had alerted them days before that a troop ship was coming into Memphis this day. What irony that they should have stood only yards from those very men. When she was with Justin,

153

she forgot everything, even caution. She must be more careful, for he made her careless and that could be disastrous in the life-and-death game she played with the Union Command. But God help her—how could she resist him?

Chapter Twelve

"I must leave you here for the hospital, but I advise you to go back to Fleur de Lys. The streets are going to be swarming with troops after that attack by what must have been Henderson's Scouts," Justin told her, reining in his horse as they rode up to the Exchange Building. "Washburn is going to be infuriated that they struck so close to the city. Every Southerner is going to be suspected of helping them."

"I think you are right," Ariane agreed, conscious of the stares she was attracting with her waist-length hair flowing down her back in a tangled mane. She had wanted to go to Felicity mother's house, but the need for caution was great after the confrontation at the Bell Tavern.

"Go then so I might have the luxury of not having to worry about you," he said with a wry smile.

With one last lingering look into his dark gaze that told her of his desire, she tore herself away and urged Dancer on down Poplar Road and away from him. Forcing an iron control over her emotions, she didn't allow herself even one glance back, but kept her eyes straight ahead. Fighting the oncoming surge of Federal troops all heading toward the river bluffs took all her attention. Justin was right, she thought, the alarm had been sounded and they were making another attempt to capture Henderson's Scouts. This would be as futile as had been the other attempts, she thought with a slight smile of satisfaction. Captain Henderson and his men would have already made their escape into the deep thicket of the heavily forested bluffs.

Hot and tired, her hair a dusty tangle, Ariane reached the sanctuary of Fleur de Lys as the afternoon sun poured down its fury. The dark shaded alley of cedars and magnolias leading to the house was a welcomed retreat from the clouds of dust on Poplar Road.

Reclining in a cool tub of scented water in her bedchamber, Ariane tried to put the worries of the day from her mind. Sable had washed her tresses with a bar of heliotrope soap and rinsed them with rainwater that she gathered in a barrel in the kitchen garden especially for that purpose. The maid swore that only a rainwater rinse could give hair the proper sheen and softness. Lying with her back against the back of the copper tub, her hair spread out to dry over the edge while Sable rubbed the long strands with a soft linen towel, Ariane relaxed for the first time in days. She had accomplished what she had set out to do—the coded message was on its way to General Forrest.

A quick rap on the door drew her from her reverie. There was an urgency in the repeated knock. Sable rose to answer the door, first pulling a screen around where her mistress bathed.

Ariane heard Caesar's voice. She couldn't make out the words, only the frantic tone. Something was wrong, she could feel it in her bones, and a chill ran down her spine even in the sultry heat of the afternoon.

"Mam'zelle, you must dress. There is trouble," Sable told her, coming around the screen.

"What is it?" Ariane questioned, seeing the worried frown on the woman's usually serene countenance.

"Mister Beau is out in the stable. He has been wounded," Sable said as she held out a huge towel for Ariane to dry herself as she stepped out of the tub onto a woven mat.

"Beau . . . here! But how? Why?"

156

"He was with the men that fired on the Yankee ship this morning. When they were making their escape, one of the sentries from the guard camp on Poplar Road shot at them as they were taking that old cotton wagon road at the edge of the estate grounds. He sent the others on and made his way on foot through the woods to the stables. He was afraid he would slow the others down."

Ariane, her heart in her throat, quickly chose a blue summer dress of light muslin. Her mind raced as she slipped on white silk stockings held up with blue satin garters with blue rosettes. Then her white kid shoes with two-inch heels, lace-trimmed pantalets, and chemise. What a fuss it was for a lady to dress, she thought in frustration, but she must appear the lady of the manor today of all days. There must be nothing to alert the Yankees that there was anything out of the ordinary going on at Fleur de Lys. She stood impatiently for Sable to lace her stays up and then help her on with her hoops, over which went the batiste petticoat and finally the blue muslin gown trimmed in ecru chantilly lace at the bodice and sleeves with an enormous tiered skirt. Her hair, still damp, was caught up in a blue silk net snood.

"Bring bandages, soap, and water, Sable," Ariane told her as they left the chamber. "And put Leroy outside the stables to watch for the Yankee doctors' return."

With Bess trailing her footsteps, Ariane hurried out of the house and down the flagstone path through the herb garden beside the kitchen house and past the privy to the stables and paddock. It was quiet in the stable yard with all the horses at graze in the white-fenced paddock. A bumble bee droned as it perused the crimson climbing roses that rambled over the stone wall of the huge barnlike structure.

"Over here, Miz Ariane," Caesar called to her from where he stood at the end of the many horse stalls deep in the barn. It was dark and pungent with the scent of horse in the long cavernous stable. Ariane made her way through the straw-strewn hard-packed dirt floor, cursing the fate of women and their ridiculous fashion as her huge skirt swung like a bell around her.

"Beau, oh Beau, honey!" she cried as she saw him on the floor on a pile of straw, the blood from his wounded leg seeping out on to the cotton sacks Caesar had put under him.

"Took one in the leg, sister," he said softly, trying to smile, but it was more like a grimace on his lean, pale face.

"Sable is coming with bandages. I must see to that wound, then we will have to think of a good place to hide you. Our 'guests' will soon be returning from the hospital," Ariane explained, kneeling beside him to examine the wound in his thigh.

It was deep and had caused quite a gash in his thigh just above the knee. She gestured for Caesar to pull off his worn boot. Her brother groaned with pain as the old black man finally maneuvered the boot from his leg. Reaching down, she tore the trouser at the seam all the way up, pulling loose material that had dried in a sticky bloodied mess to the wound. As she did, bright red blood gushed out and onto the straw.

With quiet grace, Sable appeared beside her and, without being told, began to bathe the wound with warm water in which she had placed herbs. Beau turned even whiter at the extreme pain they were causing him, but he made no sound.

"There is some brandy in that flask I brought. Give Miche Beau a good drink," Sable ordered Caesar.

Beau took several long swigs from the silver flask as they cleaned his wound. Gently with dexterous fingers Sable probed for the bullet, but the agony was too great for him. He slumped into unconscious into the cradling arms of Caesar.

" 'Tis easier for us and for him this way," Sable commented as her fingers found the Union bullet and lifted it from the mangled flesh of Beau's thigh. Quickly pressing clean cloths to the spurting artery, Ariane was with steady pressure able to stop the bleeding. She knew that she'd had only a few minutes or her brother would have bled to death.

"It must be packed and sutured, mam'zelle," Sable said calmly. "I have my herbal preparations I use on the horses, and fine sewing thread. Do you want me to try, or do you want me to send for Doctor Justin?"

Ariane stared down at her brother in an agony of confusion. Could she trust Justin, or would he turn Beau over to the authorities to end up in the hellhole of a Yankee prison. Washburn was determined to make an example of Southerners that helped the Scouts. What would he do if he had in his custody one of the Scouts that had bedeviled and embarrassed him with the Union Command? Remembering how Justin had turned Felicity over to the head surgeon, and that now she resided in the infamous Irving Block, Ariane made her decision.

"Do your best, Sable. It is what he would want. I know he doesn't want me to turn him over to the Yankees, and I don't know if I can trust Doctor Justin," she said with quiet sorrow.

Before Beau regained consciousness, Sable worked with sure quick hands, sewing up the wound with clean silk thread. Carefully she applied an herbal salve, and then wrapped the wound in clean linen bandages as she did the horses when they tore their legs against the fencing.

"I have done all I can, mam'zelle. I will make a tisane of willow bark for the fever that is sure to come." She rose to her feet after gathering up her medicines in the willow basket she carried over her arm. "Cover him with the blanket I brought when he comes around."

Ariane nodded as she held smelling salts under her brother's nostrils. Moaning, his eyelids fluttered open and he stared out of pain-filled eyes at his sister. "It's done?" he asked.

"Yes. Sable has brought laudanum for the pain. If you think you can sit up a bit, I can give you a spoonful." Pouring the liquid into a teaspoon, she helped him swallow the vile concoction that, containing mostly opium, would ease his pain.

"Where can we hide him, Miz Ariane? This place is too easy for those Yankee doctors to find when they bring in their horses," Caesar said, spreading the quilt over Beau's prone figure.

"What about Sable's drying shed at the end of the herb garden? It is out of the way and there is no reason for anyone to go there but Sable."

"Yes, ma'am. I think you're right. We should do it directly efen Mister Beau thinks he can make it with my help." Caesar agreed.

"I can make it," Beau sighed wearily, trying to stand up.

"Let us help you," Ariane cautioned.

Together they got Beau up, leaning heavily against Caesar. Ariane walked to the stable entrance to make sure there was no one around. Outside the barn all was silent and drowsing in the late afternoon sun. In what seemed like an eternity to Ariane, they half dragged, half carried Beau down through the herb garden to the small gardening shed near the spreading branches of a cedar tree.

It was fragrant inside the small structure with the scent of the herbs hanging in bunches from the rafters. Two small windows opened out to allow air to circulate, and there was a long table where Sable could work on her various projects. There was nothing else in the shed but the hard-packed dirt floor.

"I'll go 'n fetch some straw for a bed," Caesar said as he helped Beau down to the ground.

"I wish it could be your feather bed upstairs in your room, but there is a Yankee officer in it at the moment," Ariane explained ruefully.

"Don't reckon he would care to share with one of Henderson's Scouts," Beau joked, although his face was pale with pain.

When Caesar returned with enough straw for a bed in the corner of the shed, Ariane helped her exhausted brother to stretch out and try to sleep. They placed a tray with fresh water in a covered pitcher, the laudanum bottle, and some food near his reach.

"I will try and return when I can, but with the Yankees in the house, it won't be easy," she explained. "Sable will be able to come more often without attracting attention. There is something else you must know . . ." she paused, biting her lip in consternation. "One of the Union doctors staying with us is Justin Pierce."

"Justin here!" Beau exclaimed, even through the fog of the laudanum. "And wearing a Yank uniform. Well, I guess he was treated none too kindly by people in Memphis after fighting his own brother over that fast little baggage Olivia. It was a shame too. I always liked Justin, but he couldn't see what Olivia was, that she enjoyed putting men to fighting over her. Now Clay, he was as wild as Olivia, he knew her for what she was, but it didn't matter to him. He wanted her, lusted after her, as she did him. Neither one of them were capable of loving anyone but themselves, not like Justin. It always goes hardest on those who are idealists when they find out just how rotten people can really be in this world. When he came home from medical school and found she had given herself to Clay while being engaged to him, I think it killed something inside of him."

"So that is what happened. I never really knew the whole story of the duel. All I was ever told was that he challenged his own brother to a duel because he thought Clay had been flirting with Olivia at a ball. Everyone in Memphis knew that was Clay's way with anything in petticoats," Ariane commented, shaking her head, remembering the old story.

"I think you are old enough, and you sure have seen

161

enough of life since this war started, sis, not to be offended at hearing the truth. Justin caught them together stark naked in the gazebo at Cedar Rest the night of that ball. The gentleman's code forbade any mention of the condition of the lady so the story got around that Justin was a mad man fighting his own brother even when his father pleaded with him to stop. Everyone knew that Justin and his father already were estranged over the slavery issue. Justin's ideas weren't popular with most of the planters. They thought he coddled the Africans at Cedar Rest, so it was easy for Olivia to make Justin the villain in the affair to cover up her own reputation," Beau said tiredly. "The city turned on him after Olivia spread around a few lies. No, Justin has no reason to remember Memphis fondly, but Charles and I always liked him. He was a good friend and a fine man. I can only wish he could have found it in his heart to come with us instead of against us."

"He says he still loves the South, that after the war is over, the South will need voices like his to help with the healing process. He . . . he thinks we are going to lose," Ariane said quietly, with anguish etched in every word.

"He could be right, sis. God knows the Confederacy is badly wounded. If the injury will prove fatal, only time will tell. Some of the men don't even have boots. We have to steal ammunition from the Yankees we kill. Every Confederate killed is replaced by a boy or not at all, while the Yanks have a seemingly inexhaustible pool of men to pick from. Do you know that for a thousand dollars a Yank can buy a replacement to serve in his place when he is drafted? Some rich men in Washington pay two or three men to fight in their name. Their factories are working at top capacity. Sis, we barely have any factories. We can't feed our men, our horses. God, you know how awful it is to treat good horseflesh like we are forced to, and this winter . . ." He stopped and shook his head. "The land isn't being worked and men get letters

162

from their wives that they and their children are starving. They beg them to come home. How can men fight under these conditions?"

"Yet you do," she reminded him softly, tears in her gray eyes.

"It's our home, sis, our land. All we have left is our pride, our honor. We can't forsake these. We have to go down fighting or what was it all for? Why did all those good men die?" He dropped back against the straw, the words having taken the last of his energy.

"Rest. I have tired you with all my foolish chatter, but I wanted you to be aware that Justin is here and I must be very careful, for I know not how much I can trust him. Try and sleep. Sable will check on you after dinner. I will have her bring you some new clothes." She rose to her feet as she realized he had fallen asleep.

Closing the door of the shed behind her, she motioned for Bess, who had been waiting patiently outside, to come away with her. Walking toward the house, Ariane paused for a moment at the end of the kitchen gardens to stare back at the drying shed. It appeared deserted and she could only hope that it seemed that way to any of the doctors who happened to stroll outside the house.

The evening meal was a strain for Ariane since she was forced to pretend there was nothing unusual going on. But she was spared having to deceive Justin, for he was working late at the hospital. There were only the other doctors at the dinner table, her father choosing to eat in his room. She had decided not to tell her father that his son was only a few yards from the house. In his ill health she couldn't be sure that he wouldn't break down and give it away to their "guests."

After the tedium of the dinner table, everyone went their separate ways. Ariane sensed that the medical officers were preoccupied. There had been extra wounded brought to the hospital that day, and in the heat, the work was exhausting. Using the opportunity, she slipped

163

out to the kitchen house to speak with Sable and perhaps check on Beau for one last time before bed. With Bess at her heels as usual, she left the house as soon as the men had gone into the library or to their chambers.

Not a breath of wind stirred the fragrant boughs of the cedar trees that were dark sentinels casting long shadows in the silvery moon glow. The sultry air was heavy in the garden with the scent of the graceful stalks of nicotina and the heavily laden gardenia bushes. Stopping next to one of the lush bushes, Ariane picked one of the alabaster gardenia blossoms and stuck it in the vee of her bodice so she might enjoy the fragrance.

The golden light from oil lanterns in the kitchen house fell in a stream out the door on to the crushed gravel path. Inside, one of the kitchen maids washed the evening dishes in a tin sink as Caesar sat outside in the cooler night air.

"You be looking after Mister Beau?" the old man asked as Ariane came up to him.

"Yes, has Sable seen to him?"

"She be coming now, ma'am."

Turning, Ariane saw the graceful figure of Sable coming down the path from the shed. A small golden pool of light shone from the tin lantern she carried in one hand. In the other she carried a basket.

"He is doing as well as can be expected, mam'zelle. The fever has started and I have given him the tisane of willow bark, and more of the laudanum for the pain. He has fallen asleep and I think it is best if we do not disturb him again tonight."

"Thank you, Sable. Go get some sleep. I can undress myself. I won't be needing you any further," Ariane told her.

"Yes, mam'zelle." Her graceful figure faded into the shadows toward the house, for Sable slept in a small chamber on the third floor of the main house where the sewing rooms and attic storage rooms were located. She

164

had done so ever since Ariane could remember. When her mother was alive, the maid had often slept in the same room as the disturbed woman in a trundle bed that slid under the huge four-poster when not in use. Sable had come with Marie Louise Dubois when she married Ariane's father and her loyalty had been a cornerstone of the Valcour family.

Suddenly Ariane realized how for granted they had taken Sable. She was a free woman now, not a slave, but so far her loyalty to the family had not wavered. She felt a wave of gratitude wash over her. She must remember to tell her on the morrow.

"Caesar, I want to thank you for staying on here with us. I think we should begin paying you wages. I will discuss it with my father," she said, turning to the black man sitting calmly smoking his pipe.

"That would be real fine, ma'am," he replied with great dignity.

"Tell the others if you would," she said, realizing that Caesar was, and always had been, the leader of the people at Fleur de Lys. If she wanted to keep them, she would have to start paying them wages like other workers. With the Valcour Line flourishing under the Yankee business, she could afford it.

Although tired, she was afraid she wouldn't be able to sleep. Leaving the kitchen house behind, she wandered at loose ends beside the raised bed of the herb garden then on to the formal rose garden, where the white roses glowed ghostly in the streaming moonlight.

Then above the heavy perfume of the roses, she caught the scent of smoke, a familiar tobacco scent from a pipe. Looking across the rosebushes, she saw the shadow of a masculine figure strolling down the path by the lake from the direction of the stables. Justin was home and her heart sang at knowing he was so near.

He turned at the sound of the swish of her skirt against the flagstones. His breath caught in his throat at

165

the ethereal beauty of her in the moonlight. She must be exhausted, he knew, but she appeared cool and infinitely lovely in her pale blue gown, the off-the-shoulder lace bodice a perfect frame for her delicate bone structure of her ivory shoulders. He wanted to place his mouth on the soft satin of her skin where her pulse throbbed like a small trapped dove.

"What a lovely apparition to see on such a summer's night," he said in deep husky tones as she came up to him.

"You're home," she replied simply, but there was a happiness in her voice that didn't match the sadness in her eyes.

"Yes. With you here, it does feel like home." He took her hand and lifted it to his lips.

A delicious languorous warmth surged through her at the touch of his heated mouth on her fingertips, then as he turned her hand over to tenderly kiss her palm, she heard her involuntary sigh on the sultry night air that surrounded them like a caress.

"I was hoping you would be waiting for me when I returned home. All through this hellish day it was the thought of you, the feel of your skin, the taste of your mouth that kept me from despair." Gathering her to him, he held her, his lips in her hair, as if he would never let her go. It was as if by holding her he could banish the horrendous sights of young men dying by the hundreds no matter how hard he and the other medical officers fought to save their lives. The heat and disease were taking their toll, turning the hospital into a charnel house.

"Rest," she whispered, "and try for a few moments to forget."

"I need you tonight, Little Bit. God, how I need you!"

"My chamber," she whispered, shocked at the hunger she heard in her own voice.

"Yes. Oh yes," he breathed, releasing her to take her hand and lead her toward the darkened house.

166

"Bess, Bess," she called over her shoulder for the dog as they walked through the herb garden. "She was just here," she muttered, looking toward the kitchen house now dark as the servants had retired for the night.

"She's down there," Justin said, pointing to the drying shed outlined in a shaft of moonlight.

Ariane's heart fluttered as she saw the spaniel pawing at the closed door. Quietly she called her again, but the dog was intent on what she was doing.

"I best go get her. She is getting a bit deaf and it is really not safe for her to be out all night." Ariane dropped Justin's hand and hurried down the path to the shed, praying he wouldn't follow her. Her prayers, however, were in vain for his sure step was right behind her.

She grabbed the animal's collar and sternly ordered her to follow. It was then that she noticed what was occupying Bess's attention. In her mouth was Beau's leather sword belt that he wore over his shoulder. Somehow it must have dropped from his person as Caesar was helping him from the stables. Bess was chewing the leather end, and as a shaft of moonlight beamed through the branches of the cedar, it shone on the brass belt plate.

"Here, girl, let loose." Justin spoke firmly to Bess as he pulled the leather belt from her mouth. His black brows slanted in a frown as he held it out to Ariane. "Where did she get this?"

Ariane stared down at the letters C.S.A. engraved on the brass plate as panic welled up inside her. "I can't imagine, unless it belonged to Charles."

"Or perhaps to Beau," he said tersely.

"I think not. He would be wearing it." She stiffened, lifting her chin and meeting his cold accusing gaze. "She might have found it in the stables along with the saddle that belonged to Charles. I brought his things back from Shiloh. They was all that was left of him."

"Why was the belt not with his sword in the house?" Justin persisted.

"I really couldn't say," Ariane answered coldly, while her pulse raced. She had to get him away from the shed. Beau could moan or make some sound in his drugged sleep.

"What is going on here? Is that who you are sneaking out at midnight to meet — Beau?"

"What nonsense, with the Yankees all around us," she replied, trying to sound amused at such a question.

"Henderson's Scouts roam all through these woods and come, some say, even into Memphis disguised as simple farmers. What regiment is Beau's?"

"Is this an inquisition, Captain? Perhaps you would like to catch Beau and put him in a Yankee prison. Wasn't Felicity enough for you?" Ariane turned from him and, with a snap of her fingers to Bess, started for the house.

"Where are you going?" Justin asked, grasping her arm.

"To bed, alone. I find I don't care for the Yankee captain, and I certainly don't enjoy being interrogated." Pulling her arm away from his hand, she turned with a sish of her huge skirt and walked rapidly away, hoping to draw him from the shed.

"Ah, but how I wish I didn't care for the Rebel Belle," he murmured into the steamy night as he watched her swaying figure disappear into the shadows. She was keeping secrets from him, dangerous secrets. What would he do if he found them out, found her out? Would he be able to do what his duty told him he must do, even if his heart told him something quite different?

Part Two

Tenderly bury the fair young dead,
    Pausing to drop on his grave a tear;
Carve on the wooden slab at his head,
    "Somebody's darling slumbers here."

          Marie La Coste,
            "Somebody's Darling"

'Twas not the woman's heart which spoke—
    Thy heart was always true to me;
A duty stern and piercing broke
    The tie that linked my soul with thee.

          H. D. L. Webster,
          "Lorena"

Chapter Thirteen

The white-hot August sun poured down its fury upon the Memphis streets as Ariane made her way from the hospital to the Provost Marshal's office. She dreaded the task ahead of her, but it had to be done and done quickly. For Beau, she would take the iron-clad oath to the Yankees, even if she didn't intend to keep a word of it. The last weeks had been nerve-racking with Beau hidden in the drying shed. They had to get him out of the city now that his fever was down. In order to carry out her plan, she had to have a pass to cross through the Union sentries at the edge of Memphis, and all passes were issued from the Provost Marshal.

"I can allow you some time off this afternoon," Hazel Schneider had told her tersely when she explained she needed a pass so she might attend the burial of an old family friend the following day at Elmwood Cemetery outside the city.

It was a relief to get out of the hospital, Ariane thought as she stepped over the unmoving figure of a man who lay dead drunk across the wooden sidewalk, his skin a bluish color from drinking the raw gin called *blue ruin* because of the blue cast it gave to the skin of its enthusiasts. Even Memphis streets as terrible as they were since the Union occupation smelled better than the fetid wards of the hospital. The dysentery cases were up in the humid heat, the men called having it the *Tennessee Two-Step*.

The doctors worked overtime, many times to the point of exhaustion, but the death rate rose as wounds festered and disease ran rampant in the humid heat. She had seen little of Justin since the night he had found Beau's belt by the shed. Some nights the doctors didn't return to Fleur de Lys, sleeping instead on cots put up for them in the ward-room. She didn't see how they could stand spending day and night in such a place. When she had run into Justin at the hospital, as she invariably did in the routine of carrying out her duties, her heart broke at the dark circles under his eyes and how thin and haggard he appeared. He was always aloof, and only a flash of desire in his dark eyes when he was looking at her and didn't know she was watching told her that he still cared.

She tried not to think of Justin as she neared the Provost Marshal's office. For the task ahead, she had to have all her wits about her, and thinking of how much her heart ached for him would only cause her to weaken her resolve. In the next twenty-four hours nothing must be allowed to divert her complete attention from the dangerous mission of smuggling Beau out of the city.

Taking a deep breath to steady her nerves, Ariane walked into the office of the Provost Marshal. The waiting room was filled to capacity with all manner of people, from Northern speculators new to the city and eager to take what they could from the occupied South, to Southern citizens reluctantly here to get a much needed pass so they might go out into the country. It was a strained atmosphere where no one met the other's eye.

After waiting at least an hour in the hot stuffy room, Ariane was finally allowed in the office of Captain Williams. He barely looked up as she came into the small spartan chamber. Writing at the huge scarred desk that took up most of the floor space, he kept her waiting several minutes. She clenched her fists in the folds of her skirt, but kept her expression cool and aloof. The Yankee captain would not intimidate her, no matter how rude he acted.

"Yes and what do you want, Miss . . . er Valcour?" he asked, finally looking up after glancing at the paper put on his desk with her name on it.

172

"I would like a pass to go out of the city to attend the graveside services of a friend of mine," she answered coolly, staring at the bearded visage of the man in front of her. He had ice blue eyes that gave no hint of the character of the man underneath the stern gaze.

"Where is this burial to occur and when?" he inquired tersely.

"Tomorrow at ten in the morning at Elmwood Cemetery."

"You know you must take the iron-clad oath before I can sign this pass," he stated, staring up at her, a faint interest in those icy eyes as if to see what her response would be to his challenge.

"I am prepared to do just that," she replied quietly.

"Really, now that surprises me. Most of you Memphis belles would rather die than swear loyalty to the Union." His eyes swept her figure in a lingering, insulting fashion. "Perhaps you have decided we aren't so bad after all."

Ariane gave a stiff smile as she fought to control the anger she felt surging through her as he continued his lewd perusal of her person. She must not let anything go wrong for tomorrow, no matter how obnoxious the captain's manner.

"Then raise your right hand and read this card," he told her, sliding the dog-eared card across the desk, forcing her to bend down and retrieve it.

Slowly through clenched teeth, Ariane read that she would not give any help to any wounded Confederate soldier even if he was dying. The words stuck in her throat but she told herself it was all a necessary farce to parrot the outrageously cruel oath if by doing so she could help save her brother's life.

"Very nicely done, my dear. It is especially heartwarming to hear those words pronounced with such a lovely Southern accent." A cruel smile curved his stern mouth as he signed the pass. Again he slid the pass toward her instead of handing to her, and this time it fell on the floor.

Reaching down and picking it up, she said with disdain,

"I thank you almost as much as I would have if you had acted politely. Good day." Turning around, she yanked open the door, only to face a familiar face.

"What are you doing here?" Justin asked, as they both stood frozen in a stunned tableau.

"Miss Valcour is just leaving. And you had better go before I change my mind about that pass, oath or no oath," Captain Williams muttered threateningly, coming around to the front of his desk.

"Excuse me," Ariane said quietly, desperation in her gray eyes, as she motioned for him to move so she could leave the room.

With a puzzled look, he stepped back that she might exit. A trace of heliotrope perfume lingered for a moment in the hot humid air, and it struck him through like a knife. He had tried to stay away from her, but her image would come before him at intervals during the day. The nights were torture, even when he slept on the cot in the ward room at the hospital. She would haunt him even there, her exquisite form and face teasing his mind like an elusive melody.

"Come in, Captain Pierce," the exasperated voice of the Provost Marshal thundered.

"Yes, you requested to see me," Justin said tersely. He didn't like Williams — the man enjoyed his authority too much.

"You're billeted, I believe, at Fleur de Lys. And from what I understand, you were born in this town," Captain Williams said in snide tones.

"Yes." Justin's eyes narrowed in contempt at the character of the man in front of him. Everything he had heard about Williams seemed to be correct. He was a petty tyrant.

"I envy you being in the same house with that sassy Southern wench. Ariane Valcour could, however, use some instruction on how to treat a Union officer. It would be a real enjoyable task breaking that filly." He gave a lewd chuckle.

Justin wanted to strangle him with his bare hands. Even to hear her name on his lips was an insult. It was another terrible facet to this war, the fact that incapable men were put in positions of authority that they abused with glee.

"Well." Williams gave a slight cough of discomfort at Justin's contemptuous glance and silence. "That brings me to why I called you in here today. We suspect that old man Valcour, while seeming to cooperate with our office in running his steamer line, maybe in reality using his ships to smuggle guns, medicine, and salt. And to the Rebs, salt is vitally important to preserve Johnny Reb's meat. Although from what I hear, there isn't all that much meat left in Dixie," he snorted. "What I'm asking is that you keep an ear out for anything I can use to put that old Secesh bastard in Irving Block."

"I see," Justin answered in a noncommittal voice.

"This is a personal request, Captain. I want him, and I want to see that sassy daughter back in here begging me to help get her dear old father out of prison. I'm tired of these high-and-mighty Secesh families in Memphis treating our fine soldiers like dirt. They need to continually be taught who is master here. I know that this is a little out of your line of work, but I figured if you were born here and joined the Union in spite of it, that you must have some scores to settle. I'm giving you the opportunity. Now, we don't have to speak of this to anyone. You understand?"

"Precisely. Is that all, Captain?" Justin's voice was quiet, yet held an undertone of cold contempt. If the situation weren't so tragic, it would be comical. The buffoon Williams had just tried to hire General Dodge's best operative to do some petty spying. His identity, like all of Dodge's agents, was a carefully guarded secret. Not even Generals Washburn or Hulburt knew his name. All they knew was that an agent known by the code name of Falcon was operating in Memphis. His orders came straight from General Dodge through a contact in the city.

The words of the general came back to him from the day he had been told his assignment would be Memphis. Dodge had told him, "Memphis has become the biggest supply depot for the Confederacy since it surrendered. Everything that isn't nailed down, and probably some that is, is being smuggled out to that devil Forrest. You know that town and the way the people think. As a doctor at the hospital, you can keep your eyes and ears open. More damn medicine goes out of Memphis than it goes in our soldiers. No one is to know you're my spy in Memphis, not even General Washburn. This operation is strictly my show. An operative will contact you a few days after your arrival. You will know him when he says the words 'the old man told me.' Show him that pocket watch of yours with the falcon engraved upon it. Damn it, that's what I'll call you, the Falcon." He gave a raspy laugh at the expression on Justin's stony visage. "All right, 'tis a bit melodramatic, but hell, the Rebs aren't the only ones with a sense of dash." So Justin had become christened the Falcon and all his coded messages were signed with that name. He was beginning to see it all as farce, a tragic farce in which he was spying on people he had known all his life. He had not realized how difficult that was going to be to resolve in his heart, especially when he had to take orders from men he didn't respect like this idiot who sat in front of him.

Bidding the fool Williams a terse good day, Justin left the Provost Marshal's office. Out on the busy street there was no sign of Ariane, but then he hadn't expected her to wait for him. So the Provost Marshal wanted to catch Leander Valcour as well, he thought with a grim smile of irony. He was not alone. The old man was walking a tightrope and didn't even realize it. He could only hope that Ariane was not too deeply involved; perhaps she was not even aware of her father's activities. Fool, he thought in self-disgust as he walked back down the hot street baking in the late afternoon sun. A woman as spirited as Ariane was probably right up to her pretty neck in smuggling to the Rebs. What would he do if and when he ever discovered just what secrets she was hiding, he thought with a pain twisting in his gut. He had become one of Dodge's elite corps of agents at first because he thought the South was wrong. He had a list of reasons in the beginning, but finally it came down to the simple idea that if in any way he could hasten the end of this bloody war that was killing young men by the thousands, he would do it. Once back in the South, he had found that there was still love in his heart for his native land and for its people, but the war was destroying them. They could not win; the odds were against them. They, however, persisted in struggling on despite of the overwhelming evidence that they were fighting a lost cause. Suddenly he hated what he was doing—the spying, the subterfuge. It had seemed right and noble in the abstract before he'd come to Memphis, but that was before he saw Ariane and with one glance became obsessed with his beautiful golden Rebel. She was his torment and his delight.

Reaching the hospital, he knew that tonight if it was at all possible, he would return to Fleur de Lys. He had to know why she was seeking a pass at the Provost Marshal's Office. He felt deep in his bones that she was on a collision course with disaster, and that intuition had served him well as an agent in New Orleans and Vicksburg. His thin lips twisted in a sardonic smile at the irony that he was using the very skills that made him, according to Dodge, the general's best operative, to protect a woman whom he should regard his enemy. As he entered the hospital and the smells and the sounds of the sick and dying greeted him, he tried to put her from his mind, but she clung there with haunting persistence that even his strict self-control could not banish.

Ariane was filled with her own haunting memories as she rode back in the carriage her father had sent to bring her home. The sun was setting over the Mississippi River as she left the Provost Marshal's Office. It was a huge red fiery disk that hung in the west over the black, fertile bottom lands of the Arkansas bank. The rays of the sun streaked down upon the swirling ochre waters, tingeing them with gold. In the beauty of the lingering late afternoon, Ariane felt only a deep melancholy. Usually she loved this ride along the river, for she never tired of gazing upon its surging strength and power. She seemed to be able to derive some of the river's strength just from standing on its banks and watching the rushing, swirling water. Her roots were deep in the muddy soil of its banks, but today it only reminded her that the Union controlled the whole mighty twisting length of the river to the sea. The waterway that was the South's highway lay now completely in the hands of the enemy. And at that word "enemy," she closed her eyes and saw the darkly handsome visage of Justin, her lover, her beloved foe.

Exhausted from the heat and her nerve-racking meeting with the Provost Marshal, Ariane tried to rest on the ride back to Fleur de Lys. Her mind, however, was racing as she went over and over the plans for Beau's escape. Her friend Mrs. Sanderson, Felicity's mother, had been invaluable in finalizing the crucial details. When she had first suggested it to the older woman, she had been happy to help — any action against the command who held her daughter in Irving Block Prison was a strike at the tyranny she hated with all her being. They would continue with the story of her father's funeral being the reason they had to go beyond the boundaries of the city. The Union command had no way of knowing that the old gentleman had died years before. They needed an empty casket — at first they had planned on filling it with guns and medicine, but now it would serve another purpose. Staring out at the dusty trees on Poplar Street, Ariane mused on how hard it was going to be to get Beau to the bend in the road outside the estate where they were to meet the funeral procession. They would have only minutes to slip her brother inside the empty wooden casket. Just the thought of smuggling Beau out of the city in the wooden coffin filled her with revulsion, but it was their only chance. The guard around the outer boundaries of the estate had been strengthened since the day when Beau had made his way from the Bluff. It would be impossible for him to leave the same way he came.

The long mauve-violet shadows of summer twilight were falling across the stately cedars of Fleur de Lys as the carriage pulled up in front of the elegant mansion. Doves circled in the indigo sky, bidding farewell to the day before returning to their turreted dove cotes in the rose garden. All was quiet and serene, an oasis from the tumult of Memphis.

"Mam'zelle, I am so glad you have returned," Sable exclaimed as Ariane wearily placed her silk sun parasol and reticule on the hall table. Facing the mirror, she removed her bonnet and smoothed down her hair caught back in a low chignon at the base of her neck.

"What is it?" She turned with a sigh to the agitated woman.

"Your father has been told that tomorrow evening he must report to the railroad station in Lauderdale."

"Whatever for?" She stared at Sable as if she had lost her mind.

"The officer told your father that as a result of attacks on the trains along the Memphis and Charleston Railroad, General Washburn ordered forty of the most prominent secessionists placed in exposed positions on the trains. Tomorrow night there is a train leaving and your father is to be on it," Sable said in a rush, a deep frown on her elegant visage. "Mam'zelle Ariane, he is not in any condition for such a trip. When they reach their destination, he is to be held with the others till they wish him to return to Memphis on another such train, sitting again so any gunfire from Confederate troops will hit him."

"Where is he?" Ariane asked, her face gone pale.

"In the library with his lawyer. He is . . . is seeing to his will, mam'zelle," Sable said quietly, her dark eyes full of compassion.

Ariane rushed across the darkened foyer to where her father and his lawyer, George Clayton, sat calmly discussing some provisions in his will. They both rose to their feet as she entered the chamber.

"Father, I have just heard from Sable what that devil

Washburn has ordered. There must be some way we can stop this."

"There is nothing to be done, my dear, as Clayton here will tell you. I must report tomorrow evening with one satchel to the railroad station. I will ride as far as La Grange, where the train will stop and I along with some others will get off and wait for a returning train to Memphis."

"Word will be sent to Forrest. They will not fire if they know that all of you are on board," Ariane promised.

"It has been done, daughter. We can only hope it reaches the right scouts in time," he said wearily.

"And now I must take my leave if I am to be at home by the curfew," George Clayton explained as he bid them good-bye.

"I, too, must take my leave, Father, for I wish to wash the dust and dirt from my person before dinner," Ariane said as her father nodded, then walked his friend out to his horse.

None of their "guests" appeared home for the evening meal so Ariane and her father ate a simple meal alone in the huge dining room. It was too hot for more than a few cold dishes. Neither of them had much of an appetite. Leander Valcour, worn out from the tribulations of the day, excused himself and went up to bed as soon as he finished dessert.

After making sure her father had retired, Ariane left the house to visit Beau in the drying shed and go over some last-minute details. Her brother was calm, but anxious for the next morning. He had become tired of the small structure that had become a kind of prison. Assuring him it would not be long till he was on his way back to join Forrest and his men, Ariane bid him goodnight.

The house was dark and full of shadows when Ariane returned. Caesar had lit a lamp in the hall and one in the parlor beside the melodeon. It was such a hot, still night she knew it would be hard to sleep. Her nerves were taut with the tension of the coming day; there was no way she could relax. She wandered into the darkened parlor like a restless ghost in her pale rose muslin gown, the skirt like a huge swaying blossom. A small circle of golden glow fell from the oil lamp, and a moth circled the glass chimney, attracted to the flickering light.

Standing in front of the melodeon, Ariane trailed her fingers across the ivory keys. Then with a sigh she sat on the velvet padded stool and, lifting her fingers, began to play the bittersweet "Lorena." It had been the song that she had played that first night when Justin had returned to Memphis and to her. What joy she felt as he had sung the sad words to her accompaniment. Once, twice, she played the song, her eyes closing as she remembered what it was like to be held in that strong, warm embrace. How good it was to feel so safe, so protected, held against that sinewy chest, to taste his heated mouth on hers. It felt so right and was so wrong.

Suddenly without turning around, she knew he was with her in the room. As if her lonely yearnings had conjured him up so he might be with her, that she might find the solace of his touch once more. For it was his warm tapered fingers that stroked her bare shoulder and the silk of her hair that she had allowed to hang down her back to her waist, pulled back from her brow with two gold combs embossed with tiny pink porcelain roses. She reveled in his touch as she began to play the plaintive melody for the third time.

"We loved each other then, Lorena," he sang in his deep voice as he stood behind her, *"More than ever we dared to tell."* His hand caressed the slender column of her neck and down to the soft ivory curve of her shoulder. *"And what we might have been, Lorena, Had but our loving prospered well . . ."*

She stopped playing and turned toward him as his finger traced lower to the rise of her breast as it swelled above her bodice. "Justin," she gasped as he lifted her up and into his arms.

"I had to see you, touch you, kiss you," he said in a sen-

181

sual whisper as his mouth found hers in a deep kiss full of passion and need.

She responded to his wild, hungry caress, her lips parting for the velvet thrust of his tongue, her hands touching, stroking the planes of his back as she pressed as close to him as her hoop skirt would allow. Slowly, tenderly, he explored her moist waiting mouth, glorying in the knowledge that she, too, was tasting him with a passionate hunger.

He had fought his desire for her all day. Then as darkness fell across the wards, the chief surgeon gave Justin and another doctor their orders to be ready to leave the following night on a train to pick up wounded at the town of La Grange, Tennessee. Given time off till the next evening, both men had left the hospital as soon as their shift was over. Justin's heart thundered Ariane's name as he rode like the wind back to Fleur de Lys. They would have the night together, and this time she would spend it in his arms.

"I must have you," he murmured against the silken hollow of her throat, his lips having blazed a trail of liquid fire from her trembling mouth. "All of you."

"Yes, God help me, but yes," she moaned. If on the morrow she must gamble with life and death, then tonight she would experience the sweetness of existence at its pinnacle. "Come to my chamber and hold me through the night."

"If only tonight could last forever," he breathed, raising his head to stare down at her with an expression of intense desire, yet also with a shadow of great sadness in those ebony depths. Then placing his arm about her waist, he led her from the parlor to climb the curving staircase up to her darkened waiting chamber.

Chapter Fourteen

Soft, sultry night air heavy with the scent of night-blooming jasmine surrounded Ariane and Justin as they closed the door of her bedchamber behind them, shutting out the world. Here in this one room was their universe, if only for a few bittersweet hours of rapture. Existence was the circle of their embrace, the touch of their hands, the caress of heated mouth against moist trembling lips, the wonder of soft feminine curves pressed to lean sinewy manhood.

Sable had lit an oil lamp beside the bed when she turned down the bed. Its mellow light cast shadows on the ceiling through the lace canopy. Moonlight streamed in through the open windows, touching the mosquito netting around the four-poster bed till it appeared a silver cloud adding a sense of enchantment to the chamber. The heavy scent of late summer roses, a golden hue tinged with peach, lent their musky perfume to the darkened chamber from where they stood in a crystal vase on the elegant French writing desk. It was a feminine room, a room that carried the imprint of the inhabitant as personal as Ariane's signature, thought Justin with a slight smile on his stern mouth. How he loved to be here in this quiet sanctuary that was so much a part of her. Here where she sat at her desk to write in the leather-bound journal he saw next to the silver inkwell. The long pier glass she dressed in front of, checking her reflection in its wavy glass. The silk night rail that lay across the foot of the four-poster, with the absurd but delightful silk mules with the feathered toes that stood on the floor beneath the night dress. They were all part of the atmosphere that whispered the refrain *Ariane . . . Ariane.*

Bess lifted her head from her basket at the sound of their footsteps, then realizing who the people were who had disturbed her slumber, she slipped back into her canine dreams. Her contented sigh caused Ariane and Justin to smile as they turned toward each other, reaching out to feel the other's beloved touch, their hearts skipping a beat with the anticipation of what was to come.

Tenderly he placed his hands at her temples, turning her face up to him so he might examine the pale flower of her delicate visage. "Shall we make time stand still, my sweet Ariane," he whispered as he bent down and brushed her lips with a slow, dream kiss that caused her to ache with its gentleness. His mouth was surprisingly soft and sensitive for such a self-contained, often remote man, and he moved over her lips with exquisite tenderness. Then lifting his head, he stared down at her with a glint of wonder in his penetrating ebony eyes that also strangely held a glimpse of some secret pain.

"If only we could," she sighed, reaching up to pull him back so she might return his tender soul-stirring kiss with one of her own. She gloried in the gleam of joy she saw replace the pain in his midnight black eyes at her touch. The sorrow and melancholy had vanished as quickly as they had come. He now regarded her with amused delight.

"How can I release you from this armor," he teased as her hoop skirt kept him from pressing her to him as he wished to do.

"You must serve as my lady's maid," she jested in return as she moved so her back was to him. "See those small hooks—they release me."

"Ah, I see," he breathed, unfastening each hook till her gown slipped from her shoulders, revealing the perfection of her full breasts through the thin lawn of her chemise. His hands stroked the tiny peaks through the thin material

184

till they were erect and throbbing. Slipping his hand inside the material, he lowered the thin straps till her lovely globes were free to fill his hands with their soft weight. With languid sensual gestures, he traced the rose-pink nipples now marble hard between his fingers. He was rewarded with her moans and sighs of pleasure. "Still this cage protects what I wish to touch," he murmured as he kissed the hollow of her neck where her pulse throbbed with her excitement. "There is so much more of you I want to see, to stroke. I want to caress every curve of that silken skin." His voice was a low growl of desire in her ear, which he traced with the tip of his heated tongue.

"See the hook at my waist under my gown," she instructed in a voice husky with passion. "Yes, that is it. Watch." She gave a chuckle deep in her throat, and gathering up the huge skirt, she stepped from the caged crinoline and petticoat that Justin had unfastened from her waist. Stepping out of it, she said with a smile, *"Voilà,* I am free, kind sir."

With a groan he moved toward her and with one swift gesture stripped the rose muslin gown from her body. "This is inhuman," he muttered as his hands found the white and rose stays that bound her rib cage till he could reach around her waist with his hands. Turning her around, he quickly unlaced the torturous stays and pulled them from her form. "You don't need such an awful contraption. I wish all women would give them up. They are terrible for a woman's health."

"But then we could never catch a gentleman's eye." Ariane shuddered as he pulled off her chemise and bent to kiss the cruel red marks left on her skin by the corset. His hands spanned her waist, caressing the hollow underneath her rib cage as his mouth caressed her skin, then moved up to circle her sensitive swollen nipples. His tongue tantalized the buds, which were throbbing with the heat of desire.

"This is how this gentleman prefers you." He gave a low sensual laugh, raising his head as his hands stripped the lacy pantalets from her legs, till she stood in only her ivory silk stockings with their pink satin garters and her kid shoes with their two-inch heels. "Beautiful, Little Bit. How lovely you are." His dark eyes had grown fierce with his ardor as he drank in the vision of her before him. It was a sight he knew he would never forget as long as he lived. "I shall remember you like this always . . . always," he breathed.

"And you. What of you?" she asked in a husky voice that told of her passion and her happiness. Reaching out for him, she began to unbutton the brass buttons of his tunic. He had changed into a fresh uniform before leaving the hospital room that had been his sleep chamber for the last few days. There was no place in their time together for reminders of the terrible reality of a wartime hospital. He was glad he had washed away the grime and dust of the day as her tiny hands coaxed the tunic from his shoulders, and next the fine lawn of his shirt, till she could caress the bare skin of his chest, delighting in the feel of him.

"You drive me wild with such teasing," he moaned as she kissed the soft fur of his chest with butterfly kisses that burned into his skin. The feel of her moist velvet lips, the yearning and sensual courting of him in a gentle parody of his seduction of her, drove him to the limit of his control.

Sweeping her up in his arms, he carried her the few feet to the canopy bed. Pushing aside the cloud of mosquito netting, he laid her on the cool linen of the sheets, fragrant with her own special heliotrope perfume. Then he pulled off the kid slippers till she lay clad only in her silk stockings with the sassy satin rosette garters. As she watched with huge gray eyes, holding the back of her hand to her trembling mouth, he stripped the boots and breeches from his lean body, his black penetrating gaze never leaving hers.

"You, too, are beautiful," she whispered shyly, gazing on the virile symmetry of his body. He was magnificent, an Apollo brought to life. How wonderful was a man's body, she thought with a thrill of joy, so different from her own with its sinewy length, its lean planes and muscular strength, its dark masculine soft fur that covered the

186

bronzed skin she loved to stroke. How good it felt against her own smooth femininity.

"Do you know what it does to a man to hear such words from his beloved?" In one swift movement, he was beside her on the linen sheets, his lips touching her everywhere in his uncontrollable desire for his exquisite, forbidden love.

"Am I your beloved?" she asked in a trembling voice as she felt the intensity of his hunger, and knew it was matched with her own.

"Must you ask, or do you enjoy hearing that you have gotten inside my heart, a heart I had thought no one could ever penetrate." His words were almost angry as dark eyes black as onyx impaled her with the depth of his emotion. "You have become an obsession that never leaves me." He cupped the oval of her face in his hands as he kissed first her lips in a long shuddering kiss, then down to the hollow of her throat, and continuing down to circle each throbbing peak with his tongue in slow delicious circles.

The remembered thrill of ecstasy that only he could bring surged like fire through her veins as his mouth continued on down her quivering form in a rain of adoring kisses. His mouth learned the curves and hollows his hands had already traced. What a joy, almost more than the heart and soul could contain, to know that Justin, her Justin, wanted her with a passion that went beyond her girlish dreams. For in his embrace under his tender instruction she had become a woman and learned what it was to have a woman's needs. She had also learned what ecstasy could come from a woman's total fulfillment.

"You have made me vulnerable, my sweet torment, and for that I should hate you, but God help me I cannot." His raspy confession was torn from him as his mouth pressed against the tender softness of her inner thigh. His long sensitive fingers, searching, stroking, every inch of her satin skin. Slowly he pulled first one garter, then the silk stocking from her leg. Kissing, licking down her thigh to the soft inner fold of her knee. Her moan was like the sweetest music to his ears. Caressing her calf with gentle, yet deep

187

knowing strokes, he felt her relax completely, every nerve, every muscle attuned to his touch. The high arch of her tiny foot fit in the palm of his hand as he massaged it in slowly mesmerizing circles. Then his mouth was pressing kisses to her other thigh as this stocking too was removed with similar ceremony of touch, kiss, and deep message.

She was beyond speech, for his words, his mouth, his hands had excited her till she was all fiery sensation incapable of anything but the sensual rapture of the moment. Moving, arching, seeking the exquisite delight that his touch could elicit from her being, she wanted the fulfillment he, and only he, could give her. She cried out her need to him in hungry moans as she moved under his knowing rapturous caress. Her hands reached for him, pulling him to her in wanton movements that she was powerless to stop.

"Not yet, my beguiling, impetuous love. We promised to make time stand still," he reminded her in a voice harsh with barely controlled passion. "There is all the long night to spend in loving. Let us not waste any of the few precious moments left to us. We shall rest awhile, to prolong the ultimate joy we both seek." He moved slightly away from her then clasped her lightly in his arms and stretched out beside her on the feather bed. Holding each other thus, they tried to quiet the passion that was out of control so that the pleasure could be once more brought to its peak again and again. It was another facet to lovemaking he was showing her, and she followed his lead, understanding quickly how exquisite was the joy yet to come by first practicing a little restraint. "Savoring the experience is part of the pleasure," he continued against her silken hair as she lay with her head in the hollow of his neck.

The sultry night air that blew in the open windows was filled with the sounds of a Southern summer night, the rustle of the wind through the cedar branches, the peep of the tree frogs, the faraway hoot of an owl. In the distance could be heard the plaintive sound of a train whistle, a Union train leaving the station in Memphis, a train like the one her father would be forced to ride on the following evening. As Justin gathered Ariane to him to drink deeply of her mouth, she felt a stab of pain through the ecstasy of her rapture. Even here in the circle of their embrace there were haunting reminders of the real world, the reality of war.

"What is it?" He lifted his mouth from hers to kiss the tendrils of hair at her temples. "I felt your sigh, your sudden melancholy."

"Only that it is so hopeless," she murmured. "How I wish we were alive in another time, another place."

"And what time would that be, what place?" he whispered huskily into her scented tresses.

"Any time but the summer of 1864, any place but Memphis in the middle of this horrible war." She sighed aloud this time as his hands caressed down her back.

"If it were a hundred years from now, a hundred and fifty years, I should want you as I do now with every fiber of my being. Even in that strange far-off time I believe men and women will still love regardless of the circumstances, regardless of whether it is the right time in their lives. The heart has its own rules and 'twill always be so," he said quietly.

She looked at him in the dim light of the oil lamp and was entranced by his words, and the sadness in his dark understanding eyes. His insight into her feelings was one of the facets of their relationship that amazed her. Without words they were able to communicate so much, the slender invisible bond that held them seemed to grow stronger with time, but even that was not strong enough to change the immutable fact that they were still in one important way enemies, beloved enemies.

"And tonight the rules of the heart are all that matter," he told her firmly as, reclaiming her mouth, he pressed her to him and silenced for the moment all her doubts.

Parting her lips, she became lost in his kiss that was hungry, hard, and insistent. His demanding mouth was trying to banish all thought for both of them. Her arms wrapped tightly around him, she returned the touch of his tongue, lingering, savoring the taste of him, every nuance of this wonderful intimacy.

Pressing her back down on the feather bed, he gasped as he felt her fingers brush across the dark curling hair of his chest, then move on to caress the planes of his back. A mutual shudder ran along the length of their bodies crushed so close they were as one. His stomach twisted with the hard knot of his need, but he fought for control. He wanted to prolong such pleasure for he had waited so long, so very long to feel the burning sweetness of her beneath him.

Ariane molded herself to him, to the sensual heat of his skin, the caressing hands that moved with exquisite knowledge over her trembling body. She felt a painful ache built between her thighs as his fingers parted her moist woman's petals and he teased her, arousing her desire to a fever pitch with his passionate stroke that brought her again and again to the pinnacle. His powerful male hardness against her soft inner thigh filled her with the need to experience all of him deep with her, to reach that ultimate peak joined completely with him. Moving against him, she reached down to caress what she most desired.

"My love, I can wait no longer," he gasped at her touch, delight filling his soul at her tentative caress that showed him how much she desired him.

"Oh yes, now!" she cried as he entered her gently with the reverence of his tender love. Instinctively, her hips lifted in a sensuous invitation as her body opened to him. Finding his rhythm, she moved with him in circles of exquisite love and hunger. Their shadows thrown on the wall by the golden glow of the lamp showed partners in passion's dance, giving and receiving life's most splendid gift.

Clasped tightly, they moved on from deepening thrust to deepening thrust, each wishing the rapture of their total joining would never end. Caught in the spiraling climax that claims all lovers, they reached the pinnacle and in an uncontrollable explosion of ecstasy were consumed.

They lay content in the afterglow in each other's arms. There were no words to be said, no explanations needed.

For a few moments they had made time stand still, they had loved like there was no tomorrow. But the morrow would come, they knew, and with it reality. If they could pretend for a while longer, they would, and closing their eyes, they drifted off into slumber.

As the pearl-gray light of dawn pierced the dark of the night sky, Ariane thrashed restlessly in Justin's arms. Lost in the horrors of a bad dream, she moaned.

"Hush, Little Bit," he crooned, waking her from the night terrors.

Brushing the hair from her eyes, Ariane sat up, trying to wipe the memory of her dream from her mind. She gave a slight shudder as the dream refused to leave her.

"What was it that so frightens you?" he asked, stroking her back under the tangled mane of red-gold hair that he loved.

"That night . . . that night when my mother took her life," Ariane muttered, staring out into the chamber lit now only with the light of early dawn.

"Do you have this dream often, sweetheart?" he asked with concern, remembering that frightened child all those years ago that had finally come to trust him. How valiant she had been, and how heartbreakingly vulnerable, he thought with a sad smile of remembrance. There was something still of the vulnerable child in this fragile beauty who had such strength of spirit in spite of the overwhelming odds that fate threw at her. "I still dream of it sometimes when I am worried or exhausted," she said without thinking.

"And what is it that worries you? Perhaps I can help," he said, feeling her stiffen, knowing that the secrets she kept buried deep within her were once more coming between them.

Turning toward him with a sad smile, she said, "Hold me a few moments longer, then you must go. Sable would be shocked to find you in my bed."

As he gathered her to his chest and his lips sought hers, she thought, once more shall I love him. Whatever today brings, I shall have known what it is to be loved and to love in return.

As her mouth opened under his, she thought, while she could still think would Justin still want her if he knew he held a Confederate spy in his arms. How long could she continue this masquerade before she was discovered and this man she loved with all her heart learned the truth? With tears slipping down her cheeks, she gave herself up to the splendor of his kiss and became lost one last bittersweet time in the rapture of Justin's embrace.

Chapter Fifteen

"Mam'zelle, there is a problem," Sable said, a frown marring her elegant brow as she helped Ariane from the brass sit tub. "Doctor Justin did not leave this morning for the hospital. In fact, when I saw him in the hall, he told me he had the entire day off until this evening when he is leaving on a train to pick up wounded. The same train I think that Miche Valcour will be riding."

Ariane flinched at her words. It was the worst possible thing to have happen. As soon as Justin had left her as the sun rose in the east, she had pulled the bell rope for Sable. The older woman had anticipated her by having breakfast ready on a tray. Brass containers of water and her tub had been brought up while she broke her fast quickly in the tumbled bed. If Sable had noticed the appearance of the rumpled sheets, clearly showing two had shared the four-poster, she made no mention even by facial expression.

"We must get Beau out to the meeting place on the Poplar Road. I will distract Doctor Justin if need be, but Caesar must take Beau in the carriage since Father is not going into the city today. Hurry, I will have to dress in the black riding habit. I am supposed to be attending a funeral today."

"Miche Beau is waiting in the stables hidden behind a stack of hay. He thought you would be riding together, but I will tell Caesar he must ride alone in the hidden compartment beneath the seat. Perhaps I should send that huge produce basket with Caesar in case the Yankees stop him. He could tell them he is going in to the market in Memphis," Sable said with a sparkle in her soft brown eyes that showed she was enjoying the intrigue.

"Yes that would be wise. I will have to catch up with the funeral cortege further down the road if need be," Ariane sighed, her stomach churning with anxiety and frustration. Everything was going wrong and the morning had just started.

Dressed in her black linen habit, which was suffocating on such a hot, steamy morn, she slipped the all-important pass in the pocket of her jacket. In the other hidden pocket of her skirt, she placed the pearl-handled revolver. She felt a pang of regret that she couldn't smuggle medicine or at the least letters out on her person, but Beau's life was too important to risk by calling attention to herself if for some reason the Yankees decided to search her before allowing her through the lines. Washburn was tightening his noose about Memphis and Ariane was afraid to take any risks that could jeopardize Beau's life.

"Where is Doctor Justin?" she asked Sable before leaving the room.

"He was heading out to the terrace, where I have instructed Lulu to serve breakfast."

"Lulu? But she is a kitchen maid. Where is Roman?" Ariane turned from the door in surprise.

"Roman has gone, mam'zelle," Sable said quietly, looking away from Ariane as she placed her night rail and slippers in the armoire.

"To join the Yankees, I expect," Ariane replied with a sigh.

"Yes, I believe so." The older woman's voice was carefully neutral, but Ariane sensed Sable was proud of him, for Roman was her son, a year younger than Ariane. Who his father was, Ariane never knew, but Roman, like Sable, had always been a free person of color. His loyalty to the family had only gone so far and then he had to follow his conscience. She would miss him, Ariane thought with a sigh, and then a more worrisome thought occurred. How much did Roman know about her activities and would he turn in Beau to the Yankees?

"Do not worry, mam'zelle. Roman will not inform on Master Beau," Sable said quietly, turning toward her as if she could read Ariane's thoughts.

"I can only hope you are right," Ariane replied tersely. Leaving the room, she had disquieting thoughts as she made her way downstairs. She had always taken Sable's loyalty for granted as she did Caesar's. Could she continue to do so?

Justin rose to his feet as she came to join him even though she had already eaten. Somehow she must keep him occupied while Caesar smuggled Beau out in the carriage to the bend in Poplar Road, where they were to meet the funeral procession. Here Beau would be put in the empty coffin in order to smuggle him through the pickets. The plan was to meet Henderson's Scouts at Elmwood Cemetery, where Beau would leave the coffin before the burial. Inside were packets of medicine that would be unloaded as well and given to the Confederates. The empty coffin would then be buried in case any suspicious Yankees thought to check. It was a plan that had been used before to smuggle guns and morphine out of the city, but it was always risky.

"You are dressed to go riding, I see," Justin commented, staring at the black riding habit as he seated her across from him. He caressed her shoulder in a brief, yet affectionate gesture that told her of his remembrance of their night together.

"Just coffee and a croissant, Lulu," Ariane told the young maid, before giving Justin a tender smile. "Yes, I am attending a funeral at Elmwood this morning, and must wear black. Such a hot morning for dark colors," she chatted, hoping her voice didn't sound as nervous as she felt.

195

"Ah, so that is why you were seeking a pass," Justin said coolly, his dark eyes watching her intently. "It must a good friend for you to compromise your principles by taking the iron-clad oath."

"Yes, as much as I hated to swear to such an odious statement, I felt it was necessary, for my friend's mother needed me at such a time," Ariane replied, meeting his gaze with composure.

"Who is the deceased? Perhaps I know the family."

Anxiety surged through her at his question. Had Mrs. Sanderson's father still been alive when Justin lived in Memphis? Her hands shaking, she set her cup back on the saucer. "You might. It is Felicity's grandfather, old Mr. Latimer. You can see with Felicity imprisoned, her mother is quite alone. I had to be with her at this terrible time of trial to try and take Felicity's place. Even though Mr. Latimer was quite old, I fear Mrs. Sanderson is not taking it well. She has been through so much."

"Old is right. He must have been in his nineties. I thought he had died long ago," Justin said, an arched heavy black brows showing his surprise.

"He . . . he was a very old man when he died, that is true," Ariane agreed, hating the nervous crack in her voice.

"Was he ill long?" Justin persisted, his penetrating ebony eyes never leaving her face.

"No, he died peacefully in his sleep," Ariane answered, which was true, although it had occurred years before. Thankfully the real grave of the departed Mr. Latimer was in the small town of Raleigh on the banks of the Wolf River a few miles from Memphis.

"If you are going to the funeral and your father is spending the day at home, why is Caesar leaving with the carriage?" Justin inquired as they both turned to watch the carriage sway down the narrow road that led from the house to Poplar Road.

"Sable has sent him into the market in Memphis. I

196

thought it too hot to be cooped up in a carriage. I plan on riding Dancer out to Elmwood." Ariane took a sip of her coffee and this time her hand was controlled. Beau was on his way from the estate and Justin had no idea of the intrigue that was swirling around him.

"Good, then I will accompany you," he said with a slight smile that didn't quite reach his watchful eyes.

"What!" she sputtered, setting her cup down in its saucer so hard the coffee spilled on to the lace tablecloth.

" 'Tis not safe for a woman alone to ride out to Elmwood," he said tersely. "I am going with you. Thank God I have the day off from the hospital. Tonight I am leaving with a train to pick up wounded."

"I know. My father will be on that same train," she told him with a light bitterness in her voice. "He is to ride next to the windows so that if any Confederate troops fire on the train, they will hit loyal Southerners, not brave Yankee officers." Her eyes were shards of gray ice as she spat out the words with contempt.

"I am sorry, my dear, but he has angered Washburn with his refusal to take the iron-clad oath. Frankly, I am surprised he has not been arrested and thrown in Irving Block Prison. You must know that he will not be allowed to run Valcour Shipping any longer without taking the oath."

"You must realize why my father could never take that oath," she said softly, with eyes narrowed in anger, rising to her feet.

"I do, but it makes no difference," he replied softly. There was regret and sadness in his expressive dark gaze as he, too, rose to his feet.

"Good morning. I am late as it is," she said coolly, turning on her heel to walk to the stables to fetch Dancer.

"Allow me to accompany you," he told her, taking his hat up from where it lay on a vacant chair. His manner and voice told her it was not a question, but a statement of fact. Justin was going to ride with her to Elmwood.

197

One of the young stable boys saddled Justin's horse as well as Dancer. The two sleek animals stood waiting eagerly for their morning ride. As Justin helped her mount the bay mare, she wondered how they were going to run the stables without Roman. He had been wonderful with horses and the two young boys who helped him were not old enough to do everything without supervision. It seemed this morning contained nothing but problems, she thought, as they rode away from the house down through the alley of cedars and magnolias to Poplar Road.

"What is wrong?" Justin asked, hearing her sign as they rode close together on the narrow path through the cool dark tunnel of giant trees.

"Roman has left to join the Union Army." She stared out across the tranquil verdant grounds of Fleur de Lys and wondered if anything would ever be the same again.

"He spoke with me about it a few weeks ago. I think he was trying to make up his mind then. Roman is an intelligent young man; he had to do what was in his heart," Justin said thoughtfully, looking at her lovely rigid profile as she rode beside him. "The South will never be the same after this war is over, Little Bit. You had better reconcile yourself to it."

"How can I become reconciled to seeing everything I know and love destroyed?" she queried bitterly.

"Perhaps you can help rebuild it into something even better. The South, God knows, will need strong men and women in the years to come if it is to recover from this debacle."

Poplar Road, a yellow-brown ribbon of dust and deep ruts, stretched ahead of them as they left the gates of Fleur de Lys behind. There was very little traffic going out to the countryside in the morning so they had the twisting roadway to themselves. Tall oaks, cedars, and cottonwood trees shaded the dusty track, giving some relief from the oppressive heat. High in a sycamore, the music of the sad-voiced whippoorwill pierced the muggy air. Ariane gave a light shiver, even in the heat. She hoped it wasn't an omen. The sound was so mournful.

"I was to meet the rest of the cortege at Elmwood at ten. I fear I am late," Ariane said as her eyes scanned the bend where Beau was to have met the others at nine o'clock. There was no sign of the funeral procession or the Valcour carriage, but Caesar had been told to double-back to Fleur de Lys by an old cotton wagon road that was seldom used. She could only pray that everything had gone as planned.

" 'Tis only nine-thirty," he assured her, pulling his pocket watch out from his uniform and checking the time.

For a moment she stared at the gold watch gleaming in a shaft of sunlight. She was trying to remember something, but what was it? With a shrug, she brushed it from her mind as he put it away in his pocket. Signaling Dancer, they turned onto a smaller, less well traveled road that cut across the boundary of the Union lines. They had gone only half a mile when they reached the picket line and one of the Union encampments.

Ariane felt men's eyes, hot avid eyes, staring at her unabashedly as they reached the checkpoint. Hundreds of tents filled several cotton fields and the smoke from their campfires, along with other more earthy human smells, filled the air.

"Captain, if I could see you and the young lady's papers," a young corporal said, saluting Justin in a lazy manner. His gaze was directed at Ariane with lewd interest as a stream of tobacco juice trickled out of his mouth.

Justin, his stern visage a mask of contempt, handed the slovenly soldier his pass as well as Ariane's. "Has a funeral cortege recently passed this way?" His voice was cold, clipped, and full with authority.

"Yes, sir, a bunch of Secesh from Memphis passed this way a while ago. Real uppity was some of those old biddies, and those darkies they had with them was just as bad," the soldier complained. "They all had passes though so I let them through. It would have been somethin' to see those old biddies takin' the oath. Like to have seen that, sure would," he cackled, spitting a stream of brown tobacco juice in front of Dancer's hooves. "You goin' to that old Reb's funeral?" He looked at them with curiosity in his small restless eyes.

"Yes," Justin answered in terse tones, taking back their passes. Turning to Ariane, he motioned for them to continue on toward Elmwood. She tried to remain calm, but it was difficult. The crude soldier had made her uneasy. But Beau and the others had passed through here without being caught. Hopefully the worse was behind them.

Leaving the Union encampment behind, they rode down the deserted narrow path between the dense woods. Arching branches from the giant, ancient trees on either side made a verdant tunnel through the eerie stillness. The road was seldom used and long grass had grown up between the two clay ruts the wheels of a wagon or a carriage had made as they had passed through on their way to the cemetery. Only the fresh droppings from horses along the path showed that someone had been by not long before them.

Ariane caught herself glancing uneasily over her shoulder as if she was quick enough she could catch sight of Union soldiers following them from the camp. But there was no one, no one in a blue uniform but the man who rode beside her. The midnight blue plumes on his broadbrimmed hat fluttered in the warm air. Why did it give him such an ominous air, she thought, stealing a look at his tall commanding figure, or was it only her own fear for Beau that made everything seem menacing?

When a flock of red-winged blackbirds soared out of the feathery branches of an enormous cedar tree to fly past them into the dark silence of the woods on their right, Ariane was so startled she involuntarily pulled on

200

Dancer's reins, causing the mare to move skittishly away from Justin's steed. Quickly she recovered her poise and once more had the bay mare under control, but Justin was looking at her with concern in his dark gaze that seemed to be able to read every nuance of her expression.

"Is something wrong?" he asked. "You seem uneasy."

"I fear the sentry rather unnerved me," she said ruefully. "He was a most unpleasant man."

"There are many unpleasant men, as you say, in Memphis these days. I am glad you are finally aware of it. This war has worn out Chivalry on both sides, my dear. It has become a deadly fight for survival and vengeance, neither qualities that lend themselves to chivalrous actions on the part of the participants. Remember that this war is no longer a game like the ring tournaments that the South so enjoyed in those long lazy summers before the war. I am afraid that the South has found out too late that this is not some reenactment of the stories of their beloved Sir Walter Scott. It has become all too real."

Sudden angry lit her gray eyes, and she glared back at him. His tone aroused her fury, but she tried to keep her temper under control, fearing that if she spoke, she would say too much. Her nerves were stretched to the breaking point, so worried was she that they would come upon the funeral party too soon, before the switch had been made and Beau had been released from his macabre hiding place. She realized how upset everyone would be to see her arrive with a Yankee officer, but surely they would realize she had little choice in the matter.

Rounding a bend, she saw the cast iron sign mounted on two posts that was the entrance to Elmwood Cemetery. It was too late to worry about what was going to happen. In a few minutes she would know for good or ill.

The spires of ornate and impressive monuments glistening in the hot August sun greeted them as they entered the extensive cemetery grounds. Here was the final resting spot of many of Memphis's finest families.

"Where is the family plot?" Justin asked as they stopped by an enormous magnolia, the scent of the waxy alabaster blossoms heavy in the sultry air.

"There," she pointed, seeing the black plumes of the undertaker's horses at the top of a small rise. She felt a slight shiver run down her spine, for she realized they reminded her of the plumes on Justin's hat.

"Come, I think we are late," Justin said, looking up at the sun, a blinding white-hot sphere rising higher in the cloudless sky.

"Perhaps 'twould be better if I went on alone. I don't think a Union officer would be welcome at the graveside, not now with Felicity in Irving Block. You must understand this," Ariane pleaded, hoping against hope that he would accept this explanation for her not wanting him to accompany her to the grave. "Please, you can wait here." Her gray eyes begged for his compliance.

Understanding crossed his aloof handsome features. "Yes, I suppose you are right. At such a time her mother doesn't need more reminders of her . . ." His voice broke off as he stared down at the dirt road winding up toward the grassy knoll.

Dismounting, to Ariane's surprise, he held the reins in his gauntlet-covered hand while he led the horse a few feet and then bent down to touch a small dark greasy pool. Staring for a moment at the tip of his leather glove, he pulled a linen handkerchief from his pocket and dipped the corner also in the small pool in the dirt.

"What is it?" she called out to him.

Walking back to her, his face a stony mask, his eyes glittering and cold, he mounted his horse. "I am coming with you." His voice left no room for disagreement.

"I don't understand. What was it you saw?"

He urged his horse forward, not answering her question. They rode a few yards when he said tersely, "I did not come alone. You were right in feeling uneasy when we left the sentry. There are soldiers hidden in the cemetery. Washburn thinks the Confederates are using Elmwood as a meeting place with their scouts and spies in Memphis."

Ariane choked back a cry of despair as icy fear twisted about her heart. Somewhere hidden in the shadows of the cedars and heavily laden magnolia trees were Yankee soldiers.

"There was blood on the road, fresh blood," he said in a curt voice. "Stay close beside me. I don't know what is going on here, but something is wrong."

She stared straight ahead as they came upon the funeral party, afraid if she looked at him he would see the anguish and despair in her face. Two black former slaves who still worked for the Sandersons were lifting the pine casket from the back of the undertaker's carriage.

"A pine box for a Latimer?" Justin questioned under his breath as they rode up to the small party of people who stood waiting beside an open carriage.

"The Sandersons are hard up like everyone else in the South. All their money was in Confederate script and bonds," Ariane explained rapidly. They had had to use a pine box crudely made so there would be large enough spaces between the warped boards that air could get in and Beau could breathe.

Mrs. Sanderson looked up at Ariane in shock as first Justin dismounted then turned to help her down from Dancer. Mrs. Chastain, her friend, glared at Ariane as if she were the enemy. The woman had often run the sentries carrying contraband out to her family's plantation on the outskirts of the small community of Germantown near Memphis. She was such a formidable lady she struck fear even into the Union soldiers; consequently her person was never searched.

"Really, Ariane," she muttered, recognizing Justin.

"Mrs. Chastain, 'tis been a long time," he said courteously, taking off his hat to the grand dame of Memphis society.

"Justin Pierce, a Yankee!" she exclaimed, her face lifting away from him as if she had smelled something vile. " 'Tis a blessing your poor parents are not here to see such a terrible day."

"I am pleased to see you too after all this time. Isn't it amazing how some things, and some people, never change," he drawled with sarcasm etching every word.

Isabella Chastain turned her back to him and flounced off so quickly her hoop skirt swung crazily for a moment as she made her way over to where her family plot was located. They stood watching her and even Ariane had to give a slight smile at the woman's reaction to Justin. Then as the black servants stood with the pine casket in their hands, uncertain what to do next with a Yankee officer in front of them, Ariane sent an agonized glance to Mrs. Sanderson. The terrified woman gave a slight negative nod of her bonnet.

Ariane felt panic as she had never known well up in her throat. Beau had had no time to exit the casket. He was still inside the pine box the servants were carrying slowly toward the open grave. What should she do? Her mind fluttered in fear as she tried to make a decision.

"Stop! Put that casket down now," Justin ordered, stepping in front of the black men. Obeying him, they laid it gently on the wild honeysuckle vine that climbed over the long grass up the trunks of the stalwart oaks. Staring at the frightened men, he commanded, "Open it!"

Chapter Sixteen

Frozen, unable to speak or move, Ariane stared transfixed with horror as the men tried to pry off the lid of the crude coffin. As if from a far distance, she heard Mrs. Sanderson plead with Justin not to do this terrible thing. It was then she saw the blood seeping out of the corner of the pine box where the boards had slightly warped.

"No—oo!" The long-drawn-out word was torn from her throat as some primitive instinct told her what they would find. She felt Justin's strong firm hands grasp her arms as she slumped, her legs no longer able to hold her up.

"Raise it," Justin told the men tersely as the lid gave under their hands. "Don't look," he muttered, trying to press Ariane's head against his chest. Did she know what was in there?

"Beau! Beau!" Her plaintive cry soared up into the stiffling hot air and seemed to echo off the trees, sending a shiver down the spine of the others. Trying to pull away from Justin, Ariane stared down at the lifeless body of her brother. The jolting road had torn open his wound, and as they had made their way to the cemetery, he had bled to death. Guilt and anger at her own stupidity came over Ariane in waves. She should have known. She should have remembered the young soldier who had died the same way when he had been moved from the hospital to the steamer only weeks before.

"My God," Justin swore as he stared down at the body of his former friend. He had not known what he had expected, but not this, not that what they were smuggling out of Memphis would be Beau Valcour. He didn't have to examine him to tell that he was dead. Holding the trembling, distraught Ariane in his arms, he refused to let her go, refused to let her throw herself on the lifeless body of her brother.

Before anyone could recover from the horror of what had occurred, they were surrounded by Union soldiers, who, seeing Justin's uniform, came out of their hiding place in a thicket of overgrown bushes. Guns pulled from holsters, they quickly encircled the small funeral party.

"What's going on here, Captain?" a young lieutenant demanded from Justin.

His mind racing, Justin stared down at the sobbing figure he held to his chest, then his eyes met the terrified gaze of Mrs. Sanderson and the hostile one of Isabella Chastain. In that terrible moment he made a decision, a decision unlike any other he had ever made, for it was one of emotion, sentimentality, a decision from the heart.

"I was suspicious these ladies were trying to smuggle guns out of Memphis so I insisted the casket be opened," he said smoothly. "Obviously I was wrong. It has been too much for the young lady, I fear. Please close the lid quickly," he ordered the black servants.

They obeyed before the Union lieutenant could see the body. The other men looked away, embarrassed at the macabre scene and Ariane's distress.

"Proceed with the service," Justin told the elderly minister they had brought along to make it look more authentic. The man opened his Bible with trembling hands as the slaves lowered the pine box into the open grave. He tried to compose his voice as he realized with horror the funeral service was now quite real. The small group of loyal Confederate supporters who had come from Memphis to help one of their own soldiers now stood in numb shock as they attended his funeral service. It was mercifully brief, then the undertaker motioned for the black men to fill in the grave.

Ariane stood supported by Justin, her stunned mind unable to fully comprehend what was happening. A phrase kept running through her head over and over. Justin was covering for them. He was covering for them.

"Come, Miss Valcour, I fear the day has been too much for you," Justin said firmly so the lieutenant could hear. At her hesitation, he half dragged her from the grave through the crushed blossoms of the honeysuckle. Their poignant scent from now on would always remind her of Beau.

Helping her up on Dancer, Justin muttered so only she could hear, "You can't help Beau, but your friends are in danger if the lieutenant suspects anything is wrong. You must remain in control. Do you understand?"

She nodded her head, taking the reins in her gloved hand. Slowly they followed the carriages and funeral wagon from the cemetery. Ariane felt like a sleepwalker, going through the motions of riding Dancer, but nothing seemed quite real. It was more like a dream—no, she corrected herself, a nightmare.

They rode on and on, through the heat of the day as the sun rose high overhead. The dust from the carriage wheels choked them in the hot air. As soon as they passed through the sentry post, Justin motioned for Ariane to follow him away from the others down an old path through abandoned fields. It was the cotton road Caesar had used earlier, she realized dimly. She had forgotten Justin knew about it.

"How did Beau get into Memphis?" Justin asked quietly, speaking for the first time since they had left the cemetery.

"He was one of Henderson's Scouts. That day on the bluff when they fired at the Union steamer, he was shot by a Yankee soldier as he tried to escape. He made his way to the stables at Fleur de Lys and Sable treated his wound from then on in the drying shed," Ariane told him in a dull, defeated voice.

"So that is why you took the iron-clad oath, to get Beau out of Memphis," he said thoughtfully. "You must have known if you had been caught, you would have been thrown in Irving Block or worse."

"Yes," she said, her voice telling him it made no difference. "Will you tell the Provost Marshal?" There was no fear in her question. It was said almost as if she didn't care one way or the other.

"No. I see no point. Beau is dead. He was a good man, but reporting his death will make no difference to the outcome of this war. But it must stop here, Little Bit. No more intrigue, I warn you. I am trying to justify this in my mind, telling myself that it was a special circumstance, Beau was my friend. What we did today changes nothing, gives no aid or comfort to the enemy. We buried a dead man, but no more. I warn you no more deception." His voice hardened at the last sentence as he stared ahead, not risking looking at her heartbreakingly lovely visage. She had already made him compromise his principles this morning. There had been no way he could turn her over to the Provost Marshal for trying to help her own wounded brother. Uncomfortably he was discovering that this war was straining one by one all of his strongly held convictions. He was experiencing emotions he had thought he had long ago excised from his heart.

Her throat was suffocated with unuttered shouts and angry protests, but she kept her own counsel. From out of the corner of her eye she could see his grim expression as he rode beside her. Today he had saved them from the Southern Bastille, as Irving Block Prison was called by the Confederacy—she could not ask more of him. But there was a pain like a throbbing wound in her heart as she realized that she had somehow caused her own brother's death for the plan had been hers. Would it have been better to have told Justin of Beau's existence in the shed? Would he have helped him escape or would he have turned him over to the Provost Marshal? And even if he had, Beau would still be alive. The pain in her heart became a sick and fiery gnawing as guilt, grief, and despair tore through her like a knife.

"You did your best, what Beau wanted. Do not punish yourself with recriminations. Union prisons, like your Southern ones, are pestholes. With his wound, he perhaps would have died there as well, but it could have been long and lingering. If he would have made it that far, Washburn threatens to put any of Henderson's Scouts he captures before a firing squad."

Ariane turned despairing eyes on Justin. "I still feel that I killed him. You see, the plan was mine, and I never considered what a ride over the road to Elmwood would do to him. I saw with my own eyes that day at the river what a ride could do to a wounded man, and I still did such a stupid thing."

"You had no choice. You did what you thought you had to do. If Beau had been caught hidden at Fleur de Lys, both you and your father would have been imprisoned. Your father could have been hanged. They haven't hung a woman yet, Little Bit, but there has been talk since the Rosa Greenhow case and Belle Boyd's numerous incarcerations. The Northern Press has been writing about Southern women spies, calling them the "feminine desperadoes of the Confederacy." It has gotten public opinion stirred up, demanding that these women not be dealt with so gently."

Ariane had stiffened when he named two of the most famous Southern women spies. She turned her gaze away from him in confusion. Just what was he telling her? Had he guessed that smuggling Beau out of Memphis had just been a small part of her activities for the Confederacy?

The majestic magnolias of Fleur de Lys rose in front of them as they turned through the back gate and up the path that led to the stables. Ariane shuddered as she thought that she would have to tell Caesar that all his risk had been in vain. Beau was dead. She had lost both brothers to the war, to the Confederate Cause.

"Please do not speak of this to my father. Tonight he must ride that Yankee train as a target. I cannot add to the strain he is under. You see, he knew nothing about Beau being hidden in the drying shed. I was afraid he might give it away to the other doctors staying at Fleur de Lys. Later I will tell him I received word Beau was killed outside Memphis and the Scouts buried him under the Yankees' nose at Elmwood," she said with quiet determination.

"Have I told you, Little Bit, that you are quite a woman," he said with a slight tinge of wonder in his husky voice. "It won't be easy keeping this from your father. He will see on your face that something is wrong."

"Then I must be a very good actress," she replied with a bitter edge to her words.

She was lucky her father was resting when they entered the house. Justin had suggested she do the same, for she was still suffering from shock. It was there in her bedchamber that she told Sable what had happened, and sobbed out her grief in the woman's comforting arms.

Spent and exhausted, Ariane took a cool bath as Sable left to tell Caesar the sad news and that her father was not to hear a word of it. Soaking listlessly in the cool scented water, Ariane tried to come to some kind of terms with what had happened. There was no way—only time could take off the sharp edge of grief. Would she ever be able to accept what happened and not feel somehow she was at fault?

Golden streams from the setting sun filled Ariane's bedchamber, awakening her from the dream-filled nap she had taken at Sable's insistence. The air was hazy with the August heat as she sat up in the mosquito-draped bed. Her head ached and her eyes were swollen from the tears that had flowed for Beau. But she felt strangely at peace, for she knew what she must do. It had come to her as she struggled to awaken from the dreams that had haunted her slumber. Her father would not go on the train tonight; she would go in his place. If Washburn wanted Secesh families to ride the Yankee trains as targets, then she would be one of them. When they came for him, she would explain he was not in good health and that she was his replacement. All they wanted were Southern bodies to use as shields—it couldn't matter if they were male or female.

A calmness had come over her now that she was striking out, fighting in this war that had taken both her brothers. Anything was better than sitting at home waiting and worrying about what was taking place on that accursed train. If she could take some kind of action, she wouldn't feel so trapped by circumstances over which she had little control. Tonight she would strike out at the Yankees and their rules and regulations, their commands and domination over her life. On the train she could perhaps hear rumors of Federal troop movements, their strengths and weakness. Which railroad bridges were unprotected, which supply depots and railway depots were weakly garrisoned. If she was charming enough to the right susceptible officers, if she kept her ears open she could find out information that would prove valuable to Forrest. For instead of heeding Justin's warning to stay away from all spying for the Confederacy, she felt honor-bound to do her utmost, to make up for her hideous error with Beau's escape. She felt reckless, anxious to do something, anything, to keep the memory of her brother's still white face from her mind.

"Mam'zelle, 'tis dangerous what you are planning, but I imagine you already know that. You . . . you know this will not bring back Mister Beau," Sable said softly as she helped Ariane to dress in a smart traveling costume of olive green silk shot with a gold luster trimmed in black jet beads. It was the new short walking length that daringly showed her moss-green silk boots with their two-inch heels and black braid bow on the toe. When she moved, her skirt belled up to show her trim ankles in their black silk stockings with the gold leaf design up the side.

"I hate to not wear mourning, but Father must not suspect anything, and I must look my most fetching if I am to charm talkative soldiers," she commented with a bitter calculating coldness as she had Sable dress her hair loose in the back, hanging in what the French called a waterfall of ringlets. She had brushed the latest fashion in her long tresses—a gold powder scented with heliotrope that turned her hair to burnished gold. It was the latest style to resemble the color of the French Empress Eugenie's hair. It was also considered rather "fast," but then, Ariane thought, brushing Spanish papers across her lips and high on her cheeks to give herself color, that's what attracted a man's eye, and tonight that was all that mattered.

She barely touched the food brought up to her on a tray. Her nerves were tuned to a fever pitch as she pinned on a tiny dark green straw bonnet that tilted down over one eye with a curling peacock feather that brushed her cheek. A last touch of perfume to the pulse points on her neck and she was ready to do battle with the whole Union Army. Surveying her image in the long pier glass, she knew the choice had been right—the dark green set off her tawny coloring, and its rich color appeared just a bit daring and "fast." The Yankee officers would notice her and perhaps want to spend some time on the long train ride in conversation.

"Mam'zelle, I packed you a small valise. If you have to spend any time in La Grange, you will want a change of underclothes and a night dress." She held out a small tapestry bag.

"Thank you, Sable. You might be right. I don't know how long we will have to wait for our return trip."

The sound of hooves coming up the path from the main road told her it was time. The Yankees were coming for her father. They would be in for a surprise, but she wanted to speak with them first, before her father came down from his bedchamber, where he had been resting.

Gliding down the staircase, she arrived in the foyer as the pounding began on the front door. Nodding for Caesar to answer it, she waited at the foot of the stairs.

"Gentlemen, welcome to Fleur de Lys," she drawled softly, sweeping them a graceful curtsy as Captain Williams, the Provost Marshal, and several other soldiers entered the house.

"Miss Valcour, you appear to be going out," Captain Williams observed, his eyes traveling from her pert bonnet down to the tips of her boots. "Might I remind you of the curfew."

"Captain, I wish to request a favor of you if you would be so kind," she said with a purr to her voice and a flirtatious glance as she came to stand close to him.

"Yes." He waited, his eyes fixed on the vee of her neckline where she had inserted a fresh white rose. She had left several tiny buttons unfastened, for tonight was not a time for propriety.

"Could I not go in my father's place tonight on the train. He is not a well man. And it does sound rather exciting. I have seldom traveled by train." She gave a slight smile from under lowered lids at the forbidding figure who stood so still in front of her.

"Yes, I think that could be arranged, Miss Valcour. In fact, I had come with other plans for Mister Valcour since he seems disinclined to take our iron-clad oath, but that would have left us with a vacancy on board our train. How fitting that you have found a solution to our little problem," he told her with a silky menace to his words.

"I don't understand . . ." Her voice trailed off in bewilderment. She floundered before the contempt and lust she saw in his face. It was all going wrong and she seemed helpless to stop what she had put in motion.

"Ah, here is Mr. Valcour," Captain Williams said, watching the halting descent of Ariane's father. Behind him came Justin carrying a leather valise.

"Sir, I am here to make one final request that you sign the iron-clad oath that it might be published in the newspaper for all to see and perhaps convince your friends to do likewise." A silence seemed to echo in the foyer after his pronouncement.

"No," Leander Valcour said simply, holding himself erect, "I will not."

"Then I arrest you in the name of the Provost Marshal's Office and will convey you to Irving Block

Prison. Your daughter has so graciously offered to take your place on the train departing shortly." There was triumph in Williams's voice as he saw the older man's shocked expression and the slump of his shoulders in defeat when he realized there was nothing he could do.

"You are a beast!" Ariane hissed in disbelief, breathless with rage. "You can't do this. You can't arrest him for not taking an oath."

"My dear young woman, I can do anything I want," he said quietly, but with an ominous quality to his words and expression that caused a cold knot to form in her stomach.

"Don't do anything stupid." Justin's voice was a low murmur in her ear as he came to stand next to her as if in some way he could protect her from Williams. His actions were not lost on the Provost Marshal and the man frowned in anger.

"There is no habeas corpus for Southern sympathizers, Miss Valcour," he spat out, gesturing for two of the soldiers to take her father from the house. "You will go with these men, my dear, for—what did you call it? Oh yes, your exciting train ride." His cold eyes swept her figure once more in a lewd glance, then with a cruel smile, he turned and followed the men taking her father.

"Miss, we be leaving now," a young corporal told her, his manner respectful though he was obviously uncomfortable with his mission.

A glazed look of despair spreading over her delicate features, she appeared stunned then somehow, to Justin's amazement, seemed to gather her control. With a shrug of resignation, she lifted her head proudly and glided out the door to the waiting carriage. Never had Justin admired her more than to see her wonderful grace under such terrible circumstances. Never had he loved or wanted her more than he did at this moment

215

when she took on the Union Command with only the weapons of her beauty, poise, and intelligence. But never had she made him angrier than she did tonight when she began once more her games of intrigue, completely disregarding his wishes.

She was up to to something, he could sense it. He could smell it in the seductive perfume she used as ammunition in her battle of wits against the Union officers, see it in the flashy costume she wore that caught a man's eye. Yes, she was definitely up to something, for he knew her depth of feeling for Beau, and to appear in a gown like that when she should have been wearing mourning could mean only one thing. She was out to make fools of them all, a fool out of him once again. He wanted to throttle her; and he wanted to protect her. Eyes blazing, his mouth a taut line, he followed them out to the waiting carriage. She was driving him mad, he thought with both rage and despair as he got in beside her.

"You are going with us," she said with a relieved whisper, remembering with one glimmer of happiness that she would not be entirely alone on the dangerous journey. Justin would be on the train. They were going to pick up wounded.

"Yes, and I will be watching you, so you might as well abandon whatever devious plan you have in that lovely head. I promise you this time I won't cover up for you. It will be my pleasure to unmask you. What a fool you must think me, or am I just one of the dupes whom you practice your feminine wiles upon with such contempt for our easy conquest." His voice was cold and lashing, the angry retort hardening his features as he looked away from her to stare out into the long purple-gray shadows of twilight. "Was it all part of your game?"

"No, you must believe me," she pleaded in a whisper,

reaching out to touch his sleeve.

"It is too bad that I cannot believe a thing you say." He stiffened at her touch.

She sank back against the cushions, feeling weak and vulnerable in the face of his fury, for she could not refute his accusation. She had used him, even though she loved him with every fiber of her being. Conflicting loyalties were tearing her apart, and suddenly she didn't know what to do. She could not turn her back on the South and the Cause that had taken both her brothers, but she could not stop loving this proud, mercurial man that sat beside her. If she lost him, it would be like losing part of herself. How could she go on without him? Yet how could she do what she must without destroying the love and trust that lay between them? There were no easy answers, only a chill black silence in the carriage as they rode on through the Memphis twilight toward the railroad depot and the waiting train.

Chapter Seventeen

The Memphis and Charleston Railroad Station was thronged with army wagons, drays, and private carriages as they drove up in the gathering blue-gray gloaming of nightfall. Armed Union soldiers were standing in front of several of the carriages with rifles in hand. Ariane felt her spirits ebb as she realized they were escorting her other fellow Memphians ordered to ride the train.

"We shall wait here, Lieutenant, till the train pulls in," Justin told the young man who had ridden with them from Fleur de Lys.

"Yes, sir," he replied, alighting from the carriage.

"It shouldn't be long. They are coming from the railroad yards," he said quietly to Ariane. He had sensed her nervousness since their arrival. There was a somber mood about the station, a tense undercurrent that was like a palpable presence in the soft night air.

"Do you know what will be on the train besides Southerners traveling as targets?" Ariane asked with a light bitterness.

"I believe they will be carrying supplies to the various depots along the route. On the return trip we will be carrying wounded."

Clouds of white steam and a mighty roar that shook the carriage announced the arrival of the train. Opening the door, Justin helped Ariane down to the platform. She saw several older men who were friends of her father being escorted toward the waiting passenger cars. They looked at her in surprise, for as far as she could tell, she was the only woman the Yankees had ordered to come to the station.

"I will see you to your seat, then I must join the others in the private car they have attached to the train for our benefit," Justin explained as he helped her up into the second of the two passenger cars. Behind them was the private car and then several boxcars filled with supplies that would be used when empty to transport wounded back from the field hospitals to the main Union hospital center for several states in Memphis.

A confusing rush of anticipation and dread tore through her she entered the long car full of shadows. Oil lanterns swung from the ceiling at intervals down the aisle, casting a dim light. Fighting to maintain some control over her anxiety, she spoke not a word as Justin led her down to the end of the car and gestured for her to take an aisle seat on the last row.

"Next to the window," a burly, rough-featured sergeant barked before she could sit down as he entered the car from the back. He looked familiar to Ariane, and with a puzzled frown, she tried to remember where she had met him.

"The lady sits on the aisle," Justin replied in a quiet, low voice that had an ominous quality to it.

"She's Secesh, ain't she?" He leered at Ariane. "Secesh ride next to the window where they can be seen and make a real nice target for Johnny Rebs with itchy trigger fingers. I got my orders, sir." He made the title sound like an insult. He stared at Ariane as if he recognized her and hated what he saw before him.

"She is sitting here, Sergeant. I will take responsibility," Justin answered in clipped tones that forbade any argument.

"It's your neck, Captain, sir," he sneered, backing

down, but the angry look he gave Ariane told her that she had not heard the last of him.

"I will be in the next car if you need me," Justin said softly as he noticed how pale her face had become during the exchange with the obnoxious sergeant. "I know where I have seen that man before. He is the sergeant who came to Fleur de Lys the morning after my arrival. Don't do anything foolish, Little Bit. He has a score to settle. You must understand how serious this is. It is not a romantic game played by chivalrous gentlemen," he murmured as she sat down in the aisle seat. Reaching up, he placed her valise in the rack above her head, then staring down at her with an intense expression in his dark penetrating gaze, he said so only she could hear him, "The South does not need the life of another Valcour." Then he left her to her disquieting thoughts.

The car was filling with other Memphians as well as Union soldiers. There was a tense stillness in the stuffy coach as civilians were placed in the window seats and Union soldiers took the aisle seats. She sat with a hard knot in her stomach, wondering when someone would be placed next to her. She didn't have long to wait.

"Move over, girly," the sergeant growled as a young embarrassed lieutenant stood waiting behind him. "Your boyfriend isn't here to help you now."

"That's all right, Sergeant. The lady can remain seated. I prefer a window seat," the handsome young lieutenant stated firmly, moving quickly across Ariane to sit beside her in the window seat.

"You're lucky," the sergeant jeered at Ariane before leaving them.

"Thank you, sir." Ariane gave the young man her most charming smile. "And someone told me the war had killed all chivalry. I am glad to see they were wrong."

"We are not all like the sergeant," he replied, his blue eyes sparkling with intelligence and kindness.

"Yes, so I see," she drawled, the corners of her mouth turning up in a gentle, wry expression. "I must say he was right about something, however. I am lucky to have you for a traveling companion."

"As am I, kind lady." He gave a slight bow of his head, having placed his wide-brimmed hat next to her valise on the rack above.

"Allow me to introduce myself," Ariane said softly. "Ariane Valcour."

"Robert Marsh. It is a pleasure to make your acquaintance, Miss Valcour," he said with the fine manners of a gentleman.

A sudden jerk of the car and the train began to glide out of the station. The oil lamps swayed as the train gathered speed, leaving Memphis behind. Mosquitoes circled the golden lights as they flew in the open windows.

Ariane stared down for a moment at her hands clasped in their fingerless, black lace mitts. She could only pray that word had reached Forrest and Captain Henderson that on tonight's train rode Southerners as targets for Confederate guns. It was their only chance, for the Rebel partisans were expert shots, and the passengers silhouetted by the lamp light in the dark night made excellent targets. She wondered with some surprising concern if the kind young lieutenant was aware of the risk he was running. She knew that in the private car behind them, where Justin and other officers rode, all the shades of the windows had been pulled. She and the lieutenant were at the back, thank goodness, and she was shocked to realize that she was worried about the safety of a Yankee. But then, she thought with a catch in her throat, there was something about him that reminded her of her dead brother Charles. Perhaps it

221

was the patrician features or the serious, intelligent look in his kind eyes.

"It is warm tonight," Robert Marsh sighed after opening the window to its full width.

"Yes, August in Memphis can be terribly hot especially if one isn't acclimated to it," Ariane replied, touching a scrap of handkerchief to her upper lip.

"I fear it would be difficult ever to get used to this humidity," he said ruefully.

"In time it gets easier, really."

"How could I ever doubt such a charming lady," he answered gallantly.

Thus began their conversation. Gently with rapt attention, Ariane found out about his home and how long his regiment had been in Tennessee. Where they were headed and when they expected to get there. He told her about the various depots along the train track to the small village of La Grange, and which were strongly garrisoned and which were not. It had been a long time since Robert Marsh had been home or in the company of such a beautiful woman. In fact, he realized he had never seen anyone lovelier than Ariane Valcour. She was like some exotic Southern flower, and so easy to talk to. She seemed to hang on his every word.

Ariane couldn't believe her good fortune. She was learning all the information she needed about the Union troops in the area. When she had a few moments to herself, she would write everything down in the small notebook she carried in her reticule, then encode it using the cipher key in her locket. When she returned to Memphis, she would have important information to send out to Forrest. If only she knew of a Southern contact at one of the numerous stations on the way to LaGrange, she could send word right away. She must keep her eyes and ears open. Perhaps she could find someone she could trust to relay the infor-

222

mation she was learning from Robert Marsh.

"And what stop is this, Lieutenant Marsh?" she asked with a sweet smile as the train began to slow.

"I believe this is the Germantown station," he said, consulting his pocket watch as to the time. "Yes, according to the schedule, this should be Germantown."

Ariane felt her heart skip a beat for she knew the land around the small hamlet of Germantown was in Confederate hands. While the Union troops held the town and station as well as the railroad, the surrounding land was held by Rebel partisans. When stopped at the station, they would make a perfect target for any Confederate marksman hidden in the deep woods on either side of the track.

The train came to a jerking stop and she could feel the tension in the rail car, for all were aware they were in danger. She flinched as did several others when the door to their car was opened. Glancing uneasily over her shoulder, she gave a sigh of relief to see the tall stalwart form of Justin.

"Come to check on your little Secesh filly," the sergeant sneered from where he stood beside the door. "She's being taken care of by another soft-headed fool."

"That will be quite enough, Sergeant," Justin ordered in a terse, quiet voice that allowed no disobedience.

"Yes, sir," he muttered in a sullen tone.

It was as he turned to speak to Ariane that the shots tore through the open windows of the coach. She felt herself being pulled from her seat and thrown to the floor. Panic filled the car as others ducked down between the seat or in the aisle. A low moan from up front told that someone had been hit.

"Stay down!" Justin ordered in Ariane's ear as he kept her pinned to the dusty floor. Another round of gunfire had broken some of the glass in the windows and the splinters flew across the car.

223

The sound of booted feet running past the railroad cars could be heard above the gunfire. The Union garrison was returning the Confederate guerrilla's fire, but Ariane remembered Robert Marsh's words that the Germantown station was lightly guarded. They were taking a beating from the hidden marksman, who obviously had not gotten the word that Memphians were on the train.

The sudden lurch of the train told the passengers they were cutting short their stay. The click of the rails and the sway of the car almost made Ariane ill as she lay half smothered by Justin on the floor. It was only when the gunfire was a distant echo behind them that he helped her to her feet.

Shattered glass lay everywhere as men rose hesitantly to their feet. Union soldiers helped their Southern seat mates to their feet.

"Is there anyone hurt?" Justin called out as he surveyed the wreckage of the car.

"Over here, sir," a young soldier called out. "This man has been grazed on the temple. He is mostly in shock, I think."

Justin made his way to where the soldier stood next to a seated elderly gentleman. "Get my bag, and be quick about it," he ordered the sergeant, who stood gaping in the back of the car. "Now!" The burly man turned and hurried out of the car to do as he had been told.

Ariane was amazed—it was the fastest she had seen the man move all night. Torn by indecision, she didn't know what to do. The narrow aisle made walking difficult in her hooped skirt, but she felt she should be helping Justin. She had been trained at the hospital to bandage wounds.

As she started to make her way up the swaying aisle, something caught her attention. Turning to where she

224

4 FREE BOOKS

TO GET YOUR 4 FREE BOOKS WORTH $18.00 — MAIL IN THE FREE BOOK CERTIFICATE T O D A Y

Fill in the Free Book Certificate below, and we'll send your FREE BOOKS to you as soon as we receive it.

If the certificate is missing below, write to: Zebra Home Subscription Service, Inc., P.O. Box 5214, 120 Brighton Road, Clifton, New Jersey 07015-5214.

FREE BOOK CERTIFICATE

4 FREE BOOKS

ZEBRA HOME SUBSCRIPTION SERVICE, INC.

YES! Please start my subscription to Zebra Historical Romances and send me my first 4 books absolutely FREE. I understand that each month I may preview four new Zebra Historical Romances free for 10 days. If I'm not satisfied with them, I may return the four books within 10 days and owe nothing. Otherwise, I will pay the low preferred subscriber's price of just $3.75 each; a total of $15.00, *a savings off the publisher's price of $3.00.* I may return any shipment and I may cancel this subscription at any time. There is no obligation to buy any shipment and there are no shipping, handling or other hidden charges. Regardless of what I decide, the four free books are mine to keep.

NAME

ADDRESS _____ APT

CITY _____ STATE ___ ZIP

TELEPHONE ( )

SIGNATURE _____ (if under 18, parent or guardian must sign)

Terms, offer and prices subject to change without notice. Subscription subject to acceptance by Zebra Books. Zebra Books reserves the right to reject any order or cancel any subscription.

GET
FOUR
FREE
BOOKS
(AN $18.00 VALUE)

had been sitting, she saw to her horror the slumped figure of Robert Marsh. He lay with his head on his outstretched arm, a small pool of blood forming on the upholstered seat. He had been shot through the right temple. Bending down, she tried to lift up his head, but she could see there was nothing to be done for the young lieutenant. He had been killed instantly.

Ariane felt the trembling start in her legs and then move up through her till she was shaking as if with cold. Life was turning into a nightmare of death all around her. It was too much, too many young men dying and suddenly it didn't matter if they wore blue or gray. Robert Marsh's lifeless body became Beau's, and as she stared down at him, she felt a scream claw at her throat. She tried to stop it, but it tore from the depths of her being. She threw back her head as the guttural cry of anguish filled the car, chilling the marrow of those who listened. *"No—oo!"* she cried. Because of her, another young man lay dead. He had taken her place and had taken the bullet meant for her.

"Get ahold of yourself," Justin ordered harshly, coming to her side, his hands shaking her lightly by her shoulders. "I need your help. This man needs your help." He pushed her forward toward the front of the car. "Get the lieutenant out of here," he said over his shoulder to two soldiers who stood transfixed by Ariane's anguished cry. At his words, they snapped out of it and moved to obey his order.

"There's two more wounded up front, Captain," the now strangely meek sergeant told him as he handed him his bag. "The other medical officers, they are coming to help."

"Thank you, Sergeant. Send them into the other car," Justin said calmly. "Open my bag and hand me what I tell you," he told Ariane, his dark gaze capturing her tortured gray eyes for a brief moment, but long enough

225

to transfer some of his strength to her.

As the train sped on into the hot dark night, they worked in the bad light and the constant motion of the coach, patching up those men who had been hit. All but unlucky Robert Marsh had wounds that were not serious. He had been the only fatality.

"Doc, we're going straight on through, not stopping at Collierville station. Too dangerous," the sergeant confided, returning once more to their car after having seen the other two medical officers to the forward coach. "Them Rebs are like gray ghosts from hell, sneaking here and there, popping up when you least expect it. But they got some of their own tonight, by God." He smirked at Ariane as she cut the thread from the last suture Justin had sewn to close the gash in Mr. McBryde's temple. The elderly gentleman was quite pale, but the sergeant's words put an angry glint in his watery blue eyes.

"You were lucky, girl," the sergeant continued, addressing his remarks now to Ariane. "The Provost Marshal's' Office is not going to be pleased about this at all. You're going to be in big trouble when we get back to Memphis and they find out a Union officer took a bullet meant for your pretty neck. I'll make sure they hear how you charmed that poor innocent lad into taking your place. Why, maybe you were setting him up all along," he mused as the seeds of an idea grew in his suspicious mind.

"We are through here." Justin rose to his feet, addressing Ariane, completely ignoring the intrusive sergeant. "You will ride the rest of the way with me in my compartment. This coach is not fit for a lady," he said, snapping shut his leather bag. Taking her arm, he pushed her lightly toward the door, putting himself between her and the sergeant bent on revenge.

"You better be taking responsibility for this, Captain," the bullying sergeant called after them. "It's going in my report."

The private rail car was partitioned into small separate compartments off a narrow aisle. Opening the second door Justin gestured for Ariane to go inside.

It was dark and private in the small chamber. Two long upholstered benches the size of large settees faced each other. Between them was a window with the shades drawn. Two oil lamps with glass hurricane globes hung on either side of the window. The lamp had been turned low so that only two small golden pools of light shone down the shadowy compartment.

Ariane sank down on one of the velvet-cushioned benches. The terrible strain of the day had caught up with her. She was totally exhausted.

"Here, let's remove that provocative bonnet. You don't need that type of ammunition to charm me," he said dryly, but there was a sparkle in his midnight black eyes. With gentle fingers, he slipped the bonnet and veil from her head.

"I am sure I have no idea what you're talking about," Ariane protested, but even to her ears her voice carried little conviction. The swaying of the train, the rhythmic sound of the rails, was lulling her into a somnolent state. Resting her head against the back of the seat, she closed her eyes. She was so tired, but she was afraid to sleep, for with slumber came the nightmarish images of Beau's pale visage.

"Try and sleep, Little Bit, if you can. You have been through hell today," he murmured, sweeping her feet up on the seat till she was lying full length, her head on a pillow in a linen case.

"I am so afraid, but I cannot keep my eyes opened," she whispered as her own exhausted body took over and pulled her down, down into the realms of Morpheus.

227

How long she slept she had no idea, but when the dream came, she tried to wake up but couldn't. She was trapped, trapped by the terrors of her mind as she ran through a cemetery where the dead rose up to mock her and reach out for her. Ghostly young men in both blue and gray reached out to her for help, but she couldn't help any of them. She only wanted to be free, free from the horror of it.

"Sweetheart, it's all right." A deep rich masculine voice was pulling her away, away from the dark into the light.

Her heavy eyelids flew open and she was looking into the warm, understanding, beloved gaze of Justin. "They were there, they wanted me with them," she gasped.

"Who wanted you?" he asked as if he were talking to a hurt child.

"Beau, Robert Marsh. I caused their deaths," she said, her voice empty of all hope.

"Nonsense," he said sharply.

"No, 'twas because of me they died, even though God knows I didn't want such a thing to happen," she said, sitting up on the seat. "I shall always see their faces." There was a dull despairing look in her huge gray eyes that tore at Justin's heart like a knife.

"Don't say such foolishness. It is a fact of war. Men die, Little Bit, good men on both sides." He placed his firm strong hands on either side of her silken temples, tilting the pale flower of her lovely visage so she had to look into his burning hypnotic gaze.

She wanted to look away, but she was powerless. Those midnight black eyes captured her and held her fast as he looked down deep into her soul. Then as a tear slid down her alabaster cheek, she felt his mouth come down on hers with a swift act of possession and exorcism of grief.

Reclaiming her lips, he crushed her to him, his hands

228

moving to hold her trembling body to his muscular form as if by sheer force of will he could drive out the pain and guilt she felt with the strength of his passion. He wanted to pull her back from her morbid preoccupation with death to the joy and desire of life. His moist, firm mouth demanded a response in a series of slow drugging kisses that allowed no other thought but that of the strange inner excitement she experienced only with him.

A sensual languor grew within Ariane, banishing everything but the delightful shiver of wanting that ran through her. She caressed the rough texture of his uniform, wishing she could feel the warm splendor of his bare skin. He was a lifeline back to sanity and the sweet joy of life in the midst of the overwhelming despair and death that surrounded them.

His hand tangled in her hair, stroking, winding the locks around his fingers as his mouth traced her lips with his tongue then in a trail of lingering kisses down to the hollow of her throat. His other hand sought the white rose, now wilting, tucked in the low vee of her neckline. Gently he pulled it out and slipped it into his pocket. Then his long tapered fingers unbuttoned each tiny button of her jacket. Slipping it from her shoulders, he moaned as her breasts strained above her corset only thinly veiled by the lawn of her chemise.

"We shouldn't," she tried to protest, but it was only a feeble attempt. She wanted him as much as he wanted her and he knew it.

"The door is locked and we have hours till we reach La Grange." His voice was a husky rasp of hunger as he bent to kiss the nipples he had just freed by pushing down the cap sleeves of her chemise. As she lay her head back against the velvet of the high seat with a sigh of surrender, he circled each throbbing peak with his tongue, licking, sucking them lightly till her moans of delight filled the small compartment.

She didn't know if it was the rapid beating of her heart, or the throbbing of her heated blood, or the rushing sound of the mighty train that she heard. Perhaps it was everything blending together into a rhapsody that soared into the sultry air of the Tennessee night.

His hands at her waist, he loosened the hook of her skirt, then the waist of her petticoat, then the tape of her cage crinoline. With a swift downward gesture, he swept them from her figure and tossed them on the other seat.

"I want to touch and taste all of you," he whispered against one full ivory globe that was raised high by her corset. "Stand up," he ordered in a voice raspy with desire.

Drenched in the fiery passionate hunger he had awakened, she obeyed, swaying a little with the train. Mesmerized by the burning coals of his eyes that devoured the lovely sight of her, she threw back her head and gave a low sensual laugh of triumph and joy, her hands at her tiny waist, her proud breasts, their hard coral tips erect and throbbing from his touch. "Like this?"

"I shall remember this night for the rest of my life, and the sight of you here before me always, always." There was a melancholy reverence to his husky whisper as he drank in her beauty. Then he slowly turned her around that he might unfasten the strings of her stays. They, too, joined the rest of her discarded garments.

She took a deep breath for the first time since the torturous satin and lace garment had constricted her waist hours before. "That is heavenly," she sighed as his hands gently massaged the cruel red marks left on her skin by the corset. Then his fingers moved up to caress the voluptuous fullness of her breasts that he cupped in his hands, circling the peaks till he heard her breath

230

quicken.

Whirling around to face him in a graceful move, she murmured playfully, "Now it is my turn." Her fingers unbuttoned the metal buttons of his tunic and he smiled with sensual pleasure at the feel of her small hands on his chest. Shrugging out of his jacket, he pulled off his linen shirt, then unable to control himself any longer, he lifted the perfect globes of her ivory breasts to his mouth and kissed first one then the other rose pink tip.

"Oh my dearest love," she moaned, the words torn from deep within her being.

"I can wait no longer, my sweet Ariane," he told her softly, lifting his head as he slipped the delicate lace-trimmed pantalets from her hips. His eyes black and depthless in the dim golden lamp light, smoldering with the depth of his hunger and need, never left her face as she stepped out of the discarded garment and kicked it aside.

When her hands touched his belt buckle, he quickly unbuttoned the dark blue trousers and pushed both pants and boots off to join with her pantalets in a pile on the floor. His small clothes followed in one swift gesture. He stood before her, his lean, sinewy form glowing bronze in the lamp light as they swayed together in the rhythm of the train. Masculine arms wrapped around soft feminine curves, pulling her down, down to straddle his strong hard thighs. She sat on his lap, but facing him as his hands at her tiny waist held her there.

She should feel embarrassed, she thought, to sit so completely nude except for her stockings and shoes, but somehow she did not. With Justin, everything seemed right. The bond between them made their lovemaking seem natural, a spontaneous outflowing of the depth of their emotion.

Slowly they kissed, a long sensuous caress of lips and tongue, tasting, feeling, exploring the textures of the other's mouth. Hands stroked, caressed tenderly, speaking as only touch can do of what was in their hearts. Then need and overwhelming desire fueled the heat within them till their veins were coursing with the fire that threatened to engulf them.

Throwing back her head as his mouth slid down to her breasts, she reveled in the sensation of exquisite longing that was soon to be fulfilled. Never had she felt so alive, so aware of every sense, every tingling nerve. Her nails dug into the muscles of his shoulder as her hunger rose, driving her hips to move against his hard thighs covered in their delicious masculine fur. He shuddered in joy at her uninhibited pleasure in their lovemaking.

"Yes!" she gasped as his hand sought her most intimate petals, stroking them, preparing her for him. She was wild for him, holding nothing back. The depth of her need to have him inside her, to join totally and completely with him, was everything.

As he lifted her up to position himself, his eyes caught hers and she smiled a sensual smile of such other rapture that it took his breath away. Slowly, he eased her down, down onto him, erect, throbbing, and waiting for the perfection that was Ariane.

She caught his shoulders, and her moans filling the heated air as he pushed into her moist welcoming depths. With a movement as old as time, she took him further still, meeting his thrust, bearing down upon him in circles of yearning.

Neither wanted it to end, the exquisite sensation, the dark frenzy of being caught up in something greater than themselves. They moved on and on, thrust and counterthrust, till the rhythm of their bodies seemed to be one with the great pulsating engine that was driving the train through the dark, hot Southern night.

She was soaring, rising and dropping, with each powerful hard masculine thrust. They were one passionate entity and it was beyond anything she could ever have imagined. Her husky laugh of pure joy rippled out as she rode him faster and faster, higher and higher. His moan of total happiness was a counterpoint to the melody of her jubilant delight.

Then it was as if she exploded into a heart-stopping crescendo as waves of molten ecstasy shook her, taking him with her to the pinnacle. Black eyes locked with wide gray ones that were stunned with what she was experiencing, and they crashed over the edge as their souls touched for a breathless moment. This was what they had been destined for, what they had sought and not even known it, and for one split second that seemed to last for an eternity, they knew they were two halves of the same whole. The new being—the one they had made from the joining of two—was more important than war, than promises made, than anything. Holding each other, exhausted by the depth of what had happened, they spoke not a word. Yet each knew deep in their soul that what had happened could not change anything, that somehow they would have to leave this small enchanted chamber return to the separate paths life had set for them. The only question was how would they ever be able to do it? How would they live with the pain of it?

Chapter Eighteen

Ariane stirred on the bench where she lay in her chemise and pantalets, the only clothing she could stand in the heat of the compartment. Justin had insisted she try to sleep. A long night lay ahead of them, but she drifted in and out of slumber. It was only the reassuring sense of him so close to her that allowed her to relax at all. Somehow just being near him gave her such a calm feeling that everything would be all right. What an irony, she had mused in the last moments before she drifted off—that she felt safe in the company of Union officer. Whatever else he was, he would always be Justin, the perfect knight of her childish dreams

He reclined on the opposite seat, his long legs, encased once more in his blue trousers and boots, stretched out as he tried to get comfortable in the cramped quarters. The slight breeze through the open window barely stirred the drawn shade. His linen shirt clung to his back as he drew on the stem of his pipe. The smoke of the tobacco seemed to keep out some of the pesky insects of the August night. Try as he might, he could only catnap, but as an Army medical officer, he had learned to get by on short naps.

Suddenly he realized what had awakened him this time. They were stopping. The need to take on more water for the steam locomotive made it imperative that, Confederate threat or no, they stop at this station.

"What is it?" Ariane asked sleepily, pushing her

tangled hair from her eyes.

"I think we are stopping. Perhaps you had better finish dressing. 'Tis always dangerous to stop along this railway at night," he said.

"You will have to be my lady's maid," she teased, reaching for her corset and petticoats.

"I shall be happy to serve you in that capacity, however much I wish I could continue to look at you in the charming costume in which you are now attired," he replied with a sparkle in his expressive dark eyes.

The dressing process took longer than necessary, for each garment was accompanied by caresses and light kisses in the hollow of her neck, the bend of her arm, the curve of her ear. He refused at first to tighten the corset strings as tightly as she had to have them for the minuscule waist of her skirt.

" 'Tis a barbaric instrument of torture. It does terrible things to your organs. I wish I could abolish them completely," he muttered, finally agreeing to pull them tighter when Ariane told him she would never be able to don her gown if he did not.

Dressed once more, Ariane despaired of doing much with her hair except pull her brush through the unruly locks. It was difficult, for the heat and humidity made her tresses heavy and unmanageable.

"Here, let me do that," Justin said, coming to sit beside her, taking the brush from her hand. Slowly, gently, he pulled the boar bristles through her tangled red-gold tresses with long even strokes.

Ariane bent her head back, relishing each sweep of his hand. It was a sensuous, intimate experience and she gloried in it. She sensed he did also.

"I am regretting that I asked you to dress," he whispered in her ear as he slid the brush down the strand of golden silk that he held in his fingers.

A rapid tattoo on the door startled them both from

the lovely intimate circle where they dwelled far removed from the reality around them. It was what was almost mystical about their relationship that when they were alone together it seemed they entered a private universe where the rest of the world could not follow.

"I must answer that," he murmured, placing the brush on the seat beside her. Rising, he strode the few feet to the door. Opening it only a few inches, he asked, "Yes, what is it?" There was a murmured response before he answered, "Yes, two cups. Thank you."

Opening the door wider, Justin took two steaming mugs from the large tray a young corporal held in his outstretched hands. Handing one to Ariane, he closed the door firmly on the gawking young soldier.

"We shall reach La Grange in another hour. They brought hot coffee on the train from the station. I thought you might like some. I don't think either of us will be able to sleep." He smiled down at her as if he was memorizing every line of her delicate face and form. "I am sorry, but there is no cream or sugar."

"It is strong and hot," Ariane said wryly. "Right now that is enough. 'Tis more than most others have in these parts, I am quite sure." She sipped the dark brew gingerly.

"Yes, I think we crossed out of Shelby County some time ago into Fayette. This part of Tennessee has seen a lot of devastation. I wonder how we will find La Grange?" he mused, sitting across from her. Now that the world had intruded on their idyll, it seemed impossible to keep their thoughts from the uncertainty of what was yet to come.

"It was such a lovely place before the war. They called it La Belle Village. It was named, you know, after the Marquis de Lafayette's estate in France. He came through here years after the revolution, and they named the village in his honor. I went to school near there one year when there was much sickness in Memphis," Ariane told Justin as she sat lost in remembrance. "Papa was worried about me so he sent me to the Marshal Private Female Academy. It was about four miles south of La Grange at the residence of a Mr. George Wyatt. A kindly gentleman and his wife, the Plunketts, were the directors. I am afraid I didn't learn as much about the classics as Papa would have liked, for they had horses to ride and the countryside was so beautiful that summer and fall. I couldn't wait for classes to be over so I could ride free over those lovely meadows," she confessed with a light laugh. Then her visage sobered as she said, "I suppose it has much changed as has everything else with the war. All those elegant houses in La Grange and the magnificent plantations surrounding it probably are in ruins. I wish I could remember it as it was instead of having my beautiful memory destroyed with the reality of what war has done to everything."

"The South will have to cope with much harsh reality when this war is over, but then most already have had that fact thrust upon them," Justin said quietly. "The romantic dream is over, Little Bit, and I fear the awakening is going to be brutal and hard."

"Yes, the Yankees will see to that. They will want their revenge," she said bitterly, then stopped suddenly as she realized for the first time she had admitted that the South would be defeated. When had that realization crept inside her heart? When Beau lay dead in a pine box, Beau the gallant devil-may-care cavalier, gaunt and haggard in threadbare clothes, his bright wit and love of life stilled forever.

"Yes, some will, not all, but enough that the South will suffer greatly if the ones who do have their way. That is why, my brave, beautiful rebel, I want you to

237

become my wife as soon as possible. It is the only way I can protect you and your father from what is sure to come. I offer you the shelter of my heart and my name." He placed the mug on the small narrow table in front of the window and leaned across to take her hand. His extraordinary eyes burned above the hard bronze planes of his intense face. Those black orbs showed the entire man. They were luminous with the gentle strength inside him, contrasting with the fierce visage that often appeared remote and implacable.

It was what drew her to him, she thought with a pang of love that was almost like pain. How could she resist such words? Could she marry him to save her father and to give herself the perfect cover to help her poor beleaguered South? For no matter how strong her love for him, she would not go back on her word to her compatriots. She would fight with her friends till the last man surrendered even if the cause was already lost. Her sense of honor would not allow less, but would it allow her to marry a man she would deceive, and perhaps put in danger if she was discovered by his comrades to be a spy for the Confederacy? She felt torn in two by her love for Justin and her love for the South.

"I . . . I don't know. What you say makes sense, but I don't know . . ." Her voice trailed off as she found the strength to look away from those eyes that held her to him like bonds of steel.

He felt the rapid throb of her pulse in the delicate wrists he held in his hands. He knew she was not wanton, that she did not give herself lightly to him, but there was something stopping her from accepting him. It was what would always stand between them. He felt a cold anger build within him. Her precious, foolish cause meant more to her than anything between them. It was that same stiff-necked Southern pride in Memphis society that had turned against him after the duel with his brother and believed the lies of shallow Olivia Whitlaw. His own father would not believe that his favorite son Clay would be less than a gentleman and dally with his own brother's fiancée, but his other son, the one with the radical ideas, yes, he would gladly believe anything about him. One must always behave a certain way, play by the rules in Southern society, or risk banishment and disdain. He had never played by the rules and so he had been cast out. It had hurt, but he had recovered and hardened his heart. What a fool he had been to expect this pampered belle to risk anything for him. She was a product of her class and heritage. He wore the uniform of the hated enemy, the enemy who had killed her brother Charles and indirectly caused the death of Beau. Her father was being held in a Union prison on a flimsy trumped-up charge. How could he expect her, under such circumstances, to marry a Union officer? Her friends and family would consider it an act of treason.

"We will make no decision tonight, but think about it. Your father's health will not allow him to survive long in the hellhole of Irving Block Prison. Do not take lightly the stories you have heard about the prison they have called the Bastille of the South, for they are all true. Even though President Lincoln sent a team of investigators down here last spring and temporarily cashiered the Provost Marshal for the conditions they found there, not much has changed. General Grant intervened, and as you know, George Williams was reinstated as Provost Marshal and commandant of the prison. He has a grudge to settle for the humiliation of being cashiered," he warned, letting go of her hands and leaning back against the seat.

Ariane knew what he said was right. She gave a light shiver—Sable would say it was a premonition of bad times ahead. There was a sick feeling in the pit of her stomach at the thought of her father at the mercy of the prison guards. If there was a way to get him out of such a place, shouldn't she take it, for it he had to stay there very long, she knew it would cost him his life. He did not have the stamina to endure many days in the "Bastille of the South."

The next hour was spent in a strained silence as Ariane pretended to nap while Justin read through some papers he had brought with him from Memphis. Even with her eyes closed, she was so aware of him, she thought with a sad frustration. The scent of his pipe tobacco, the slight rustle of his papers, the merest brushing of his boot against her skirt as he shifted position, they were all constant reminders of Justin, her bittersweet love, her betrayal.

"We are slowing down," Justin announced, breaking the long silence, "we must be coming into La Grange. Stay close to me and say nothing. I have told the others you have volunteered to help nurse the wounded. In this capacity you will be under my command."

Ariane nodded, her nerves too taut to speak. She watched as he rose and went to the window, lifting the shade slightly to look out. La Grange was safely in Union hands. They would not have to fear being shot at by Confederate partisans when they disembarked. She could only wonder how much of the lovely village was still intact after being occupied so long by the Yankees.

It was pitch black when they left the train. There was only the dim light of the kerosene lanterns on the depot to show them the way over the rough boards of the platform. Carrying her own valise, Ariane walked beside Justin. She was aware of the stares from the other medical officers as well as the other Memphis hostages as they straggled behind them.

"We will be taken to a house that is being used for a hospital. It is why you must make good my story about volunteering as a nurse; the other Memphis passengers are to spend the night in the depot," he explained tersely. "It could be several days before we return to the city. I am afraid your fellow Memphians are going to be very uncomfortable until they return home."

Ariane's hands tightened on the handle of her valise. She fought to keep her anxiety under control. Justin was beside her, her bulwark against the frightening unknown that seemed to lurk just outside the small circle of light thrown by the lanterns.

Leaving the others at the depot with Union guards, she, Justin, and the other medical officers were met by a sergeant and several young soldiers, who stood beside several horse-drawn Rucker ambulance wagons. They were new and the first ones Ariane had seen having been built by the Union right before the Battle of Gettysburg. A great improvement over the springless converted freight wagons that had been used, they were obviously much more comfortable for the patients. She thought with a sinking heart that the Confederacy didn't even have enough medicine while the Yankees had new, luxurious vehicles for their wounded. Suddenly a terrible bitterness and sense of defeat came over her in waves. How could the South continue to fight against such odds?

In a daze she allowed Justin to help her up into the high canvas-covered wagon. They sat along the side on boards with the other doctors. The other ambulances were quickly filled with supplies from the train and they were off into the still hot night.

"Does anybody know where we are going?" one young doctor inquired as he slapped at a persistent mosquito.

"Tranquillity Plantation on the edge of La Grange,

sir," the corporal driving the mule team yelled over his shoulder.

"Did he say Tranquillity?" Ariane asked Justin in a low voice.

"Yes. Why, do you know the place?" he replied.

"It is the home of a girl I knew at the Marshal Academy, or at least it was before the war. I visited her once there on vacation and we wrote for a while, but with the war, correspondence was impossible." Ariane's voice trailed off, remembering the elegant Greek Revival mansion that had risen majestically from the end of a long alley of enormous cedar trees. Did the Paytons still live there now that the Yankees had taken over, she wondered. With a flash of irony, she thought of how surprised her friend Eugenia would be to see her again, especially with her blue-clad escort.

There was a thin gray line of light on the eastern horizon as they rode down the main dirt road that led through the village of La Grange. As the black of night began to fade to the pearl light of day, Ariane was able to see that most of the houses she remembered still stood, although some of the neat white picket fences were missing. Lawns were torn up by the hoofs of the Yankee horses and flowers and shrubbery were trampled. Tents were pitched in some of the yards and the wood smoke of camp cooking fires hung in the sultry early morning summer air. In front of one elegant mansion the remains of an armoire stood in solitary splendor beside several army tents. The soldiers had obviously looted the house before setting up camp. Ariane trembled when she thought of what they would find when they came to her friend's old home. The medical officers were silent and avoided meeting Ariane's eye. Justin's firm jaw was clenched, his mouth grim as he looked at the belongings of the owners scattered about the lawn.

242

The sun was rising as they turned into what was left of the gates of Tranquillity Plantation. One gate sagged on broken hinges while the long white fence connected to it had broken boards and sections torn out of it. A rooster crowed his salute to the day from somewhere behind the house as they rode down between the giant cedars, their fresh astringent fragrance perfuming the air. There were no tents pitched on the grounds of Tranquillity, but a huge Union flag hung from over the front door. On one of the soaring pillars, someone had tacked a crude board sign with the words U.S. HOSPITAL scrawled across it.

Ariane felt weary tears prick at her eyelids as she stared at where a sword had cut a gash across another column in what appeared to be a deliberate act of vandalism. The house had been so beautiful once, so fitting of its name, but now one could hear the moans of the wounded coming through the open windows. She felt dizzy for a moment as Justin helped her down from the ambulance. The fetid smells of a front-line hospital in the heat of August reached her nostrils, almost making her retch from the overpowering stench. A mockingbird trilled in a cedar tree behind them, and the normalcy of it seemed almost absurd in the face of such suffering and horror.

"Thank God you're here, we can use all the help we can get," a gruff voice greeted them as a bewhiskered army surgeon appeared on the threshold of the door of Tranquillity. The cloth he had tied around his waist was dark with bloodstains. "Those damn Rebs have been raiding every station along the railroad, and with this new drive of Smith into Mississippi looking for that devil Forrest, we can expect to be full up. We need those that can travel to be taken out of here as soon as possible to Memphis."

"That's why we are here," Justin said quietly. "I am

243

Captain Pierce, these are Captains Blake, Anderson, and McSwain. Miss Valcour is a volunteer nurse from Memphis," Justin explained in a voice that allowed no further comment as the surgeon's eyes swept over Ariane's face and figure with contemptuous surprise. "And whom do I have the pleasure of addressing?"

"Captain Silas H. Kruger," he said wearily. "Welcome to Tranquillity, gentlemen." A brief twisted smile of irony curved his stern mouth, then was gone as he gestured for them to follow him.

Ariane would never have recognized the elegant house she had once visited. Wounded men lay everywhere on pallets spread on the heart of pine floor that was dull and stained with blood. All the graceful imported English furniture was gone; dark patches on the smudged wallpaper were all that was left of where paintings had hung in gilded frames. Over a marble fireplace mantel in what had been the dining room still hung an enormous mirror in a curved gold-leaf frame. It was still in good condition if streaked with dirt and dust, but as the sun streamed in through the long windows, it caught the glass and reflected the macabre scene of sick and wounded men lying below. A chandelier hanging in the center of the room had been used by someone for target practice — all the crystal pendants had been shot out.

Ariane stared about her in mute horror, realizing how lucky they had been at Fleur de Lys. Houses in Memphis had received some damage from their Yankee "guests," but nothing like what had been done at Tranquillity. Then a disturbing thought struck her through — if this is what they had done to the house, what had happened to the Paytons? She had to ask.

"Captain Kruger," she called after the harried surgeon, "what has happened to the family that used to live here?"

"They're living in the overseer's house. Just a young woman and her mother. The old lady is sick so for humanitarian reasons we let them move in there. The staff is staying in a few rooms upstairs, but I am afraid the rest of you will have to move in with the Paytons. I don't know if there is enough room, but there were several bedrooms. If there is not, the old lady and her daughter can move into one of the slave cabins that haven't been burned."

Ariane seethed with mounting rage that had begun when the surgeon had said he had let the Paytons stay on their own property for humanitarian reasons. He had smirked with self-righteousness as if he should be commended for his good deed. Justin, as if he read her thoughts, gently touched her arm in warning to keep her anger from showing to the captain.

"The sergeant will show you out to the overseer's house. Leave your bags. There is coffee and breakfast in the kitchen house. We are expecting more wounded today up from Mississippi and Smith's campaign according to the telegraph transmission received this morning at the rail depot," Captain Kruger told them as he led them through the house to the back door opening on to the ruined kitchen garden. "God knows where we are going to put them."

The sergeant led them through gardens trampled by dozens of horses, past the still standing brick kitchen house now taken over by the army cooks. The stables that had housed the Thoroughbreds of Tranquillity Plantation were now housing army mules and horses. A few chickens and one old rooster still ran around an enclosed pen, but all the other livestock were gone. In the distance, Ariane could see ruined cotton fields, the plants trampled or burned to the ground. She felt sick at the sight of the once prosperous plantation in ruins and realized that she had seen few negroes since they had entered the grounds. Where had all the slaves gone?

The overseer's house stood at the end of the ruined rose garden. It was a raised-cottage-style house, and here in the side yard inside a patched fence someone had planted a vegetable and herb garden. As they approached the small veranda, a black woman in the gingham dress and tignon of a house servant came outside, a broom held in her hands like a weapon.

"What yo' want?" she questioned, a scowl creasing her round face.

" 'Tis all right," a soft cultured voice reassured her from around the corner of the house. A thin, tired-looking young woman with auburn hair pulled back in a chignon low on her neck came from the direction of the garden, a basket on her arm. Her dress was of a faded muslin without hoops, and to Ariane's surprise she saw the woman's arms and face were sunburned. "Yes, can I help you?" The young woman's voice was polite, but wary as she approached them.

"Eugenia!" Ariane gasped in sudden recognition. This was her friend dressed in rags and sunburned from working outside. Lovely Eugenia with the delicate complexion of a redhead. She had always been the belle of every school ball where the young gentlemen from surrounding academies and plantations had flocked to dance with the fair Eugenia.

"Yes . . ." The young woman's voice trailed off as she held her hand up against the rays of the morning sun to see who had called her name. "Ariane, Ariane Valcour, is that really you? Whatever in the world are you doing out here with a Yankee escort?" Eugenia Payton cried out, dropping her basket and running to embrace an equally tearful Ariane.

"These officers and the lady are to be billeted with you and your mother, Miss Payton," the sergeant said awkwardly, interrupting the reunion between the young women. "If you could show us what bedrooms are theirs."

"Yes, Sergeant," Eugenia replied, wiping the tears from her cheeks with the corner of her threadbare apron. Taking her basket from Justin, who had quickly retrieved it from the ground, Eugenia gave a smile of thanks and led them into the house.

The heavyset black maid called Myrtle followed them with a suspicious frown as her mistress showed the four men to two bedrooms on either side of the front door. They had belonged to the overseer's sons, both long gone with their father into the Confederate Army.

"I am sorry but we will have to double up. This cottage is not as large as the main house," Eugenia explained, "but there is a trundle bed underneath each four-poster. Ariane, honey, you can stay with me. Mama is staying down below in the room next to the summer dining room. It is cooler down there, and she had been feeling so weak and ill. My room is the former master bedroom. Mr. Adams was a widower so we shall have plenty of room now that he and his sons are gone with Forrest's men."

"They are with Forrest," Ariane repeated softly, glancing back over her shoulder to make sure Justin and the other doctors were moving into their bedchambers.

"Yes," Eugenia repeated, and a light came into her weary blue eyes. "Honey, you are up to something, I can tell, and I can't wait to hear what it is," she whispered with an excited giggle that reminded Ariane of the high-spirited Eugenia of old.

As Myrtle unpacked Ariane's valise and hung her night rail and peignoir in a pine armoire, the two young women traded confidences of what had been happening in their lives since the hardships of the war had changed everything so irrevocably. Eugenia's eyes filled once more with tears as she explained her father had been killed at Shiloh and her brothers were with the Army of the Tennessee. She had not heard from them in months. If it hadn't been for the food given to them by the Yankee doctors, she and her mother might have starved. The fields were in ruins, the slaves except for Myrtle and a few other house servants had all left, and the livestock had been killed by the first wave of marauding Yankees and bands of roving deserters.

"It has destroyed my mother's mind, Ariane. When they took the books from Pa's library and burned them in the front yard along with his portrait, she just went crazy. She took after them with an old hunting gun that had belonged to Pa. They took it away from her before she could hurt anyone, thank goodness, or they might have shot her right there. Then they took it all . . . furniture, dishes . . . they chopped up the piano and burned it. They even took the old cradle from the attic, and that broke Mama's heart, for she had sat by it and rocked and sung to her babies as they lay in that cradle. You know, the last of her babies, my little sister, died in that cradle so to her it was kind of sacred. She begged them, Ariane, got down on her knees and begged them not to burn it, but they wouldn't listen. She was never the same after that," Eugenia said in a trembling voice, her hands clenching and unclenching nervously. "They would have burned the house too if a Yankee major didn't ride up and decided because it was so large it would make a fine hospital. They, the doctors, took pity on my mother and allowed us to live here in the overseer's house. It hadn't been touched so we took what clothes we could recover from where they scattered them over the front lawn and moved in here. We did have the foresight to bury some of the silver in the ground and hide some of our clothing, Mama's wedding dress, and some heirloom jewelry in the attic.

They never found that, and if we are lucky, it will still be there when they leave—if they don't burn the house," she sighed.

"It has been bad in Memphis, though not so much destruction of property," Ariane confided. "But Eugenia, I need your help. Is there any way I could send a coded message to Forrest's men? I have information that would be very useful to them. You see, I have a cipher key," she explained after Myrtle had left the room to press one of the dresses Sable had packed in case Ariane needed it. Ariane was thankful the woman had been so far-seeing, for it looked like they could be in La Grange several days.

"Yes, there is a way," Eugenia admitted in a low voice. "If we have information about troop movements or some such thing, we leave it in a small tin box placed inside a stone urn in front of a certain grave with a bouquet of flowers placed on the gravestone. Every Saturday night it is checked by one of the raiders who ride all through the woods between here and Holly Springs and harass the Yankees along the railroad. We have circulated the story that the graveyard is haunted so most of the soldiers don't go there, especially at night."

"And tomorrow is Saturday." Ariane smiled with satisfaction.

There was a sharp rap on the chamber door, startling both women. Eugenia rose to her feet and glided to the door, opening it a crack. "Yes?"

"Please ask Miss Valcour to come to the door," Justin said politely.

"One of the Yankee officers wants you, the handsome one," Eugenia told her after shutting the door behind her. "There is something about him that quite makes one forget his uniform," she mused, watching a blush tinge Ariane's cheeks. Her friend had not told her everything, Eugenia thought with interest.

"Yes, you wished to speak with me," Ariane said softly, coming out into the hall and closing the door behind her so Eugenia could not hear their conversation.

"Please change into more suitable attire if you have it and come with us to the hospital. I have told them you are a nurse and we require your services. You are being carefully watched, Little Bit. Do not do anything foolish. I shall wait here; be quick." His voice was terse and cold.

"Yes, sir," she answered with an angry flash of her gray eyes, turning on her heel and slamming the door shut as she went back into the bedchamber.

The sun was high in the sky, sending down unmerciful heat on the hospital, as Ariane and Eugenia tried to make themselves useful to the Union doctors. Ariane followed Justin, writing down the names of the patients who were to be moved to Memphis and then pinning a corresponding tag to the remnants of each man's clothing. Eugenia carried water in an oaken bucket and helped the wounded drink from a tin dipper. The women tried to close their ears to the pitiful moans from those men in the throes of fever's delirium, and to endure the stench of wounds festering in the humid heat. After several exhausting hours, both women agreed it no longer mattered if the men were Yankees. Most were suffering young boys, some who had never been off their family farms, some newly arrived immigrants who barely spoke English and certainly had no idea what they were fighting for, having been paid to fight for some wealthy man's son. They were all in pain, frightened, and homesick.

"Are you all right?" Justin asked Ariane after she had helped to prepare the body of a twenty-year-old for burial. She had held the boy's hand as he died. Gently she closed his eyes and crossed his arms over his breast and then pinned the toes of his stockings together. As the other men watched with haunted eyes, she pulled the sheet over his face.

"The terrible thing is I don't feel anything but numb," she murmured, staring up at him, her gray eyes huge in the pale weariness of her delicate visage.

"Come away from here. There is nothing more you can do for him now," Justin said softly, his hand on her arm, leading her firmly from the parlor through the maze of pallets containing wounded men. "I could use a cup of coffee and I am sure you could too. Your friend Eugenia has gone outside to fetch more water from the well," he told her as he noticed her frantic glancing around the foyer for the other woman.

In the shade of the trees it was a bit cooler than inside the stifling hospital. Ariane took a few deep breaths of the fresh, scented air. She sat on the remains of a garden bench as Justin went into the overheated kitchen house, where army cooks prepared meals for the soldiers. There were always several pots of strong black coffee hanging over the coals in the huge brick fireplace.

"Good Lord, what are they doing?" Ariane asked, taking the mug of coffee Justin handed her. It was thick and sweet with real sugar. The Yankees had everything, she thought with a sigh, knowing that the Confederates didn't even have coffee. She pointed to where several soldiers were starting smudge fires of burning tar in barrels outside the open windows of the hospital.

"There have been several deaths from malaria, what the men refer to as the 'Ague,' or bone shake fever. Some believe that the disease can be prevented by burning tar around the hospital, but the only medicine that seems to work once the disease progresses to the shaking fever is quinine. Some doctors are taking a small

251

amount each day as a preventive against coming down with the fever. The Northern troops, not being acclimated, seem to be more susceptible, but I have heard from Southern prisoners that they, too, are coming down with the disease, if not in such great numbers," Justin explained as they sipped the strong, hot coffee.

"And the South does not have quinine," she muttered in bitter tones, "nor sugar, nor coffee."

"No, they do not," he answered quietly, turning to look at her with sadness in his dark eyes. "Perhaps you can understand now what I have been telling you—that the South cannot win against such overwhelming odds. It is only a matter of time, and time is on the side of the Union."

"That smell is awful. It will make the men feel worse," Ariane complained, gesturing toward the burning barrels of tar.

"Did you hear what I said?" he asked, setting down his cup. Taking hold of her forearms with firm hands, he made her face him. His black eyes captured her tortured gray orbs, holding her gaze by the force of his will as he waited for her answer.

"What do you want from me?" she hissed, fury and despair almost choking her.

"I want you to face the truth so you won't do anything foolish," he told her, his fingers pressing into the flesh of her arms.

"I will never turn against my own people, no matter what, no matter how easy it might be for you." She watched as his face paled as if she had struck him.

"You are a stubborn little fool to throw yourself away on something that is already lost." His voice was quiet, yet held an undertone of contempt as he released her and rose to his feet. "We are needed inside." He turned and left her to follow him to the hospital, which was becoming a charnel house in the humid heat.

The long afternoon finally died into the purple shadows of twilight, and the medical officers from Memphis, as well as Ariane and Eugenia, were allowed to seek the sanctuary of the overseer's house and the evening meal. Too hot and tired to talk, Ariane and Eugenia stripped the clothes from their bodies and, standing in two tin washtubs in their bedchamber, poured pitchers of tepid water over their heated forms as they made use of the scented soap Ariane had brought with her.

" 'Tis heavenly," Eugenia exclaimed as she held the perfumed soap to her nostrils. "I thought I'd never smell perfume again," she sighed.

They heard the doctors outside swimming in the small lake that was behind the house. It seemed they were not the only ones seeking relief from the heat and stench of the day.

"I declare, now that I have bathed, I feel quite human—human enough to want to take a peek at those men outside," Eugenia teased as she donned clean underclothes.

"Eugenia, really! After all, they are Yankees. Look what Yankees did to your house," Ariane reminded her with a frown, trying not to think of Justin's lean body and the delight it had given her.

"Well, it wasn't *those* Yankees. Why, they seem like gentlemen, and it has been so long since I have seen any Southern gentlemen," Eugenia explained, trying to rationalize even to herself. "I have seen you with that Captain Pierce. The sparks positively fly whenever you two are together," she said. "And the way he looks at you when you are not aware of it. Honey, his eyes smolder, really they do. It has been so long since any man looked at me that way."

"Eugenia, have you anything else I could wear?" Ariane asked, trying to change the subject. "It is really

253

too hot for the green silk gown I wore on the train, and the dress I wore today was all I brought with me."

"They are all pretty threadbare, I am afraid, but you are welcome to anything that will fit," she said generously, throwing open the doors to the armoire. "When the war is over, I am coming to Memphis for a new wardrobe, if I have any money, that is." She gave a resigned shrug.

"And you will stay with me at Fleur de Lys," Ariane said, giving her a quick hug of reassurance. Eugenia would have a new wardrobe—she would make sure of it. It broke her heart to see her friend, who had always been so elegant and stylishly dressed, in worn, patched gowns. But for now she also would wear one of these much-washed dresses. Picking out a pale blue muslin with patched lace at the neckline, she stood while Eugenia helped her don the garment. Worn over her hoops, the ruffled skirt billowed prettily from a tiny waist, but the bodice was tight, for Eugenia was flatter in the bosom. The neckline was indecently low with her breasts mounding above.

"You will turn their heads at dinner tonight," Eugenia giggled as they stared at Ariane's reflection in the pier glass.

"Perhaps they will be too tired to notice," Ariane muttered, her delicate brows drawn together in a frown. Her cameo looked indecent nestled between her breasts, calling attention to the décolletage of her gown.

"They would have to be dead not to notice you," Eugenia teased, then they both looked stricken as they realized they had been joking about death, and it was all around them.

"I reckon if we don't laugh, honey, we will cry," Ariane told her friend. "Sometimes in Memphis at the hospital we will laugh over the silliest things just to break the tension."

"Maybe if you left off the locket. It is rather large," Eugenia mused, looking at her friend.

"I can't let this out of my sight. Here, let me show you," Ariane whispered, opening the locket to show the small brass cipher code wheel inside.

"Lord almighty, you really are a spy," Eugenia breathed, her blue eyes enormous in her small heart-shaped face.

"We must find time tomorrow to go to the cemetery and leave that note. Who could we say we were visiting?" Ariane queried as she closed the lid of the locket.

"My father's grave," Eugenia said softly.

"Oh honey, I am sorry, but yes, it would be the perfect cover."

"Then that is what we will do. He would be happy to think he was still helping the Confederacy," Eugenia said sadly, her eyes misting.

The medical officers were dressed and awaiting them in the small parlor. Eugenia, a magnolia blossom tucked in her chignon, swept into the room as if it were the splendidly furnished parlor of the main house in the days before the war. Justin's eyes darkened as he saw Ariane and the seductive neckline of her gown. Her hair was piled in loose curls at the back of her head, since her head ached too much for a chignon. Eugenia had insisted she pin two gardenia blossoms on either side of the curls.

"We are honored by two such lovely ladies," Justin drawled as he rose to his feet at their entrance.

"Why Captain, I could swear I heard a Southern accent in those words," Eugenia trilled, giving him a flirtatious smile. "You have been in the South too long. Whatever will your family think."

"Sadly, my family is all gone, but since they were Southerners, I think they would be happy I kept a trace of my homeland in my speech, Miss Payton," Justin replied politely but with a cool edge to his words as if he were waiting for her reaction.

"What part of the South are you from, Captain?" Eugenia continued, her blue eyes darting from Ariane's uncomfortable visage to Justin's frozen mask.

"From right outside Memphis, ma'am," he replied tersely.

"Of course, the Pierces of Cedar Rest," Eugenia mused. "Although I have heard of your family, sir, I am sorry to say I never had the pleasure of their acquaintance, and I truly regret to hear that will not now be possible." Turning toward the other officers, who stood in embarrassed silence, she gave a pretty social smile and said, "Shall we retire to the dining room, gentlemen."

Captain McSwain moved quickly to her side and held out his arm. Justin with a swift step was beside Ariane, claiming his right to be her escort. Stiffly she placed her hand on his rigid arm and they followed their hostess down the short hall to the small dining room.

Ariane sat at one end of the pine table and Eugenia at the other, the men taking the side chairs. Myrtle and the old butler began to serve from a crude pine sideboard as if they were all at table in the Tranquillity mansion before the war, only the quality of the furnishings, the dishes and the food, showed that unmistakably times at changed.

A thin vegetable soup was the first course, served in plain white crockery bowls with flatware of pewter instead of silver. Remembering the days when she had visited the plantation in its glory, Ariane was saddened at the difference, but she admired Eugenia, who was the perfect hostess, acting as if nothing had changed.

The conversation was stilted despited Eugenia's best effort. Captain McSwain seemed thoroughly captivated by his hostess and tried to lighten the atmosphere with banter and jokes she alone seemed to find engaging. Ariane was conscious of Justin's brooding presence on her right, and although he spoke little, she felt his intense gaze sweep over her from time to time. Their previous conversation still rankled her, and perversely she wanted to punish him, hurt him as he had hurt her. With a lovely smile, she turned to Captain Blake on her left and began to engage him in conversation. She could sense Justin's anger and she reveled in it. Why couldn't he see that she could never turn her back on the South? It always came between them, their divided loyalties. With a pang as sharp as a knife, she realized it always would, that it would never allow them to be totally committed to each other. But she would never allow the heartache to show on her smiling face. She had learned the social graces of a Southern hostess and lady at the same academy as Eugenia. It was a most effective armor to keep the cruel world at bay, but it did nothing to stop her heart from breaking.

It was as they were finishing the last of the rather meager meal that there was a sharp rap on the front door. Signaling the old black butler to answer the door, Eugenia asked Myrtle to serve the coffee in his stead.

"Captain Pierce, a young lieutenant is here to see you from the depot," Eugenia announced after the butler whispered a few words in her ear.

Placing his much-mended napkin on the table, he excused himself and went out into the hall. The others stared after him with curious eyes, all wondering if this was the order that they would all have to load the tired wounded men on the train for Memphis. They had hoped for another day's grace, that the wounded from Mississippi would not arrive so soon. Trying to pick up the thread of conversation, they tried to pretend that they weren't dreading finding after such a long day they might have to spend an equally long night on a train.

"Miss Valcour, if I might have a word with you." Justin's commanding voice turned all eyes to where he stood in the portal. In the golden glow of the tall bayberry tapers on the table, he seemed to dominate the entire chamber, even somehow to diminish it.

The smudged gray of her eyes were dark with apprehension as she stared back at him and rose slowly to her feet. Something was wrong—she could feel it. The bond between them was so strong that she sensed his agitation. He was frightened for her. She knew it suddenly as if he had spoken, but he had said nothing. It happened like this sometimes between them, their thoughts, their hearts, communicated without words.

Her red-gold curls caught the light and sparkled like gold coins in the candle glow as she moved toward him. He clenched his fists at his sides to keep from reaching out and pulling her to him, shielding her with his body. There was no other course he could take if he wanted to protect her. It must be done. The mere thought of another man's hands on her lovely ivory body made him wild with rage. No matter where her loyalties lay, no matter how wrong others might see it. It must be done and done quickly.

Stepping aside so she could leave the chamber, he followed her out into the darkened hall. The young lieutenant stood waiting, turning his wide-brimmed hat in his hands, and he cleared his throat nervously.

"Tell her what you just told me, Lieutenant," Justin ordered, his voice grim, each word spat out in terse tones.

"There is going to be an order for your arrest presented to you when you leave the train in Memphis. The sergeant has been bragging about it all day and wired the Provost Marshal to be waiting for you when the train arrives from La Grange. I thought the captain

258

should know," he finished, nervously stroking his mustache.

"That will be all, Lieutenant. Thank you for the information," Justin said in dismissal. He waited for the young man to leave before he turned to Ariane. Reaching out, he pulled her to him, his firms hands holding her possessively to him. She trembled both from fear at the lieutenant's words and the nearness of Justin.

"What shall I do?" she whispered, staring up at him.

"You shall become my wife here in La Grange. There is a small church. I saw it when we came in, and there is a chaplain attached to the hospital. I know how you feel about the uniform I wear, but my name is a fine old Southern one and I offer it to you as protection. But in return I ask for your complete loyalty. No longer shall you engage in any activities that could be construed by the Union Command as aiding or abetting the South. I wish I could turn away, let you suffer the consequences of your foolish allegiance, but God help me, I cannot. You have gotten inside me, Little Bit, and no matter how hard I try to excise you, the thought of you, the feel of you, lingers till I think I shall go mad. It is an insane time for us to be drawn together, but fate is capricious, and I have stopped trying to question it. What is between us is there, it exists." His voice was a husky rasp as his eyes blazed down at her with desire and something that looked almost like anger.

Numbly she stared back at him, knowing within the deepest part of her being that what he said was true. They belonged together, no matter how impossible it seemed. She was no fool, and had no desire to suffer at the hands of the Yankee guards, who would show no mercy. She could not help the South or her father inside Irving Block Prison, but the thought of marrying Justin and continuing to deceive him tore at her heart.

259

She knew, however, that no matter what vow she made to him, she would never turn her back on the South, even if it meant beginning her married life with a lie.

Pressing her with a maddening arrogance, he asked, "Well, my dear hot-headed Rebel, what is it to be, marriage to this Yankee devil, or the hell of Irving Block Prison?"

Chapter Nineteen

The late afternoon sun slanted through the open windows of the small master bedchamber in the overseer's house, falling across Ariane as she stood quietly in the center of the room. Eugenia and Myrtle slipped the delicate ivory silk and lace wedding gown fashioned in the style of over twenty years before over the stiffened silk crinoline petticoat around Ariane's waist. The petticoat and the gown stored for years in a trunk in the attic of Tranquillity were to be worn once more by a bride. The stiffened crinolines felt strange to Ariane—they had been fashionable in the 1840s, when the wedding gown had been made. They felt very different from the huge cage steel hoops of the 1860s that she was used to.

" 'Tis beautiful," Eugenia breathed as the silk gown, faded a delicate ivory with time, belled out from Ariane's tiny waist. "And it fits so well. I wish Mama was able to understand what is going on today. It would make her very happy to see her wedding gown worn once more."

"Thank you for allowing me to wear a gown I know your mother kept for your wedding day," Ariane said softly as Eugenia fastened the many tiny buttons up the back of the low, off-the-shoulder bodice with its deep bertha of fine duchesse lace.

"At least it will be used again for a wedding. Little did I guess when I hid it in the attic that it would be used so soon. But Captain Kruger was most understanding when I explained why I wanted to go up and fetch that old trunk. I think it helped immeasurably that 'twas a Yankee officer you were marrying," Eugenia said with a light laugh as she remembered Captain Kruger's face when she explained why she needed two soldiers to go up in the attic with her to carry down a trunk. "Please take the gown and veil with you and keep it for me in Memphis. If I am lucky when 'This Cruel War Is Over,' as the song goes, I shall find I am need of a wedding gown," she sighed, turning for the veil Myrtle held in her hands.

"You don't think what I am doing is wrong?" Ariane asked in a low voice as her friend placed the veil of fine duchesse lace on the fall of curls that rippled down her back to her waist. Carefully Eugenia pinned a wreath of honeysuckle and gardenia blossoms to the veil so that it encircled Ariane's red-gold hair resting above her forehead where tendrils were curling from the heat and humidity across her brow.

"You love him, you said so yourself, honey. I am just thankful that he is here and can keep you from that awful place when you get back to Memphis," Eugenia said briskly, handing her the fingerless ivory lace mitts for her hands. "You will not be the only Southern woman to marry a Yankee before this war is over, or afterwards for that matter. I sometimes wonder if, when the bloodletting is done, there will there be any men left at all to marry North or South. Take your happiness when you can find it, for too soon it can be snatched away."

Ariane's somber gray eyes met Eugenia's in the long silvered pier glass. "You have put the message on the gravestone?" she asked, for today was Saturday, and in spite of everything, she had to leave the coded message for Forrest's men, the message that told which rail depots were heavily garrisoned and which were not, and which roads into Memphis were heavily guarded and which were not. The information she had gleaned from the poor dead Lieutenant Marsh had to be relayed to the general.

"Yes, when I took flowers to the church, I took a nosegay to the cemetery. I told the sentry at the gate that this was my father's birthday and I wanted to honor his grave," Eugenia explained, handing Ariane her wedding bouquet of gardenia blossoms. "I wish for your wedding the flowers could have been roses, but with the garden destroyed, I am afraid we had to make do with what was left."

"They are beautiful, and gardenias are my favorite flower," Ariane reassured her, lifting the bouquet to inhale the seductive fragrance.

"Good. Well, then, I think we are ready. I would like for Mama to see you, but Myrtle says she is having one of her bad days."

"Yes, ma'am, that's right. Poor Miz Claire is real confused today. 'Twouldn't help to add to it," the maid said, shaking her head.

Eugenia, dressed in an old ball gown she had found in the trunk with the wedding dress, accompanied Ariane as her attendant. It was years out of date, but the lavender silk was in quite good condition and looked lovely on her with her auburn hair. Ariane noticed that several of the medical officers were unable to take their eyes off the fair Eugenia as they rode to the church as an escort. The women rode in the old carriage the soldiers had left untouched when they tore through Tranquillity. Decorated by the Payton butler with shafts of cedar branches and magnolia blossoms, it appeared almost like the pre-war wedding carriages of happier days.

As the sun set in a brilliant blaze, the carriage

263

swayed under the spreading branches of the cedars along the narrow path to the small chapel. It was surely the strangest wedding procession the village of La Grange had ever seen. As they rode past several houses, only the moving of a lace curtain at a long window told them they were being observed. Soldiers in Union blue rode before and behind the bedecked carriage containing the two Southern women dressed in bridal finery.

"When you are gone, everyone will want to know the story of what happened. I will be deluged with questions," Eugenia giggled. "Why, Tranquillity might become as famous as Lucy Holcombe Pickens House. Did you know they call her the 'Queen of the Confederacy,' what with her having her picture on the Confederate one-dollar and hundred-dollar bills. The Yankees are letting her family's house stand even if she is married to the governor of South Carolina. I thought they would have burned it for sure, but then you can never tell what they will do," Eugenia prattled on, trying to distract Ariane, for she could see how tense and pale her friend had become as they rode up before the small church which had been vacant since the war. The circuit-riding preacher had not come to La Grange since the fighting had begun.

Set in a grove of cedars, the small chapel was lovely as long streamers of dying sunlight fell through the myriad branches of the tall trees. The door stood open and a line of blue-clad soldiers stood out in front. Ariane felt her hands tremble as Justin appeared in the doorway of the church then in a few lithe strides was beside the carriage. After helping Eugenia out onto the carriage block and down to the ground, he turned and held out his strong firm hand for Ariane's lace-clad trembling one.

"Since your father is not here to escort you, I shall

do the honors," he said softly, helping her to the ground. "Always I shall remember how beautiful you looked on this our wedding day."

She looked up at him through a mist of tears. This was not the way she had pictured her wedding, but it was the man she had always dreamed of as her husband all those years ago when she was standing on the brink of womanhood. It might be all wrong, but this was in many ways her childish dreams coming true. This was Justin, her knight come once more to rescue her, even though instead of shining armor he wore dark blue. He was her beloved Justin, her enemy, and soon to be her husband.

Her hand on Justin's arm, she followed Eugenia and Captain McSwain into the church. Her mouth curved into a smile as she saw how much care Eugenia had taken in so little time to make the chapel quite beautiful. Vases of curving branches holding exquisite alabaster magnolia blossoms nestled in their shiny dark green leaves stood everywhere. The lemony fragrance of the huge blooms perfumed the sanctuary. A tall brass candelabra stood on the altar with flickering tapers adding their golden glow to the streamers of rose-tinted light from the setting sun coming through the stain-glass windows.

As they started down the aisle, a soldier rose in the back of the church and began to play the haunting song "Lorena" on the flute. Ariane glanced up at Justin and gave him a sweet smile of thanks for remembering.

The army chaplain stood waiting at the altar. The words of the marriage service joining her to Justin seemed to echo in the tiny church and her heart. As the chaplain asked for the ring, she was startled to see Justin take a gold band from his pockct.

"My mother's," he whispered. "She left it to me for my bride. I have kept it always with me as a talisman."

265

After repeating his vow, he slipped the ring on her finger.

Then as the chaplain declared them man and wife, Ariane felt Justin's strong arms pull her to him and the wondrous safety and rapture of his embrace. As his lips slowly descended to hers, he whispered, "You are mine, Little Bit, now and always."

Her mouth met his and she quivered at the sweet tenderness of his kiss that reached down, down into the depths of her soul. They were now man and wife, and no matter what lay ahead for them, for this one perfect moment she knew total and complete happiness.

The ride back to Tranquillity through the mauve-violet twilight was filled with the flirtatious laughter of Eugenia and Captain McSwain and a quiet joy between Ariane and Justin. Their hands were clasped, and a warm current seemed to run between them, connecting them with an invisible bond. Tonight they would spend their first night as man and wife in a small guest house deep in the woods of Tranquillity that had been used as a bachelors quarters before the war, in what was called a *garçonnaire* in Louisiana. Eugenia had insisted they spend their wedding night there in privacy. Although only two rooms, the structure and its furnishings had been left virtually untouched by the soldiers, for it was well hidden in a dense grove of trees on the other side of the small lake. Their fingers entwined as they rode toward Tranquillity through the soft lavender haze of twilight, the newlyweds were both filled with a wild yearning for the night to come.

"You can't leave us yet," Eugenia teased as they drove up in front of the overseer's house. "Captain Kruger was able to get hold of a chicken, a tough old bird I am sure, but tonight we will have roast chicken for dinner, and the last of my father's brandy."

The dinner was filled with laughter as Eugenia played

the perfect hostess, and the Union officers responded to her hospitality with fine manners and good spirits. To Ariane, the evening had a feeling of unreality about it. A wedding dinner where there were only two women present without a single member of her family, and all the guests were Yankee officers. As if Justin could read her thoughts, he placed his hand over hers as it rested on the patched lace tablecloth. The warmth from his touch seemed to flow into her. Turning toward him, she met his compelling gaze that told her he understood, but nothing really mattered except that they were beginning their life together on this strange night, in these unusual circumstances.

At last the meal was over and the toasts drunk in the last of the fine old French brandy from Eugenia's father's wine cellar. The carriage was brought around once more and several of the officers left to make one last round of the wounded at Tranquillity. Seated next to Justin, dressed still in her wedding gown, Ariane waved a farewell to Eugenia standing in the light of the open door of the overseer's cottage, Captain McSwain at her side. Then they were off riding the short way through the overgrown road to the guest house hidden deep in the woods.

The sultry Southern night was full of the sounds of summer as Justin helped her down from the carriage and nodded to the old black driver to leave them. The sounds of the peeper frogs filled the humid air around the still dark lake as the moon rose over the water, casting sparkling silver streamers across the pond as if in their honor. Several oil lamps lit by a servant sent to straighten the cottage cast a welcoming mellow glow through the open windows as they stepped on the tiny veranda encircling the structure. The guest house was a tiny Greek temple, a replica of the mansion of Tranquillity. Opening the door, Justin turned to her and, with his devastating smile, swept her up in his arms, her full skirt trailing down his blue clad legs, and carried her over the narrow threshold.

"Eugenia has seen that everything is in order," he murmured as he closed the door behind him with his foot. He carried her into a small parlor with fine English furniture in the style of Queen Anne. Lace curtains hung at the windows and several glass hurricane lamps had been lit on the walnut tables. A huge basket of magnolia branches had been placed in the empty fireplace, and a wicker picnic basket covered with a linen cloth was on the carved mahogany pedestal table, used before the war for bachelor guests' card games that went on into the night.

Letting Ariane down slowly, Justin kept her close within his embrace. The memory of their night on the train from Memphis had made his sleep restless the night before, despite his exhaustion. Now that they were alone in this enchanted place, he felt his blood pound with anticipation for the rapture that lay ahead of them.

"I have waited long for this night, even when I didn't realize what I needed to fill the empty place inside my heart was you," he said, his voice husky with need and desire.

"I, too, dreamt of this night from that first time when you rescued a frightened mixed-up girl and showed her a caring and compassion that she had never known was possible. I thought I'd never see you again when you walked out of my life so many years ago, but like one of my childish dreams, you came back to me. And now here you are once more rescuing me like the knights of Sir Walter Scott. How does one say thank you for always being there at precisely the time I most need you," she whispered through the ache of emotion caught in her throat.

"I want more than your gratitude, my dearest Ariane, my wife," he demanded in a rasp of barely controlled passion, his words a faint whisper of air on her cheek as he cupped her soft visage in his hands so he might look deep into her eyes. "Tonight I want to feel you under me, the soft warmth of your body, the silken touch of your skin, the sweet taste of your mouth."

When his lips came down on hers, she reacted with all the strength of the desire he had aroused within her. Her arms wound around his neck as she flung herself against him, her mouth opening under his like a parched flower to the rain. With a moan, he crushed her to him, her skirts a rumpled impediment to be torn away with his hands, shaking with need and hunger. Buttons and hooks were unhooked, or torn open, till the gown fell open down her back. Tapes and hooks on her petticoats were similarly torn open. Caught up in the whirlwind of passion and emotion, she helped him, twisting and turning till her garments lay in a pile on the polished boards of the wooden floor, the veil and flowered wreath having fallen beside them.

Sweeping her up in his arms, he strode in a few lithe steps into the other shadowy chamber to the enormous mahogany four-poster with its soaring emerald-green satin canopy. The bed was draped in the fine ivory mosquito netting so it appeared to float in the room as if in a cloud.

"One moment, I want to see you, every beautiful inch of you," he murmured as he struck a Lucifer stick and lit the tall bayberry tapers in the brass candelabra. "There," he said, staring down at her, his black eyes becoming glowing coals of desire in the candlelight. Then his hands were everywhere, stripping her of the last impediment her corset, chemise, and pantalets.

She stretched against him like a languid kitten, the warm, humid air caressing her skin as did his wonderful, knowing hands. Her blood was aflame with the fire he had ignited with his words, his touch, the feel of his mouth. She wanted to feel all of him, the heated skin, the sinewy muscles. Small hands pulled at the buttons of his tunic, to his wondrous delight. Driven by his need to feel naked skin on skin, thigh on thigh, chest against soft full breasts, he pulled his clothes and boots from his body till he stood nude before her. His long, lithe masculine form glowed bronze in the light of the tall fragrant tapers, his midnight black eyes smoldering down at her, touching her everywhere with his intensity.

"Feel my heart, how it is beating like a wild trapped thing." His voice was a raw husky whisper of hunger as he caught her hand and held it to the soft black fur of his chest. "Touch me, sweetheart. Know how much I want you."

Her hands caressed the masculine fur of him, the sinewy satin of his muscles, down, down, learning the contours of his beloved body. Then she felt his hands on her shoulders, bending her back so his mouth could trace down the ivory column of her throat in a trail of fevered kisses.

Lifting her up, she felt her feminine softness pressed for a moment against the hard warmth of his body then she was swung up and across the dark green satin of the counterpane. The cool touch of the fabric was another sensuous delight on her fevered skin. Then he was beside her after pulling the gold cord that held up the mosquito netting. It fell silently around the bed till it engulfed them in a hazy soft ivory fog.

How beautiful she looked with her red-gold tresses spread out on the green satin, the dark verdant color a magnificent contrast to the peach-ivory of her skin, he thought, his blood pounding in his veins, a tightness in his loins that was almost pain. He wanted to prolong each moment of this night in this enchanted oasis in the midst of war. For a brief rapturous time they could pretend none of the horror outside these walls existed. This was their world bordered by the ethereal cloud of netting that encircled the bed. For a few brief rapturous hours they would make time stand still and love like there was no tomorrow, for the morrow would bring only the pain and heartache of reality. Tonight was magic, a wondrous respite that few were ever given when they were allowed to experience the joining of two into one, body and soul. They were both aware of how lucky they were, of how kind fate had been to allow them to find one another and celebrate, for this splendid night, the perfect joy of being together.

She stared up at him as his hand spread out the glory of her hair against the emerald satin. His dark eyes were fathomless in the dim light of the tapers filtered now through the filmy net. His gaze swept down from the pale oval of her face across her body as if he was memorizing every curve. Then one bronzed hand caressed her cheek, gently down the hollow of her throat and on to the soft curve of her breast. Encircling the pear shape, he caressed the throbbing coral peak in a light sensual motion, never taking his gaze from her smoke gray eyes, which were wide with wonder and arousal. Her hand, as if it had a will of its own, lifted and she stroked his chest, teasing him as he had her.

"Ah, yes, Little Bit." He gave a ragged sigh. Then as he moved his hand lower across her tiny waist to her slender hips, she followed his lead on his sinewy body. When his long fingers found the sensitive velvet of her womanhood, she reached for his throbbing shaft. Wrapping her tiny fingers around him, he moaned with joy as he stroked her with a sensual touch, showing her what rapture was to come.

Then his mouth was on hers, their tongues entwining with the fever of their passion. They clung, sucking, bruising, unable to get enough of the taste and feel of the other. Their bodies were at the peak of their desire held at bay only by force of will from seeking the complete fulfillment both wanted with a dark frenzy that threatened to overwhelm their resolve.

She saw the smoldering fire in his black eyes as he left her burning mouth to trail his kisses down to the erect rosebuds of her breasts, which she lifted, twisting her body as if presenting him with a gift. Her nails grazed the skin of his back then cut into him as she reached to press him closely to her as if she could never get enough of his mouth and tongue. She felt as if she had never been so alive as she was at this moment. And she was aware of everything around her—the smell of the sultry summer night, the heady perfume of the gardenias in a bowl beside the bed, the masculine scent of Justin's silky raven-black hair as he bent lower to trace the curves and hollows of her form till he reached the silky intimate curls he brushed with his lips, the fur of his mustache a sensual caress against the skin of where her thigh met her hip. There was only the hot molten flow of her desire, the wet of his burning mouth, and the dark, steamy perfumed night.

He could wait no longer. He had to have her, feel the silken warmth of her around him. Rising over her, he lifted her slender hips and pressed into her waiting depths as she arched up to receive him. "My love!" It was torn from deep within him as she moved with him. They were one, she part of him, he part of her. Together they were the very essence of life, flying, soaring, becoming the very affirmation of life in the midst of a deadly war. Shudder after shudder of soul-reaching joy flooded them as they found their ecstasy, forgetting that there would ever be a tomorrow. They were invincible in their love, like all lovers since the beginning of time.

It was as they were lying entwined in the bittersweet

afterglow that they heard the shots, a rapid burst of rifle fire from somewhere quite far away in La Grange. As Ariane lightly stroked the fur of Justin's chest and he kissed a tendril of her hair, the candlelight caught the gold of her wedding ring. As she stared at the golden circle, she knew the cause of the gunfire. Forrest's Scouts were checking the cemetery, having seen the signal left by Eugenia. Had they gotten her coded message signed "the Swan," or had they been caught?

A cold chill cut through her like a knife. What would Justin think if he knew that his new bride had, on her wedding day, broken the vow she had given him? She had begun her married life with a lie, and she was beginning to realize how it would haunt her. What had she done in marrying Justin, knowing that she had no intention of stopping her spying for General Forrest and the Confederacy.

"Is there something wrong?" Justin asked, caressing her arm.

"No," she lied softly.

Do not worry about the gunfire. 'Twas probably just a sentry firing at shadows."

"I am sure you are right," she sighed, staring at her wedding ring against Justin's chest. The war had once more intruded on their lives, and she realized with a heartbraking certainty that there was more to come. Tears misted her gray eyes as she wondered if the war would destroy her marriage as well as everything else in the South.

Chapter Twenty

Steamy late-afternoon heat pressed down on Tranquillity Plantation and the Federal hospital, compounding the already difficult work of loading patients into ambulances. Justin stood bare-headed with shirtsleeves rolled up under the blinding sun, directing stretcher bearers, some of whom were convalescent men who were able to walk. In the Union Army, the movement of the wounded was the responsibility of the Army Quartermaster Corps, not the medical staff, but they, having no medical training, had been particularly rough on some of the more serious cases. In his frustration, Justin had taken over, insisting on better care of the patients. It had earned him some black looks and complaints from some of the rougher-looking soldiers of the Quartermaster Corp, but they had sullenly obeyed him.

Ariane, having said her good-byes to her friend Eugenia, stood on the veranda, checking off the name of each man carried out of the hospital on a list of those who would be leaving for the Memphis train. From time to time, she would look up to stare for a brief moment at her husband of only twenty-four hours. His commanding presence, and calm voice, reassured her in the chaos of the loading of the patients, and she was aware that he had the same effect on the men.

She stood lost in thought, staring at how a shaft of sunlight gleamed bronze across the arresting planes of his handsome, strong visage. His hair was dark as a raven's wing even in the penetrating afternoon light. Had it only been hours before that she had been held in those arms, against that chest. Their wedding night seemed to have happened eons ago, for with the first light, they had been brought breakfast by Myrtle and the Paytons' butler, as well as brass containers of water for bathing and a fresh change of clothes. Insisting Eugenia keep the green walking costume in which she had arrived, Ariane donned the gray dress she had brought with her and worn to work in the hospital. Myrtle had washed and ironed it so it was presentable for the trip back to Memphis. There had been tears when she told Eugenia good-bye at the overseer's house. She had made her friend promise to come to Memphis whenever she wanted, and that Fleur de Lys was always to be considered her second home. Eugenia agreed, explaining that she and her mother could not leave Tranquillity at present, or it would be considered abandoned by the Union troops, as had so many other plantations, and sold to some eager speculator who followed in the wake of the army.

"Miss Valcour, er . . . Mrs. Pierce," an embarrassed Captain Kruger interrupted her musings.

"Yes, I am sorry," she said, turning away from the compelling sight of Justin.

"That is the last of them. You and the others will be leaving in the last ambulance," he told her, wiping the sweat from his forehead with a crumpled much-used handkerchief. "Give that list to your . . . your husband," he said awkwardly. "They will need it once you get to Memphis."

"When will the new wounded arrive?" she asked, more to break the strain between them than anything. She felt the captain's disapproval of her, and wondered for the first time how other people would react to the news of their marriage once they got back to Memphis. Everything had happened so fast, there had been little time to think of the many ramifications of what she was doing.

"According to the telegraph, a few hours after your train leaves La Grange. Ah, here is Captain Pierce to escort you to the station," the medical officer said with obvious relief to be rid of her.

"Good-bye, Captain Kruger," Justin said as he picked up Ariane's bag, the other man already having turned to go back inside.

"Er . . . good-bye. Thank you for all your help. Hate to lose such able doctors." He stumbled over his words, avoiding looking at Ariane. Holding out his hand, he shook Justin's saying, "Good luck. Heard there was some business in La Grange last night, some sentries thought they saw some Rebs prowling around the cemetery of all places. They shot back and then took off like the gray ghosts they are. Hope they don't bother you on the way back into Memphis."

Ariane felt her pulse pound at Captain Kreuger's words. Forrest's Scouts had seen the signal placed by Eugenia. Had there been enough time before they were spotted by the Yankees to retrieve the coded message? She imposed an iron control over her emotions to keep the two men from seeing her excitement and concern.

"The train will be heavily guarded, Captain, but that has not stopped them before. Perhaps we will be lucky and they are otherwise engaged," Justin said with an edge to his voice. The Union Army seemed to have trouble even finding these Confederate Scouts that made lightning raids on the railroad and then disappeared into the countryside they knew so well without a trace.

The ambulance in which they were to ride contained several patients with fractured legs suspended in new devices that kept the men from suffering excessively on the bumpy roads. Helping Ariane up next to the driver, Justin swung up beside her, giving the signal for them to leave for the station.

As they rode down the shaded alley under the boughs of the stately cedars, their fresh astringent scent a welcome respite from the stench of the hospital, Ariane took one last look back at the mansion, still elegant despite the treatment it had suffered under its new occupants. The house glowed alabaster in the intense white light of the sun at the end of the jade tunnel, and for a moment she remembered it as it had been in those carefree golden days before the war.

She turned away from the sight, and from the bittersweet memories. Eugenia was right to stay and protect her land, her heritage, but Ariane trembled for her friend, for all of them. How could the South stop such well-equipped invaders? They believed as strongly as did the Southerners in what they were doing, and they had such limitless supplies of men, horses, food, medicine, and weapons. An almost overwhelming sense of hopelessness came over her in waves. She had to grip the edges of the hard wooden seat to gain control and keep from crying in despair.

"Eugenia will be all right. I know Captain Kruger seems a hard man, but he will see she and her mother are not harmed. Tranquillity has too much value to the army to be burned," he said softly, leaning so his words were not heard by the others.

"How thankful we should all be to the Union Army," Ariane muttered in bitter tones. She felt him stiffen beside her. He had only been trying to be kind, having sensed her pain. She felt a pang of remorse that she had snapped at him, but her anguish was so great that, despite her love for him, she couldn't help hating the uniform he wore and venting that despairing anger in his direction.

They rode the rest of the way through La Grange in a tense silence. Ariane was, after having spoken with Eugenia, much more aware of the damage to the village. She saw with a heavy heart the site where the La Grange Synodical College had stood. The entire male graduating class of 1861 had volunteered for the Confederate Army. When Federal troops had entered La Grange, they'd torn the college building apart to get the bricks. Some of the bricks were used to make flues for the fires that warmed the Yankee squads assigned to the lonely hazardous duty of guarding the tracks and bridges of the Memphis and Charleston railroad against Confederate raiders. Nothing remained of the college. She could only hope Tranquillity did not come to the same fate.

The small rail station was crowded with Union soldiers, and the ambulances backed up to where they were unloading the pale sweating men on stretchers into the boxcars that had held supplies from Memphis. There were so many sick and injured that some were placed in the parlor cars with the men who were hostages from Memphis. Ariane noticed how tired and worn her fellow Memphians looked from their days spent held in confinement in the small crowded depot. She also noticed to her dismay the looks she was getting from her fellow hostages. It was clear they had heard of her marriage to a Yankee officer, and their disapproval was a palpable presence in the sultry air filled with gritty smoke from the steam engine.

"This way," Justin said firmly, his arm about her shoulders as if protecting her from the hostility of the other Memphians. He led her through the confusion of soldiers and patients to the private car for officers.

As she placed her foot on the first step into the car, she looked up into the familiar disagreeable face of the sergeant. A wave of revulsion came over her as he placed his hand under her arm to help her up into the car.

"Well now, if it ain't the captain's new wife," he sneered, his fingers pressing hard into the flesh of her arm. "A real quick worker you are, but it's not going to save you from what you deserve. I'll see to that," he hissed low in her ear so Justin couldn't hear.

As their gaze met for a brief moment, she felt a shock run through her at the hatred she saw in those porcine eyes. Pulling her arm from his grasp, she recovered her wits enough to glare back at him. It was impossible, however, to still the anxiety that surged through her at the certain knowledge that the sergeant meant to do everything in his power to cause her harm. His enmity was a black aura of hate that seemed to reach out for her with invisible tentacles of malice.

"Ariane, what is it?" Justin questioned from behind her as she stood transfixed by the sense of danger that came from the man who stared at her with such loathing. She had not realized before how much the Yankees could hate their enemy, as strongly as any Southerner who felt his home was being invaded. For one brief moment, she realized that the war had come down to the two of them, and to the Union sergeant, she was the embodiment of evil. It struck her to the depths of her being.

"Nothing, 'tis nothing. I just felt giddy for a second. I am all right now," she said with a catch to her voice, turning away from the sergeant. Quickly she moved down the narrow passageway to the sanctuary of their small compartment.

" 'Twill be cooler once we get under way," Justin commented as he closed the door behind him then crossed to the window, opening it wide so what little air was stirring could freshen the small chamber. "Is there anything else wrong?" he asked, sitting across from her

279

after putting her valise and his portmanteau under the benchlike seats.

She gave him a wan smile that did not touch her sad silver-gray eyes. "You know me so well." She spoke in a broken whisper. "The way they looked at me . . . as if I were a traitor," she said with a great weariness, pulling out her long hatpin and removing her straw chip bonnet. She felt a throbbing in her temples, the result of the heat, tension, and despair.

"Did you not think that might be the reaction of your fellow Southerners," he said gently, leaning toward her and taking both her hands in his, stroking her fingers in a slow, tender caress. "I wear the wrong color uniform," he teased lightly, his dark eyes capturing hers, seeming to probe and penetrate into the hidden corners of her soul.

"Yes, I have noticed," she answered with a bittersweet smile. "Somehow I didn't consider, didn't even think of what others would say, not even my own father." She stopped, looking away from that all-seeing gaze that threatened to consume her with its intensity.

"Has that not been the way between us from the beginning, nothing mattering but this bond that binds us together. I am not saying it will not be difficult, but my dear, you had no choice. You are not a traitor because you choose to help your father out of that hellhole or because you followed your heart. Did you follow your heart when you married me?" his deep-timbered voice asked in a velvet murmur that was edged with steel. His mesmerizing black eyes would not allow her to look away.

"Yes, God help me but I did," she gasped, almost in anger.

"Then it cannot be wrong, for always, my sweet Ariane, we will have this." With these words he was beside her, pressing her to him, molding her soft trembling mouth to his as if to sear her body with the memory of what rapture they knew when they were in the private world of their embrace.

Her hands reached for him, caressing the muscles of his back through the rough tunic as she clung to his burning mouth, as if only here in the circle of his arms was she safe and sure of her course. He caressed her lips with his tongue, tracing their outline and then inside as she savored the taste of him.

The sudden start of the train caused them to pull slightly apart with a dazed expression that soon turned to a low sensual laugh. They had been so lost in each other they had forgotten for a few delicious moments where they were and why.

"You drive me wild, my bewitching Rebel," he whispered against her hair, his breath warm on the shell of her ear. "I want to take you here and now, again and again. Do you want me, my sweet wife, as I want you?"

"Yes, oh yes!" she moaned, pressing herself to the heated ecstasy of his mouth once more, entwining her tongue with his in a deep, devouring kiss.

The knock that sounded on the door was an intrusion they at first tried to ignore, but as the rapping became more insistent, Justin reluctantly lifted his mouth from hers. "Yes, what is it?" he called, not letting her go from his embrace.

"Captain, you're needed up front. A man broke open his sutures in the front passenger car. He got in some kind of argument with one of those Memphis men. The other doc sent me for you. All hell's breaking loose up there, blood all over," the soldier called through the door.

"I will be right there," Justin answered, looking down with regret at Ariane's lovely upturned face. Touching his finger to his lips then to the tip of her deliciously sassy retroussé nose, he whispered, "Till later, Little Bit."

Leaning back against the seat, she watched him rise to his feet, straightening the rumpled tunic, placing his wide-brimmed hat on the slightly curling raven-black hair. Reaching for his worn leather medical bag, he gave her a smile of regret.

"Do you want me to go with you?" she asked, thinking of being some use to him as a nurse.

"No, I think for now 'tis best if you stay away from the other good people of Memphis," he said with a glint of humor in his black eyes. Then as he opened the door, he paused and said with a somber tone, "Stay in here. There is a dangerous atmosphere on this train. 'Tis not safe for a woman, especially a Southern woman. Promise me you will pull the latch on the lock after I leave."

"I promise," she said, rising to her feet, remembering with a shudder the sergeant with the eyes full of hate.

With one last brief kiss on her lips still burning for him, he was gone. She quickly locked the door after him. Sighing, she sat back down on the seat and, adjusting the shade so she could look out at the passing scene, tried to rest her overwrought nerves. Her hunger for Justin was still strong, making her restless in the sultry heat of the setting sun. Staring out at the wild beautiful terrain of the Tennessee countryside, she tried to calm the fevered desire her husband had awakened in her blood. Soon she was lost deep in melancholy thoughts of the war, of Beau's recent death, and the necessity of keeping the news of his son's death from her father till he was strong enough to bear it. She could only hope that Justin was able to get her father released from Irving Block Prison as soon as they returned. The thought of her frail father in that terrible place tormented her. If marrying Justin would make the

Provost Marshal think the Valcour family was not a Confederate threat to the Union Command, and they released her father, she could stand the snubs of her fellow Memphians—her friends would know that her heart was still with the Southern Cause. In fact, she thought with a leap of excitement, she might even be better able to aid Forrest and Henderson's Scouts as the wife of a Yankee officer, for she would not be under such scrutiny by the Union Command. A part of her heart ached at the thought of betraying Justin even that little much, but he need never know if she kept her head about her. Hadn't they been together this long, and while he might have suspected, he had no definite proof she was a Confederate spy. And it wasn't as if she was really doing anything to him personally—why, he was a Southerner born and bred, she tried to rationalize, but there was a part of her that hated the need for such subterfuge. Why, oh why couldn't fate have been kinder and allowed Justin to return to his Southern heritage instead of following his mind and conscience?

The heat of the setting sun and her exhaustion soon caused her to fall into a light slumber sitting up, her head back against the upholstered seat. She didn't know at first what had awakened her, but as she fought to raise her heavy eyelids, she heard the insistent sound of someone trying to open the door. Getting to her feet, she walked to the locked door. "Justin?" she asked, her hand on the latch.

"Open the door," a raspy male voice demanded.

"Who is it?" she answered, her pulse quickening in fear. She had an idea of who was on the other side of the door, and it terrified her.

"I'll make a deal with you, Reb, but you have to let me in."

"Go away, Sergeant!" Ariane hissed, realizing she had

been right. The sergeant who had threatened her when she got on the train was now trying to enter the compartment.

"All right, girly, then I'll just go get the key," he snarled, walking away.

With her heart pounding, she stood overwhelmed with panic. He was coming back and she was terrified even to guess what he intended to do. Her eyes sweeping the compartment, she saw her valise and knew what she had to do. Quickly she pulled it out from under the seat and, opening it wide, reached under her clothing till her fingers found the revolver. Checking to see if it was loaded, she closed the valise and placed it back under the seat. A sense of calm came over her as she knew what she would do if she had to, if the sergeant forced her. Sitting down, she faced the door, the loaded gun pointed at the portal.

It was only a few minutes before she heard footsteps outside the door and then the turning of a key in the lock. Slowly the door opened till she was facing the brutal visage of the sergeant.

She watched with satisfaction as he paled at the sight of a pistol pointed directly at him. "Yes, Sergeant, what is the 'deal' you wanted to make with me?" she inquired, her mouth curved in a mocking smile of triumph.

"Where did you get that gun?" he snarled, his eyes narrowed in frustration and anger.

"I don't think that is any of your business. It is sufficient for you to know that I have it and will use it without hesitation." Her voice was cold, exact, as she ground the words out between her teeth. Her stormy gray eyes never wavered from his sneering countenance.

"You will pay for this, you little Secesh bitch. You can count on it," he growled, but it was empty posturing. He backed out of the compartment, quickly slamming the door shut behind him.

Ariane sat holding the gun in her outstretched hand, but now her hand began to shake as she stared at the closed door. Slowly lowering the gun to her lap, she sat in the gathering shadows of twilight, trying to stop the spasmodic trembling within her. She knew that what the repulsive sergeant had threatened he had meant. Somehow, someway, he would make good his threat.

Suddenly she heard the sound of a man's boots coming toward the compartment. With a shaking arm, she raised the gun toward the closed door. When she heard a light rap on the portal, she said nothing, only cocking the trigger. She moistened her dry lips with her tongue as she heard someone try the handle. Slowly the door opened.

Chapter Twenty-one

"My God, Little Bit, what the hell is going on?"

"Justin, oh Justin," Ariane gasped, lowering the pistol to her lap.

"Why didn't you lock the door after me?" He ripped the words out impatiently. "I believe with the door bolted, you would not have need of a pistol."

"I did lock the door, but you Yankees don't let that stop you. If you want in, you simply push your way in," she retorted, her eyes gray thunderclouds of anger. "You come and force yourselves upon us, taking whatever you want like the barbarians you are," she continued, seething with indignation at the unfairness of his remark.

"What happened?" he inquired softly, coming to sit beside her. She was so overwrought she would not allow him to calm her.

"That buffoon of a sergeant wanted to make a deal with me, but first he said I must let him in so we could talk over what I had to offer him. I refused. He went and got the key that opens all the compartment doors."

"And you were waiting with the gun aimed in his direction." His voice was full of admiration for her courage, but in his eyes there was a cold rage directed at the man who had been so bold as to approach Ariane in his absence.

"Yes, he left in a hurry," she said with satisfaction.

"I am sure he did," Justin replied in dry tones, rising to his feet. "Put the gun away, Little Bit. I will see to the sergeant. You will have no need to endure his attentions again."

She watched as he walked with an intent stride to the door. There was a dangerous look to those narrowed black eyes, the clenched jaw, and tight grim mouth. A raw power barely held in check was evident in the way he carried himself, the fluid grace of his movements like a wild predatory beast that was coldly, methodically stalking his prey.

She gave a light shudder as he closed the door behind him. It was a side of Justin she had never seen before, and didn't wish to see again. That cold ruthless expression on those handsome features was a revelation. Justin Pierce was not a man to be crossed. And as she put the gun back in the valise, she remembered the old stories about his duel with his brother, Clay. Yes, her husband had many facets to his character. With a sudden chill of premonition, she wondered what other sides to his personality he had not revealed to her.

Within minutes he was back in the shadowy compartment, bolting the door behind him. Crossing to the window, he struck a Lucifer stick and lit the hurricane lamps. Pulling the shade down to cover the window, he said, "We do not want to be a target for your Reb sharpshooters."

"No, there are other people from Memphis in the forward cars who have that honor," Ariane replied without thinking.

"Is this how it is to be between us, the war brought into our marriage?" Justin queried, sitting across from her. Those dark eyes measured her with a cool speculative gaze.

"How can it be kept out," she stated, and there was a sadness in her voice. "Even if we wished otherwise, it is

287

a fact that cannot be ignored."

"No, we will not be allowed to ignore it; others will see to that." There was a light bitterness to his tone.

They sat gazing across the narrow space between the seats, wide sad gray eyes caught by the intensity of burning black orbs that said more plainly than words that he would allow nothing to come between them. The silence lengthened in the warm shadowy compartment, underscored by the surging sound of the train speeding through the lush wild Tennessee countryside. Soft sultry air crept in under the drawn window shade to caress them and stir the blood with sensual yearnings.

"Remember last night," he murmured, his voice low, husky, and intentionally seductive. "I shall never forget it. The velvet touch of your skin, the golden fan of your hair as you lay under me, the desire in your smoky eyes. You wanted me then, my hot-blooded Rebel. There is no blue uniform between us when we are naked together in our marriage bed. There is only skin against skin, mouth against mouth. When I am inside you, there is only me, hard and throbbing with my hunger and passion for you, all for you. Do you remember, my sweet angry Rebel? Do you remember how nothing matters but the splendor and the rapture?" The sound of his voice, his carefully chosen words, floated across on the humid, warm night air to caress her, seduce her while his ebony-black eyes held her ensnared, challenging, devouring, consuming, making an exquisite love to her that was the most erotic experience of her life. He had aroused a fire in her till she was totally entranced, breathless with the desire that was racing through her.

"Yes, I remember," she whispered as a hot ache grew in the back of her throat. There was a warm heavy aching in her limbs that grew to an almost unbearable

288

throbbing in the center of her womanhood. Her face burned with the memory of being held against his strong burning body; her lips tingled in remembrance of his mouth.

"Can you tell me that you could live in this world and never want to feel me inside you, never want to experience what we have between us. If you can, then ours will a marriage of convenience, a battleground where the war between North and South can be played out one on one. But if you want me as I want you, then you know that is impossible. Do you want me, Ariane?" His question was a husky rasp that hung in the air like a challenge as his dark eyes bore into her, drawing out her deepest desires.

"Yes! Yes!" she cried out, her voice angry that he could elicit such a reaction from her. Lifting her hands, she pressed them to her trembling mouth as if to keep from saying anything else. He had won—what more did he want? She shuddered with embarrassment as resentment and passion warred inside her.

"Say the words, sweet love, say the words," he ordered hoarsely, eyes blazing, his fingers gripping the seat till the knuckles turned white.

"I . . . want you. God help me, but how I want you," she gasped with a moan that was torn from deep within her. She stretched out her arms to him, but whether she was reaching for him or pleading with him, she never knew.

Justin rose without a word and swept her up into his arms. They stood pressed together, weaving back and forth from the motion of the train. His lips were in her hair as he murmured fiercely, "Never forgot this joy that is almost pain. Never forget what it is to experience such a love."

His hands moved to her chignon at the base of her neck, pulling the pins from her hair till it fell in a glorious red-gold waterfall of silk to her waist. He slid it through his fingers, reveling in the cool feminine caress of it against his heated skin.

As the train rounded a bend, they were thrown against the bench. Her hoop collapsed against her waist and under her, and her skirts flew up, revealing her pantalet-clad legs. She felt his hand reach up under her skirt and tear the lace-trimmed underpants from her body. His mouth was on her inner thighs tasting, circling the skin with his tongue till she was aflame. Twisting, arching under the rapture of his mouth, she was unaware of anything but the wild frenzied hunger he evoked.

"Yes! Oh yes, there!" she cried out in her ecstasy as his fingers parted her, stroked, caressed, and carried her to the heights of desire. Her hands reached down to where his dark head lay against her lower hips. Tiny fingers wound in the black satin of his hair as she moved against his mouth and hands in circles of delight.

He had never been so aroused. Her abandonment thrilled him in a way he had never thought possible till this wondrous moment. There was no embarrassment between them, just the glorious hunger that drove them on to experience every sensual nuance of lovemaking.

She moaned as he took her almost to the pinnacle with his knowing touch, but she had a stronger need, a need to feel him deep inside her, filling her with his thrusting length. The frenzy of her hunger amazed her—tonight she felt wanton, wanting to enjoy all the new strange delights her body could give her under Justin's expert instruction.

"I must have you," he muttered, his voice hoarse with his overwhelming desire as he rose above her, unbuttoning the fly of his breeches.

She arched up, giving a sigh of relief as he entered

her. This was what she wanted, what her body craved—those hard, powerful strokes again and again. Looking up at him, she was thrilled by the play of passion on his handsome features, the softening of the stern mouth, the fire and wonder in his dark eyes. She reached up, her fingers digging into his muscular forearms as he braced himself, taking his weight off her delicate frame. He became consumed by her as he thrust and retreated, then thrust again in a rapturous movement of love.

Together they found a rhythm that was both new and old as time. There was no reality but this enchanted moment when they were no longer separated by war, by right or wrong. They were one soaring entity united by the force of the flame that flared between them. Higher and higher they soared till they reached the heights, transfigured by the glory of life's sweetest gift, the touching of two souls at that perfect moment of fulfillment.

Later as they half reclined on the seat, Ariane's head against Justin's chest listening to the beating of his heart within the circle of his arm, he whispered into the silk of her hair, "Forgive me, but I had a wildness in me that could not be controlled."

"I am glad you lost control," she replied, turning her face up to look at him with a mischievous smile, "even if I have to find another pair of pantalets in my valise. Every woman wishes that she could drive the man she loves beyond his control. It is such a lovely compliment, although I don't know what Sable will think when she finds those torn pantalets when she unpacks. Perhaps she will realize I have a most passionate, impatient husband."

"And you are a most bewitching wench," he said ruefully, lightly touching the tip of her nose in a playful gesture.

"I feel like a wench when I am with you, a very wanton wench," she sighed, stretching against him like a contented kitten. "I am sure a Southern lady should never confess such a thing."

"Every Southern lady should feel like a wanton with the man she loves," he assured her with a husky chuckle of pleasure, "especially if he is a barbaric Yankee. Isn't that how you describe me?"

"I really wish you didn't remember everything I say. 'Tis most disconcerting to be quoted from a fit of temper," she sighed in exasperation, a gentle smile curving her mouth.

"Ah, that is what that was, a fit of temper," he mused, the teasing quality still in his deep voice.

"Yes, hot weather and rude Yankees always rile my temper, be forewarned," she murmured, tracing the delightful cleft in his chin with the tip of her finger. "So take care and not rile me, sir, for I have a fearful temper."

"I thought Southern ladies weren't supposed to have anything so common as a fit of temper," he teased, capturing her finger and lifting the hand to his lips.

"We are many-faceted, we Southern ladies."

"So I am finding out," he murmured ruefully, bending his head to lightly kiss her soft lips. Gently he pressed her head down onto his chest. "Rest, Little Bit, it is going to be a long night till we reach Memphis."

Exhausted and safe within Justin's embrace, she slumbered against the rock-steady security of his chest. Whenever they stopped at a station to take on water for the steam engine, she would stir as the lulling motion of the train ceased. Her fatigue was so great that she couldn't lift her eyelids and so she would nestle back into Justin's embrace like a sleepy kitten.

Justin, however, did not rest so easy. The sergeant's threat to report Ariane to the Provost Marshal worried him. The man had a score to settle and he knew his warning to leave his wife alone had only fueled the man's need for revenge. He could only hope that being his wife would save her, but he knew the depth of the Provost Marshal's hatred for the people of Memphis. Their complaints about Irving Block Prison had been so insistent to the Northern newspapers that President Lincoln had been forced to send an investigation team to Memphis. Their findings had caused Williams to be suspended for a time as commandant of the prison, but now he had wormed his way back and was out for blood.

Looking down at Ariane's delicate profile, he felt a cold chill at the thought of her in such a place. Sometimes she seemed to him to be that scruffy little waif he'd found dressed in boy's clothes the night she had run away from the tragedy of her home. She had always brought out this protective feeling in him, even more now that she was a beautiful, alluring woman.

There had been no shots from snipers till they stopped at the Buntyn Station. Then as they were preparing to leave, a burst of gunfire came from a thicket of trees. At the first sound, Justin pulled a sleepy Ariane to the floor, covering her with his body till they were under way again.

"Where are we?" she asked, rubbing the sleep from her eyes as he helped her back up to the seat.

"That was Buntyn Station, and those were Reb snipers. It's amazing that we had no trouble till we got closer to Memphis. Henderson's Scouts are like quicksilver, and they seem to know which stations are undergarrisoned," he mused out loud. "I think some of your fellow Memphians have discovered ways to send information out of the city to the Scouts. In fact, I am beginning to wonder if the whole damn town isn't one vast espionage network." His dark eyes flashed at her intently.

"They are Southerners," she said with a shrug, as if to say how could he expect anything else. He did not know how close he came to the truth.

"Yes, they are," he answered in cryptic tones.

Her eyes misted as she thought of Beau and how never again would he ride with the brave men of Henderson's Scouts. In the confusion and excitement of the events that took place in La Grange, she had been able to push Beau's horrible, needless death farther back in her mind, but now that they were returning to Memphis, she was filled once more with an overwhelming sense of guilt, that somehow she could have prevented it. A deep depression like a cloud seemed to engulf her as the awful memory of seeing Beau's still white visage came back, crowding out everything else. Did she have the strength to keep such a dark secret from her father till somehow he was strong enough to learn the truth? She sat staring ahead of her, not seeing anything but that awful afternoon at Elmwood Cemetery. It had marked her and she knew that she would never forget the horror of it for the rest of her life.

"Do not dwell on it, my dear. It was not your fault. You did everything you knew how. These things happen in war. With Beau's wound, it was a wonder he didn't die sooner. You have worked in a hospital, you know how serious his injury was," Justin reminded her in his deep-timbered voice, his dark eyes filled with a warm compassion.

"How did you know what I was thinking?" she asked with a sad, bittersweet smile.

"I could feel your pain, see the sorrow in your eyes," he said softly. "I know you, Little Bit. Let go of the guilt. Beau would not want you to carry it, and it will not bring him back."

"You are right," she sighed. Nothing would bring

Beau back, but she could still help his friends and comrades. If she allowed herself to become immobilized by grief, she could be of no use to the Confederacy. She would find her way out of the morass of sorrow over Beau by helping Henderson's Scouts and General Forrest.

There was no way she could return to slumber. The sniper fire had broken the spell of contentment within the small compartment. The reality of the war and all its complications for them had intruded. As Justin lit his pipe, Ariane picked up her hair pins from the floor. With a few quick twists, she wound her long tresses back into a chignon at the base of her neck and secured it with the pins.

"I know it must be cooler worn that way, but I do so enjoy the sight of it hanging loose down your back," Justin told her as he watched her put up her hair. It was an intimate gesture and one he was looking forward to watching daily as her husband.

"You will see me every night with my hair loose," she said shyly, coming to nestle once more in the curve of his arm.

"I shall look forward to it every day when I return from that charnel house of a hospital, to see you across from me at the table and later in my bed. I shall help undo your hair. Sable's services will not be needed at night," he whispered huskily against her temple.

They sat quietly together as the train sped through the dark sultry Tennessee night toward Memphis. The closer they got, the uneasier both became, as if some sixth sense was alerted to an impending danger. Unconsciously, Justin tightened his arm around Ariane as if to protect her from some unseen danger.

It was after midnight when they pulled into the Memphis Station. A fine misty rain had begun to fall as Justin helped Ariane step down from the railroad car.

The platform was chaotic, thronged with Union soldiers helping to unload the patients.

"Go inside the depot and wait for me there. I must see that all are loaded onto the ambulances. It was insanity to bring these men to Memphis in the middle of the night, but the trains carrying wounded have a lower priority with the Federal Command than supply trains," Justin muttered in disgust, carrying their luggage toward the two-story depot. Ariane followed in his tall wake as he made a path through the jostling humanity who all seemed to be going in the opposite direction.

The humid air was stifling inside the depot, what with the heat and the rain. Placing their two pieces of luggage in a corner, Justin turned to her and said, "This, I am afraid, is the best we can do. You can sit on my portmanteau. I shall return as soon as I can, and then we'll look for a hackney buggy to take us out to Fleur de Lys." With a brief kiss on her forehead, he was gone, pushing his way out of the crowded depot.

The minutes seemed to drag as Ariane first stood, then took Justin's advice and sat on the edge of the portmanteau. She received curious stares from the soldiers, but none approached her, for which she was thankful. She watched as the hands of the station clock crept across its fly-specked face. The heat and humidity were unbearable, and she had to take a handkerchief from her reticule several times to wipe the moisture from her face.

After an hour had crept by, and she had almost given up any hope of seeing Justin before first light, she heard a quick-booted step behind her coming from the main door. Standing up and turning around with a smile, she felt her heart skip a beat as she saw a tall lieutenant come toward her with the repulsive sergeant from the train at his side. There was a smirking grin on the sergeant's sweaty visage.

"That's her," the sergeant said in triumph to the officer beside him. "That's Ariane Valcour."

"Miss, I have a warrant for your arrest," the young lieutenant said as he touched his broad-brimmed hat with his gauntlet-clad hand.

"I . . . I don't understand. Why? For what reason?" she asked, icy fear twisting her heart and drying her mouth.

"Aiding and abetting the enemy in the murder of Union Officer Marsh," he said in solemn tones, but she saw a flicker of regret in his brown eyes.

"But that is ridiculous," she gasped in dismay. "I had nothing to do with Lieutenant Marsh's death. He was a fine young man. We talked, that is all. There must be some mistake."

"Please follow me, miss," the lieutenant insisted.

"But where are you taking me?" she asked, her voice trembling.

"Where you belong, you Secesh bitch, to Irving Block Prison," the sergeant sneered in contempt, spitting a stream of tobacco juice onto her skirts.

Chapter Twenty-two

"That will be enough, Sergeant," the young lieutenant ordered sharply. "Come quietly, miss. It will go easier on you." He stood back, gesturing with his hand that she was to precede him.

Ariane stood paralyzed for a moment, feeling like a trapped animal with no way to turn. "May I take my valise, Lieutenant?" she asked, reaching for the bag.

"No, miss. Later your family might be allowed to bring you some personal items, but not now. If we might proceed to the wagon outside," he said firmly.

As she started toward the door with a faltering step, joy and relief flooded her being as she saw the beloved face and form of her husband entering the depot. She saw the wary look come into his black eyes as she approached him, flanked on either side by the lieutenant and the sergeant.

"What's going on here, Lieutenant?" his terse voice, ringing with authority, queried the young soldier.

"Escorting a prisoner, sir," he replied, giving a respectful salute to the senior officer. The leering sergeant reluctantly touched his hand in a sloppy imitation of a salute to Justin.

"That prisoner happens to be my wife," Justin responded icily.

"Sir . . . are you sure . . ." The lieutenant stumbled

over his words to the cynical amusement of several soldiers watching the proceedings.

"Lieutenant, I know my own wife," Justin said, his tongue heavy with sarcasm. There was a dangerous look in his cold, narrowed black eyes that caused the young soldier to turn pale.

"I am sorry, sir, but I have a warrant for her arrest," he tried to explain to the icy remote mask that was Justin's visage.

"This is ridiculous. On what charge?" he demanded, ripping out the words impatiently.

"Aiding and abetting the enemy in the murder of a Union officer, Lieutenant Robert Marsh."

"I was with her and she had absolutely nothing to do with it. He was killed by a Reb sharpshooter." His furious stare drilled into the lieutenant.

"You can explain that to the Provost Marshal, Captain. I have my orders, and I must carry them out." The lieutenant took Ariane's arm to lead her away from Justin.

"I am coming with you," Justin replied in a low voice taut with anger.

"Then you will ride up front with me, sir, for I cannot allow you to ride in the back of the prison wagon," the lieutenant said stiffly.

"You are new to the Army, aren't you, Lieutenant," Justin replied, his voice quiet yet holding an undertone of cold contempt.

"Yes, sir. How did you know?"

"You go right by the book. You're still impressed by regulations," he answered tersely.

The light rain had turned into a misty fog as they walked out of the station with Ariane between them. The sergeant brought up the rear. A few carriages for hire waited to pick up the last of the soldiers. Ariane felt as if she were sleepwalking through a nightmare

299

as they crossed the dirt road, now becoming a muddy morass, to the high closed prison wagon with its wooden sides and top. The only window was a small barred one in the back door.

"Where are you taking her?" Justin demanded as the lieutenant unlocked the door.

"Irving Block Prison."

"I will get you out of this, Little Bit," he promised, taking her by the shoulders, his fingers pressing into the fine bones as she turned huge frightened gray eyes up to his. "Courage, my fiery rebel," he whispered hoarsely, then she was gently pulled from his grasp and thrust up the iron steps into the dark bowels of the prison wagon.

The hot fetid darkness surrounded her as she was pushed on to a hard wooden seat along the side, and the door slammed shut. She sensed in the blackness that there were others with her, but she was unable to see them in the gloom.

"What they get you for, honey?" a raspy feminine voice called out from somewhere near the front of the wagon.

"They said I was helping the enemy and was responsible for a Union officer's death," she murmured, reaching out for some human contact in this hellish place.

"Good for you, honey. One less Yank. Memphis is a better place for it," the voice cackled.

"I didn't do it," Ariane protested weakly.

"Sure, honey. None of us did it," she snickered.

"Why . . . why are you here?" Ariane inquired, trying to divert the attention from her.

"They say I struck my fancy man. Course I didn't, even if the bastard needed to be taught a lesson or two," the voice drawled, mimicking Ariane's explanation.

300

"Tell that to cock-eyed Charlie now that he's colder than yesterday's mash potatoes," another feminine voice cackled.

Ariane flinched and shrank back against the wall of the wagon. Her companions were obviously prostitutes of the lowest caliber. A sensation of intense despair and desolation came over her. She closed her eyes, feeling utterly miserable, and tried to block out the lewd conversation of her companions.

There was a jolt as the wagon started on its way to Irving Block Prison. Ariane could only pray that Justin was sitting up front with the driver and the lieutenant. The ride in the ovenlike prison wagon seemed interminable. Even the coarse women that rode with her seemed to have their spirits sapped by the heat and humidity. Soon the only sound inside the hellish wagon was the creak of the boards and the cadence of the mule's hooves on the hard-packed dirt road.

When they suddenly jerked to a stop, Ariane's eyes flew open, her heart pounding with hope. Now perhaps this nightmare would end and she would be exonerated.

"All right, ladies," a male voice called out in sarcastic tones as the door was flung open and a bright, blinding lantern was shone in their face. "Get out."

Her arm raised against the blinding light, Ariane stumbled down from the wagon. She felt a strong arm catch her as she almost fell in the mud of Second Street. The prison was located in a row of office buildings on Second Street across from Court Square, one of Memphis' parklike squares. A bust of Andrew Jackson stood in the midst of the leafy verdant square. Under the bust, the words "The Federal Union It Must And Shall Be Preserved" had been chipped by a small hammer in defiance of the Union occupation. Because of that, the small park was closely guarded. Lanterns hung from posts in front of the prison, casting a harsh glare.

"Courage, 'tis almost over," Justin whispered in her ear as he half carried her across the wooden sidewalk and into the main lobby of the prison.

Ariane stood huddled within the circle of Justin's arm as she watched the two women whose voices she had heard in the prison wagon. They were coarse, garishly dressed women, missing most of their teeth. They were streetwalkers from the meanest cribs in Pinch Gut. They were more pathetic than dangerous, Ariane thought with a shudder as she watched them being led away, vanishing down a long, dimly lit hall.

"Miss Valcour, if you would follow me to the commandant's office. There are some forms that must be filled out," the young lieutenant said, having taken care of the prostitutes.

"The name is Pierce, Lieutenant, Mrs. Pierce," Justin corrected him vehemently, his voice cold and lashing. "I have the papers signed by the army chaplain who married us in La Grange."

"You may bring them. Captain Williams likes for each prisoner's file to be correct. This way." He motioned for them to follow him.

With Justin's arm steadying her, Ariane followed him, shaking so violently she could hardly stand. The chamber into which he led them was stark, with only a scarred desk and a few cabinets for furnishings. Motioning for them to be seated in the only two other rickety chairs, the lieutenant seated himself behind the desk.

"If I might have the marriage certificate, Captain," he said, addressing Justin coolly. This was his domain. He wanted them to realize that fact.

"I would like to speak with the man in charge tonight as I am sure Captain Williams is in his bed,"

302

Justin demanded in sharp tones, his eyes blazing.

"You are right, sir. Captain Williams is in his suite at the Hotel Gayoso asleep. I am in charge here in his absence," he replied. "The marriage certificate, please."

"It is with my belongings back at the station. You may send someone for them," Justin suggested through clenched teeth, his visage pale with rage.

"Yes, well, that will take time, but no matter. I cannot release Mrs. Pierce tonight anyway. That, I am afraid, is a matter for the Provost Marshal. Since I see that you are a lady, ma'am, I have brought you in here to explain that you will be taken to the upper floor, which is the women's floor. In time perhaps, with your husband to vouch for you, you could be released, but for now, there is nothing I can do," he said quietly, but one look at his determined eyes told her he could not be moved from his decision.

"I see," Ariane murmured, her anger and pride finally coming to her aid. "Well, I shall at least not be alone, Lieutenant, for I understand the Provost Marshal has locked up many of my fellow Memphians on equally trumped-up charges." She felt Justin's hand on her arm to quiet her, but she was determined to have her say. If she must be imprisoned, she would not beg—she would handle herself with dignity and pride as she had been taught to behave all her life. "And I believe my father is also one of your guests."

"If you will excuse me, Captain, Mrs. Pierce. I will call the guard to take you upstairs," the young lieutenant said stiffly, rising to his feet, anger and respect warring in his eyes as he left them.

"While I admire your courage and bravado, Little Bit, be warned that these qualities will be not appreciated in this hellhole. Cooperate and keep that lovely mouth shut till I can get you and your father out of here," Justin cautioned, sounding curt, distracted as his mind worked furiously on a plan to secure her release.

"I will never cooperate with them, never!" Ariane spat out the words contemptuously. "It is not so easy for some of us to turn traitor as it is for others."

"Don't be a foolish romantic. This is deadly serious. Do you think these men care about abstract values like chivalry, nobility, and gallantry toward ladies? This war has turned nasty on both sides. The Confederate prisons in Richmond and Andersonville are certainly no models of courteous behavior toward an enemy. I know the South has no food for its own people, let alone prisoners, but that cannot excuse some of the cruelty, and the stories of treatment there have been printed in the Northern newspapers. The North will treat their own prisoners in kind, believe me. There is a deep anger against the South, a wish to punish them for their transgressions. Remember what I tell you and conduct yourself with some wisdom and plain common sense, for God's sake, till I can get you out of here."

There was no time to reply, for the lieutenant had returned with a surly-looking corporal. His small restless eyes were bloodshot, and he had a day's growth of beard on his florid visage, which told of his frequent bouts with alcohol.

"Lieutenant, would it be possible for me to see my father, Leander Valcour, before I am incarcerated?" Ariane asked, rising to her feet.

"No, that would not be possible. There is no visiting allowed between the men and women's floor," he answered tersely.

"Then might I inquire about his condition?" she continued, despite the warning hand Justin placed on her arm.

"Corporal, this is the prisoner. Take her to the women's floor," the lieutenant ordered, not answering her question.

"That will not be necessary, Corporal. I will accompany you," she said quietly, and with as much dignity as she could muster, pulling her arm away from the corporal's rough grasp as he pulled her from Justin's side.

Never had Justin loved or admired her more as she swept from the office, her golden head held high. He followed them with a swift step and stood watching as she walked down the long dim hall to the first locked door. As the corporal fumbled for the key, she turned and looked back.

Smoky-gray eyes enormous in the magnolia blossom of her delicate face reached across the dingy, dimly lit corridor to touch Justin. They reminded him of a doe he had seen as a boy, when hunting with his brother Clay. The deer had been drinking at a creek, and when she caught wind of their scent, she had raised her elegant head to stare at them, realizing it was already too late—she was trapped. His brother Clay had gleefully raised his rifle, quickly fixing her in his sight. As he pulled the trigger, Justin had knocked the gun so the shot went wild, allowing the graceful doe to escape into the woods. Clay had been livid, swearing furiously at him, but he had not cared. The lovely doe with the expressive eyes had escaped. But there would be no escape for his beloved Ariane, and his anger and frustration became a scalding fury. His fists clenched at his sides to keep him from pulling his sidearm from the holster at his waist and firing at the corporal. It would be a futile effort at best, solving nothing, but perhaps getting them both killed. His black eyes blazed across the few yards separating them, boring into her soul, saying without words that he was with her always, if not at her side physically then with his spirit. The bond between them would always be with her to give her strength.

"In here," the corporal said, standing back so she could enter the open portal.

His words caused a momentary rush of panic to course through Ariane as she tore her gaze from Justin's intense dark eyes, which seemed to be flowing out to her, reassuring, caressing, lending his strength to her terrified heart. She raised her trembling fingers to her lips in a brief gesture of a kiss, and he returned it, the fierceness and depth of emotion in his ebony orbs searing the distance between them. Then the door was slammed shut behind her.

Her first reaction as she walked with the corporal was to the terrible smell that seemed to permeate everything. It was the scent of unwashed bodies, sickness, human excrement, death, and other less tangible things such as fear, hopelessness, and despair.

"Without your slaves to bring you bath water, you fancy stuck-up Rebs stink just like the rest of us in this heat," the corporal said in disgust. He wanted to bring this one down a peg or two with her snooty manner. After a few days in Irving Block, she wouldn't be so high and mighty. He chuckled, thinking how much he was going to enjoy seeing her like the others.

"Up these steps," he ordered, grabbing her arm once more, now that there was no Union officer to see, and pushing her in the direction of a dark, steep, airless staircase.

Lifting her skirt, she stumbled as she started up the stair, the fetid, alcohol breath of the corporal a hot wind on the back of her neck as he followed close behind, poking her now and then sharply in the back as if she were an animal to be moved along.

306

"I am going as fast as I can," she muttered, already out of breath as they reached the second floor.

"Keep going, lady. You have three more flights to go."

Out of breath, sweat running down her face in rivulets, she tried to fix her mind on the memory of Justin's face. If she could think of that and blot out the pain in her side where her stays were cutting into her skin, making it even more difficult to breathe in the stuffy stairwell, she could find the strength to go on.

"Guess all your friends will be waiting to welcome you to the four floor," the corporal taunted her. "It's real deluxe accommodations, the four floor. There's fresh meat, if you can catch it," he guffawed at his own humor. "You ever eat rat, lady? They say it's real tasty if you're hungry enough."

"Please, Corporal, is this real necessary?" Ariane questioned dryly, trying to use her anger to give her the energy to climb the last flight of stairs.

"Why, you're real polite, ain't you, lady. Well, polite ain't goin' to get you nothin' on the fourth floor. You'll see," he taunted her, giving her a shove up the last step till she almost fell. She caught herself by grabbing on to the iron bars that formed a door a few feet from the top of the landing.

"Welcome to the women's floor, lady," the corporal said as he took his ring of keys from his pocket and opened the door. Ariane peered down a long dim hall, with bars where there should have been doors on the rooms opening on to it.

At the sound of the opening door, wraithlike creatures came to the bars and stood staring at her from pale, sweaty, dirty-streaked visages. The heat and fetid smell were horrendous, but the most frightening aspect were those haunted eyes that stared back at her

307

as she waited for the corporal to give some papers to a sergeant sitting behind a battered desk.

"Down here, lady. You're goin' in with some Secesh friends of yours," the corporal jeered, bored now with Ariane and anxious to get back downstairs where it was cooler, and where he had a bottle of whiskey hid away.

In the dim light from the oil lantern hanging outside the iron bars, Ariane could make out several figures slumped on the floor. They looked up as she entered the small room bare of any furniture or even boxes. There was only loose straw scattered about the floor, mounded here and there for use as beds by the prisoners.

"Sweet dreams," the corporal crackled, pushing her inside and slamming the door shut. The sound of the key turning in the lock echoed like a death knell in Ariane's tortured brain.

"Yes, who are you?" a tired, yet cultured voice called out from a few feet away.

"Ariane Valcour," she answered, forgetting in her fear and turmoil that she was now married.

"Ariane, 'tis Lavinia Davis," the voice replied, coming closer till Ariane could see the wan, weary face of Mrs. Davis. She was an older woman, her husband a friend of her father's. Ariane remembered she had been arrested in June for smuggling letters to Confederate soldiers.

"Mrs. Davis, how are you?" she asked. The woman had been in this filthy pesthole over two months.

"My dear, I am alive—that is more than most can say who have spent any time in the Bastille," she said in wry tones. "But then I come from old pioneer stock. My family came to Tennessee with Davy Crockett. We are a tough lot." She gave a wan smile and gestured for Ariane to come sit beside her on the

308

straw.

"Are there no chairs, no beds?" she whispered, not wanting to disturb several women she could see were sleeping, stretched out in the dirty straw.

"None, and fresh straw only once a month. Even the chamber pot over there is dumped only in the morning. I hate to tell you, my dear, but you are in hell."

"I thought they were to have cleaned this place up after Lincoln's commission ordered them to," Ariane said, still stunned. The conditions were even worse than what was rumored about the place. If this was the women's floor, what must it be like where they kept the men?

"They did for a while, then things began to slide back into what they had been before, I am afraid."

"Have you seen anything of Felicity Sanderson?" Ariane asked.

"But, my dear Ariane, she is in here with us, asleep. She is exhausted, poor thing, with a touch of the fever, but she will be so cheered when she awakens to see your face. Her spirits have become rather low after the death of her cousin Camelia day before yesterday."

"Camelia dead!" Ariane gasped, tears misting her eyes as she realized that both Beau and Camelia had become casualties of the bloody war. Where would it all end? she thought in despair.

"Yes, the poor thing had consumption, you know, and with the terrible conditions and the diet here of coffee, cold potatoes, a bit of salt pork, and a few stale crackers, she could not survive. She was so delicate in health, but not in spirit. She refused to the end to tell them where she got the ten yards of gray material and gold buttons and braid she was smuggling out of the city to her brother for a new uni-

309

form."

Ariane was assailed by a terrible sense of bitterness at Mrs. Davis words. Camelia had died because of ten yards of material, some buttons, and gold braid. The darkness seemed to press down on her as Mrs. Davis helped her out of her hoop skirt then her petticoat, which she would use as a sheet on the dirty straw that was to be her bed. Although most women removed their stays in the dark, they couldn't undress down to their chemise and pantalets despite the humid heat, because they had no privacy. The Yankee guards came by and stared in at them at any time.

As Ariane stretched out on her petticoat across the mounded straw, she felt too empty for tears. The horror of it all, the ache for poor dead Camelia, the worry over her father in this awful place, the overwhelming depression that threatened on the edges of her mind—she tried to put it all from her, bury it in a hidden corner of her mind. She would deal with it later, for now she was beyond pain, beyond sorrow—she was simply hanging on to survival.

Closing her eyes, she tried to find escape in slumber, but her nerves were too overwrought to allow her that solace. Her body was exhausted, crying out for sleep, but her mind was too overstimulated. She had to relax somehow if she was to keep her wits about her on the morrow. Slowly she willed herself to forget where she was, the heat, the stench, and travel to another time, another place. The cottage at Tranquillity—that's where she wanted to be, with Justin. They were riding through the sultry summer night to their honeymoon tryst deep in the fragrant cedar forest. She could almost smell the woods' astringent perfume, feel the soft night wind on her body as Justin peeled her wedding gown from her hungry body. Slowly, savoring every remembered nuance, she submerged herself in the memory of the splendor and the rapture of her wedding night. Her mind floating in a haze of remembered delight finally allowed her tired body to find wondrous release in slumber. Her head resting on a curve of her arm, she dreamt of her husband, her husband who wore the same blue uniform as her jailers, her husband who was her only hope of escape from the hellhole of Irving Block Prison.

Chapter Twenty-three

The burning rays of the sun slanting through the bars of the one window in her cell forced Ariane awake. For one awful moment, she had no idea where she was, and then like a heavy weight in the pit of her stomach, it came to her, all of it.

"Wake up, ladies," a rough masculine voice called out as he moved down the corridor. The sound of him unlocking and then locking the bars echoed down the hall.

"He is bringing what passes for breakfast in this place and water," Lavinia Davis explained as she sat up next to Ariane.

They both turned at the sound of a feeble moan coming from the corner. Several of the other women had also been awakened by the sun and the din of the soldier. They rose and stretched stiff muscles. Then as the moaning increased, Lavinia walked over to see what was wrong.

" 'Tis Felicity," she said. "Her fever has risen again in the heat of day. Come, we best see if there is anything we can do. What we need is quinine, but the Yanks refuse to give us any. I don't see how they think we would smuggle it out of here to the Confederacy." She shook her head in disgust.

Ariane realized as a stream of sunlight fell across Mrs. Davis that her hair had gone completely white. She had been a woman in good health when she was arrested. Ariane's father, however, had been in a weakened condition. How could he withstand such a place? She shuddered inwardly at the thought of what he must be going through.

"Good morning, ladies. Time for breakfast." The insolent private grinned as he unlocked the door and entered, carrying a pail of water with a tin dipper floating in it. His companion carried in a pot of coffee, some chipped mugs in a basket, and a container of gray-looking crackers as well as some fatty pieces of salt pork. This unappetizing mess was breakfast. "Eat up," he said with another twist of his mouth that was meant to be a smile. "I'll be back soon for the dishes."

"There is a woman sick with fever here. Shouldn't she be taken to the hospital?" Ariane called out as the men turned to leave.

"Nobody leaves here, Reb. You're new here, so I'm goin' to overlook your sassy question, but I don't want to hear no more askin' for favors unless you have something to trade. You understand?" he leered, then followed the other man out of the cell.

Ariane's mood veered sharply from despair to anger. Breathless with rage, she stared after him with contempt. The rage, however, pulled her from her depression.

"Come, my dear, eat. You must keep up your strength. Help me try and force a little water between Felicity's lips," Lavinia called from where she knelt beside the sick woman's pallet.

Felicity's fever was so high she was delirious. She didn't recognize her friend. Ariane and Lavinia quickly ate the moldy crackers and some of the awful salt pork, washing it down with mugs of the weak, lukewarm coffee. After breaking their fast, they took turns swishing off the flies and mosquitoes that bedeviled the debilitated Felicity. The insects, terrible during that

313

time of year in Memphis, were attracted to the unsanitary conditions of the prison and flew in through the open barred window in swarms, biting the sweating women. Felicity tossed and turned in fever then began toward late afternoon the terrible shaking with shivers running up and down her spine that told Ariane she had malaria, what the soldiers called the "ague." She knew with a grim certainty that if Felicity did not start on quinine soon, she would die, so weakened was her body by her time spent in prison.

Never had Ariane felt so helpless or experienced such a wretchedness of mind as she did sitting by her friend in the long hot suffocating August day, unable to give her even the smallest comfort or relief from pain. It was as she sat there losing hope that Justin could secure her release that a cold unrelenting hatred began to grow deep inside her heart toward the cruel inhuman men who ran Irving Block Prison. If she ever got out of here, she would do anything in her power to bring about their defeat. She wanted vengeance for Camelia and for poor Felicity, who, it appeared, would soon join her cousin in death. Her hatred and determination that somehow, someday, she would find a way to achieve her revenge saw her through the following night.

When the burning sun again awakened her from a restless sleep, Ariane no longer believed that Justin would come to her rescue. What she had always feared, known deep in her soul, had come to pass—the war had torn their love apart. How could she ever love a Yankee after being their prisoner, after suffering at their hands, after watching the still, dead body of her friend be carried from the cell, having died quietly in the night while they all slumbered exhausted from the heat. She was numb, her heart a lead weight in her chest. She had seen too much, suffered too much, to

314

feel anything. The numbness was a welcome relief. She hoped she never felt anything again.

It was late in the afternoon of the second day of her captivity when they heard the unaccustomed sound of booted feet coming down the hall. It was not time to be fed, and they knew that the Yanks kept to a strict schedule. The women stirred, wondering if another poor soul was to be put in with them. Most of the women were too hot and tired to more than lift their weary, pale faces up listlessly to see who had entered their cell.

Ariane didn't even do that. She stood at the barred window, trying to see out into the street below, the patch of green that was Court Square. It was all that kept her from giving into despair like several of the other women, who simply stared into space, lost in some happier time and place.

"You there by the window, you're lucky, your husband's come to fetch you," a rough male voice called to Ariane.

She had ignored the sound of the booted feet and had not listened to the sergeant calling to her. She did, however, notice a stirring among the women who sat near her.

"Little Bit, I have come to take you home." Justin's deep, strong voice sounded in her ear as his hand touched her shoulder.

Slowly, she turned around to stare into dark eyes that were gentle and filled with concern. "You came," she whispered, lips dry and blistered from not enough water and too much salt in the pork.

"Did you doubt me, dearest?" He brushed a piece of straw from her hair, which had long come undone and hung down her back in a snarled tangle.

"Yes," she replied with such despair in her gray eyes that it smote his heart.

"Come, we will leave this place," he said softly as if to a hurt child, leading her to the door, his arm around her waist. They walked through the stunned women, and as they reached the door, she heard the whispered hiss "traitor" from behind her. She turned and saw the hostility and envy on some of the women's faces and shock on others at hearing Justin in his Union uniform was her husband. Then firmly, Justin led her out of the cell and down the hall. She moved like a sleepwalker through the opened barred door and then down another hall to a wider staircase than the one she had been forced up the night of her arrest.

"We will take it slowly, my dear. Lean on me. You will be relieved to know that your father has been released also and waits in the carriage," Justin informed her, talking low and as one does to a convalescent. He was shocked by her appearance, and even more so by the stunned expression in her eyes. The prison was still a hellhole even after the commission's supposed attempt at reform, but he felt a cold knot in his stomach at her condition. He had seen that same look in men's eyes when they had been in combat too long. It was in Leander Valcour's as well, and his physical health was deteriorating rapidly. He could only wish she didn't have to see her father before they got him home and cleaned up.

When they walked outside into the fading twilight, Ariane stopped for a moment to breathe deeply of the fresh air. She could smell the magnolia blossoms in the park. Tears filled her eyes at the beauty of the trees and the mauve-violet of the night sky.

"Caesar is here with the carriage," Justin told her, guiding her with his hand about her waist down the wooden sidewalk to where the closed carriage stood waiting.

"Father, oh Father," Ariane sobbed as she got inside

316

and saw Leander Valcour huddled in the corner, a light quilt wrapped around him, for even in the heat he was shivering. He had already drunk half the flask of brandy Justin had given him.

He clasped his daughter to him with tears running down his wrinkled cheeks, stroking her tangled hair with his shaking hand. "You have gotten yourself married while I was gone. Wait till your brother hears you were married without either of us being there, you little minx," he tried to jest.

Ariane felt a stab of pain go through her like a knife and had to bury her face in his ripped dirty shirt for a moment while she fought for control. Her father had been through too much—she couldn't tell him about Beau.

"Yes, Papa, Beau will be mighty vexed, but then he always liked Justin," Ariane said lightly, moving across to sit next to her husband for her father's body was stretched out on the seat.

The strong masculine hand of her husband clasped hers tightly, telling her he was with her, and understood how hard it was for her to continue this charade that her brother was alive. Lacing his fingers with hers, he put his other arm around her shoulders, but she pulled lightly away from him.

"I am such a mess. I need to bathe," she explained with a brief smile of apology, but it did not reach her cool remote gray eyes. She held herself away from him, stiff and withdrawn. The ride to Fleur de Lys was a quiet one, for Leander Valcour, exhausted and filled with the brandy, soon fell asleep. Ariane said not a word, staring out the window, never looking at Justin, her hand limp and unresponsive in his grip. He glanced from time to time at her delicate profile, her cheek smudged with dirt, straw still clinging to her hair, and he felt anger and apprehension. Something

317

had changed between them since her stay in prison. He wondered suddenly if all she saw when she looked at him was the blue uniform instead of the man. It was a disquieting thought.

"Felicity Sanderson was in my cell," she said in flat tones after they had turned in through the gates of Fleur de Lys. "They carried her body out this morning. She had died in the night while we all slept. They would not give her any quinine for her malaria, nor would they call a doctor, or take her to the hospital."

"I am sorry you had to see such a thing and that your friend is dead," he told her softly.

"Really, how strange, since you were the one to send her there," Ariane replied coolly in a distant voice, but as she turned to look at him, he saw the fury and desolation in her misty gray eyes.

"These terrible things happen in a war, Little Bit. It is not pretty or romantic, but brutal and cruel, inhuman most of the time. I must confess I knew Irving Block was a pesthole but even I did not realize just how awful it is."

"Yes, 'tis inhuman, as are the men who run it. I shall never forget it or them." The tone of her voice struck him through with a dark premonition that nothing between them was ever going to be the same again.

He had been a fool ever to think it could work. Hadn't he experienced enough rejection because of that stiff-necked Southern pride? Whatever had happened to her in prison had left its mark. She was not the fiery Rebel belle, not now. Beside him sat a cold, tormented woman balanced, like many soldiers he had seen, on a thin line between anger and despair. Their only grip on sanity was their hatred and need for retribution.

"Home," she breathed, and for a moment he saw a glimpse of the old Ariane.

"Yes, home, and rest for you and your father. You

318

will both be my only patients, so you will get my undivided attention," he told her, reaching out and cupping her chin so she had to look up into his intense searching gaze. "Do you want my undivided attention, Ariane?"

"I . . . I don't know," she answered, her crystal-gray eyes bordered by tears. "There has been so much, I have seen so much, that I don't know how I feel about . . ." Her voice trailed off as the carriage came to a stop in front of the house, which looked to her like a wonderful sanctuary. She turned away from him to stare longingly at the elegant mansion that was Fleur de Lys. More than shelter, it was a symbol of her lineage, of her past, and it was her anchor in the storm of war, her splendid refuge.

Justin stiffened, knowing that she had to have time to heal. She was coming back to Fleur de Lys like a wounded animal to its lair, but when she had recovered in body and spirit, would there be anything left between them? He reached across her and opened the door, swiftly stepping out and then extending his hand to help her down. Turning to awaken her father and help him disembark, he heard her gasp of pleasure.

As he and Caesar half supported, half carried her father out of the carriage and up to the front door, he saw Ariane run to one of the giant magnolia trees that shaded the front of the house. Helping Leander Valcour in through the front door opened by Sable, he watched from the corner of his eye as Ariane picked one of the huge waxy blooms and held it to her nostrils as if the fragrant flower could wipe forever from her mind the stench of Irving Block Prison. Her dog bounded out the door, Bess's tail wagging enthusiastically as she ran to greet her mistress. He watched as she placed the flower gently on the ground and bent down to embrace and fondle the beloved pet. He gave

319

a sigh of relief—it was the first show of positive emotion she had shown since he had taken her out of that hellhole. Turning, he went inside to help his more critical patient. Leander Valcour's sickness was of the body, hopefully easier to treat than that of a tortured mind.

"Dearest Bess, how good it is to see you. I have missed you so, darlin'," she crooned, stroking under the dog's silky ears the way she enjoyed it. The simple act of giving the animal affection and receiving it in return seemed to bring a slight ray of light into the gloom that hung over Ariane's mind. "Come, let's go inside," she whispered to her pet, picking up the magnolia before rising to her feet.

Holding the blossom carefully in her hands lest she touch the fragile petals and cause them to turn brown, as magnolia blooms did when they came in contact with anything, she walked into the house with Bess trailing at her heels. From now on, she would fill her bedchamber with fragrant flowers. Then a frown furrowed her brow as she realized Justin would expect to share her bed now that they were married. She experienced a gamut of perplexing emotions at the thought. Wishing she could be stronger, she knew that there was a part of her that wanted him, no matter what uniform he wore. Then with a shiver of vivid recollection, she remembered the whispered accusation as she'd left the prison cell. *Traitor,* someone had called her. Was she a traitor to enjoy the feel of Justin's embrace, the touch of his heated mouth on her own? She sighed, weary of the argument that went round and round in her tired brain. Her whole body was engulfed in tides of exhaustion, leaving her feeling drained, hollow, and lifeless. Sable greeted her with concern in her brown-velvet eyes as she observed her usually immaculate mistress's condition. "Come, *ma petite,* a good refreshing

320

bath and some nourishing food and you will feel much better. I will come as soon as I get your father settled. Doctor Justin is with him now. There is a tray in your room. Leroy and one of the kitchen maids is bringing the water for your bath."

"Thank you, Sable. And please put perfume in the water, a lot of perfume. Later if you could have someone pick more magnolia blossoms, I want my bedchamber filled with them," Ariane said, starting up the stairs. "I want to check on my father before I eat."

"Miche Valcour is bathing now, and then he is to be examined by Doctor Justin. Rest, *ma chère,* and eat. There will be time later when you are feeling more yourself to talk with your father," Sable told her in a troubled voice. The lifeless look in Ariane's eyes bothered her. Something had happened to the young woman she had cared for all her life, something that had damaged her spirit in a way that was terrible to behold.

"Perhaps you are right," Ariane said dully, stopping at the top of the stair, then turning and walking with Bess into her bedchamber.

Sable stared for a moment after her then, with a sigh, hurried down to the doctor's room for his bag, thinking now that they were married, she must move his belongings into Ariane's bedchamber. A slight smile curving her lips, she mused that that was what the young woman needed to pull her from her depression, a few nights in the four-poster with that handsome, intense husband of hers. She was glad Ariane had Justin for a husband. In the hard, vengeful times coming in the South, a Yankee husband would be heaven-sent. Perhaps this would end her sweet chile's dangerous work for the Confederacy. The war was lost, but the fools couldn't see it, Sable thought. And yet they were her fools, her family for so many years she couldn't leave them. But she thought with a smile of triumph about her boy, her Roman. He was wearing blue now and that was something. Pride swelled in her breast as she thought about Miche Valcour's three sons—two had fought for the Confederacy, and one was fighting for the Union. Then arranging her face in its usual placid mask, she strode down the hall to see to the man she had loved all her life.

Inside her room, Ariane peeled the dirty clothes from her body. Then taking a wrapper from the armoire, she sat at her desk, touching the locket that still hung about her neck. All the time she had been in prison she had worn a Confederate cipher key about her neck. Unfastening the clasp, she took it from her neck and placed it in the hollowed-out romance novel she used for a hiding place. Then taking the covers from the dishes on the tray, she began to eat, but not from hunger. She ate so that she might regain her strength, for without strength, she would not be able to help the Confederacy and strike a blow at the men who she now hated with a cold fury.

As she was eating, Leroy and Susie brought in the brass containers of water. After Leroy helped her bring the brass tub from behind the screen, Susie dismissed him and began to fill the tub at Ariane's request.

"Thank you, Susie, that will be all," Ariane said to the young woman. Then after she left, she took a bottle of heliotrope perfume from her dressing table and poured a large amount along with bath salts into the water till it turned lavender. Taking the bar of scented soap from where Susie had placed on the towel, Ariane shed her wrapper and slid into the warm fragrant water.

Sitting there for a moment, she enjoyed the sensual feel of the water on her tired body and the wonderful clean smell of the perfume. Then taking up the soap,

322

she began to scrub every inch of her body. Perhaps if she scrubbed hard enough, she could wash away the memory of Irving Block, and the misery she had seen there.

"Sable, help me with my hair," she called out as she heard the door open.

"I would be glad to," a deep masculine voice said, sending a sensual ripple of awareness up and down her spine.

"Justin!" she gasped, turning around, the bar of soap clutched in her hand. "What are you doing here?"

"At the moment I am going to wash your hair, but as for later, we shall have to see," he told her, taking the soap from her hand. "Sit up now so I can pour the water. Close your eyes so you do not get soap in them," he murmured, his voice velvet-edged but strong and determined. Lifting the large porcelain pitcher of warm water, he poured it over Ariane's head while she sputtered in protest.

"Stop it," she complained. "I want Sable. What would she say if she saw you in my bedchamber." She quickly closed her mouth as he poured more water on to her hair.

"She would think what a considerate husband I am," he said. "Now tilt your head back like that, and close your eyes. Relax." His voice was soft and hypnotic as he began to soap her long tresses, massaging her scalp as he moved his fingers up and down in delicious, mesmerizing strokes.

With her eyes closed, she gave in to the wonderful sensual feel of his hands, the warmth of the water, and the scent of heliotrope. She was in an enchanted garden of sweet-smelling flowers, floating on a warm cloud. As warm water flowed once more over her hair, rinsing away the soap, she thought of rain, warm soothing rain, falling down over her tired muscles, her tense back, relaxing rain washing away all the dirt and ugliness.

"There, your hair is done, but I think your back could use some help. Yes, you are so tense. Allow me to wash it all away," he murmured in a low, composed voice that was deep, dusky, lulling as his hand soaped her back, then poured a stream of warm water down her spine. She sighed with pleasure. His fingers followed the water, stroking, kneading the nerves and muscles of her long exquisite back.

"I think that is enough," she managed to say as his hands reached the curve of her bottom. "If you will leave, I can finish dressing," she said primly, opening her eyes but staring straight ahead, not looking at him.

"No, my sweet wife, that is most definitely not enough," he told her, his voice uncompromising yet oddly gentle as one hand slipped under her bottom and the other around her waist. With one quick movement, before she knew what was happening, he had lifted her up and out of the tub. Her wet body dripped water all over his clothes.

"What are you doing?" she exclaimed in annoyance. She didn't want to feel anything. If she started to feel, it would all break loose. She didn't want to go through all of it again. She wanted to bury it deep, deep, where she didn't have to face the pain of it.

"I am going to dry you although you feel so delicious wet." His voice had a trace of laughter in it as he set her down on her feet. As she stood glaring at him, water running off her in rivulets, he picked up a towel and began with her hair. Standing behind her, he rubbed the long strands between his fingers, then on to her back and then gently her breasts, taking a long time with her breasts.

"I think they are dry," she said through clenched

teeth, trying not to feel the convulsive tremors that ran through her at his gentle, oh so seductive touch. "Don't do this. I do not want this," she breathed, her words shakier than she would have liked.

"But, my sweet Ariane, my golden fiery Rebel, this is what you need. What I need. Don't be afraid to feel," he whispered, his tongue circling the contour of her ear.

"But I am afraid," she shuddered.

"I am with you, there is nothing to fear. Let me show you the way back to life." His dark liquid voice was a seductive promise as he dropped the towel and reached for her with strong, caressing, knowing hands.

Chapter Twenty-four

"I . . . I don't want to feel anything," she protested. "Do not make me feel."

"Ah, but 'tis so wonderful to feel. Do not close yourself off. Remember how exquisite it can be between us," he murmured, turning her around slowly in his arms till she faced him, his mouth touching hers lightly, teasing the sensitive contours.

His lips were warm and gentle, molding her trembling mouth to his with a sweet fierce determination that allowed her no retreat. The velvet of his tongue was tracing, soothing, seducing away her stubborn refusal to relax. She tried to fight him and her own arousal, but he persisted with a gentle yet ardent patience till she parted her lips with a sigh and he tenderly invaded the sensitive moist cavern. She swirled around the honeyed banner of his desire, responding despite all her resolutions. Swaying against him, she succumbed to his touch, his taste, the intensity of his passionate resolve to reach her, to bring her back from the depth of her despair.

A sigh shuddered through him as he felt her soften, mold her body against his lean hardness, her arms reach around him. His mouth caressed the fullness of her lips then slowly, almost reverently, he kissed each eyelid, each temple where her pulse throbbed like a trapped hummingbird, then down her soft cheek to the curve of her neck, fragrant with heliotrope, the scent that to him would always be Ariane.

She wished dimly she could tell him to stop by a gesture, to pull away, tell him to leave, but she could not. The aching need made her limbs feel heavy with a languor that had nothing to do with the humid heat of the afternoon, the hunger that throbbed deep within her would not be denied. This was an affinity of body and soul that claimed a precedence over ideals, over a concept of honor, over war. This yearning desire to bond once more with a man who was a mate of her soul, a twin of her heart, overwhelmed all her resolve. He might wear the uniform of those she hated, but he was in the deepest, hidden recesses of her heart not one of them, never could be one of them.

"I want to feel the silk of your skin on mine," he whispered against her throat. Then lifting his head, he joked gently, " 'Tis warm this afternoon for so many clothes."

"Yes," she replied, her voice shaking, for she, too, wanted to feel the strength of him against her, inside her. If she could lose herself in the splendor of his touch, his thrusting glory, perhaps she could forget everything. As he began to unbutton his tunic, she reached out to help him. His burning black eyes radiated his joy as together they pulled his clothes from his body.

"You make me wanton to act so," she murmured as he pulled her against him, pressing her so she felt his erect arousal against her thigh.

"But it is so delicious to feel wanton, to feel wild and free. You and I make our own rules," he said.

The sultry afternoon air swirled around Ariane's nude body, drying her skin, teasing her like Justin's caresses. "When I am with you, there are no rules," she sighed ruefully. "What would Sable think if she came in?"

"That we are enjoying each other, and that 'tis beautiful and right that we do so," he murmured, stroking down her back to the saucy silk mounds of her bottom.

So exquisite were the sensual sensations he aroused in her, that she tilted back her head and gave him a seductive smile as he pressed her against his erect manhood. Her legs wrapped around his sturdy fur-covered thighs like the honeysuckle vine to the massive cedars.

"This is life, this is feeling, my lovely wanton," he breathed, his dark eyes holding her, willing her not to look away as his gaze burned into her, thawing the last frozen parts of her soul. "Do you feel the fire, the wanting that is beyond anything?"

"Yes . . . yes!" she moaned, the words torn from her aching throat.

Lifting one hand to cup her chin, he said, "Look, look and see the beauty of a man and woman together celebrating life and all its joyous pleasures." He turned her head to the right, where they were reflected in the long mirror over the mantel.

Ariane felt a flush of rose stain her face at the sight of their two naked bodies pressed together in the late-afternoon light. She tried to turn away, but his hand held her chin with gentle, but firm fingers.

"Do not be embarrassed, my sweet, shy love. There is nothing to be ashamed of in the glory of our pleasure. This is what man and woman are meant to do, to join together, to enjoy the differences and the beauty of each other's body. There is nothing furtive or wrong about it. It is right, and more than that—it is magnificent."

"Yes 'tis splendid," she whispered, meeting his ebon eyes in the mirror. And she realized it was beautiful and unbelievably erotic, her feminine gold-ivory smooth skin against the bronzed, furred, sinewy masculine

328

form. The hazy, burnished light gilded them both till the sensual tableau in the mirror seemed to glow like exquisite Greek sculpture touched by Zeus himself and brought to life. Did all lovers in the heart-expanding thrill of their passion feel like gods and goddesses brought down from Mount Olympus to enjoy the pleasures of their flesh, she wondered as she watched Justin's hand stroke down the curve of her back.

"See how lovely you are," he breathed, gently turning her so she stood in front of him. "Like soft doves are your breasts." His voice was a velvet murmur as his hands lifted each alabaster mound up and his finger and thumb caressed and teased each coral peak.

She stood mesmerized by the sight of what was giving her such exquisite pleasure. The dark bronze of his male hands, the long tapered fingers plying their magic on her opal breasts. It was intoxicating to see this woman arching up against the man who stood enraptured behind her. Her head thrown back against the raven-black fur of his chest, eyes wide with desire, her hands reaching behind her to stroke his thighs till his moans of pleasure joined hers. Twisting, turning, arching up into his hands that she might experience every nuance of his knowing touch.

He shuddered with the effort to keep control, for the sight of her in the mirror reveling in the ecstasy his hands brought her was a sight so sensual and erotic he knew the image was burned into his brain. Slowly, as one hand continued to caress the throbbing rosy peak, the other trailed down the soft curve of her rib cage to linger a moment at the indentation of her tiny waist then on down across the moonstone of her belly to the silky golden curls at the vee of her thighs.

"Oh," she gasped, and her misty-gray eyes widened further till they were enormous in her pale visage with

329

the rose flush of passion on her high cheekbones. Unable to tear her gaze away, she watched as those long sensitive fingers stroked through those intimate curls to find the center of ecstasy. She was swept by a dark frenzy, moving, arching, wanting more and more of him till she felt like some wild creature riding the crest of a wave of erotic sensation.

"Yes, yes, my sweet Ariane, feel it, delight in it. Look at how beautiful you are, how good it is between us." His voice was a hoarse rasp in her ear, his smoldering night-black eyes adoring her in the silvered glass that reflected back their passion in to the shadowy chamber. The last dying rays of the sun caught them in a shaft of mellow light till their bodies seemed to be as on fire on the outside as they were within.

Suddenly she was soaring as contraction after contraction swept through her. The pearl of her fingernails dug into the muscles of his thighs as he took her over the edge with his deft unyielding touch. She shook with waves of molten voluptuous joy as her cry of release soared into the air like a released dove.

"My God, how incredible you are!" he breathed as she slumped back against him, her legs shaking from the intensity of her plunge into fulfillment.

"I did not know such a thing was possible," she whispered, turning her face against his chest. "You did not . . . enter me."

"There are many ways to give pleasure and that is only the beginning, my sweet," he murmured, kissing the silky top of her head. "I have till twilight, then I must return to the hospital. We have time for another lesson."

"You make me a wild thing," she whispered, blushing at her own wanton excitement.

"Then I am happy, for that is exactly what I set out to do." There was the sound of satisfaction in his voice. Lightly he stroked down her hair, soft and silky from the shampoo but tangled, a golden mane that gave her the appearance of a small sensuous feline with her eyes still heavy-lidded with the remembrance of her unrestrained passion.

"Come, we must rest awhile," he told her, leading her to the bed. Sable had turned it down in case Ariane cared to nap.

With languid movements, Ariane slipped under the linen sheet, but it was too warm. She flung it from her body as Justin joined. To her amazement, her blood began to pound in her veins once more as she mused on what was to come. Justin had been right—it had been only the beginning. Her body wanted him again, only this time she wanted to feel him inside her, joining with her till they were one.

He pulled her to him, his mouth on hers, kissing long, slow, deep kisses till her lips felt swollen from the fiery massage. Then his burning, teasing mouth was everywhere, in the hollow of her throat on down to each hard, aching, rosebud nipple, lightly circling each peak with his tongue, fanning the flames of her desire once more. She writhed as his tongue circled her navel then down to the soft roundness of her belly.

Justin felt control slipping away but he fought his desire, rolling away from her. Then reaching back for her, he pulled her up and astride him as he lay this time under her. His fingers gently opened her to receive him. His hands at her rounded hips, he lifted her on to the throbbing length of him.

She tossed back her golden mane with a deep sensual laugh of excitement and utter joy. Her hands caught his shoulders as she stared down at him, watching the play of passion across his handsome features, the fierce hunger in the black eyes as she began to move, taking him deeper into her body with each of

331

his powerful thrusts.

She was beauty incarnate, the passionate symbol of femininity with her red-gold sunset hair wild and loose about her ivory shoulders, her soft gray eyes languid and heavy-lidded with desire. She was his woman, and he gloried in it as she took his savage thrusts, riding him hard, giving no quarter. She was his mate, his lover, his Ariane.

Never had she felt so alive in every nerve, every pore. This was almost primitive, elemental, the joining with the man she seemed to have been waiting for all her life. Nothing existed for her but the feel of his hot swollen shaft moving inside her, carrying her to heights she could find only with him.

"Ride me, Little Bit," he murmured hoarsely, his hands holding tightly to her waist as he surged into her moist velvet depths, withdrawing and plunging, till she was panting, meeting him, anticipating each thrust with a moan of relief that soon she would feel him again.

This was madness, she thought while she could still barely think, but what divine madness. Another wild laugh of rapture was torn from her throat as she kneaded the sinewy muscles of his shoulders, scraping her nails across his skin. In her frenzy, she bit him lightly on the upper arm, and he groaned with the thrill of it.

"Yes, this is life, my sweet love, feel it, taste it. Take it, take me deeper, all of me," he muttered huskily, caught up now in the passionate hot frenzy that drove them both.

Sensing he was losing control, he held her waist, and with one swift movement, she was on her back and he was on top of her, still thrusting deep inside her white-hot honeyed sweetness.

"Yes, now!" Ariane cried out, her blood singing as

once more the molten waves swept over her, carrying her higher, higher, till she soared with a pleasure that was total, all consuming, and healing.

When his shuddering release came and he cried out her name, she held him to her as together they found contentment. He had been right—there were so many wonderful ways to celebrate their passion, she thought. Feeling reborn, she closed her eyes, so heavy now with sleep, and for the first time in days, she found a deep peaceful slumber still locked in his embrace.

Justin held her to his chest, relieved that somehow he had penetrated the barrier she had erected. Her hideous time in prison would eventually fade to a dim memory as soon as the war ended. He sighed, staring out across the feminine chamber. It had taken all his ingenuity and fast talking to secure her and her father's release. He had had to wire General Dodge, intimating that it was of great importance that they be released, that through them he would discover the leaders of the Confederate spy ring in Memphis. His mouth twisted into a cynical smile—whose side was he on? But he was wearying of it all, the bloodshed, the young men dying on both sides, the petty tyrants who ruled over their individual domains, terrorizing the civilian population. He still believed the Union was right, but he was not so sure that his spying on the people of Memphis would end the war any faster as he had once thought. It was not a question of who was working for the Confederacy among the old guard of the city, but rather who was not. His feelings and emotions where Memphis was concerned would always be confused, a mixture of love and hate. Where would it all end, he thought with a sense of unease. What would his high-minded wife think if she knew her husband was a spy for the Union? What would her highly developed sense of honor think of the fact that General Dodge thought he had married her so he might discover what Rebel activities her father's steamboat line was involved in? Would she sleep so peacefully in his arms if she knew the truth, he wondered, brushing a silken strand of gold from her temple. He had to leave her for now, since he had had to take night duty at the hospital in order to get the day off to fetch her from prison.

When she opened her eyes, it was late the next morning. She had slept almost twenty-four hours. As she lay staring at the hands of the pretty little French clock on the mantel, she inhaled the heady fragrance of magnolias and gardenias. Turning her head, she saw a single perfect gardenia blossom just beginning to fade on the pillow next to her. The room was filled with shallow bowls of fresh magnolia blooms floating in the water. Lifting the gardenia to her nose, she smiled. Justin—it had to have been Justin who'd placed the flower on the pillow beside her. Gardenias had been her wedding bouquet.

Sable confirmed her suspicion when she brought her breakfast tray. "He picked it himself when he came back from the hospital at dawn, and insisted I have the room filled with magnolia blossoms for you when you woke," the woman told her with a twinkle in her brown eyes.

"My husband, where is he?" Ariane asked, sitting up in bed so Sable could put the white wicker bed tray across her lap.

"He is sleeping in his old room for today. After he awakens, I shall bring his things in here with you. The night duty was only for last night. He will return to the hospital on the morrow."

"I see," Ariane said with a troubled frown. "Did my husband request to move in here with me?"

"Yes, *ma petite,* he did. Does this trouble you?"

"No, only that I have some items in here that my husband should not see," Ariane said quietly.

"You mean the cipher key," Sable stated softly.

"He must not find it, but then he has not noticed anything yet, so perhaps I am safe," she mused, sipping rich, hot coffee.

"Hide it. Forget it ever existed," Sable pleaded, her usually calm exterior shattered with the force of her emotion.

"I cannot. I . . . I love Justin, but I also love the South."

"You are making a mistake, *ma chère*. The war is already lost for the South, but your marriage, it is just beginning. What if you are forced to choose between them?"

"Pray that day never comes," Ariane said grimly, placing her cup back on its saucer.

"La, but you were always hardheaded," Sable sighed, shrugging her elegant shoulders in defeat as she walked to the armoire to fetch Ariane's gown for the day.

"Sable, how is my father?" Ariane asked, her voice filled with concern.

"He is resting. Doctor Justin has given him a sedative, thinking that if Miche Valcour rests, gets good food, and keeps his mind untroubled, his body will heal itself. Doctor Justin is a very wise man," Sable told her as she took an ivory muslin gown printed with pink rose sprays and narrow lavender stripes off a scented satin hanger from the armoire.

Ariane nodded that she would wear it. She felt a pang, realizing that she could not wear mourning for Beau, not if her father's mind was to be kept at peace. Her mouth a grim line, she thought that her work for the Confederacy would have to be her way of honoring Beau's memory.

"A note was sent around this morning from M'sieur

335

Barbierre's shop by his boy. It was addressed to you, *ma petite,*" Sable said quietly, but there was worry in her brown eyes. She knew that Joseph Barbierre, who owned a liquor and sundry shop and worked for the Barbierre Brothers of Marseilles, France, was also an agent working for the Confederacy. He was Forrest's contact in Memphis, and Ariane's as well.

"He must have a job for me," Ariane mused. "Good."

"Think carefully what you do," Sable cautioned, handing her the letter sealed with red wax and pressed with a seal that contained the letters J.B.

"I do what I must," Ariane said with grim determination as she opened the letter with a brass letter opener in the shape of a sword. "My spectacles please, Sable."

Giving her the needlepoint case from the desk that contained her spectacles, the older woman said, "I have made a powerful gris-gris to keep you from harm, for I know you, *petite chere.* How stubborn you are, and how you think you must continue with this madness because of Miche Beau's memory. I shall sew it at the top of your corset where it shall lie near your heart." The woman took from the pocket of her voluminous apron a tiny heart-shaped bag made of soft white linen. It resembled a sachet, but it contained secret ingredients known only to Sable. As a high priestess in the Memphis Voodoo Cult, she was known to have great powers. She would use those powers, her strong magic, to protect her child. She had watched over this high-spirited girl-child since she was born, as she had promised her mother, the tragic Marie Louise.

Even if she hadn't loved the headstrong Ariane, she never went back on her word. It was a point of honor with Sable; the quadroon woman was in many ways as much an aristocrat as Ariane, for Sable's father had been Ariane's great-uncle. Her child, of course, knew nothing of this. White women, plantation mistresses, had long ago learned to close their eyes to such things, and Ariane had never visited her mother's family in Baton Rouge. The gossip of nearly fifty years before had never traveled upriver to Memphis. Yes, she thought, threading a needle, there were many reasons for her loyalty to Ariane. Knotting the thread, Sable began to sew the tiny bag to the silk and lace-boned corset.

"Thank you, Sable, for caring," Ariane said softly, realizing that even though the woman obviously wanted a Union victory, she would protect the young woman whom she had raised from babyhood. The war had caused many strange alliances and torn so many families and loved ones apart. If they had known what it was going to cost on both sides, would they have rushed in with such enthusiasm? Putting on her spectacles, Ariane began to read Joseph Barbierre's note.

The sentences were harmless enough to any Yankee soldier reading them. Ariane, however, understood that the innocent announcement—that her order from France had finally made its way to the shop, and would she please stop by and see if it was to her liking—meant he needed urgently to speak with her. That Forrest had a job for her, a most important job or he wouldn't have sent for her so soon after leaving prison.

"Sable, has the Provost Marshal's Office put a guard on the house?" she asked.

"No, they have not. Doctor Justin said you are free to go as you please about the city, but that like everyone else in Memphis, you would need a pass to go outside the Union lines," she said, finishing her sewing.

"See that one of the kitchen maids is free to sit with Father. You and I are going to Joseph Barbierre's shop. Have Caesar bring around the carriage. We must

337

stop at the Valcour Line offices as well," Ariane said with determination, moving the breakfast tray to the side. Flinging back the sheet, she got out of bed.

"A Yankee officer along with Sam Riley, since he is back in port, are running the Valcour Line," Sable told her, pouring water into the tub for her bath. In the heat a bath was needed to find some way to cool off. The humid heat poured into the chamber along with the unrelenting rays of the sun. " 'Tis a hot day to go into the city," she commented, playing her last card.

"Sable, I am going and that is all there is to it," Ariane announced firmly, sinking into the cool fragrant water.

"Doctor Justin won't like it, he won't like it at all," Sable said with one last parting shot as she left the room to carry out Ariane's orders.

Staring out the window at the tops of the majestic cedars and magnolias, Ariane felt congested with doubts and fears. She had depicted to Sable an ease with the situation she didn't really feel. Her commitment to the Confederacy was unwavering, but she was not a fool—she had seen what the Yankees did to those they considered traitors. She wasn't anxious to return to Irving Block Prison, but it had not been easy for Beau and for Charles. The men that carried on their fight were doing so under the worst conditions— she couldn't let them down. Then as she stared down in the water to soap her legs, she saw her wedding ring catch the light and glow with a gold fire.

Justin, her husband, her enemy, her delight, and her despair. She was caught between two conflicting loves, between two loyalties. In a way she felt as if she was betraying them both. Her heart ached with the agony of being torn between her love for the South and her love for her husband, but she could not let either of them go. It would require a balancing act of the greatest delicacy to continue on as she must. Today would be the first step along the dangerous path she chose to walk as Confederate spy and wife of a Union officer. She hoped Sable had created a strong gris-gris charm for her. She knew she was going to need it if all was not to be lost.

Chapter Twenty-five

The sultry heat of the afternoon was at its peak, the sun an unmerciful, white-hot sphere in the cloudless sky as the carriage rolled down Poplar Road to Memphis, somnolent in the August heat. The dust and mosquitoes were so bothersome that Ariane had had Caesar put up the hood, so it was stifling inside the coach.

The magnolia trees drooped in the heat along Front Row, their leaves seeming to be covered in a fine ochre dust that was everywhere in the muggy town. Even the Union drays had slowed to a crawl in the humid, suffocating air. The river simmered below in the blinding sun like a great coiled yellow-brown reptile. Mosquitoes were everywhere, swarming from the Bayou Gayoso into the heart of the city to bedevil the Union troops unaccustomed to a steamy Memphis summer.

Stopping in front of Joseph Barbierre's store, Ariane noticed that the sidewalks seemed unusually empty for the afternoon. Everyone with any sense, or instinct for self-preservation, had gone indoors. She lifted her rose silk parasol against the sun rays with satisfaction. It was the perfect time to come to Barbierre's Sundries. Sable followed, carrying a large basket. They had to make it look authentic, as if, indeed, they had come to Memphis to shop. She had to remember to buy something, she thought as they walked into the darkened interior of the store.

"Madame Pierce, how good it is to see you again. I trust you are feeling well." The deep French-accented voice of an elegant man of medium height impeccably dressed with black hair, mustache, and goatee greeted them as they came into the shop. It was empty of all customers except two elderly women, who before the war had been grand dames of society. Today they simply appeared tired and worn, their clothes clean but having seen better days.

"Good day, Mrs. Winchester, Mrs. Breckenridge," Ariane said with a polite smile. They stared at her for a long silent moment as if they were looking through her, not at her, then turned and filed out of the shop without saying a word.

"Do not mind them, they do not know the courageous woman I have had the honor of coming to know and respect," Joseph Barbierre said softly in gallant tones, seeing the pain in her gray eyes.

"I see the news of my marriage to a Yankee officer has flown around town," Ariane commented with a light bitterness.

"Not only a Yankee, my dear Madame Pierce, but Justin Pierce, black sheep, rogue, and a man whom many in Memphis consider a traitor," Joseph Barbierre reminded her, compassion in his black eyes.

"Yes, and now I am considered one also," she said with more than a tinge of regret.

"But I, my dear lady, know differently."

"Why do you say that? Why do you not think me a traitor for marrying a Yankee?"

"I know what risks you have taken for the Cause, and also being French, I understand we don't always have control over the dictates of our heart. You love this man, no?" he asked, watching her delicate features intently. She was so important to their plan, he had to trust her. Somehow he was sure he could do just that.

"Yes, I do, but that does not change my love for the South. It only complicates everything," Ariane explained, a wistful expression crossing her face like a shadow. "My devotion to the Southern Cause is unshakable, you can be sure of it." Her chin came up and she met his gaze with a sad determination in her misty-gray eyes.

"Good, that is what I wanted to hear. I have been informed about your gallant brother's demise and I wish to offer you my condolences. I understand why we must not speak of it, but in my position, Madame Sanderson thought I should know since other arrangements must be made for your new contact. I, my dear lady, shall be your Confederate liaison in Memphis. As a French national, I am not suspected by the Provost Marshal."

"Yes, it would seem to be a good cover," she agreed, staring at him as he stood in a stream of dusty light filtered through the large many-paned glass display window.

"Precisely. Now I will come to why I requested your presence. If your serving woman would wait for us here, I would request that you follow me into my office." He gave a slight formal bow and indicated a closed door at the back of the store.

"Wait here, Sable," Ariane told her, not missing the frowning glance the woman gave her from worried amber-brown eyes.

She followed her host down the narrow aisle between rows of bottles, of all shapes and sizes, some dusty from long being on the shelves. There had not been money in Memphis from his old customers to purchase fine wines and brandies as they did in the old days. The Yankees speculators and soldiers found their liquor in saloons and bawdy houses; only a few officers came in now and then to purchase a fine brandy. The boxes of French chocolates sold a bit better, as did the cigars and pipe tobacco.

"I would not have insisted you come back here alone, but what I have to tell you is of the utmost importance," he murmured, closing the door behind him as they stepped into a small room that contained a desk and a bookcase full of record books.

"How can I be of help?" she asked, turning to face him.

"General Forrest has need of the services of his Swan," he told her, gesturing for her to be seated in a chair in front of his desk.

"What does he need me to do?" she said quietly.

"We need you to look at some diagrams of the inside of Irving Block Prison," he replied, looking at her intently.

"They are going to try a rescue," she deduced, excitement lighting her crystal gray eyes.

"Yes, but I cannot tell you more, only that your information about which roads were heavily garrisoned and which were not was received in La Grange and was most important. Now, will you try to the best of your ability to remember the layout of the prison?"

"Yes, although I was not in every part of the prison. I can show you where the staircases are located, and on what floors are housed the men and women. They are suffering terribly. Something must be done to help them."

"Something will," he said tersely, rising to his feet. Quickly he crossed to a large black iron safe and turned the dial till the door sprung open. Reaching inside, he lifted out several papers and brought them to the desk. Spreading them out on the surface, he motioned for Ariane to come stand with him. "These are old architectural drawings of the building when it was first erected. The Yankees have made modifications—

that is what we want to know about, and on which floors they keep the prisoners. If you can remember anything else, such as guard routines, it will be helpful."

Slowly, Ariane marked on the drawings the information needed. She told him as much as she could recollect about the prison routine, feeling somewhat of a release inside her as she took some action against those she hated, and helped those who had not been as lucky as she and were still inside the walls of Irving Block.

"This will be invaluable to General Forrest. I will see it is sent immediately. If you hear anything that you think would be of use, come to the shop and ask for a bottle of Napoleon Brandy. I shall answer that there is one in the back of the shop and ask you to accompany me to see if it is to your liking. Report anything, no matter how small. Forrest is fighting for his life. The Yankees are closing in on him down in Oxford, but you know the Wizard of the Saddle—he always has something up his sleeve. Be prepared for one of his most daring maneuvers yet," Joseph Barbierre said in cryptic tones.

"I shall, believe me, I shall," she murmured, fervently watching as he strode to the safe and carefully placed the drawings inside. "Now, I think I should buy several bottles of brandy for my father and perhaps some pipe tobacco for my husband. It must look as if I have been shopping," she told him as they exited the office.

Her next stop was the Valcour Line headquarters. A silence fell over the large chamber as she walked into the building. Furtive, curious stares were cast her way as she walked up the spiral cast-iron staircase to the owner's office.

"Saints preserve us!" Sam Riley exclaimed, rising to

his feet from behind her father's desk. A Union officer rose from his chair on the other side, turning to face her with a surprised look.

"I had to come by to see how everything is going. I am no longer allowed to serve as a nurse in the Union hospital since my incarceration. My father is quite ill, but I will be coming to the office in his place till he is well enough to take up his duties again," Ariane explained, clasping Sam's outstretched hand with affection.

" 'Tis a welcome sight you are, lass, and welcome news you bring," Sam said with a heartfelt fervor. "The lieutenant and I have been trying to keep things going, but everyone will breathe easier now that a Valcour is at the helm."

"Thank you, Sam," she said softly.

"I was not aware you were returning to run the Valcour Line," the Union officer interrupted sharply.

"Must I clear every move I make with the Provost Marshal, Lieutenant?"

"As a recent prisoner of Irving Block, I would think that would be in order, Mrs. Pierce," he said in terse tones, "or has your husband already done that for you?"

"My husband is not my jailer. I have left one prison and I have no intention of entering another," Ariane replied coldly.

"Isn't that exactly what he is, Mrs. Pierce? You do not think the Provost Marshal would let you out of Irving Block without being sure that you behaved yourself." There was triumph and a tinge of scorn in his voice.

"Please leave us, sir. I wish to discuss a private matter with Captain Riley, and I noticed when I came in that the name 'Valcour' is still on the door of this company."

"We are watching you. One false step and you will find yourself back in prison so fast it will make your pretty Secesh head swim," he shot back as he stormed out the door, slamming it behind him.

"They didn't take any of your spirit away from you, lass, I am glad to see," Sam said with admiration in his Irish-blue eyes, pulling out a chair for her.

"No, I wouldn't allow that, Sam, but I fear they did father's. He is a very sick man, broken in body and spirit. I did not want to say this in front of our Yankee friend, but he may never return to his office at the Valcour Line," Ariane told him with a sad sigh, placing her reticule on the desk. "I shall endeavor to take his place, and my first task is to see if we can resume our running of the Union blockade up the smaller rivers that feed into the Mississippi."

"The Yankees are tightening the noose about the Confederacy, lass. Every steamer leaving Memphis has a couple of guards on it. But we are still able to bribe a few with a couple of bales of cotton. The price is sky-high and many Billy Yanks like to add the sale of a bale to their pay for looking the other way when we load at Memphis. Medicine, salt, items of clothing, those are easier to hide inside a bale of cotton than guns although we have done that. Why, Ward and McCellan Pharmaceutical Company has smuggled over sixty thousand dollars' worth of medicine alone to the Confederacy, but Forrest needs guns, and they are hard to come by in Memphis. The Provost Marshal has issued an order that no guns may be sold to anyone suspected of being a Secesh sympathizer."

"Well, we must do what we can. The South needs everything, so whenever a Valcour steamer leaves Memphis, I want something on it for the Confederacy. What system are we using to alert the partisans?" she asked.

346

"When we know we are in an area of the river where there are some of our people, we signal with flags if it is in the daytime. If at night, and it usually is at night, we signal with lanterns from the Texas deck. The night is better because the Yankee patrol boats can't see as well and they don't know the Mississippi like we do," Sam explained, leaning back in his chair. "But the Yanks do have someone snooping around down at the wharves. Some tall officer has been down going through the steamers at night, talking to the roustabouts in their dives in Pinch Gut. He seems real familiar, some even say he has a bit of a Southern accent. Sounds to me like he is working for the Provost Marshal, trying to find out about our operation. I will try to find out more about him and head off any trouble he is out to make for us."

"Yes, they are looking for anything they can use to put me back in Irving Block," she mused. "Take extra precautions, Sam. If they can't defeat General Forrest on the field of battle, they can try and starve the South into surrender. They have already done a good job of it in some places," she said, her lips thinned with anger, staring at some terrible sight only she could see. Then as if shaking it off with a light shudder, she stood up and said, "Now I must be going, but I will try to come in on the morrow if that is possible. I know you are anxious to return to the river." She gave him an understanding smile as she moved toward the door.

"Aye, that I will. A steamer wheel is more to my liking than this desk," he acknowledged as he bid her good-bye.

The ride back to Fleur de Lys was a silent one as Ariane stared out at the hot dusty road, not really seeing it, seeing instead the horrible conditions of the prison they passed by on their way out of Memphis.

347

Would it always haunt her? It must not be allowed to continue—somehow those men must be stopped. She would do anything to stop it, anything. Perhaps then she would stop feeling guilty that she walked out of there alive while Felicity had left in a crude pine box. Yes, whatever it took, she would do it to avenge Felicity's death and the deaths of her other friends and family killed in this bloody war. Suddenly Justin's darkly handsome visage swam in front of her, blotting out the horror she had seen, and she was filled with the dull ache of despair. Love him though she might with all her heart, she could not allow her feelings to interfere with what she must do, the pledge she had made, even though it broke her heart in the process.

The last golden rays of the dying sun were streaming through the cedars as the carriage came to a stop at the portico of Fleur de Lys. Stepping down on the carriage block, Ariane sensed someone was watching her from the shadows. Turning, she saw a figure next to the shaggy bark of a cedar tree. The glare of the sun was in her eyes and she could see only his long lean form.

"Yes, what are you doing?" she called without thinking.

"I might ask the same question of you, my dear wife," the deep sardonic voice asked as the figure came strolling toward her.

"Justin!" she cried.

"Yes, did I startle you, or did you think to slip into the house without my knowing you had been gone?" There was a note of cynicism in his voice and a watchful, speculative look in his dark eyes.

"Are you my guard now, as well as my husband?" she demanded bitterly.

"Do you need one?" he asked.

She had forgotten for a moment how close the bond

was between them, close enough that they could sense when the other was troubled or evading the truth. She felt a sinking feeling in her stomach as she realized how hard marriage to Justin was going to be, sleeping in his bed every night, yet keeping an important part of herself secret from him. Somehow she must keep her guard up so this discerning enigmatic man didn't read her like an open book.

"If you mean, do I need a guard against crude Yankee soldiers that mean me harm, then yes I guess you could say I need a guard. But there is a difference, my dear husband, between a guard and a jailer. I do not, will not, have a jailer telling me where I can go and when. Memphis has the Union Command and Provost Marshal to do that and it is a job they seem to relish. At Fleur de Lys no one tells me what to do," she retorted. "This is my home."

"Perhaps 'tis time we find a home of our own," he said in a low taut voice.

"I cannot leave Fleur de Lys," she answered stubbornly.

"Cannot or will not?"

They stared at each other across the silence of the sultry late afternoon, frozen in an angry tableau. The sun had darkened behind a bank of black clouds, hinting at the coming storm. A wind began to blow across the small lake, rippling the water. Suddenly their attention was diverted as the air was filled with the flutter of wings, the black and white swans taking off from where they had been feeding next to the lake. They soared together till they reached their nesting spot on the tiny island in the middle of the lake.

"Come," Justin ordered, taking her hand firmly in his and striding with impatient steps down the curving pathway that followed the lake.

" 'Tis a storm coming," she protested, but he pulled

her along, not letting go of her hand. Having no choice, she stumbled after him, her skirt belling crazily around her in the wind, now gusting as sudden summer storms would often do in Memphis. Her bonnet sailed off and flew out over the water.

As the first drops of rain began to fall, she saw where he was taking her. When she was child, she had often played in the small one-room structure designed by the landscape architect her father had brought all the way from England. Built to resemble a miniature ruined tower from the Middle Ages, it was all the fashion in England to have such a "ruin" created for the garden. Ariane had always thought it resembled a romantic tiny castle out of one of Sir Walter Scott's novels. The small tower room with the long arched many-paned windows had been used by her brother Charles as a studio, for it had an excellent north light, and being located on the far side of the lake away from the house, it had been a quiet retreat. Charles had been an amateur artist, finding enjoyment and relaxation in oil painting. When it became his studio, Ariane had never come unless invited, for she hadn't wanted to disturb him. She had sat for a portrait in the last days before the war, but it had not been finished when Charles's regiment had left for the battlefields of Shiloh. She realized as Justin pushed hard against the door, for it stuck in the heat and humidity, that she had not been in the studio since Charles had left. The servants had come and dusted, but they were the only visitors to the quaint structure. Fragrant white roses climbed the stone walls around the heavy wooden door, their perfume heavy in the sultry air.

"You came here with Charles, didn't you. I had forgotten," Ariane said softly as they dashed inside to escape the rain, now coming down in torrents.

"Yes, and I wanted to talk with you away from the

house. The other officers will soon be coming home from the hospital," he explained, going to the casement windows and opening them so some air could come into the stuffy, long-unused chamber. The scent of the rain and roses floated in on the wind from the storm.

Ariane stood for a moment in the middle of the room, overcome by memories of her brother and the time she had spent here sitting for her portrait. She saw with a start that the easel holding the canvas of her portrait stood with a cloth thrown over it as it had the day Charles had left with his regiment. Walking over as Justin opened the windows, she pulled off the cloth. There it was as he had painted it over two years before.

" 'Tis you," Justin said with a husky catch in his voice. The lovely oval of her face, the pensive gray of her eyes, the gold with a hint of red in her hair. He had captured it all including the vulnerable wistful expression that cut through his careful defenses straight to his heart. Only the visage, elegant neck, and shoulders were finished in oil. The gown, her arms, as well as her hands, were only sketched in with charcoal.

"Yes, Charles was finishing it when he was called up to leave for Shiloh. He never returned to complete it and it was too painful for Father and I to come here. The maids dusted, and made sure the door and windows were shut, but it has stood empty since that spring. In many ways it seems a lifetime ago—so much has changed—but then for a moment there when we first entered, I could see Charles at the easel, his wife Alissa sitting over there sewing a layette for the baby she was soon to give birth to." Ariane sighed as she stared about the room, the chairs and daybed covered in white muslin sheets. The sense of abandonment and melancholy loss seemed to permeate the place.

"His wife?" Justin questioned, for he had not corre-

351

sponded with Charles in the last few years before the war.

"Yes, she died in childbirth, along with the child, only days before Charles died at Shiloh," she explained with a light shiver.

"I am sorry. We should not have come here," he said quietly, coming to stand in front of her. He cradled her gently in the circle of his arms, his lips against her hair.

The touch of his hand against her back was almost unbearable in its tenderness. She stood with her head bent against his chest, deriving strength from the warmth of his body.

"You bring out a wildness in me, Little Bit," he muttered against the silk of her hair. "I want to love you and I hate you for making me feel so out of control."

"And you do the same to me," she sighed, caressing the planes of his back through the rough material of his tunic.

"We cannot leave here till the storm passes over," he whispered, lightly kissing her temples.

"No, we cannot," she agreed huskily.

"What shall we do to pass the time?" he asked, his voice simmering with barely controlled passion.

"I believe you said you wanted to talk about something you wanted no one else to hear," she reminded him, raising her head, her gray eyes wide with a teasing, seductive quality that made his blood pound.

"There will be plenty of time to talk . . . later," he murmured thickly as his mouth claimed hers and there was no more need for words.

Chapter Twenty-six

The heady perfume of the roses climbing outside the window surrounded them as they shed their clothing, dropping it to the floor like the fallen petals of a flower in the wind. Their anger before, the sudden fury of the storm, the isolation of the studio, all combined to fan the flames of their ardor.

The feel of the moisture-laden air on their heated skin, the touch of the other's hand, the slightly salty taste of their beloved's skin on their lips — everything was overpowering in its eroticism. They moved almost as one to the daybed that stood near the windows.

Pulling the sheet from the couch, Justin revealed a silk shawl in brilliant colors of indigo, emerald, amethyst, and gold thrown across the surface. Turning to Ariane, he stepped behind her to take the pins from her chignon, allowing her long waist-length tresses to ripple to her waist, the pins falling to the floor. Gently he stroked his fingers through the silken locks till they fell around her like a golden aureole. "Yes, that is perfect," he whispered huskily. "Come lie with me. I want to see your beauty against the silk."

Drawing her with him, he pulled her down beside him on the bed. Tenderly he spread her hair out around her on the deep colors of the silk. The brilliant shades of emerald and indigo were a spectacular counterpoint to the peach-ivory of her skin and the red-gold of her hair. His hand lifted a lock of the golden

353

tresses to his lips, then placed it so it curved around, not covering, one alabaster breast. His ebon eyes smoldering with his intense passion seemed to devour the sight of her breathtaking beauty.

She lay unashamed, glorying in the reflection of adoration she saw in his consuming gaze. It was wonderful to know that she was the inspiration for the almost savage desire she saw on his usually remote visage. There was nothing remote about his expression now. The mask was gone, and the naked hunger of his obsession could be clearly seen.

With a controlled delicate touch, he traced the curve of her lips, swollen from his insistent mouth, till she opened them, sucking the tapered finger lightly, sending a burning flame through his body till he trembled with his hunger for her. Moving the finger down, he traced the delicate line of her jaw down to her throat, his eyes never leaving hers till he circled the taut nipple of her right breast. Teasing her with his touch, he bent down and reclaimed her burning lips with his mouth.

A sigh shuddered through Ariane as his mouth followed his hand down from her lips to her breasts, sucking, circling each throbbing rose peak. A wonderful languor traveled like warm honey through her veins till she was only aware of sensation, the feel of Justin's heated mouth, his sensual touch, the scent of the rain, the roses, and the ebony silk of his hair.

A man entranced by her beauty and his need to touch, taste, and feel every beloved inch of her femininity, he explored the curves, the hollows, the softness that was Ariane. There was the scent of heliotrope and roses, wind and rain, in the sultry air and on her skin. It was if he could not get enough of her. She felt the aching, the yearning in her heated loins. There was an emptiness inside her that could only be filled with him. After so much ugliness, so much horror, he was

354

life's rapturous essence. She wanted him to take her once more to that soaring splendor.

As his mouth trailed burning kisses across the mound of her belly to the silky curls of her womanhood, he heard the soft moan coming from the back of her throat, the siren call of love that told him of her complete arousal, and her need as great as his own.

Her hands stroked down the hard planes of his back, and as he rose over her, she trailed her fingers over the soft dark hair that covered his flat, taut belly. His body was so different from her own, the lean muscle, the bronze skin, the silky black masculine hair, so wonderfully different. She had first wanted him as an innocent young girl filled with strange yearnings she did not understand, but now she wanted him as an awakened woman. She wanted him inside her, filling her, transporting her to that rapture she found only with him. She wanted to hear the deep moans of pleasure torn from his throat that told her she was driving him to the same wild frenzy she was feeling in every pore of her moist heated skin.

"Please," she implored him as he rose over her, his fingers stroking, preparing her honeyed depths for him.

"What do you want?" he asked, his voice a thick rasp of barely controlled passion. "Tell me what you want."

"You, I want you inside me," she moaned, her fingers digging into the silk beneath her as he lifted her hips up to receive him.

"Yes, yes, as I want to feel you all around me," he breathed. He could wait no longer. He would take her again and again till this elusive woman understood she was his and his alone.

When he plunged into her, the half-sigh, half-moan that was torn from her filled the chamber like the

355

sweetest music. His part-savage, part-gentle assault was everything she wanted, and she met it with an arching, undulating motion of her hips, wanting him, taking him deeper, and deeper still.

Burning mouth pressed to burning mouth, soft ivory feminine body molded against hard bronzed masculinity, they moved in circles of ecstasy, thrust and counterthrust, a duel of insatiable rapture. Swept by a dark frenzy, they reached their shuddering, soul-searing crescendo and together they rode the top of the wave to the ultimate joining of man and woman.

Later as they lay arms and legs entwined on the silk shawl, Ariane wished they never had to leave this bower. She sighed, thinking how much easier it would be if instead of a replica this was indeed a small British castle in the time of Sir Walter Scott. She longed for a time when there was no war, only long golden days to be spent in the simple pleasures of the hearth and home.

"Why?" he asked softly, stroking the silk of her hair as it trailed over her back and across his chest.

"What do you mean?" she replied, looking up at him with sad gray eyes.

"The heavy sigh, the sadness in your eyes."

"Here it is so peaceful, only the music of the rain, but out there is the real world, a world that frightens me."

"You are right to be frightened," Justin said in somber tones. "I wish to protect you as much as I can. That is why I was so angry when I found you had left the house without telling me."

"Am I to be a prisoner once more, only this time in a more luxurious cell?"

"It always comes between us, the uniform I wear," he said with a troubled resignation.

"Yes, I fear it does."

"What shall we do, my dearest Little Bit?" There was a harsh, raw quality to his voice that spoke of his frustration and his pain.

"I do not know." The intensity of his gaze tore her apart, eating away at her resolve that what she was doing was the right and honorable decision.

"I cannot give you up," he said, his voice hardening ruthlessly. "I will not give you up, Ariane, not now that I have found you. Cupping her chin with his warm firm fingers, forcing her to look at him, he said, "You cannot escape me, for I would follow you to the ends of the earth."

"Even into the Confederate lines, into Dixie, as you Yankees so quaintly put it?"

"Yes, even into that hell," he replied with a cold contained voice that still showed his fury. "You are mine and you best remember it."

"I am your wife, not your possession, and you best remember that," she retorted, rising to her feet, leaving him to don his clothes.

He lay watching her through narrowed eyes, enjoying the beauty of her slender body, her graceful movements, even though she infuriated him with her stubborn loyalty to a dying South. There were times he wished he had never returned to Memphis, and yet deep in his heart he knew that he could never leave again without Ariane. She had become his torment and his delight. And he feared that somehow she was changing him, the enjoyment he had found in his work for General Dodge and the Secret Service in Vicksburg and New Orleans was gone. There it had been a game, a dangerous, ruthless game where each small piece of information that he gleaned as a spy was somehow a personal victory against the Southern society that had cast him out, against the father who had never tried to reconcile with him. But here in Memphis it was differ-

357

ent, different because of a golden-haired beauty with big soft gray eyes that could tear him apart with one glance.

"What is that pinned to your corset?" he asked, letting her know he was watching her.

"A gris-gris charm Sable made me for my protection," she said without thinking, turning her back to him as she donned her garments.

"Why do you need protection?"

"From Yankees," she said tersely.

"Touché, Little Bit. You scored your point," he murmured, "but there is one Yankee you needn't fear."

"I am leaving, for he is the one I fear the most. With him I am my most vulnerable," she said with a sigh, turning around to face him fully dressed. Carefully she wound her tangled tresses in the semblance of a chignon, having picked up the hairpins from the floor. With a few quick gestures, she secured her hair, then headed for the door. She had to get out of this seductive place, had to leave before she gazed too long at the enticing sight of Justin's long lean form reclining on the daybed where she had experienced such sensual joy.

"It is still raining," he commented softly. "Come back here to me."

"I . . . I cannot," she murmured, her voice breaking as she made for the door through a mist of tears. She had to have time to think. When she was with him, all that mattered was Justin and the sheer bliss of being within the circle of his arms.

The storm had slackened to a fine warm mist as she left the studio. Walking toward the house, she saw one of the kitchen maids in the vegetable garden, a basket over her arm, selecting items for the night's meal. The young woman was hurrying to get out of the weather. Ariane, however, took her time. She was already a mess, her hair straggling out of the hasty chignon, her bonnet gone forever, most likely at the bottom of the lake. A little rain couldn't hurt, and she needed to think.

Stopping under the large overhanging branches of a giant cedar tree, she inhaled the fresh astringent scent of cedar pungent in the rain. Perhaps it would clear her brain of the scent and feel of Justin. Looking out over the lake, foggy now from the rain, she sighed, knowing that nothing would ever drive Justin from her mind, her heart. He was in her blood, an obsession since she'd been a hurting child. He was the standard by which she measured other men, and compared to Justin, they all came up a poor second.

"You shouldn't be standing out in the rain," a low achingly familiar voice said from behind her.

"Dinner will be ready soon. We should return to the house and change," she said, trying to keep her tone light, but there was a catch in her voice as she turned to face him.

"You can't run away from me, I will always be right behind you, no matter how hard-headed and stubborn you are, and you can be contrary, God knows," he told her, a faint twinkle in the depths of his black eyes.

"I see I have met my match," she commented in wry tones, a smile trembling on her lips.

"So I have been trying to tell you, Mrs. Pierce," he responded, holding out his arm to escort her to the house.

"This doesn't mean you have won," she said, determined not to let herself fall under the spell he seemed capable of weaving around her whenever they were together.

"Shall we call this one a draw," he bantered, his smile as intimate as a kiss.

"You are the very devil," she said with a wry smile, shaking her head as she placed her hand in the crook of his arm.

"So I have been told," he answered as they walked back to the house in the gentle, warm rain.

If Sable was surprised by their rumpled damp appearance, she gave no sign. The only indication was when she ordered one of the maids to fetch water for Ariane's wash basin.

"I have taken the liberty, Doctor Justin, of moving your things into Madame Pierce's bedchamber. Is that all right?"

"Yes, Sable, that will be just fine," he answered, giving Ariane an amused glance.

"It seems I cannot fight you both," she said dryly as they climbed the stairs to change clothes before the other officers arrived home.

"Sable is a very wise woman," he said solemnly, but his mouth quirked with humor and there was amusement in his dark gaze.

"You mean you have managed to wrap her around your finger," she quipped as they reached the door of the bedchamber. "Go on in. I must see first to my father," she said, more seriously.

"Do you want me to come with you?"

"No, I will send for you if I think he needs medical attention. I just would like to let him know I am thinking of him, and that I saw Sam Riley at the office today."

"That is where you went, into the Valcour Line offices," he said sharply.

"Yes. I thought it was time someone from the family put in an appearance, although the Yankee lieutenant assigned as liaison officer by the Provost Marshal wasn't glad to see me."

"Did he give you any trouble?" He was watching her

intently and she sensed he was worried about something connected with the business.

"He told me the only reason they allowed me to leave prison was because you were to keep an eye on me," she replied with an edge to her voice. "Is that true?"

"The lieutenant talks too much, but I will not lie to you. He speaks the truth. You would have never been released if your husband hadn't been a Union officer, nor would your father." His dark watchful eyes that missed nothing stared down at her, telling her without words that he understood how hard it was for her to hear this, but her anger would change nothing. He was not only her lover, her husband, but also her guard and jailer.

"I see, then I must watch my step since you will be observing my every move," she said quietly, her eyes cold gray glass that flashed her annoyance and something like pain.

"If you do nothing wrong, then you have nothing to fear," he murmured, staring at her with deadly concentration.

"But right and wrong are a matter of interpretation," she reminded him, then turned away and walked toward her father's chamber.

He stared after her with a strange feeling that they were both being pulled down a path neither wanted to go by events outside their control. To a man used to being in command of his own destiny, used to answering to no one but his own conscience, it was a disconcerting thought. A wave of gray uneasiness passed over him, a kind of dark premonition that jolted him, for he was a man of medicine, of logic. This feeling had no basis in fact, but was so strong it left him shaken.

"Father, I spoke with Sam Riley today," Ariane said with a smile that didn't reach her eyes. She tried not to look shocked by her father's appearance as she came to sit by his bedside. It was very difficult, for her father seemed to have trouble focusing on who she was and why she was here.

"Missy, you should let your brothers handle the business. A lady shouldn't concern herself with such matters. Why, you tell Charles and Beau to come in here. I want a word with those boys. What were they thinking of, letting a little girl go down to Front Row. You go back to your school friends and let your brothers worry about the Valcour Line till I am recovered," he said fretfully, plucking at the sheet with weak, restless hands.

A glazed look of despair spread across her pale visage as she realized her father's bruised and battered mind had refused to accept the horror of the present and had retreated back in time to happier days before the war. Perhaps, she thought with the sickening feeling of suddenly being quite alone, he was better off in the safe world his mind had created for him. She realized with a sad clarity that their roles had reversed—she had become the parent and he the child.

"Yes, Papa, I will tell . . . tell my brothers," she said, swallowing the ache in her throat that cut like a knife. She couldn't say their names. Rising to her feet, she bent down and straightened the sheet about him. "You rest, and Caesar will be up soon with your dinner tray." She kissed him lightly on the brow, biting her lower lip to control the sobs.

"You send Charles and Beau up to me the moment they come home," he called to her as she walked to the door.

"Yes, Papa, as soon as they come home." She closed the door tightly behind her and stood for a moment leaning against the portal, her head bowed, her body slumped in despair. Was she to be spared nothing? Was this war going to take everything from her that had any meaning?

Swallowing the sob that rose in her throat, she fought hard against the tears she refused to let fall. She didn't have time to cry, could not allow the tears to start for, if they did, she feared they would never stop. Taking a deep breath, she walked with a faltering step down the hall, full of shadows now that night had fallen. Sable had lit the lamps, and the small golden pool of light that fell from the glass globes was a beacon lighting her way to her bedchamber and Justin. Justin, her safe harbor in a sea of madness.

Flinging open the door, Ariane rushed into the darkened room, seeking the solace of Justin's embrace, only to find it empty. Bess lay slumbering in her basket at the foot of the four-poster. The faint scent of Justin's bay rum and the aromatic fragrance of his pipe tobacco hung in the damp night air. He had been in here. She stood for a moment in the center of the chamber, at a loss. She had been so sure he would be here.

It was then, as she stood unsure of what to do, that she heard the sound of a horse's hooves galloping away from the house. Hurrying to the window, she could just make out the figure of a man riding away before he disappeared in the mist that was rolling in over the grounds.

"Come in," she called in answer to the rap on her door.

"Doctor Justin wanted me to tell you he had to leave suddenly," Sable said as she came to help Ariane out of her damp crumbled gown.

"Did he say where he was going?"

"No, ma'am, I know only that a messenger rode up to the house and requested to speak with him."

"Who was this messenger?"

"A Union soldier. He left immediately after speaking with Doctor Justin."

"And my husband didn't say where he was going?"

"No. Only that he would not be back till late."

"Perhaps he had to return to the hospital," she mused as Sable helped her out of her dress.

"I don't believe 'twas the hospital, because when I reminded him that Miche Valcour was almost out of his medicine, Doctor Justin said that he would bring some home tomorrow night when he returned from the hospital."

"I think I will have a tray in my room tonight, so just put out my nightrail and peignoir, Sable," Ariane said, her mind preoccupied with the whereabouts of her husband.

After bathing and dressing in her night garments, Ariane finished the food on her dinner tray. She barely tasted the meal, for she was in a hurry to finish a task she had wanted to do since returning home from Irving Block Prison. With Justin gone, she could write the piece for the *Memphis Appeal* about conditions in the prison. She knew Joseph Barbierre would somehow smuggle her copy out to the Confederate lines, where it could make its way to wherever the plucky newspaper staff was located now. She had even considered sending a copy of the piece to one of the Northern newspapers so that they could see nothing much had changed. It would have to be anonymous, but they just might print it. Putting on her spectacles, she wrote as fast as she could, not sure when she would hear the sound of her husband's horse. By ten o'clock she had finished placing the sheets in the bottom of her lingerie drawer. In a few days she would return once more to Joseph Barbierre's shop and give him the article.

Restless now that she had finished her writing, she

walked to the open window to stare out at the foggy night. The cedars seemed like ghostly sentinels in the gray mist that covered Fleur de Lys.

Where was Justin, and why had he been gone so long? Suddenly a remembered scrap of conversation with Sam Riley floated across her tired, troubled mind. What had he said? Oh yes, that there had been a Union officer prowling around Valcour steamers at night and talking to roustabouts off the boats in their dives in Pinch Gut. She tried to remember his exact words. A tall Yankee officer speaking with a slight Southern accent who seemed to know the river and the men who worked it. Strange and disquieting thoughts began to race through her mind. Could this officer be her Justin? He knew the river and he knew the Memphis riverfront. But only a Yankee spy would do such a thing, an agent for their intelligence network. Her brain was in tumult, remembering how Justin had insisted on following her that day to Elmwood Cemetery, how he had been able to get her released from prison. No, no, it had to be some other tall Yankee officer who spoke with a slight Southern accent. There must be others in the Union Army, there had to be, she thought in despair, staring out into the dense haunting fog. It couldn't be Justin.

Chapter Twenty-seven

The oppressive August heat held Memphis in its grip, exhausting the weary citizens, including Ariane as she made her way down the wooden sidewalk of Front Row from the Valcour offices. Throngs of soldiers and the inevitable prostitutes that followed them were already beginning their Saturday night carousal, even though it was only four in the afternoon. If you were drunk enough on cheap whiskey, perhaps you didn't notice the steamy heat wave, she mused as she passed reeling men and their garishly clad companions. The women made her think of the streetwalkers who had shared her ride in the prison wagon, and even with the high temperature, she gave a light shudder.

She had one more stop to make before she could go home. This was the most important stop of all, for she was meeting the contact from Ward and McClellan, the Memphis pharmaceutical company, at the Gayoso House for tea. It would appear to be an innocent meeting, for the contact was a woman, and she would give Ariane the vital information on where Sam Riley could pick up the medicine they were donating to the Southern Cause. He was free to take out a steamer now that she was coming to the office in her father's place. Ariane wanted that medicine on the *Memphis Cotton Princess* when it left on its trip to New Orleans. There would be Confederate boats waiting at the mouths of various rivers and

366

streams feeding into the Mississippi to intercept the *Memphis Cotton Princess* and unload the desperately needed medicine for the Confederacy. She had heard that Confederate doctors were being forced to perform amputations without anesthesia. They needed chloroform, ether, and morphine, as well as quinine for all the malaria cases now that they were in the fever season.

Approaching the Gayoso House, Ariane felt a whisper of terror run through her as she saw all the blue-uniformed officers coming and going from the lobby. She knew Justin was at the hospital so she didn't have to fear running into him, but she wished this contact had agreed to meet somewhere else. The woman in question was said, according to Joseph Barbierre, to be one of their best operatives, fraternizing with the Yankees constantly and having gained their trust. She also had a strange sense of humor in that she liked the idea of arranging clandestine operations right under their nose. Entering the busy lobby, where she attracted the stares of quite a few men, Ariane wished this woman was less flamboyant, but then she had a point—who would expect two Southern ladies to be planning how they were going to smuggle hundreds of dollars' worth of medicine to the Confederacy in the hotel housing most of the Union Command staff?

Walking so swiftly across the lobby toward the Ladies' Tea Room that her hoop skirt swayed, Ariane ignored the advances of some of the more aggressive men. Holding her folded silk parasol like a sword, she glided into the tea room set aside just for ladies. Here they did not have to worry about men missing the brass spittoons when they spit out a stream of tobacco juice and hitting their skirts instead. The air was free of cigar smoke and drunken men. It was perfect, there was not a Yankee officer in the room—some of their wives and daughters, but no men.

Quickly scanning the room, Ariane looked for a

woman wearing a black straw hat with red and white ostrich feathers and a black spotted nose tip veil. There couldn't be many women wearing such deep colors on such a hot day. Then she saw her over in the corner by the window beside a tall potted palm. Intense astonishment touched Ariane's pale face under the lilac veil. Her contact was Olivia Whitlaw Pierce, Clay's widow and Justin's sister-in-law. The woman who had driven Justin from Memphis all those years ago was the woman she was to meet. What game was she playing, for she had known she was meeting Ariane, but she had refused to allow Joseph to tell Ariane her name. Her nerves stretched to the breaking point, Ariane made her way to Olivia's table.

"Good day, Ariane, won't you sit down," Olivia said from red lips curved in a malicious smile.

"Thank you," Ariane said coolly, taking the chair across the linen-draped table. "Now I understand why you would not let Joseph tell me your name. You thought I would not come."

"It did cross my mind, but I thought sisters-in-law should get to know each other, and you have to admit it makes our meeting seem natural to the Yankees. They know nothing about the old gossip concerning Justin and myself," Olivia said, her black eyes gleaming with curiosity. "Besides, I wanted to make sure you came. I wanted to see how you had turned out, Ariane. Clay kept me out at Cedar's Rest most of the time, and we never really ran in the same social circles. You were just a child the last time I saw you, but you have grown up, I see. Tell me, my dear, are you woman enough for that exciting husband of yours? He always was so deliciously intense." There was a cruel, taunting edge to Olivia's voice, and deep dislike in her eyes as she stared at Ariane. She was playing with her like a cat with a mouse.

"I will not discuss my husband with you, for you

threw away any claim you had to Justin years ago. I believe it is a decision you came to regret. It was very foolish of you, but then I think you got what you deserved in Clay Pierce. He was a charming man, but a weak one," Ariane said softly, her eyes gray ice as she stared at the still attractive, but aging woman across from her. Olivia was a rose that had lost its full bloom, a bit wilted around the edges.

"Ah, the kitten has sharp claws," Olivia said with a wry twist of her lips, but there was a begrudging respect in her eyes. "And here is our tea. I took the liberty of ordering for both of us."

"Good, then we can get down to business," Ariane replied as the waiter brought a pot of tea and a tiered silver dish of cakes and sandwiches. Waiting until he left she said, "How soon can we count on the merchandise? We have a ship leaving in three days. And most importantly, can we trust you?"

"I don't know if you knew or not, but my father had invested money in Ward and McClellan. Now that he is dead, I inherited some shares in the company, but not enough that I don't have to sell myself to the highest Yankee bidder, who at the moment happens to be a revolting man by the name of Major Horace Osgood. Every time I help the Confederacy, I strike a blow at Horace. It doesn't make up for how he treats me, but it helps," Olivia said, her eyes glittering with hate. "No, my dear, this isn't just for the glorious Cause, this is also intensely personal. Not all men are Justin. They are not all exquisitely tender lovers. They are, in fact, quite brutal."

Ariane felt an uncomfortable flush stain her cheeks at Olivia's words. And as she looked at her, she also felt strangely sad for the woman who sat across from her with the expression of despair and loathing on her once delicate face. "I think you have answered my question about trust," she said quietly.

369

"Good. I shall gather together a package and put it in a small trunk. I can send the trunk down to the wharf with one of the young men that carries bags here in the hotel. He has run errands for me before so it would not seem strange. What is your captain's name? I could put a tag on it stating that it was one of his pieces of luggage."

"Sam Riley, and tell the boy he is to carry it to the captain's suite," Ariane replied, speaking softly so she would not be overheard.

"Yes, I think that will work out very well," Olivia said. "Those Yankee fools think that since the owners of Ward and McClellan took the oath after they were imprisoned and then were allowed to resume business, that they are Union men." Her words were edged with venom and her lip curled in disgust.

Ariane was anxious to leave Olivia now that their business was concluded. Lifting her napkin to her lips then placing it by her half-finished cup of tea, she reached for her reticule and parasol. "The ship sails on Tuesday afternoon at four. 'Tis the *Memphis Cotton Princess,*" she said, repeating it slowly as Olivia nodded that she would remember the name.

Rising to her feet, Ariane said, "Thank you for the tea and for . . . everything. Good luck." As she turned to leave, Olivia stopped her, placing her hand on Ariane's sleeve.

"Justin's a good man. I wish I had known that years ago, but I was foolish. Don't you be. I know what you're doing for the Confederacy is because of deeply held convictions, but don't let him get away. If you do, you will regret it till the day you die. Believe me, I speak from experience."

"Good-bye," Ariane whispered.

She hurried through the hotel lobby and out into the street, the rays of the setting sun streaking down in a mellow saffron light, giving the dusty street a hazy glow.

Opening her parasol against the last of the dying light, she quickened her step. Caesar was supposed to come fetch her with the carriage at five, and it was almost that time.

Arriving back at the Valcour Line, she had only a few moments to tell Sam about the arrangements she had made with Olivia before Caesar appeared with the carriage. On the ride home through the streets coming alive with early evening revelers, Ariane sat lost in thought. She had wanted to get home before her husband. Tonight she would speak with him about what was bothering her, what had been eating away at her for the last two weeks. They would retire early, and after he thought she was asleep, he would slip from the bed and leave the house. She heard the sound of his horse on the drive outside, and would get up and go the window. Last night by the light of the almost full moon, she had seen him clearly. Lying awake in the four-poster, she would hear him return several hours later and slip back into bed. She usually pretended to be asleep, but not tonight. Tonight she was going to follow him.

After seeing to her father, whose mind was still lost in the past, Ariane bathed and dressed for dinner in a cool-looking gown of azure mousseline de soie, a lovely silk fabric with a texture like muslin, and trimmed at the bodice and short puffed sleeves with heavy blond lace. Her hair was pulled back from her temples with antique combs of tortoise-shell and gold and allowed to fall in silky curls to her waist.

"You are a lovely sight for these weary eyes," Justin said huskily, coming down from their chamber after washing up, having just returned from the hospital. "Where are you going with that basket?"

"To pick fresh roses for the dinner table," she replied, moving toward the door. "Come with me, 'tis cooler outside."

"How can I refuse such a beautiful lady," he said gal-

371

lantly, his dark eyes glowing with his response to her beauty.

They walked together out into the pearl gray and violet of twilight. There was just enough light to see as they strolled in the sultry air heavy with the sensual scent of gardenias, nicotina, and night-blooming jasmine, and the delicate fragrance of the rose.

"Did you stay long at the Valcour Line offices today," Justin asked with anticipation, as if this was more than a casual question about her day.

"Till five. Why?"

"Someone saw you walking into the Gayoso House in the late afternoon," he said matter-of-factly, but there was an underlying tension in his voice.

"I see you are having me watched," she said with a sigh, playing for time. How much had they seen? There was no way around it—she would have to tell some of the truth without revealing the real intention of her visit.

"Not me, the Provost Marshal," he told her softly, with a tinge of regret in his tone.

"You might have told me," she replied in a broken whisper. "You might have shown that you trusted me enough to tell me."

"Why did you go the Gayoso House?" he persisted, a faint tremor in his voice as though some emotion had touched him. It was as if he hated to hear her response, but was intent on hearing it just the same.

"If you must know, I was invited by my sister-in-law to tea. She wanted to speak about you," Ariane told him in a cool throaty voice.

"Olivia invited you to tea," he muttered, astonished. Something Ariane could have sworn was embarrassment shadowed his handsome features for a brief moment.

"Yes, she really seems quite lonely with all her family gone. Her . . . her life with the major is not a happy one, I think. She also seems quite remorseful for what she did to you all those years ago." Ariane stopped be-

372

side one of the white rosebushes profusely laden with large creamy blooms. Taking her garden shears, she cut a half-dozen flowers, placing them in her basket.

"I am sorry she bothered you. You are right—Olivia is not a happy woman," he said in terse tones, taking the basket laden with alabaster roses from her hand. Lifting one so he could breathe its perfume, he murmured huskily, "These remind me of the studio. Remember, my love, how it was there between us?"

"How could I forget," she whispered. "How could I forget any of our nights together?"

"After dinner, I must spend an hour with the other officers—we have something we must discuss concerning the hospital. But then, my sweet Ariane, I shall come to you in our bed. Wait up for me?" His deep voice simmered with the urgency of his desire as he stared down at her, his black eyes searching the pale flower of her face as if he could reach down, down into the very depths of her heart and soul.

"Yes, oh yes, my love," she whispered, lost in those magnificent eyes that saw so much more than the mere surface of a person. Her yearning for him, her desire, was overwhelming in its intensity, and she swayed toward him in the gathering shadows of twilight. From somewhere near the river came the jagged flash of lightning and the roll of thunder.

"Come, we best return to the house before the rain comes," he said thickly, holding out his arm for her.

She placed her hand in the crook of his arm, and they started up the flagstone walk as the storm seemed to gather force over the river. The black-and-white cat called Pirate emerged from the kitchen garden and, as if also sensing the coming storm, followed them into the house.

Justin's fellow officers had arrived home also, and as Ariane handed the flowers to Susie to put in water, voices raised in conversation could be heard coming from the library. "Join them," Ariane murmured to Justin. "I must make sure Father has had his dinner."

"Till later tonight," he whispered, bending down to caress her ear lightly with his tongue.

"Yes, till later," she echoed as he left her, walking toward the library with his own proud, graceful saunter.

The tapers in their silver candelabra flickered in the damp gusts of wind that blew in through the open windows. As the servants poured the wine, everyone listened to the mournful cries of the wind through the boughs of the cedar trees.

"What an eerie sound," one of the medical officers remarked with a grimace. "Sometimes I think all of Memphis is haunted. Never have I known such a lush landscape, but there seems to be an almost overripe, rotting quality about the place."

"Really, Captain, I have never heard my home described in quite that manner." Ariane's voice was cool, and she stressed the words "my home."

"I am sure he did not mean to offend, Ariane," Justin insisted in a low composed voice.

"No, I meant no offense, was just stating a fact," the rather pompous captain, new to Memphis, said stiffly. He had been recently transferred there to the hospital and billeted at Fleur de Lys only the last three days.

Justin knew that stormy look in Ariane's gray eyes. She had taken a dislike to her new "guest" almost from the beginning, and was itching for a fight. While he admired her spirit, she could be a real handful, but then, he thought with a gleam in his dark eyes, that was part of her allure. The angelic ethereal facade masked the fiery hellion beneath all that beauty, those exquisite manners.

She did complicate things for him, with the Union Command in Memphis, but then they saw him as only a Medical officer, a doctor at the hospital. Even General Washburn was not privy to the names of General

Dodge's field agents.

General Grenville Dodge felt that the best way to protect his elite corp of 117 agents operating from Memphis to Mobile and from Atlanta to Richmond was to give them complete anonymity. Generals Hurlburt and Washburn might know there was an agent with the code name "the Falcon" operating in Memphis, but they had no idea of his identity. Justin preferred it that way. As the husband of a Secesh wife, his loyalty to the Union might be suspect, but never did anyone surmise that there was more to his activities in Memphis than those of a doctor. It was a perfect cover—that of a Southern-born doctor working for the Union Army, but with a Southern wife who was unabashedly for the Confederacy. He could win the trust of those who had no qualms about taking a bribe from those who wished to smuggle goods to the Confederacy. They thought if he was not one of them, then he could at least sympathize, since he had a Southern wife. Yes, marrying Ariane had been advantageous to his cover as Dodge's field agent, and had been the reason he was able to wire and request he go over the Provost Marshal's head and have her and her father released from prison. His superior, however, had no idea of the depth of his obsession for his beautiful wife. Justin had led him to believe that this was a marriage of convenience, and that after the war, it would end. In his work in New Orleans and Vicksburg, he had gained a reputation as being ruthless, so the idea of such an arrangement did not seem too far-fetched to Dodge.

Tightening his hand around the stem of his wineglass in an unconscious gesture of the conflict that raged inside of him, Justin knew that he could never leave Ariane. She had found a place inside his heart so secure that she was as necessary to him as food and drink, as elemental as breathing. He knew with a sense of foreboding that she was an irresistible compulsion and had been since that hot June day when their eyes met across the crowd of stunned people at the surrender of Memphis. In a strange way he knew he had come as a conqueror but had instead been conquered and subjugated by a pair of stormy gray eyes and red-gold hair.

"Gentlemen, I shall leave you to your cigars and brandy. The storm seems to be getting worse and I wish to check that the servants have closed the windows. Good night," Ariane said softly, rising to her feet as did they, standing till she swept from the room. The men watched as she paused for a moment at the door, her eyes meeting Justin's with a smoldering promise that sent a wave of jealousy through them. They saw his burning black eyes rake her with a fiercely possessive look and her mouth curve in a sensuous smile of recognition of that desire. There was not a man among them who did not envy Justin his right to climb the staircase to her bedchamber. The look of scorching intent that passed between them left no doubt of the passionate interlude that was yet to come on this sultry, stormy Southern night.

Chapter Twenty-eight

The tall ivory taper flickered in the draft of air from the slowly opening door. Turning the knob of the heavy portal, Justin stepped into the darkened chamber. Ariane was stretched out like a tawny cat on the linen sheets, her lovely nude body gleaming in the golden light.

"I have been waiting for you," she murmured in a throaty voice that lit a fire in his blood. Her hair in a sensuous tumble about her shoulders caught the light from the taper. Her lithe, peach-ivory legs and full breasts glimpsed through the haze of the mosquito baire tantalized and fanned the flame of Justin's arousal.

"You shall wait no longer," he promised, quickly stripping the blue uniform from his body. Desire overwhelmed him at her seductive surprise. To see her nude and waiting for him with a look of dreamy passion in her eyes reminded him of all the glorious times they had lain together, and it was his undoing.

She caught her breath at his virile beauty. Then the mosquito baire was pulled aside long enough for him to slip in beside her. He reached out to caress her hair, then as hunger drove him, he pressed her down, down against the feather pillow and mattress. His eyes stared down at her as if he were memorizing every feature, then his hands reached for her ivory breasts cupping first one then the other, lifting them so his wet-hot mouth could tease and caress each rosy peak. She heard her moans of wanting fill the room.

Then his knowing hands and heated mouth were everywhere, exciting, eliciting sensations from her trembling, hungry body that carried her to that wonderful plane of rapture where there were only the two of them. Nothing existed in this special world but the joy that they found in the taste, the sight, the feel of the other.

He looked down at her, reveling in the sight of her head flung back against the pillows in wild abandon as she writhed under the magic of his touch. Driven by the sensations he was evoking, she reached out for him, digging her fingernails into his shoulders as she pulled him to her, slender hips moving and arching against him till he felt his control slip away. He had to have her. It was a force driving him that could not be denied.

"I cannot wait," he gasped as he lifted her hips up and rose above her, holding her eyes with his own night-black gaze.

"Yes, oh yes, fill me with you!" she cried out as he thrust himself inside her waiting, honeyed depths. Then she was all moving, pulsating sensation, moving in wanton circles against him as he cried her name again and again.

Thrusting, pulsating waves of ecstasy shook them as they reached their pinnacle, unable to withhold the full force of their emotion. It was as if tonight there could be no limits. They had to have each other wildly, with an urgent primitive passion allowing the full range of their desire till they felt they were totally consumed by the other.

They lay side by side, panting with light gasps, stunned by the force of what had just occurred between them. Their fingers reached out and touched, then intertwined.

"Never has it been so between us," he murmured, lifting her hand to his lips. "I was a man obsessed."

"Then I, too, was consumed with the need for you," she whispered, turning her head on the pillow so she could give him a shy, gentle smile.

"How lucky we are, Little Bit, to have found each other," he said. "It makes me feel sad for all those who will never know what we have experienced. No matter what happens, we have had nights, afternoons too" — he paused and smiled down at her — "like only a few lovers have the privilege ever to experience." There was a bitter-sweet sadness in his expressive, penetrating gaze.

"What is it, my love?" she asked, reaching out to touch his cheek in a gesture of concern and aching tenderness. It was as if he were seeing some premonition of the future, a future where they might not be still together. It cut to her heart and made her tremble in fear.

" 'Tis nothing but a melancholy that sometimes comes over me of late," he whispered, taking her hand and placing a soft kiss on the palm.

"It frightens me to hear you speak so," she told him. "I lost you once long ago when I was just a child with a child's love; to lose you now that I love you as a woman would destroy me."

"Then we will speak no more of such matters. We will slumber in each other's arms and dream of long, lazy summer days after the war when we have nothing to do but while away the hours making love." Pulling her down beside him, he curved his body around hers so they lay with the soft mounds of her bottom fitted up against the flatness of his belly. His head nestled in the tangled silk of her hair.

Soon the darkened chamber, lit only with the flickering taper, was filled with the sounds of silence and the even breathing of two lovers caught in the arms of Morpheus, or so it seemed. But Ariane and Justin were both feigning sleep, he because he must leave her for an appointment he had with a Confederate informer in a gambling den in Pinch Gut. The informer was a double agent who the Rebs thought was one of theirs, but who in reality worked for the Union. He had little liking for using women agents but this woman was supposed to be one of the best. She was to be wearing a scarlet dress with red and black plumes in her hair. He was to walk up to the table she would be sitting at and ask if she knew A. Lincoln in St. Louis. She would reply, "Yes, he is a friend of mine." She was a paid informant, and he never trusted an agent whose loyalty was bought with greenbacks, but she claimed to have information about smuggling on the riverboats leaving Memphis for various stops downriver. She told their contact she would speak only to Dodge's top agent in Memphis and she had heard that was the Falcon. She wanted a draft for three thousand dollars on a St. Louis bank as well as a steamer ticket to St. Louis for the morrow. He had both tucked away in the pocket of his tunic.

Ariane pretended to slumber for she was determined to follow Justin. His melancholy words had only strengthened her resolve that she would find out what mysterious errand compelled him to make these midnight excursions from Fleur de Lys.

She heard the grandfather's clock in the hall strike eleven and felt Justin slip quietly with a minimum of motion from the bed. She lay still, her pulse pounding, forcing herself to breathe slowly, with deep regular breaths as if she were sound asleep. She did not move or open her eyes although the temptation was great as she heard him don his clothes. Bess stirred in her basket and she heard Justin whisper reassuringly to the dog. Then the door opened softly and he was gone.

Opening her eyes, she looked about the darkened chamber lit now only by the stub of the candle. Seeing it was, indeed, empty, she sprang from the bed and hurried to the armoire, pulling out her black riding habit. She wanted to blend in with the night. Dressing as fast as she could, she had a bit of trouble pulling on her high leather boots over her silk stockings but finally she managed without Sable's aid. Pulling her hair back in a black net snood, she pinned on the silk black top hat and pulled the black spotted veil down about her face. Pulling on leather riding gloves, she crossed to the chest of drawers that contained her lingerie and pulled out the bottom drawer. Fumbling around under a pile of delicate folded chemises, she found the pearl-handle colt revolver. Holding it for a moment in her gloved hand, she closed the drawer and rose to her feet. Checking to make sure the chamber was loaded, she clicked on the safety catch and slipped the gun in the deep pocket of her riding habit. Opening her locked jewelry case, she selected a forged pass she had been given by Joseph Barbierre in case she was stopped by a Union sentry. The scrawl was illegible on purpose and would never stand up to intense scrutiny, but it might work if the man was careless. Glancing at the clock, she knew she had to time this just right. She couldn't go to the stables too soon or she would meet Justin, but she couldn't wait too long or he would get too far ahead of her.

The house was dark and quiet as she slipped down the stairs and crossed through the parlor to the long French doors. Gliding out through the door, she made her way down the terrace and around the side of the house. The rain was over but there was a misty fog that made it easier to not be seen, but made it harder for her to find her way through the maze of the kitchen gardens.

Waiting in the shadow of the kitchen house, Ariane saw a lantern burning in the stable and knew that Justin was inside saddling his horse. She stood with pounding heart as she heard the sound of a horse's hooves on the hard-packed earth of the stable yard.

Then as he rode past her, she ran to the stables and Dancer's stall. She was grateful that Beau had showed her how to saddle a horse even though they had always had plenty of slaves to handle the horses. Dancer nudged her in pleased surprise as she saddled the bay mare, then leading her to the carriage block, Ariane stepped up and on to the horse. They were off, out of the stable yard, and down a shortcut Ariane knew would take her to the front gate just minutes after Justin. Reining in Dancer in the shadow of the trees, her hooves muffled by the layer of wet leaf mold that carpeted the ground, she watched as he turned his horse out the front gate and down Poplar Road toward Memphis.

Giving him a few minutes' head start, Ariane nudged Dancer and they were off down the fog-shrouded road behind Justin. She could only hope if he heard the sound of a horse's hooves behind him he would think it was one of the Union patrol. She was thankful for the cover of the dense fog—a full moon would have made it much harder to follow him without being seen.

She met no one on the muddy road; it was as if she rode through a cloud. Her stomach churning with anxiety and frustration, she could only hope that Justin did not turn off the main road to Memphis, for she could not see him through the dense fog that turned everything a misty gray.

As they entered Memphis, Ariane could make out the figure of her husband ahead of her in the glow from the street lamps. She was able to urge Dancer closer to him, for the streets even at this late hour were not empty. There were soldiers both mounted and on foot, but none stopped her. They were all more concerned with going from tavern to tavern. Prostitutes hung on some of the men's arms and most were the worse for drink.

Ariane touched the pistol in her pocket for reassurance as she followed Justin into the meaner, more crowded streets of Pinch Gut. Rowdy drunken laughter and loud music floated out onto the foggy streets from the open doors of the various saloons, gambling dens, and bawdy houses. She gave a light shudder of apprehension and disbelief as she followed Justin farther into the Pinch district. What could he be doing here after midnight?

Although it was the very early morning hours of Sunday, the streets were crowded with revelers left over from the precious Saturday night. They hardly noticed her as she slid off Dancer's back and tied her to a hitching post a few yards away from where Justin was doing the same to his horse in front of Lily Walker's Gilded Lily Saloon and Gambling House. Ariane was just another woman prowling the misty streets of Pinch Gut—a feminine wraith in black.

Justin strode into the noisy saloon smoky with the blue haze of the cheap cigars. A tinny piano played by a black man thumped out a raucous tune as Justin made his way past the many games of chance to where the tables were located in front of a long mahogany bar. The gilded mirror reflected the scene of the Gilded Lily, and as Justin looked in its wavy reflection, he saw a woman in a scarlet dress with red and black plumes in her high-piled raven locks. Turning around, he strode to where she sat by herself. He didn't see the woman dressed in black come in the saloon or the stricken look of panic on her white visage beneath the black veil.

"May I sit down? I believe you know a mutual acquaintance of mine in St. Louis, an A. Lincoln?" he asked of the woman who had her face turned from him in the murky light of the saloon. Even so there was something familiar about her, and he felt a flicker of apprehension go up his spine.

"Yes, he is a friend of mine," the sultry voice drawled as the woman turned her triangular visage up to his. The amber eyes widened then filled with a malicious humor. "What a strange world this is," she purred. "Won't you please sit down."

"Olivia?" He ground her name out between his teeth.

"Yes, of course, 'tis me," she said softly, "but I am equally surprised. I didn't really think you would do something so furtive. You always prided yourself on your honesty and—what did you call it—oh yes, your honor. It seems we all can be had for a price." Her eyes

383

glittered like those of a savage cat closing in for the kill.

"Not all. I don't do this for the money. I do it to end this bloody war," his voice grated harshly.

"Not maybe a little bit for revenge," she said with a laugh of cynicism. "You have no reason to love Memphis. They turned on you, remember? I know I do. You always liked to go against their conventions. They didn't like your attitudes, your beliefs, and I am sure they still don't."

"I am leaving, Olivia. You are not to be trusted. You had better go back to your major," he said ruthlessly.

"What about my information?" she asked, her eyes narrowed to slits.

"Do you really think I would believe anything you had to tell me? I know what you are capable of, the extent of your loyalty. How do we know you aren't playing us against the Rebs? You are lucky I don't have you thrown in Irving Block, which I will if you ever cross my path again. You are out of the spy business, Olivia. I suggest you return to your patron and the business you are so much more suited to." He turned to leave and it was then that he saw Ariane standing only a few feet away, staring at him out of haunted eyes.

"My God, what are you doing here?" he asked, reaching her side and taking her by the arm.

"You were always leaving late at night," she said dully, as if in a waking nightmare. "I wondered where you went so tonight I followed you."

"We are getting out of here. I will explain everything later," he told her tersely, leading her from the saloon out on to the wooden sidewalk.

"You were going to meet her, meet Olivia," Ariane gasped as the full realization of what she had seen came over her.

"Yes, but not for the reason you think," he said with exasperation, untying the reins of his horse and leading him down to where she pointed to Dancer. "I cannot believe you followed me all the way from Fleur de Lys. Don't you realize how dangerous it was to do such a foolish thing."

"Why did you go to meet her and in such a place?" Ariane persisted, apprehension filling her as she realized Olivia was up to something.

"She sent word to me that she thought she had some information about smuggling out of Memphis and that since I was the only Union officer she trusted, she wanted to tell me," he said, hoping the half-truth would pacify her.

"Why did she not tell this major she is . . . is involved with?" Ariane queried, allowing Justin to help her up on Dancer.

"As I said, she does not trust him, did not want him to think she might be involved with the Rebs. Also she thought maybe I could get money from the Provost Marshal for her information. I believe she would like to leave the major," he replied as they headed out of Pinch Gut.

Ariane sat stiffly in the side-saddle. If what Justin said was true, then Olivia was a traitor to the South. She was playing both sides for the money. She would have to alert Sam not to accept the trunk of medicine. It might be a trap set by the Yankees. Unwittingly she had stumbled on the plot. She wondered if Olivia had seen her. It made no difference—she would have to alert Joseph that Olivia was no longer to be trusted. They would have to get the medicine some other way.

"That explains tonight, but what about all the other nights?" she inquired as they turned their horses down Poplar Road. It was then that they heard it, the rapid sound of gunfire and heard the frantic shouts of men coming from the direction of Front Row.

Justin never answered her question, for to their stunned amazement, they were met by a Cavalry charge of men riding wildly through the streets. They wore Confederate uniforms, or what passed by that time in

385

the war for uniforms.

"Rebs! Rebs!" several soldiers cried as they ran down the streets half dressed, having been roused from their sleep by the daring raid.

Ariane tried to quiet Dancer, made skittish by the excitement and the thundering sound of the horses that raced past. Her blood was pounding as she remembered Joseph Barbierre's words that Forrest would do something about the Southerners in Irving Block. They were attempting a rescue by riding into the very center of the Yankee garrison that was Memphis.

"Forrest rode into the Gayoso, right up to the front desk, horse and all. They want General Washburn and Hurlburt," a Union soldier shouted as Memphians now roused from their slumber came to their windows and cheered the Confederate raiders on.

"We have to get out of this," Justin told Ariane, riding up close beside her. "All hell is going to break loose with Forrest's men on the street. As fast as the horses can go, I want us on our way out Poplar to Fleur de Lys. Now!" he cried, slapping Dancer on the flank so she took off.

Hanging on to Dancer, Ariane sensed Justin and his horse at her side as they rode like the wind out of the melee that was Memphis. The sound of gunfire and the shouts of men and cheering Memphians echoed in their ears as they left the city behind, not slowing their pace.

It was as they had almost reached the gates of Fleur de Lys that they saw him, a young soldier in a threadbare gray uniform with one side of his broad hat turned up and stuck with a jaunty plume riding a roan horse. He was in the shadows of the magnolias, hiding from several Yankees who had just ridden past.

Justin pulled his pistol from his holster before Ariane could say a word. Pointing it at the Confederate he said, "Throw down your rifle."

There was a long silence that seemed to last forever. Every sound seemed so distinct that Ariane would remember them always, the panting of the horses, the creak of the other man's saddle as he shifted position, the drip of the rain off the green leathery leaves of the magnolia. Then, instead of throwing down his gun, he lifted it slightly—to do what, they would never know, for Justin fired his pistol and the man fell from his horse to the damp, moldy ground.

"No!" Ariane's cry rent the still sultry air, for at the last moment she had recognized him as a friend of Beau's. Had he come by simply to pay his respects to his fallen comrade's family, or to seek sanctuary from the Yankees, having gotten separated from his regiment? They would never know, for he lay dead under the spreading branches of the magnolia.

They were surrounded by a Union patrol, who had heard the single shot. Ariane sat trembling, her eyes enormous as she watched Justin dismount.

"Yes, he is dead," Justin told the others after examining the fallen man.

"Murderer!" she cried, and she heard her own voice as if she were a bystander observing the scene from afar. She would never forget the anguish in Justin's black eyes as he looked up at her. Then unable to stand any more, she slapped Dancer lightly and they were off, racing down the main path through the trees to Fleur de Lys.

Tears blinded her eyes so she could not see and it was only Dancer's knowledge that she was near her barn that led them through the fog-shrouded trees of the estate to the stables. Lifting her hat and veil from her head and tossing them aside, Ariane wiped the tears from her cheeks with the back of her hand before tending to Dancer and rubbing her down. It was as she was vigorously brushing the mare down, as if she could forget in hard physical work the horror of the night, that she heard the sound of Justin's horse returning to the stables.

The pearl-gray of dawn was lifting the dark of night

in the east as Justin strode into the stables. He stood for a moment, his tall masculine form silhouetted by the light of the lantern hung from a peg on a rafter overhead. "I must talk to you." The rich timbre of his insistent voice echoed through the long straw-strewn stable.

Ariane stood silent, continuing to brush Dancer's satin coat. Tonight she had seen the side of her husband she had tried to pretend didn't exist, but she had been forced to see him as the Union officer. The reality of war had intruded on their idyl and had shattered her romantic illusion that they could somehow keep their private life from being touched by their conflicting allegiances.

"You knew him, didn't you," Justin said tersely, coming to stand in the front of Dancer's stall.

"Yes, I knew him," she replied, brushing the mare with long strokes. Her knuckles were white from clutching the brush so tightly.

"He could have shot us, Little Bit. We will never know if he recognized you, or saw only my blue uniform."

"No, we will never know," she answered bitterly.

."Do not do this to us." There was a silken thread of warning in his voice.

"I did not pull the trigger," she spat out with contempt.

"Look at me, for God's sake," he demanded. He grabbed the brush from her hand and pulled her from the stall till she was pressed against his long length.

"Let me go," she countered icily, her eyes blazing up at him in the dim light from the lantern. "Let me go, Yankee."

"Don't be a little fool," he warned, holding her hands by her wrists, forcing her body tight against his hard lean muscle.

"Better a fool than a murderer," she said, throwing back her head and staring up at him with impotent rage.

" 'Tis no good with your anger, your misplaced loyalty, between us. Perhaps, my stubborn misled Rebel, you will think differently when I am gone."

"Gone?" she whispered.

"Yes, I am being transferred from Memphis. You will have a long time to decide how you feel about your Yankee husband, but remember this, my fiery Rebel," he told her in voice husky with need, anger, and something like sorrow.

She felt his mouth come down on hers in a kiss that was punishing, burning, ravishing her lips with a searing fire that meant to brand her as his. Forcing her lips open with his thrusting tongue, he caressed and tasted the moist velvet warmth of her till she melted against him. He released her hands and they came up and around his neck as she succumbed to the forceful domination of his burning mouth.

Somehow he found the strength to pull away from her, taking her hands from his neck and holding them tightly, his eyes blazing down at her as he said, "Remember that, my sweet wife, till I return." Then he turned and walked out of the stables.

"Justin!" Her despairing cry echoed after him in the soft warm air.

Part Three

In a Civil War the firing line is invisible,
it passes through the hearts of men.

Saint-Exupéry, *Wind, Sand, and Stars*

Who would give a law to lovers?
Love is unto itself a higher law.

Boethius,
The Consolation of Philosophy

Chapter Twenty-nine

April 1865

Fluffy white clouds sailed across the wedgewood blue of the spring sky as the Valcour carriage rolled past the huge magnolias standing majestically along the river bluff on Front Row and descended the rough cobblestones to the docks. The levee was busy at even this early hour, Ariane noticed, gazing out the window at the sight of black roustabouts heaving the heavy burlap sacks of produce up the long swaying planks and onto the decks of the waiting steamers. Union soldiers driving army drays and soldiers on foot swarmed everywhere. She still after all these months looked closely at every soldier dressed in blue disembarking from a paddle wheeler, searching for Justin's handsome visage. She was always disappointed.

As Caesar drove the matched grays through the throngs of drays, army wagons, and wagons piled high with produce and army supplies, she leaned back against the cushioned seat, lost in bittersweet memories. It had been over seven months since that early August morning when Justin had walked out of her life. He had gone to the house after leaving the stable, gathered his belongings, and ridden away. In her hurt, anger, and confusion, she had not gone after him. It was only later on those long winter nights that she thought twice about how much her pride and stubbornness had cost her.

With a clearer head, she had known that Justin had shot the young Confederate because he had thought the man was reaching for his gun to shoot them. Once again their divided loyalties had torn them apart.

Where was he, she mused, as she did over and over with never an answer. The Army had transferred him, but where, she didn't know. It seemed no one knew, or wouldn't tell her. She was not privy to the confidence of the Union Command. Once a month, she received a letter delivered by a Union courier with no postmark and only the same words written in a scrawling masculine hand.

Remember how it was between us.
J.

How could she ever forget those nights in his arms, that last bittersweet night when he had hinted that they might be parted. She would search each letter for some clue to his whereabouts, but there was nothing. Then at Christmas had come a package in a box from a shop in New Orleans. Inside was a small ornate silver jewelry box that played "Lorena" when the lid was lifted. Nestled inside on the red velvet was a delicate pin of fine porcelain in the shape of a gardenia blossom. The card, however, said the same haunting words.

Touching the gardenia pin she always wore now on a ribbon about her throat, she tried to put it all to the back of her mind and concentrate on what she must do today, the dangerous yet vital task that lay ahead of her. As the director of Valcour Line now that her father's mind was firmly in the past, she was responsible for all facets of the business, and she was using that capacity as an excuse for the trip she was taking on the *Southern Lady*.

The steamer was leaving today for Helena, Arkansas, some miles downriver, loaded with supplies for the town, plantations along the way, and supplies for the Union Command. She had managed to convince the Provost Marshal to give her a pass to leave Memphis, stating that she had kin in Helena and wished to visit them as well as check on the service her passengers received on the *Southern Lady*. To her surprise, they had agreed and issued her a pass.

The Union Command had had complete cooperation from the Valcour Line in the last six months, and so had begun to ease up on them. Little did they know that it had been to Ariane's advantage to pretend to accommodate the Union Army when they wished to use her steamers to ship supplies. Many of those supplies never got to their destination without a stop along the way when some were taken off by Confederate blockade runners waiting at the mouths of rivers and streams emptying into the Mississippi. That was her plan today for the *Southern Lady*, but this was to be a special rendezvous with an agent from Forrest.

As Caesar came to a stop in front of the white carved gingerbread confection that was the *Southern Lady*, Ariane took a deep breath and smelled the medicine, coffee, tobacco, whisky, and salt to be turned over to Forrest's men at an abandoned plantation on the Mississippi side of the river. When Caesar opened the door, she stepped out into the bright morning sunshine to meet her fate.

"Have my portmanteau put in the owner's cabin, Caesar. And you and Sable keep an eye on Father while I am gone," she told the elderly man as he closed the carriage door behind her.

"We will watch after him, don't yo' worry none, ma'am," he assured her, turning to direct a burly roustabout where to take Ariane's bags.

"You ready, lass?" Sam Riley asked, having seen her arrival from the deck of the steamer and hurried down to greet her. No matter if she was now running the Valcour Line, to Sam she would always be his lass.

"Yes, has all the merchandise arrived?" she inquired casually, but Sam knew to what she was referring. The medicine had been the hardest to obtain from Ward and McClellan in the large amounts needed without alerting the Yankees. Ever since the night Olivia had been unmasked, the Confederacy had not used her, considering her untrustworthy. Olivia had left Memphis within a few days of her meeting with Justin, and she hadn't been seen since. It had complicated getting the medicine from the pharmaceutical company, but Ariane had found a clerk willing to run the risk of discovery by the Provost Marshal. She always worried, however, that this time they would be discovered. "Everything is ready then?"

"Aye, it is loaded safe and sound. We are ready to push off in a few minutes. Allow me to escort you on board," he said gallantly, extending his arm.

"Thank you, Captain." She gave him a sad smile as he placed her hand on his arm, following his lead up the gangplank. She couldn't help remembering that summer day when she and Justin had worked frantically over the young Confederate soldier as he bled to death on the long grass waiting to be carried aboard this very ship. She gave a slight shudder, trying to put that morbid picture from her mind. There had been so much death these last years that thinking about it would surely drive a person mad.

She looked tired, did his lass, thought Sam as he glanced at the lovely pale woman beside him. It was that husband of hers being gone that had put that sad look in her gray eyes. Well, he mused with a sigh, there were a lot of women wondering where their husbands were on both sides of this accursed war.

"I think I will stand up here on the deck outside my stateroom, Sam, and watch us cast off from here. You go do what you have to, I will be fine," Ariane told him, holding on to her wide-brimmed Dolly Varden hat of ecru straw. The wind had begun to gust as they reached the deck where her stateroom was located, swaying her violet silk hoop skirt like a giant blossom of some exotic flower.

Standing at the teakwood rail around the deck, Ariane felt a rising excitement at the coming trip. Whatever danger lay ahead of her, she was ready for it. Somewhere out there was Justin, perhaps on one of the new hospital ships the Union had commissioned. She saw them docked at the wharves in Memphis and always eagerly scanned the decks from her office with her father's telescope.

The high melodious notes of the ship's whistle sang out and the *Southern Lady* slipped away from its moorings at Memphis, heading out into the main channel of the long, muddy, inland sea that was the Mississippi. It was a treacherous river with "boils" that could whirl a man to his death, hidden sandbars that could beach a steamer, and floating trees that could rip the bottom of a boat in minutes. But to Ariane, that was part of its allure, for it was an intoxicating, golden-brown highway that never failed to intrigue her whenever she sailed up and down its mighty turbulent waters. Now with her mission to Forrest, and the Yankees patrolling the river, a new element of danger had been added to the rich gumbo of travel on the Mississippi.

Leaving the bluffs of Memphis behind on one side and the flat Arkansas bank of the other, the *Southern Lady* glided down the rushing ochre waters, joining the motley traffic of steamers, rafts, flatboats, and shanty boats, all scurrying to get out to the main channel. She marveled at how there was no perceptible motion of the vessel, so steady that it seemed the boat was not moving, but rather that it was the riverbank that was in motion.

There were few passengers on board, for it was dangerous to travel by riverboat during the war. Confederate raiders had control of the countryside outside the towns along the Mississippi and often shot at the steamers as they glided past. It was just as well, Ariane thought, staring out across the water—fewer people to question why they were stopping at a plantation wharf that looked so deserted. While the steamers stopped at any plantation dock that had its flag raised, as was custom, Ariane knew that the main house of Mimosa Bayou Plantation might be visible through the trees, and it was obviously deserted.

She had no desire to leave the tranquil scene in front of her for the closed confines of even the large, luxurious owner's stateroom. The gentle lapping of water against the boat lulled her into a mindless serenity. It was the most at peace she had been since the morning Justin rode out of her life.

She watched from her vantage point all morning as the river widened and the banks lowered as they sailed farther downriver from Memphis. They had stopped once already at a plantation landing on the Mississippi side that was crowded with people waiting for the riverboat. It would not seem unusual then when in the late afternoon they stopped at the landing of Mimosa Bayou Plantation. She was to meet Forrest's scout inside the abandoned mansion with important information that they had gleaned about Yankee troop movements in West Tennessee and Northern Mississippi. Her beloved South was bleeding, on its knees. She had to do anything she could to help the valiant men who rode with General Forrest, the man who astounded even the Union Command with his daring strategy. There had been so many double agents used by the Yankees in the last months that Forrest was leery of trusting anyone he didn't know completely. It was why she had to go in person. The Wizard of the Saddle knew he could trust his beautiful Memphis belle, the spy he called the Swan.

"Could I interest you in a spot of food?" Sam Riley asked her, joining her on the deck.

"Yes, I have lost track of time," she answered, turning to face him. "Although I must confess I hate to leave this magnificent view."

"Why, lass, the view is just as lovely through the windows in the dining room, especially from the captain's table," he told her.

Sam was right, Ariane decided, seated at the linen-covered table beside a long window that looked out on the river and the wild lush vegetation of the passing bank. The dining room was magnificent with its intricate carved white and gold ceiling and long Brussels carpet under their feet. Tall palms in brass pots shaded the tables dressed in white linen with crystal goblets, delicate china decorated with the steamer's picture, while the heavy silverware by Reed and Barton bore the ship's monogram, which was also inlaid in lighter wood on the dark mahogany paneling on the walls.

"Sam, when will we be docking at Mimosa Bayou?" Ariane asked in a low murmur, for there were two Yankee soldiers on board the steamer. They made her nervous, even though Sam assured her they had been paid large bribes not to check too closely whenever they stopped at a plantation landing.

"Late afternoon. 'Tis the best time when the shadows are long about the place. There will be a flag flying and a couple of field hands from other plantations standing on the dock with baskets and a wagon back under the trees hitched to a mule team. I thought we could explain your disembarking, if anyone asks, by saying you knew the owner and wished to pay a short visit while we unloaded the supplies they ordered."

"Yes, that sounds plausible," she agreed, stirring uneasily in her chair for one of the soldiers continued to stare in her direction.

"Don't mind him," Sam reassured her with a wide grin, sensing her anxiety. "He is just admiring a pretty woman."

"I have not felt like a pretty woman in a long time," Ariane confessed ruefully, lifting the glass of wine to her lips. Perhaps it would give her courage. She had been experiencing a feeling of foreboding ever since they left Memphis. It had been quieted somewhat by the lulling serenity of the water when she stood out on deck, but now it had come back over her like a heavy fog.

"I won't tell you not to be nervous about this afternoon. 'Tis dangerous, there is no doubt about it, especially now that the Yankees are doing their damnest — er, excuse me, lass — their darnest to stop the smuggling out to Dixie, as they call it. They caught some of our scouts down near Helena not a week ago. We can't know for sure that they haven't been able to sneak one of their agents, a Southern traitor, in among our people. It's how they are infiltrating our intelligence operation. There is a rumor out that one of their best agents is working this area — 'tis why Forrest is being so careful, taking no chances."

"How will we know that the man is from Forrest?" Ariane queried, and to her dismay, her voice broke slightly. The specter of Irving Block Prison rose in her mind to haunt her at Sam's words of warning.

"I shall tell you the code when we disembark. There are too many listening ears aboard this ship," he murmured, sipping his coffee.

The rest of the long afternoon Ariane spent sitting in the ladies' lounge watching the passing scene and pretending an interest in the book she held in her lap. She was alone, for there were few women who wanted to risk steamboat travel on the Mississippi in the midst of war. As the hours dragged on, Ariane struggled to overcome the anxiety that hung over her like a black cloud. When she heard the *Southern Lady's* whistle blow sharply, it startled her and she dropped her book.

"What was that?" she asked as Sam walked into the lounge.

"If you look out that window on your left, you can see a Union hospital ship passing us on the left. It must be coming from downriver," he told her, pointing to where a steamer passed by.

She stared out at the large steamer with a catch in her throat. Could Justin be on it, just yards away across the yellow-brown waters of the Mississippi? She suddenly felt bereft and desolate. If anything happened to her on this most dangerous assignment, would he ever realize that in spite of everything she loved him still? What she wouldn't give to be able to speak with him for just a few minutes, to tell him what was in her heart, but it was, of course, impossible.

"We will be at Mimosa Bayou Plantation in a few minutes. It would be best, I think, if you came up on deck. Leave your book here, perhaps, as if you will return soon," Sam murmured as she rose to her feet.

Once out on deck with the other passengers, who gathered to watch any stop along the river, Ariane said as loudly as she could without sounding unladylike or strained, "Is this Mimosa Bayou Plantation where we are stopping? I declare 'tis been an age since I saw May Beth Haydel. Really, Sam, I must pay my respects. Now don't fuss and say no—I insist. It won't take that long. While you are unloading their order, I will just saunter up to the main house," Ariane trilled while Sam put on a show of objecting then finally giving in to her flirtatious pleas. They both noticed the Union soldiers listening and grinning at what they thought was Sam's discomfort at being put in such a position by a capricious Southern belle.

Watching as a former slave stood out on the dock waving a cloth flag as a signal, Ariane felt a thrill of frightened anticipation touch the bottom of her stomach. Gracefully the huge steamer glided into place next to the long rotting dock with a wash of muddy water.

Lifting her parasol above her head, Ariane waited impatiently at the head of the gangplank as it was carefully lowered in place. Playing the spoiled, flighty belle to the hilt for the benefit of her Yankee observers, she felt a panic unlike any she had ever known.

"Listen carefully," Sam whispered as they walked down the gangplank. "Our man will say 'Liberty or death,' and you will reply 'Never surrender.' I shall wait as long as I can. If you do not return in an hour, I will tell everyone you decided to stay and we are to stop on our way back. I shan't want to leave you, lass, but if you don't return, I will know something has gone wrong or you have decided 'tis safer to go with Forrest's man. I can't help you with those Yanks on board, so you are really on your own. Remember—after one hour I will sound the whistle three times and then wait ten minutes before we push off. God speed," he said with a catch in his voice.

Ariane nodded her understanding while she continued to smile a vapid smile for the benefit of anyone watching. Even in the balmy April warmth, she felt a chill, a chill of fear.

"Be back in an hour, Mrs. Pierce, or I will know you decided to stay for a visit," Sam called out loudly after escorting her down the gangplank, across the dock, up the grassy bank toward the house, which was barely visible through the thick forest. From the steamer, one could see only the gleam of ponderous white shafts soaring through the trees to a second-story roof.

Ariane hurried up the path through the long grass, hoping that nothing reptilian slithered across her way. Once away from the riverfront, it was obvious it had been a long time since the Haydels had lived at Mimosa Bayou. There was an almost jungle-like atmosphere about the grounds, which had been kept to manicured perfection before the war. Fever had taken May Beth's father, and when her brothers left to serve with the Confederacy, she and her mother had struggled to work the plantation. The Yankees had stopped on their push

402

downriver two years before and all the slaves, except for a few house servants, had left with them. May Beth and her mother had given up and moved in with relatives in Natchez.

Ariane shivered in the dark coolness of the near tropic vegetation gone wild. Creeper vines wound from roots to top branches on the trees. Daffodils struggled through the long grass and matted vines. She could barely see the formal stepping stones that led from the overgrown driveway to the front veranda. The soaring pillars of the Greek-style mansion were spotted green with moss, and the glass in most of the windows had been broken out. There was a rotting, haunted quality about the place that hung in the air like the many enormous spider webs that hung from the tree branches.

Trying to control the spasmodic trembling that threatened to overwhelm her, Ariane forced herself to step up on the vine-covered veranda. Lowering her sunshade, she hung it from a cord about her wrist. She wanted to run from this macabre place, which in its desolation seemed to represent what had happened to the South that she had known, and a way of life that was no more. It was a rotting shell that could only hint at what it had once been, and would never be again. There was no future here, only decaying reminders of the dead past.

Forcing herself to cross the threshold with its sagging door half-open, she stood in the long hall that bisected the once elegant mansion. Faded wallpaper stained by the rain peeled in the corners. A mirror, the glass cracked, hung crookedly over a spot where there had once been a table, long gone now, having been carried off by some vandal. There was an eerie stillness about the place like the inside of a tomb. Every instinct told her to leave this haunted place, to run as fast as she could back to the safety of the *Southern Lady* and Sam Riley. She wanted to leave and never look back, but her sense of honor made her stay. She had a job to do, a mission to carry out, so stay she must, no matter that her legs were trembling as she waited in the deserted hall. Where was her contact from Forrest? He should have seen the steamer dock and her walk up the path from the river.

Her heart thumping madly, she slipped her hand in the pocket of her skirt and pulled out the colt revolver. Releasing the safety catch, she called out, "Is there anyone here?"

A creak from somewhere in the back of the house was her only answer as she stood with the gun pointed in front of her. After a long chill silence, she heard footsteps, the sound of a man's boots on the wooden floor. Turning toward the sound, she held her gun in trembling hands, her breath coming in shallow, quick gasps.

"Never surrender," she called out, her words trembling more than she would have liked.

"Yes, I can certainly believe that," drawled a deep, familiar masculine voice from the past.

Chapter Thirty

"What are you doing here?" she exclaimed, intense astonishment in her pearl-gray eyes, her oval visage white with shock.

"I might ask you the same question, but unfortunately I fear I know the answer," he replied, his voice deep, velvet-edged, and strong. Only his burning gaze betrayed his passionate hunger at seeing her once more.

She experienced the sound of him like a caress up her spine, turning her knees to water. His night-black eyes traveled over her face then, meeting her gaze, seemed to search within her for some sign. She could feel the fiery yearning to be held in those arms, pressed closed against him, growing with her till she feared she would lose control. Just to be in his embrace once more, to know his touch, her whole being cried out for him, for Justin.

"Could you at least put down the gun, Little Bit. I find it unsettling to converse with anyone, even my own wife, when she is pointing a pistol in my direction."

"Where is the man I am supposed to meet?" Ariane asked in a choked voice, surprised at her own presence of mind.

"Someone got here before the both of us, and was waiting for him. He is in the back garden. Whoever shot him has stolen his horse."

"How . . . how do I know that it was not you?" She still had not lowered the gun.

"You don't. But I think you know that even if I did, I

405

could never harm you, even though you are Forrest's Swan." His gaze darkened with some unreadable emotion. Could it be hurt?

"Why do you say that?" she queried, playing for time. Shocked that he should know her code name she still knew deep within her soul, that no matter they stood on opposite side of a deep chasm called war, he could never hurt her.

"We have been able to break your code and intercepted your courier, sending on one of our own agents to take his place. Yes, we have known all about this meeting, but we wanted to catch Forrest's agent in the act for although we had your code name we didn't know who was the Swan. I must confess once I heard the name I had a good idea. I wish I had been wrong," his voice was uncompromising yet oddly gentle.

Suddenly, she lifted the gun up once more till it pointed straight at him. "And you seem to have a hidden facet to your character as well," she said with surprise and bitterness.

"As I told you once before, my sweet Ariane, we are different sides of the same coin. Are you planning on using that on me? Could you kill me, Little Bit?" he asked softly, his expression grim as his black eyes bore into her. There was a waiting quality in those eyes, and a sadness that seared her heart.

All those years of bloodshed and pain, when brother fought brother, and friend turned against friend, all those years of war when abstract values of loyalty, honor to country and cause had unleashed a horror until then unknown, now came down to this moment. These were not armies of faceless men against faceless men, but a man and woman alone in a deserted rotting plantation house. They could no longer avoid confronting what had stood between them since that long ago hot June morning at the surrender of Memphis.

There was a long brittle silence when Ariane looked

406

into the depths of her soul and saw the truth. Gazing at him in despair, she clicked off the safety on the Colt and lowered it to her side putting it in her pocket in a gesture of utter defeat. Then lifting that same hand to him in supplication she called in desperation, "Justin!"

With a few lithe steps he was in front of her pulling her roughly, almost violently, to him. She clung to him tears blinding her eyes, choking her voice, as she murmured "Justin, my love," over and over.

"Yes, oh yes, my sweet Ariane. 'Tis all right. We are together that is all that matters," he whispered into her hair, holding her against him as if he would never let her go.

She wound her arms around his broad back caressing him through the material of his tunic, wishing that she could feel the sinewy warmth of his skin. Suddenly it didn't matter that they were on different sides, all that was important was the magnificent man in her arms.

There was no time. He knew they had to leave this place; he had arranged to come first so that the Rebs would be taken by surprise. The other soldiers from a detachment off the hospital ship were just upriver a mile. They were to come when he signaled, but there would be no signal. He was leaving with Ariane; somehow he would explain it later. Someone had killed the Reb Scout, whether a newly freed slave with a need for vengeance or a roving band of deserters, either Union or Confederate—the South was full of them. Who was to say that he had not had to flee from the same murderer? The Swan had escaped, but the Union Command would never know that one of their own had helped her.

His mouth covered hers hungrily, devouring her burning lips as she returned his kiss with reckless abandon, pressing her body against his till he moaned, pulling away, "We must leave now. There is no time. They are coming for you. Follow me. I will explain later." His voice was rough with anxiety and the need for haste. He

407

looked down at her for one brief moment, his heart and soul in his smoldering night-black eyes. Then taking her hand, they started for the back door.

"Wait." She stopped him, pointing to her hoop skirt swaying around her.

"Yes, for God's sake, take it off and the parasol, and the hat. Leave them as a calling card that the Swan escaped," he said with a brief, humorless laugh.

Dropping the cage hoop petticoat from under her voluminous skirt, she placed the parasol and the huge floppy hat beside it on the floor. Then she was beside Justin, hurrying out the back door and across the back garden toward his horse. She stopped for one brief moment as she saw the scuffed boot of a man lying in the long grass. A Forrest Scout, she thought with a pang.

"Come, hurry, we don't have much time. I want to be far away from here," he told her as they both heard the whistle of the *Southern Lady* alerting her that it was time to leave.

Sam would have to go on without her, she thought as Justin pulled her up in the saddle in front of him, her long skirt hanging on either side as she sat astride the horse. They were off down a faint old wagon trail. She remembered that Justin had come to Mimosa Bayou Plantation as a boy to hunt and fish with the Haydel sons.

The woods were thick with giant cypress trees, their knots pushing up into the swampy water of the bayou for which the plantation was named. In the summer, the banks were dense with mimosa trees in bloom, their shaggy pink flowers fragrant in the sultry heat, but it was spring and they were not yet in bloom. Ariane shuddered as they saw a sluggish water moccasin sunning itself on a limb of a cypress tree hanging over the olive green water.

In the far distance, they heard a series of gun shots from the direction of the abandoned plantation house.

Leaving the faint trail, Justin headed through the swampy undergrowth until they reached a higher rise in the ground that seemed to follow the river as it wound its way downstream. They were heading south, away from the plantation, away from Memphis into the wilderness.

Quietly Justin explained to her whom they were running from, that he was taking her away from the Union troops—the soldiers that were coming to arrest her and Forrest's dead scout.

"You planned it this way because you thought I was the Swan and you were trying to rescue me," she said with wonder in her voice, leaning back into the warmth of his arms around her as he held the reins loosely in one hand.

"Yes, Little Bit, you have made what some people would call a traitor out of me," he murmured ruefully into the scented silk of her shimmering hair.

"Never to me," she whispered. "To me, you will always be my valiant knight even if you wear blue wool instead of shining armor."

"When, and if, we get out of this, my impetuous Rebel, we are going to have to talk about your activities on behalf of the Confederacy," he murmured, circling her ear with the tip of his tongue.

"And you. Where have you been? Seven months with only those cryptic notes and the . . . the pin." She stopped her complaints as his hand touched the gardenia pin on the lavender ribbon about her slender throat.

"Up and down the river on the hospital ship you passed earlier this afternoon," he explained softly, kissing her temple in featherlike kisses.

"But that ship stopped in Memphis several times since you left. I saw it," she said, turning around to accuse him with hurt in her dove gray eyes.

"It took every shred of willpower not to come to you, my sweet, but there was so much pain between us. If you had known what else I was doing beside my position as medical officer, I knew I would lose you. So I stayed away, hoping that the war would end and with its finish we could find a new beginning."

"So you were also involved in . . ." Her voice trailed off.

"Yes, I, too, am a spy, my dearest wife."

"You are the Falcon," she said softly, understanding lighting her gray eyes.

"Yes."

"Did you hate the South that much that you would spy on your own people? Is that why you did it?"

"I thought, like you, that in some way I would help the war end. At first, to be honest, I think I did have a need for vengeance. I had painful memories of Southerners and of Memphis. What I didn't realize was that there was also a part of my heart that still loved the South. I had forgotten its seductive lure, how once it gets in your blood, it never really leaves. And I lost my heart to one of its most beautiful belles that very first morning of my return."

"Why did you come to me now?"

"Serving on the hospital ship was good cover for what General Dodge wanted me to do, and that was to find out how supplies were getting out of Memphis to the Confederacy and particularly Forrest and his men. We made our contacts along the river, buying information when we had to, and soon a picture began to form, and that was of steamers leaving Memphis and meeting Rebs at the mouth of streams feeding into the Mississippi. The Union Command wants to make an example of soldiers being bribed by Southern steamer captains. When we were able to capture one of your couriers on his way to Forrest's man and break the code, we knew we had them. When I heard, however, that the contact was a woman spy from Memphis called the Swan, I knew in my bones the identity of Forrest's most trusted spy. I knew I could stay away from you no longer."

"How glad I am that 'twas you," she sighed, "my Yankee spy, my Falcon, my love."

"They are serious this time, Little Bit. The war is all but won and they will want retribution for all the Northern dead. I know it hurts to hear this, but I care only for saving your life. I am sick of war, of the useless dying of young men.

When I get you back to Memphis, however, your activities must stop, for the next time I might not be there." There was a warning in his voice that sent a shiver up and down Ariane's spine. She knew that he spoke the truth and how close she had come on this spring afternoon to capture or perhaps death.

"Where are we headed? It's almost sundown."

"Spanish Bend Plantation. 'Tis been deserted since before the Haydels gave up and left Mimosa Bayou. No one comes around since a Union soldier was killed there. On the way to Vicksburg, a Union gunboat anchored at their dock and took over the house as headquarters for a while. The owner was too old for the Confederate army but his son had joined up. Seems he was killed at Shiloh and the old gentleman was filled with hate. When they tried to take over Spanish Bend, he shot at them from the second-story gallery. They shot back and he was killed, but before he died, he claimed to have seen the ghost of a Spanish galleon the night before they came so he knew he was going to die. According to legend, a Spanish ship sank a hundred years before in the bend in the river near the plantation.

"If anyone sees the ghost of the ship, they will die within twenty-four hours. Of course they laughed at the old man, thinking he was crazy and, after burying him, moved into his house. The next night a lieutenant walked out on the gallery because he couldn't sleep in the heat. The next morning he was raving about seeing a four-mast ship sailing by out of the fog. They all thought he had been drinking and had dreamed the whole thing. That afternoon his horse threw him and he broke his neck instantly. They packed up and left, the slaves scattered, and vandals carried off most of what was left. Spanish Bend is quite deserted, for the story of its being haunted is known up and down the river," he told her as the last rays of the dying sun slanted through the gnarled branches of the cypress trees.

"I can't say I am looking forward to spending the night there myself," Ariane murmured uneasily. "But then 'tis better than the swamp or a Yankee prison."

"My sentiments exactly," he agreed, turning the horse through the dense trees until they came to a faint path through the tangle of weeds and grass that was the front lawn of Spanish Bend Plantation.

The house had an air of seclusion, of hidden secrets, about its tall doric pillars gleaming gray-white against the dark green of the surrounding, encroaching forest. There was an overwhelming silence, an eerie stillness that permeated the seemingly tranquil scene.

Ariane's unease grew as they neared the shadowy gallery of the empty mansion. The house soared two stories high in front of them. The white plaster was cracked here and there from the elements to show the red bricks underneath. The glass still remained in most of the windows, for even vandals had been eager to leave a haunted landscape.

"We will be safe here. As you can tell, no one comes here, especially after sundown," Justin said, dismounting and then reaching up to help her down.

A flock of black birds flew out from underneath the eaves as they stepped foot on the gallery that ran across the entire front of the house. Ariane, startled by the flock, stepped back, but Justin's reassuring arm about her waist pressed her forward to the massive double doors, closed, it seemed, against all intruders.

"Perhaps we shouldn't," Ariane whispered as Justin

412

put his hand firmly on the bronzed doorknob turned a gray-green by time.

"There is no one here. I have used Spanish Bend before as a stop on my, shall we say, travels," Justin said, his mouth twisting into a wry smile.

"I see. This is a safe house for the Yankees."

"Just for one Yankee. The others don't know about it or I would never have brought you here, Little Bit," he told her, pushing open the door with a shove of his shoulder for the wood was swollen shut from the changing temperatures of the seasons.

"When was the last time you were here?" she asked, following him inside the dark and shadowy hall that ran the width of the house from front door to back.

"A few weeks," he replied, striding into the chamber on the right.

Dim light from the gathering twilight filtered through lace curtains that hung in tatters at the long windows. Ariane stood at the entrance of the empty room, watching as Justin crossed to a fireplace mantel where a stub of a candle stood in a wine bottle. It was cool and damp inside the house and she shivered as she saw him light the taper.

"Why were you here only a few weeks ago?" she continued as he turned to light an oil lamp on the far end of the mantel.

"In pursuit of my duties as a Union agent, my dear. I shall not tell you any more nor will I ask you about your activities on behalf of the Confederacy. Shall we declare a truce between North and South here in this private place?" His voice was a sensual promise as he turned to her in the shadow room.

"Yes," she whispered, "a truce."

"Come to me," he said, his voice husky with need, holding out his arms. "I have been too long without you."

She ran with a small moan into his embrace, flinging

413

herself against the solid wonderful strength that was Justin. He enfolded her into his arms, rocking her back and forth gently, allowing all the repressed emotion and desire he had suppressed for so long to flow to the surface.

He kissed her temples, the silky tendrils that curled across her brow, the rounded curve of her soft cheek. As she raised her head from where she had buried it in the hollow of his neck, he stared down into her misty gray gaze with a wonder in his black burning eyes that told her of his joy in being united with her once more.

Shyly, she reached up and touched the swarthy planes of his beloved visage as if to reassure herself that he was here with her. She sighed, a smile trembling on her lips as she realized that in this deserted place they had the entire night to become reacquainted with the splendor of the other's wondrous being.

"There are only the two of us and time, so much glorious time, to be together," he whispered, cupping the pale oval of her face up tenderly with his warm hands.

" 'Tis been so long," she sighed, drowning in his nightblack eyes.

"I know, my love, but the waiting is over for us." His lips brushed against hers as he spoke, then he was pressing her to him, demanding more, caressing her lips, tracing their fullness with his tongue, leaving a burning trail that made her quiver with need.

Wrapping her arms around his neck, she gave in to the currents of desire that ran through her, making her veins feel as if they were filled with hot molten honey. She was all passionate languor, crushed to his sinewy lean strength, mesmerized by his slow, drugging kisses.

When the storm first rattled the loose shutters, they paid no attention, but when the wind gusts blew open the heavy front door, Justin lifted his head with reluctance. "I must see to my horse. There is a stable out back. I will bring in some firewood I secured in the barn the last time I was here. Take the lamp and go upstairs.

There is a large bed in one room, too heavy for anyone to carry off. It has been stripped of all coverings, but in the massive armoire are clean army blankets I left the last time I was here. I shall join you as soon as I can. You are not afraid?" he asked, staring down at her, concern in those ebony depths.

"With you I am not afraid of anything," Ariane said, a soft loving curve of happiness and wonder touching her lips. She felt as if she were wrapped in a silken cocoon of love where nothing could harm her.

Lifting her hand to his lips, he pressed a kiss into her palm then was gone out into the storm. She stared at him for a brief moment then, remembering his instructions, walked over and picked up the oil lamp. Holding it in one hand and her skirt in the other, she started up the shadowy stairs. Reaching the top landing, she saw flashes of lightning through the long, many-paned window that looked out on what once had been the back garden. Seeing Justin lead the horse into the shelter of the barn, she walked down the hall, looking into several empty rooms. Some still had heavy armoires—remnants of the fine furnishings that had once been part of the mansion. The third room that overlooked the front must have been the master bedroom for it had two French doors that led out to the second-floor gallery. A huge mahogany four-poster with an ornate carved canopy stood against the far wall. The bed hangings and bedclothes were gone, as Justin had said. Only the mattress stuffed with Spanish moss remained. Placing the oil lamp on an enormous dresser, also of mahogany, she crossed to the armoire, which stood like a monolith against the other wall. Inside were several folded Union Army blankets, and a bottle of brandy.

Ariane spread one blanket across the mattress of the four-poster, tucking it in as Sable had always directed the housemaid. She placed the other across the foot of the bed. The bottle of brandy she placed on the marble-topped dresser.

With an impish smile, she slipped out of her clothes, leaving them in a pile on the heart of pine floor. The air cool on her naked skin, she climbed on to the blanket-covered mattress, pulling the other blanket up to her shoulders against the damp chill of the chamber. Watching the fury of the storm outside the French doors, she heard Justin's booted step coming up the stair. Remembering how he liked her hair down about her shoulders, she pulled the pins from her chignon, then realizing she had no place to put them, she jumped out of bed to put them on the dresser. She stood with her back to the door as she heard it open, her waist-length red-gold hair her only garment.

Chapter Thirty-one

"What a lovely sight to greet a wet and weary man."
Justin's voice was thick and unsteady as he stood on
the threshold of the room. Over his broad shoulder he
had slung his saddlebag, and in his hands he carried a
canvas sling full of firewood.

"I hoped to surprise you," she said with a slight seductive smile that lit up her silver gray eyes with an inner fire.

"You accomplished your goal splendidly," he replied,
his voice raspy with desire. Crossing to the fireplace,
he set down the wood and his leather saddlebag. As he
turned toward her, his eyes swept over her figure glowing ivory and gold in the light from the oil lamp. "Let
me divest myself of these sodden garments, my beautiful tantalizing wife, so I might show you my appreciation of your surprise."

She stood transfixed by his words and the language
he spoke only with his dark eyes. There was no need
for false modesty between them. They gloried in the
knowledge that the other enjoyed the sight, the feel,
the taste of the beloved's body.

Stripped of his uniform, he stood before her and she
was unable to take her eyes from his lean, sinewy,
masculine beauty. Men had a beauty all their own, different from a woman's, but glorious in its length of
line and hard planes. He had the muscular grace of a
proud jungle cat, aloof, yet intent on what he desired,

what he would take if need be, to have what he wanted above all else. A flash of lightning showed what she had not noticed before, a tinge of silver at the temples of his blue-black hair. When had that come, she thought, and she was suddenly conscious of the time they had been apart. She wanted to stroke the heavy, still-damp silk of his hair, learn the feel of him again, curl her fingers in the fine dark curls that matted his bronzed chest and down, ever downward, across his lean hips to the very symbol of his passion for her, the throbbing erect length of him.

" 'Tis for you," he whispered, following the direction of her gaze.

She lifted her gray eyes, enormous in her pale face, her lips trembling. "Then come to me," she told him, her voice breaking with her desire.

With a few lithe steps he was beside her, then taking her hand in his, he led her to the bed. They sank down onto the mattress, arms entwined, heated mouth on heated mouth, soft feminine thighs wrapped around the hard planes of muscular masculine thighs.

Her hungry mouth was full of his delicious probing tongue and she drank her fill of his honeyed sweetness. She reveled in the touch of his hands learning the contours of her body once more. Arching up, she pressed the aching fullness of her breasts into the silk fur of his chest, her soft hips against the lean plane of him. His erect manhood strained for her moist velvet depths.

Then they were rolling over and over on the blanket till he was beneath her, and with his strong hands on her narrow waist, he was lifting her up till her soft thighs straddled him. "I can wait no longer, but I want to see you, caress you," he murmured as his hand reached down to part her soft feminine petals and prepare her for him. Feeling her hot moistness and knowing she wanted him as much as he wanted her, he lifted her up and then plunged slowly, rapturously into her pulsating depths.

"Oh yes!" she gasped, placing her hands on his shoulders as she took him into her, deeper and deeper still. The pearls that were her fingernails pressed into his skin as the fire grew within her to a blazing fury.

His hands stroked down the hollows of her back to cup her buttocks as she moved in circles of ecstasy, her head thrown back till her long red-gold hair fell across his thighs. She was woman, his woman, and he gloried in the beautiful sight of her lost in the rapture she had found in his lovemaking. Her body and hair were a golden glow in the dim light from the lamp.

Her wanton moans joined in the sounds of the thunder, the wind, and the rain on the roof. She felt one with the elements of nature as she rode him like some wild creature, driven by a need so deep within her that nothing would satisfy it but total abandonment to sensation.

Caressing up to her full breasts, circling the hard rose nipples swollen with desire, Justin drank in the vision that was Ariane. It was worth everything to be joined once more with this extraordinary woman who had haunted his days and obsessed his nights every minute that he had been away from her. Nothing would ever part them again, he vowed. Whatever it took, he would do it — he would never lose her again.

Then she felt his hands at her waist, and with one fluid motion, she was pressed back against the mattress and he was over her and deep inside her. His mouth was raining kisses down on her temples, her closed eyelids, her tangled hair, the throbbing pulse at the base of her neck. His whispered words burned into her skin as he muttered, "Mine, all mind. Never will I let you go. Never. I will follow you to the ends of the earth, through all eternity if I must, but we will never be parted again."

He took her mouth with a savage intensity that was more than a kiss—it was, in effect, the sealing of a vow. She responded with all the force of her long-pent-up need for him, for his presence in her life, the touch of his hand on her yearning body, the taste of him on her mouth, the sound of his voice in her ear that was the sweetest music. She knew that there was nothing more important in life than this magnificent man and the love she held for him in her heart. If she had learned nothing else in this bitter war, it was that life was short and one should treasure each moment when one's existence was touched by the wonder of love.

They moved together, arching and surging, silken fire and thrusting passion, in a sensuous rhythm that burned away the memory of the empty hours when they had been apart. Joined body and soul, they found their ecstasy, soaring to the peak and over into the infinity that only true lovers have ever been privileged to experience. In rapturous reunion, they achieved total fulfillment, complete commitment one to the other.

Slumber came to them as they lay entwined under an army blanket. What peace, Ariane thought as she listened to the steady beating of her beloved's heart, and the rain above them on the roof.

It was the early hours of the morning when they woke to a foggy gray sky as first light streaked into the chamber. They had slept the night through, exhausted by the previous day's events and the intense emotion of their reunion. Both were reluctant to leave the bed, but they were ravenous.

"I shall make a fire to take some of the damp from the room. I have some coffee and army rations in my saddlebag. 'Tis not much but will fill the empty places," he said, slipping from the warm sanctuary of the four-poster to don his clothes. Soon he had a fire blazing in the fireplace and it gave the shadowy chamber a more comforting atmosphere.

Ariane watched in amazement as he soon had water boiling in a battered pan he had taken from his saddlebag. He poured the ground coffee beans mixed with sugar into the pan, and the chamber was filled with the wonderful fragrance of rich hot coffee.

"No, don't dress," he told her as she started to slip from the bed. "We shall have our breakfast in bed."

Spreading a large linen handkerchief on the rumpled blanket, he placed some pieces of chocolate and squares of corn bread on the makeshift tablecloth. Pouring some of the brandy into a battered tin cup with the hot coffee, he held it out to Ariane for the first sip. " 'Tis not much, but it's all I brought from the hospital ship."

"Hot and sweet. 'Tis wonderful," she murmured, brushing the tangle of her hair from her eyes.

Sitting beside her on the bed, Justin took sips from the mug as they ate in a companionable silence till there was not a crumb left. Leaning over, he kissed her on the tip of her nose and said, "You look lovely this morning, Mrs. Pierce."

"And you are a bare-faced liar," she joked with a wry expression. "I look dreadful. If only there was some water and a bit of soap," she sighed.

"I have some soap, but I will have to go outside to where I saw a rain barrel in the overgrown garden. After last night's downpour, there should be plenty of fresh water. I saw a bucket in the stables."

Watching him leave the room, she gave a slight shiver. Perhaps if she stood over by the fire, she could get this chill from her bones. Wrapping the blanket around her, she padded across the floor, stopping to pick up her garments, which she had so casually discarded the night before. Shaking out the wrinkles as best she could, she draped her clothes over the bed. Starting back for the fireplace, she stopped to look out the long French doors. In the morning light, she could see the river. They had come up the long overgrown drive the night before and she hadn't realized in the gloom of twilight how close they were to the Mississippi.

Walking closer to the French doors, she stared out at the haunted scene below her, of tangled overgrown vegetation and trees. Nature was reclaiming Spanish Bend Plantation. She could just make out through the branches of the towering trees the rotting dock that jutted out into the rushing waters of the river. Once steamers had stopped there to take on the white-gold cotton from the fertile fields of the plantation, but no more. The grayish-white fog swirled in from the river, hanging in the cool of morning in the low places. It was then that she saw it, and a primitive fear raced up her spine. There in the fog of the river she saw a ship. Were those masted sails or only her imagination? She stood frozen, she didn't know for how long, staring out at the now empty river. Had she seen the ghostly apparition of the legendary Spanish galleon, or had it only been her overwrought mind?

"What are you looking at?" Justin's deep familiar voice cut into the frightened stupor that had paralyzed her.

"The Spanish galleon, I saw it!" she gasped, turning to where he stood in the doorway holding an oaken bucket of rain water.

" 'Twas only the fog and your imagination working overtime," he reassured her. Crossing to the dresser, he placed the bucket upon it and took a square of flannel from his saddlebag along with a bar of soap. "I shall leave you to your toilette, madame. There is something

422

I must do so we do not have to spend another night here."

"Don't leave me," she cried as he started for the door.

"I must raise a flag on the dock. There should be a steamer passing this way this morning and I want it to stop here and pick us up, horse and all."

"A Yankee ship?" she asked, concern making her voice quiver.

"No, 'tis another kind of ship I make use of, the way I do this abandoned plantation. I knew it would be passing this way today and arranged with the owner, Molly Cook, to check the dock to see if my flag was flying. If it was, she promised to stop."

"Molly Cook's steamer?" Ariane asked in incredulous tones. "That is a brothel boat."

"Yes. It makes excellent cover, and she asks no questions. You see, I treated her and her family years ago when they were ill with fever. Although her mother and father died, she and her sister lived, and she thinks I was responsible for her survival. 'Tis not the *Southern Lady,* Little Bit, but for our purposes it will serve us well," he said quietly, moving toward the door. "Dress while I am gone. I will only be a few minutes. You can see me from the French doors."

Knowing what he said was true, she tried to recover her control. Dropping the blanket, she quickly washed with the soap and rainwater, shivering in the cool damp of the chamber. Wrapping the blanket back around her shoulders, she took her clothes and carried them to the fireplace to dress, basking in the warmth of the flames. When she had finished donning her rumpled smallclothes and gown, she started for the bureau to pin up her long tangled hair. Just then she heard steps coming down the hall outside the door.

Turning with a welcoming smile for Justin, she froze

as she stared into the grimy, leering face of a stranger. Dressed in a mud-spattered blue uniform and battered blue fatigue cap, he watched her from where he stood on the threshold. Thinking they were quite alone at Spanish Bend, Ariane had neglected to close the door.

"So the lady of the house is still here," he muttered in sarcastic tones. There was a mean vile expression on his grizzled countenance.

"What do you want?" she demanded, stalling for time, wondering with a sinking heart if he had a gun on him.

"Well, now, Reb, it depends on what you have to offer. Seems there is nothing much left about this place."

"Where are the rest of your men?" Ariane fought to maintain some kind of control, to show no fear.

"I'm all alone, missy, just like you," he said, coming into the room.

A deserter, she thought, relieved that at least the detachment from the hospital ship had not tracked them down. This was just one Yankee deserter, but from the looks of him, that didn't minimize the fact that he could hurt her.

"I have nothing of value, as you can see. Others have been here before you," she said coolly, playing along that she was the mistress of the house. "My house servants will be back from their quarters directly, and they can show you that everything of any worth was taken long ago."

"You're a cool one, ain't you," he said with a flash of respect in his small, mean eyes. "We both know the slave quarters are deserted. Looks like they haven't been lived in for a good long time. Although some Fed soldier left you his horse. What did you have to give him for that fine animal, or did you steal him? I'll take the horse, pretty Reb, and there is something else I want. Can you guess what that is? I'll give you a little hint — I'm looking at exactly what I want." He started toward her.

Panic welled up in her as she backed slowly away from him. Where was Justin?

"Now don't run away, Reb," he snarled, reaching out and grabbing hold of her arm.

"Let go of her!" Justin ordered, pushing open the French doors from where he stood on the gallery.

Ariane whirled around, joy flooding her frightened visage. The deserter took a step back, dropping her arm, astonishment whipping the lust from his beady eyes. He looked at Justin as if he could not believe the apparition that stood in the doorway. Staring at his blue tunic, he seemed suddenly to make a decision and pulled his service revolver from under his coat.

Ariane gasped, realizing that Justin's sidearm and holster lay with his gauntlets and wide-brimmed hat on the dresser. He had not donned them, thinking they were alone at Spanish Bend and he would finish dressing after he'd raised the flag on the dock.

As the deserter raised his pistol to fire at Justin, Ariane felt the weight of her father's colt in her pocket. She had forgotten that she had put it there before leaving the *Southern Lady*. Quickly, she released the safety and, with only the thought that her beloved husband was in danger, fired.

The man staggered forward, knocking an oil lamp to the floor before slumping dead at her feet. She stood transfixed by the knowledge that she had killed a man, and then shock turned to horror as Justin hurried to her side.

"We have to get out of here," he told her in terse tones, pointing at the oil that was seeping out of the broken lamp into the fireplace. His arm around her waist, he pulled her from the room as the oil caught

425

fire, blazing up in a trail across the floor to the tattered lace curtains.

Hurrying down the long hall, they heard the fire crackling in the chamber they had just fled. Down the stairs and out the front door they ran. Outside in the foggy morning they stopped for a moment to stare up at the fire they could see gathering strength in the upstairs bedchamber.

Ariane felt an overwhelming sense of despair as she stared at the stately mansion ablaze. One Yankee had finally succeeded in destroying the house that had made a slow descent into ruin. It had taken it a long time to die, but it was perishing before their eyes and they were helpless to stop it. The man she had killed in the upstairs chamber she tried to put from her mind. He would have killed Justin if she hadn't shot him first. She had no regret over her action, only regret that it had been necessary.

"Come, Little Bit, there is nothing that can be done. I must see to my horse. We will wait down on the dock for the steamer."

Silently, hand and hand, they walked to the stables, leaving the empty hulk of Spanish Bend Plantation to its fate. Ariane stood numb as Justin saddled the horse and then, taking the reins, led him outside. The air was now filled with the smell of smoke, and the animal became skittish at the scent.

Skirting the burning house by taking a far path at the edge of the overgrown lawn, they reached the rotting dock that jutted out into the Mississippi. "We will wait here on the shore. I don't want to take the horse out on those boards till the steamer is docked," Justin explained, keeping a tight hold on the reins of the skittish animal.

"Sooner or later everything is destroyed because of this accursed war," Ariane mused, staring back at the

426

flames shooting up into the misty fog. Had the ghostly ship she thought she saw that morning indeed been a warning that someone was to die? She wondered if the deserter had seen the same apparition.

"Don't think about it, sweetheart," Justin said softly. "Remember only that you saved my life. I never realized how lucky I am to be married to a fiery Rebel. This old Yank will spend the rest of our life together trying to show his gratitude." His voice was husky with emotion as he pulled her to him so she rested in the curve of his arm, the other hand holding the horse's reins. "Don't look back, Little Bit. Look out there to the river."

"Why were you out on the gallery?" she asked, leaning her head on his shoulder, staring out at the mist rising from the water.

"I heard two voices when I came in downstairs. Suspicious that a deserter had made his way to Spanish Bend, I entered the gallery from one of the other rooms that opened on to it. When I saw him touching you, I thought I would go mad."

"I could only think that just when we had found each other again, fate could not be so cruel as to tear us apart," Ariane sighed with a shiver of vivid recollection.

" 'Tis in the past now, my sweet. We shall put it behind us."

They waited for what seemed like hours, nervously looking back at the house that in the lightly falling rain had turned to a smoldering hulk. They had seen no ship pass by on the rushing water.

Ariane shivered in the cool April mist. She was drenched, and her light dress gave little protection or warmth. Even in the circle of Justin's arm, she felt a chill.

"There is a blanket rolled on the back of my saddle," he said as he felt her tremble. Handing her the reins, he moved to unstrap the blanket and drape it about her shoulders.

" 'Tis much better," she told him with a wan smile.

"Good," he murmured huskily as he gently brushed a strand of wet hair from her cheek.

"I must look a fright," she sighed.

"You are beautiful, Little Bit, never so beautiful as you are at this moment. My God, I am proud of you, of your strength, your courage, your fiery spirit." His black eyes caressed her delicate face, glowing with his love for her.

It was then that they heard the clanging of a steamer bell out on the water. Turning their gaze from the other's beloved visage, they saw the outline of a ship coming toward them out of the mist.

"Wait here, I will go to the end of the dock and wave the flag to make sure they see us," he told her. She stood holding the reins of the horse, watching the great shape of the steamer come closer. The tan waters of the Mississippi churned up and over the paddle wheel. Soon she could see the gilt words of the name, *Molly Cook*. It was the infamous brothel boat that sailed the serpentine river, stopping at all the most notorious ports along the Mississippi.

"Doc Pierce! Is that you?" the booming voice of an enormous woman with flaming red hair called from the first deck as the intricately carved gothic confection pulled up to the dock.

"It's me, Molly. I thought you would never get here. You're going to have to take my horse on board," he called, grabbing hold of the thick rope a roustabout threw him.

"Looks like a horse ain't all you brought with you this trip," she shouted, gesturing with a grin at the huddled figure of Ariane. "Don't I have enough ladies

428

on the *Molly Cook* for you?"

Ariane stiffened at her crude humorous shouts, but it was something else that caused her gray eyes to widen with astonishment. Another figure had joined the flamboyant Molly Cook, an amber-eyed, raven-haired woman she knew only too well. Staring down at her with cool disdain was Olivia Whitlaw.

Chapter Thirty-two

"You certainly are well acquainted with Molly Cook," Ariane said coolly as they walked up the gangplank. Molly's girls were all on deck to watch them come aboard.

"Why, I do believe you're jealous," he teased, helping her on to the deck of the steamer.

"Do I have reason to be?" she replied in taut low tones as the buxom owner sauntered over to greet them.

"None at all," he said quietly, turning his serious gaze upon her. She knew that he spoke the truth even if Olivia was on board.

"Well, dearie, I don't know what this handsome man has been doing to you, but you look like a drowned kitten," Molly said frankly, her ice-blue eyes traveling over Ariane's bedraggled figure with a calculating gaze. "Best get you in a warm cabin right away. We can scare up some clothes for you. That gown could stand a good cleaning."

"Thank you," Ariane managed to say through teeth chattering with the cold and damp.

"The Natchez cabin," Molly called to a young black woman who came gliding out of a door with the word *Office* on it. "All my cabins are named after towns on the river," she confided to Ariane as Olivia stood observing her like a cat watching a mouse. "Lucy here will take you on up. I need to speak with your gent a moment," Molly said in her whiskey-rough voice, placing a plump beringed hand on Justin's arm.

"Go with her. You are freezing. I will be up directly," he said to Ariane, touching her cheek in a gesture of reassurance.

Picking up her skirt in one hand and holding the wet blanket around her with the other, she followed the young servant up the iron staircase to the next deck. There was a scene of Natchez painted on the door and the name printed above it in flowing gold script. Inside, the chamber was large and warm if rather garishly furnished.

Red velvet curtains dripping gold fringe hung at the small window. An Oriental rug, also in red and gold with touches of indigo, covered the floor. Red-and-gold-flocked paper covered the walls. White-and-gold-gilded chairs curved in the French manner stood beside a marble-topped mahogany table. An armoire stood against one wall as did a chest with a china pitcher and bowl painted with enormous red roses standing on the white marble top. The room was garish and overdone, but on such a damp gray day, it was a cheerful sanctuary.

"You step out of those wet things, mizzy. I get you something real pretty out of the armoire," the black servant Lucy told her, opening the mirrored doors. "I reckon you will be needin' undergarments as well."

"Yes," Ariane answered reluctantly. "I am soaked to the skin."

"These be real pretty, silk from New Orleans," Lucy said, taking out an emerald-green gown with a raised skirt that showed the gold tissue lace petticoat beneath. It looked more like a ball gown than something to wear in the daytime, but then Molly's ladies dressed to attract the male eye, Ariane thought with a wry smile.

431

" 'Tis lovely, thank you," Ariane told Lucy as the maid helped her out of her mud-spattered gown.

"I believe it will fit. The gal it belonged to ran off with a gambling man, didn't take half the nice things Miz Molly had bought her," Lucy confided.

"How short-sighted of her," Ariane replied dryly.

"Oh, he was a handsome gent, but fickle. You could tell that man was goin' to break Miz Suzanne's heart. But she jes took off, leaving these silk undergarments she never had worn," Lucy explained, shaking her tignon-clad head as she lifted out chemise, pantalets, and a corset of gold silk trimmed with black lace.

Ariane stood stunned, and then had the most uncontrollable desire to laugh. She was going to don the cast-off undergarments of a whore. Her life, after so much tragedy, had become a farce.

"Don't you look pretty," Lucy commented, standing back and regarding Ariane with sparkling black eyes after helping her into the emerald gown. "Let me do your hair. That gent of yours will plumb have his eyes bugging out when he sees you," she said, reaching for a silver-backed hairbrush and comb.

Justin's eyes might not have bugged out, as Lucy put it, but he did take notice as Ariane was shown into the main saloon where he sat at one of the gaming tables with his hostess, Molly. He rose to his feet as she swept into the elaborately furnished room, her emerald silk hoop skirt swaying as she walked. She saw his eyes fasten on the porcelain gardenia, which she wore on a length of emerald ribbon Lucy had found to match her dress.

"How lovely you look," he said gallantly as his dark eyes moved down to the extreme décolletage of her gown. The ivory mounds of her full breasts pushed up and over till only the rosy nipples were covered.

432

"It belonged to one of Miss Cook's girls," Ariane replied with a wry twist to her mouth.

"Molly, honey, call me Molly. Miss Cook sounds like a schoolteacher and I sure enough ain't one of those," she cackled, lifting a long thin black cheroot to her rouged lips.

"Thank you for the gown . . . er, Molly," Ariane stammered, sitting down in the chair Justin held out for her at the table.

"You're welcome, honey, that no-'count trash Suzanne won't be needing it. I never knew a more stupid gal in my life—she actually enjoyed her work. Believed anything a man told her as the gospel truth, now that's a stupid woman," she told them in her husky voice, blowing out a ring of blue smoke.

"You're a realist, Molly," Justin said, gazing at Ariane with a grimace of good humor.

"In my line of work, you have to be," she replied philosophically. "Now that new gal I picked up in St. Louis, that's a real cold hard one."

"Yes, we are acquainted with her," Justin said with distaste in his voice.

"You know Desirée then?" Molly inquired, her hard eyes suddenly alert.

"Is that the name she gave you?" he asked quietly, watching the tense look on Ariane's delicate visage.

"It's the name I gave her. I name all my gals and that one looked like Desirée to me. She is supposed to be French, up from New Orleans. The gents, they like these little romantic stories, especially the Yanks. They don't know a French Creole from a horse's behind so they believe our little story about her being a French Aristocrat down on her luck. She can play the part real well, probably would do all right on the stage, that one." Molly mused, taking another drag on her cheroot.

"Yes, she can be quite an actress," Justin told her in a contemptuous tone.

"Don't trust her an inch, though. I had a cat like her once—beautiful but a real huntress, enjoyed torturing her prey for a while before she killed it."

Justin and Ariane never had time to reply, for their conversation was interrupted by the sharp pierce of the ship's whistle and then the clang of the bell. They all knew the river well enough to know that meant a ship was passing them or trying to come alongside.

"What the hell is going on, Arlo?" Molly called out to the black man who was her chief steward and oversaw the gaming tables when they were in port.

" 'Pears a Yankee gunboat coming up alongside," he hollered back from where he stood next to the window. "We're stopping, Miz Molly."

Ariane's frightened gray eyes met Justin's as they all rose to their feet. Why were the Yankees trying to board the *Molly Cook?* Were they looking for her?

"Molly, Ariane is one of your new girls, if anyone asks," Justin said in a low voice as the door that led to the deck was wrenched open and two Union officers strode into the saloon.

"Might I help you gents?" Molly called out as they stared in stunned amazement at the sight of Justin in his Union uniform standing beside Ariane and the flamboyant figure of Molly.

"Or perhaps you can help me," Justin said smoothly, returning their salutes. "Miss Molly has been so kind as to pick me up and take me to Memphis. I got separated from my men downriver."

"Sorry, Captain, we are going in the opposite direction," the one lieutenant explained. "We stopped you, ma'am, because we are looking for Rebs who shot up one of our boats pretty bad not far upriver. We saw some of them take off in a small dinghy riding the

434

current into the fog. They must have passed this way. Have we your permission to search your ship?"

"Of course, I have nothing to hide," Molly lied smoothly, meeting their eyes with a bold glance. "But we haven't seen anyone in that pea soup out there."

"Yes, ma'am, we will want to make sure of that."

"Could I be of some assistance in showing them around the steamer?" Olivia inquired in a sultry drawl as she swirled into the saloon in a billow of scarlet silk.

"Why, that would be real fine." The young lieutenant smiled down at the seductive, triangular face gazing up at him with such invitation in her amber eyes. "Perhaps the blond lady would care to accompany my partner," he said, sweeping his eyes over Ariane's low neckline.

"The lady is taken, Lieutenant." Justin spoke softly, but there was menace in his deep voice.

There was a flash of dislike and suspicion on the lieutenant's face as he regarded Justin standing with his arm around Ariane's waist. Then giving a sharp salute, the two officers, with Olivia in tow, strode out of the saloon. Pausing in the doorway, she turned and gave them a smile that could only be described as vicious and triumphant.

"Molly, do you have a small boat on the port side of the ship? One that could be lowered quietly without attraction attention?" Justin asked in a low, taut voice.

"Yes, hurry. Arlo will show you, but be quick. Remember my cat—she liked to toy with her victims, but not for too long before she moved in for the kill. Desirée knows something she is going to use against you. I can see it in her eyes," Molly muttered, leading them to where a single door in the back of the saloon led outside to the deck. Arlo was right behind them.

"I'll make a commotion with Lucy and the other

435

girls to distract the Yanks, but hurry and slip into the fog before they see you. If those two nosy officers ask where you've gone, I'll say you two are otherwise engaged in the Natchez suite," she whispered as Justin gave her a quick kiss on her rouged and powdered cheek. "Go on, Doc. I don't know what you're up to, but God speed."

"I owe you, Molly," he said.

"No you don't, Doc. You paid me years ago when you saved my life. Now, for God's sake, hurry!"

Following Arlo down the staircase, Ariane felt awkward as her skirt billowed and dipped, but she held fast to the top hoop and eased her way along as best she could. Reaching the bottom deck, they heard Molly yelling at the girls and Lucy's high-pitched wail as the servant girl played along. Near the middle of the deck, they saw a small wooden emergency boat used by the crew if they wished to go ashore or if the steamer should blow a boiler and catch fire, an all-too-common occurrence on a riverboat. The paddlewheeler had thus earned the nickname "flaming coffin," a term used by many old rivermen.

As Arlo unfastened the gate, Justin slid the small boat into the water, holding fast to the rope that was attached to the prow. Handing the rope to the black man, Justin turned to Ariane and said, "I will get in first and then Arlo will help you down. Slip out of that hoop. Arlo will hide it."

Reaching under her skirt, she quickly untied the tapes and let the cage crinoline drop to the floor of the deck. Then as Arlo whisked it behind a heavy barrel of supplies, Ariane leaned down, took Justin's hand, and stepped into the rocking boat.

This tiny vessel was to be their method of escape from the Yankees, who at that very moment were probably hearing all about Justin and his Southern spy wife. She shuddered as she sank down on the bottom of the rocking boat. They were going to float down the powerful, rushing waters of the Mississippi in this fragile craft. It was a nightmare.

Justin caught the rope Arlo threw to him. Then he was working the oars, paddling away from the steamer and its powerful paddlewheel that could suck a small craft in its wake, for even though the steamer was stopped, the wheel was still turning.

Ariane tried to keep her fragile control as Justin moved the boat around and away from the steamer and into the cover of the fog. Quickly they were caught in the swift current of the mighty river and were floating faster, and faster, away from the two anchored boats.

It was like a journey through a dream, thought Ariane as they traveled southward on the liquid highway through the wispy gray fog. They dared not speak till they knew they were far away, for voices carried a remarkable distance across the water.

"Are you all right, Little Bit?" Justin finally asked over his shoulder, his deep steady voice cutting through the still unearthly fog.

"Yes," she answered, staring at the broad set of his shoulders as he sat in front of her.

"Good. We are making for Helena. If we're lucky, the *Southern Lady* should still be there. Molly said we were near there, only on the Mississippi side, when they picked us up. We had not gone that far when the gunboat stopped us, but it might be a rough ride. This skiff isn't made for a long trip down the Mississippi."

Ariane had lived all her life on the banks of the Mississippi and her family ran a steamer line. She had grown up on stories about the treachery of the river. It was why she sat so still and cramped in the tiny boat tossed about by the swirling, rushing water. Floating logs, barrels, branches could, if they hit just right, overturn the skiff. And in the fog, Justin didn't have a clear view of the water. They were sailing blind through the misty fog. Another steamer could be upon them before they saw it and they would be sucked under the paddle wheel.

Losing all track of time, Ariane sat behind Justin, marveling at his strength and will as he kept them in the channel of the river and away from the flotsam and jettison of the Mississippi. Shivering in the silk dress, she tried to think of other things, of other times, to keep from losing her courage.

The memory of the first time she had seen Justin after all those years on that hot June morning when Memphis had surrendered came flooding back to her. She had hated him as a conqueror of her beloved city till she had looked into those wonderful, penetrating night-black eyes that could see into her soul. So many lovely memories—the first night they made love and she had known the fulfillment of a woman for the first time in his arms, the erotic night of lovemaking in the tower, the dangerous and tragic ride on that terrible train to La Grange, and their wedding night. She would never forget the love she saw shining in his eyes as he slipped his mother's ring on her finger.

Looking out into the lifting fog, she thought that despite the horror of the war and all the losses she had sustained, she had found Justin. Through the good times, and the bad, he had been there for her. Even though everything in their lives had decreed it wrong, their love somehow had always been so right, so good. If she lived to be a very old lady, she knew she would always have the memory of when she had experienced life to the fullest, fought with everything she had for what she believed in, and known a love that only a precious few were ever privileged to enjoy.

438

Whatever lay ahead on her life's journey, she had had this splendid time, when anything and everything had seemed possible. She had lived and loved with no restraint as if there would be no morrow beside this magnificent man who had let her into his heart. Their love had been only strengthened by the fires of war, forging them together till their souls were one.

"The fog is lifting. 'Tis a good omen," he called to her, allowing himself to turn a little so he might gaze upon her for a brief moment.

"Yes, oh yes," she sighed, turning her face up to the golden streams of sunshine that were streaking out of the parting clouds. The sun was burning away the fog, turning the chocolate water into a sparkling prism.

"We are going to make it, Little Bit," he told her, his dark eyes shimmering with his triumph and overwhelming love for her.

"I never doubted it, my love," she said with joy and laughter in her voice.

They reached Helena, Arkansas, as the sun was setting over the fertile Arkansas bank. As Justin paddled them in toward one of the smaller docks, they were amazed to hear band music, the sound of pistols being fired in the air, and the drunken laughter and singing of men.

Throwing the rope to a young black boy who stood whittling a stick on the dock, Justin called, "What is going on?"

"Old Bob Lee surrendered. The war's over," he called out with a grin.

Ariane felt a sick, sinking feeling in the pit of her stomach as Justin helped her out of the boat and up onto the dock. He held her against him for a moment, for he knew what this news would do to her.

"I cannot believe it," she told him, looking up at him with tears turning her eyes a crystal gray. "What was it all for? All those good men lost? Why?"

"So now we can become one nation again, strong, with no more divisions, sweetheart."

"But at what a cost," she said, and shuddered.

"Yes, the pain will not forgotten, but perhaps now the healing can begin," he murmured, pressing her to him as he felt the strength ebb out of her. "Is the *Southern Lady* still in port?" he asked the young boy.

"Yes, sir. Half her crew are drunk as Cotter Brown, celebrating they are, sure enough." He laughed, pointing down to where the gleaming steamer was docked.

"Come, my sweet, let us go back to Memphis. Let us go home," Justin whispered against her silky hair.

A sad, if relieved, Sam Riley welcomed them on board. The Union officers were ashore celebrating so there was no one to see Ariane and Justin come up the gangplank. They decided to tell the men that Ariane had caught another steamer from Mimosa Bayou Plantation, which took her as far as Helena so she might join the *Southern Lady* for the trip home. About Justin, they said nothing, for when the two men returned for the next day's sailing, they had such hangovers they were aware of very little.

After a good night's sleep in Justin's beloved embrace and dressed in her own clothes, Ariane felt more able to face the reality of the South's defeat. Standing on deck in the late-afternoon sunshine, she stared into the rushing water below and seemed to see all the faces of those she had loved and lost. Could she ever learn to live with the sheer waste of so many young lives? Men, and women too, who would never laugh, or love, or hold their children to their hearts.

"What is it, my sweet Ariane? You sighed such a heavy sigh," Justin asked in a voice as warm as the sun that streamed down upon them.

"How can we ever be the same again?" she replied

440

in a low, tormented whisper.

"We cannot, the South cannot, but together we must all try to make something worth all the suffering, all those lives lost. I am with you, my dearest wife, and there is nothing we cannot do, no storms we cannot weather if we are together," he promised her, taking her hand in his, entwining their fingers.

"Yes, at least we are together once more," she said softly, her throat aching with a threat of tears. But these were tears of joy that at least now there would be nothing to separate them ever again.

"Look, Little Bit, 'tis Memphis. We are home," he said. This time it was his voice that was thick with emotion as they looked toward the city rising out of the muddy surging waters of the Mississippi. "There is our future, my sweet Ariane, my wife. I came down this river filled with hate, and found instead love and meaning for my life. I found you. There is nothing that will ever change my love for you. Like the river, the bond between us is ageless, constant, eternal."

She looked up at him and smiled, her soul flowing out to him and joining with him as he lifted her hand to his lips. Then they turned and looked across the water at where they would again begin their life together. Memphis, place of good abode.

We have shared the incommunicable experience of war. We have felt, we still feel, the passion of life to its stop. . . . In our youths, our hearts were touched by fire.

Oliver Wendell Holmes, Jr.

Epilogue

July 1865

Sultry summer heat engulfed the grounds of Fleur de Lys with not a breath of air stirring, not even now that the long mauve-violet shadows of twilight slanted across the still glassy lake. Ariane stood on the bank watching the graceful ivory mother swan glide with her two tiny cygnets across the moss green water. The black male was right behind as if guarding his mate and their young.

It was Bess who alerted her that someone was coming as the dog turned and gave a frantic wag of her tail. Turning away from the tranquil aquatic ballet, Ariane saw him walking toward her down the path from the house. His tall, lean masculine form was bathed in the bittersweet purple haze of eventide. Justin was home.

Her heart ached with longing as she saw him. The depth of her emotion whenever she was reunited with him at the end of the day always startled her with its intensity. The sheer male beauty of him would hold her spellbound for a breathtaking moment as she realized how lucky she was to have this magnificent man as her own beloved. Watching him come toward her, she thought how much she adored the curve of his mouth, the gentleness that was strength in his night-black eyes, the sinewy grace of his movements and his touch that set her aflame.

"You're not in uniform," she said with surprise as she realized as he came up to her that he was dressed in civilian clothes. The gray breeches and fine ivory linen shirt gave him a dash that sent an unexpected tremor of pure desire through her.

"My service with the Union Army is over as of today, Little Bit," he explained, cupping her chin with the firm, yet gentle hands she loved. His dark eyes caressed her oval face, delicate as a gardenia blossom in the dusky light. "I am simply Doctor Pierce once more, your husband." His words were absorbed into her heated mouth as his lips brushed across hers in a kiss that was a tantalizing promise of further delights. Her seductive heliotrope perfume floated up to him, the fragrance that would always be Ariane.

"Welcome home, Doctor Pierce," she breathed as his whisper-light kiss seared a path down to the hollow of her alabaster neck, where her pulse beat wildly with her awakened passion. "I am happy the Yankee captain is gone, and once more I have back my Southern gentleman, my errant knight."

"Ah, yes, my bewitching wife, we may have won the war, but you have won the peace. Through you I have come to realize that the South is still lodged deep within my heart," he said huskily, lifting his head, his raven hair gleaming in the last dying light of the day. "I am here to stay, for you have made Fleur de Lys and Memphis truly the place that holds my heart. If the people of Memphis will have me, I should like to begin my practice of medicine here once more. The times ahead are going to be hard for them; perhaps, in some way, I can be of service. This Yankee has come home to stay." His dark eyes stared down into her misty gray ones, touching that private place within her that only he could see.

444

"I am glad the Falcon has been tamed," she teased gently, touching his bronzed visage with the tips of her fingers.

"By such a beautiful Swan—how could he possibly resist?" he whispered, capturing her hand and turning it over to press a kiss to the palm. "Come walk with me. I seem to remember a private trysting place on the other side of the lake. A private rose-covered nook that holds wonderful memories for me. Although your father is a fine man, I think he might look askance if we adjourn to our bedchamber before the evening meal, and my sweet temptress, I cannot wait any longer."

" 'Twill always be our private place, my love, where we can be alone," she murmured, smiling up at him as she placed her hand inside the circle of his arm. "What lovely new memories we shall make there tonight."

The black and white swans with their two cygnets sought the verdant sanctuary of their island in the middle of the still lake as the long perfumed Southern twilight encircled them. They sensed instinctually that it was time to put the day's cares behind them. It was the same with the man and woman walking with arms entwined toward the beckoning studio shimmering as the rising moonglow touched the white climbing roses till they shone like a beacon to welcome the two lovers. For a few short enchanted hours, there would be only the rapture found in the joining of two beloved bodies, two beloved souls.

"Have I told you how beautiful you look tonight and how much I love you," he murmured as they reached the heavy door under the arch of white roses.

"No, my love," she answered as he opened the door, "but you must tell me again and again. We have all the long splendid night ahead of us."

445

Author's Note

It has been said that the Civil War saw more espionage, more spying by men and women on both sides, than any other war in our history. The brave, romantic agents for both blue and gray came from all walks of life, all levels of society, but it seemed those who captured the imagination of the public at the time were the Southern women. They certainly received a lot of publicity in both the Northern and the Southern press, and many became legends during the war. Southern women spies were written about in Northern newspapers as "feminine desperadoes of the Confederacy."

The exploits of real-life Southern spies Belle Boyd and Rosa Greenhow would make fictional accounts pale in comparison. Memphis had its own courageous female agents — Virginia Moon, who carried a pearl-handled revolver, and Belle Edmondson, who smuggled information and medicine through Union lines to the Confederacy. Belle Edmondson's poignant published diary and letters give a moving account of what it was like to be a female spy for the Confederacy. She died shortly after the war under unusual circumstances and is buried today in Elmwood Cemetery in Memphis.

It was a romantic age when dashing men believed in a gentlemanly code of honor toward women spies. As the war dragged on, and grew more bitter, male agents when caught were hanged or shot. The women, however, were imprisoned or threatened, but a lady was still a lady. No man, North or South, could bring himself to order a woman's execution. The women knew it and took shameless advantage of that fact, making them often the most effective spies.

In *The Falcon and the Swan,* I have tried to follow the historical events of Civil War Memphis. A single shot was fired at the surrender of the city to Union forces, but no one is sure who did the firing. The author would like to think it might have been one of the impassioned belles of the city who never surrendered in their hearts. Irving Block Prison did actually exist and the conditions were so dreadful that President Lincoln sent a team down to Memphis to investigate if what had been written in the Northern press was true. After they sent him their findings, the Provost Marshal and the warden of the prison were suspended for a short time, but conditions didn't improve very much and it became known as the Bastille of the South. Prominent Memphians were forced to ride the railroad cars of the Memphis and Charleston Railroad as targets for unknowing Confederate sharp shooters. The presses of the *Memphis Appeal* did leave town on a railroad car hours before the city surrendered, and the editors traveled through the Confederacy for the duration of the war, publishing their newspaper under difficult circumstances. The paper was the forerunner of the modern Memphis newspaper known as the *Commercial Appeal.*

General Nathan Bedford Forrest is a legend in military history. His daring raid into Memphis in the early-morning hours of an August Sunday is part of the city's colorful history, and did much to bolster the sagging spirits of the citizens. He was considered by historian Bruce Catton to have been "one of the authentic military geniuses of the whole war." It has also been said the Nazi high command during World War II studied Forrest's brilliant military tactics when developing their swift military offensive known as the *blitzkrieg*.

The small village of La Grange, Tennessee, still exists about fifty miles east of Memphis. It is a lovely hamlet of restored historic homes. A church and cemetery dating from before the Civil War still exist. There is a legend one mansion was used as a Union hospital during the battle of Shiloh.

Many Union soldiers who came to Memphis as conquerors were conquered by the city and decided to stay after the war was over. They married, reared families, and made a great contribution to the growth of the city. Perhaps like Justin and Ariane, there was an actual Yankee officer who fell in love with a beautiful Memphis belle and stayed to live happily with his beloved for the rest of their days. As a true romantic, the author would like to think that even in those dark days love triumphed over all bitterness.